"YOU CANNOT GET AWAY, MADAM. I HAVE BOUGHT YOU. YOU ARE MINE."

His voice was <u>soft</u> against the howl of the wind. Dark. Strong. Dangerous. This was Michael Langssonn, and according to all the laws of the land, she belonged to him.

"Let me go, lord, so that I may help my people."

"Nay, I need you. I have wanted you since I first set eyes on you."

"Don't come any closer," Cait warned. "Or I shall be forced to hurt you."

Michael laughed. "Killing me is the only way you'll stop me."

He pressed her into the ground and covered her mouth with his in a hot, demanding kiss.

"My mountain cat," he murmured. His voice had become low, sultry, stroking away all her resolve. "I want you to purr for me, to rub against me, to sit in my lap . . . because you want to. I shall be gentle with you, little wild cat, and tame you . . ."

" 'Tis possible *I* shall tame *you*, lord."

LORD OF THUNDER

EMMA MERRITT

An Avon Romantic Treasure

AVON BOOKS ◆ NEW YORK

LORD OF THUNDER is an original publication of Avon Books. This work has never before appeared in book form. This work is a novel. Any similarity to actual persons or events is purely coincidental.

AVON BOOKS
A division of
The Hearst Corporation
1350 Avenue of the Americas
New York, New York 10019

Copyright © 1994 by Emma Merritt
Inside cover author photograph by F. E. Alexander
Published by arrangement with the author
Library of Congress Catalog Card Number: 94-94066
ISBN: 0-380-77290-6

First Avon Books Printing: August 1994

AVON TRADEMARK REG. U.S. PAT. OFF. AND IN OTHER COUNTRIES, MARCA REGISTRADA, HECHO EN U.S.A.

Printed in the U.S.A.

RA 10 9 8 7 6 5 4 3 2 1

Chapter 1

Kingdom of Glenmuir
Scottish Highlands
A.D. 626

Lightning flashed across the storm-darkened sky of the Scottish glen, illuminating the lone warrior who stood at the forest's edge. A fine rain fell like silver. The wind swirled his black hair from his shoulders and whipped his clothing against his body. Like the oaks that towered around him, he seemed impervious to the inclement weather.

Tall, formidable, his arms akimbo and his brow furrowed, he looked about him as if he knew she was hidden there, spying on him. Hugging the trunk of a massive tree, Cait nea Sholto peered at him through the fine mist and dense autumn underbrush.

Several days worth of stubble blurred his jaw and chin but did nothing to soften his sharp, angular features. Like the grim clouds that were bringing an early end to the afternoon, his dark and forbidding countenance mirrored the fury of the gathering storm. He frightened her.

A gust of wind, blowing with renewed fury, billowed open his black mantle at the same time that a blade of lightning sliced downward from the sky.

1

Its brilliant glow reflected off the silver latchets of the black leathern girdle he wore and off the black-enameled dagger and silver-hilted sword strapped around his waist.

Silver mail stretched tightly across his broad shoulders and massive chest. His arms bulged with muscle. Beneath the short-sleeved chain mail, he wore a long-sleeved black shirt. Tight-fitting trousers, the same color as the shirt, encased legs as muscular as his shoulders. Yet he was a lean man, as hard and tough as the black leathern scabbard at his side. His stance, his physique, his countenance, all bespoke power and might.

He turned in her direction, his gaze seeming to focus on her. Cait caught her breath, but didn't move. She watched and prayed that he would soon return to his ship so she could question the few inhabitants nearby and learn more about what had brought him to Glenmuir and why he'd anchored his fearsome ship in one of the kingdom's little-used coves.

Finally the warrior lowered his arms, turned, and walked toward the loch. Emitting a long sigh, Cait wilted against the tree trunk. As though he had heard her, he abruptly swung around, his hand returning to his sword hilt. She crouched lower.

Long, determined strides brought him back to her. The thud of his footfalls on the hardened pathway rang out menacingly. The wind was cold and biting, but a sheen of perspiration covered her body. She hoped the thinning foliage was enough to shield her from the warrior's piercing gaze. She didn't dare move for fear the slightest noise would alert him to her presence. He was within six steps of her when he halted. Cait flattened herself against the oak trunk and shivered.

Eventually she heard the soft crackle of leaves, the snap of twigs. He was moving away from her again. Taking a deep breath, she eased her head around the tree, keeping her gaze focused on him as she slipped backward among the trees.

Abruptly she halted, the hair prickling along the back of her neck. Someone, or something, was watching her. Chills chased up and down her spine. Her heart beat so fast, she felt light-headed.

Cautiously she slid her arms beneath her mantle. She had been trained to defend herself with a whip and blades, but having had no idea she would need her whip for protection, she had packed it in her satchel and sent it ahead with her companions. She would have to rely on her blades instead.

She reached into the leathern carrying case belted around her waist and extracted a small silver dagger—one of twenty that she kept precisely arranged there. Crafted by the same silversmith, they were identical in design, measurement, and engravings.

Armed, she spun about . . . and stared into the snarling face of a silver-white wolf. Its eyes were fixed on her, its teeth bared. For a moment fear froze Cait in place.

She swallowed, then whispered, "I mean you no harm, wolf. Move and let me go my way."

The wolf growled deeper in its throat. Its teeth seemed to grow longer and more pointed, its grin more menacing.

Perspiration beaded Cait's forehead. Growling louder, the wolf crouched, ready to spring.

"Ulf!" commanded a low, masculine voice.

Cait jumped. The wolf ceased growling and relaxed his stance, though he kept his gaze pinned on her.

A puff of lightning, like smoke, billowed from behind heavy clouds, followed by a muffled rumble of thunder. The warrior strode toward her. The richly embroidered hemline of his mantle slapped against his knee-high boots.

"Why are you lurking about, woman?" he demanded. His voice was low, but Cait heard the ring of iron in it. Although he spoke Gaelic fluently, she detected a slight accent and sensed it was not his native tongue.

"I wasn't lurking." Holding on to her dagger, her heart pounding so loudly that Cait wondered if the stranger could hear it, she gazed into the beard-stubbled face. "Even if I was lurking, this is where I live, and *I* have a right to be here." Her tone questioned his own presence there.

His eyes flicked over her before they rested on her face. He was so big and formidable, he could have been hewn from stone.

She glanced over her shoulder at the ship hidden in the cove. It was as fierce-looking as the warrior standing before her, as threatening as the men who had disembarked earlier. "That is a warship, my lord, its dragon-head prow designed to strike fear into people's hearts."

"I have my reasons for being here," he answered, not refuting her charge, "but war is not among them. You have no need of your weapon. I won't harm you." He reached for her dagger.

Cait jerked back her hand. "Until I am satisfied that I don't need it, my lord, I shall keep it."

"Do you know how to use it?"

"I'll let you be the judge of that."

Cait lifted the flap of the leathern carrying case and pulled out four more daggers. Deftly she balanced one in her right hand between her thumb and index finger. With a twist of her wrist, a flick of her hand, she flung it. In a silver blur the blade twirled through the air and thudded into the earth, hilt upright, directly next to the toe of the stranger's boot. As quickly, the other four blades followed until the entire front half of his foot was outlined.

He stared down, then squatted and pulled each blade from the ground. He held them in his palm, studying them.

"They're small."

"Big enough for me, and superbly crafted," Cait answered.

Still kneeling, he ran his hand around the sole of his boot.

" 'Tis not damaged," she assured him.

"Nay," he agreed, "not a mark on it."

He rose, stepped forward, and handed the daggers back to her. She found herself looking into startling, vivid blue eyes framed with long, dark lashes. Their vibrancy and beauty drew her, but also unsettled her. They were cold and emotionless, as sharp and cutting as the blades of her daggers.

"You're good with a still target," he said. "How about a moving one?"

Pushing aside her apprehensions, she taunted softly, "Run, my lord, and I'll demonstrate my skill."

The warrior laughed, the rich sound wrapping around her and lulling her apprehension. "I think I have had enough demonstration for one day, my lady."

Suddenly Cait had the feeling that she had seen him someplace before. Something about his eyes, his face . . . his stance . . . his voice. But she could not fix his image to a particular place or time. And she surely would have remembered had she met such a cold, hard man before.

"Why do you stare?" he asked.

"Your face is familiar. Perhaps you have made a religious pilgrimage to the Shelter Stone?"

"I travel frequently," he answered, "but I don't make religious pilgrimages, and I don't recall having heard of this Shelter Stone."

" 'Tis a holy place, my lord, a natural stone bridge hewn out of the mountain at the beginning of time by the twin gods Night and Day."

"Ah," he drawled. "I do remember, madam. 'Tis said it is one of the most richly endowed shrines in all the land. Pilgrims are noted for leaving the gods extremely valuable gifts."

Concerned because he associated wealth rather than worship with the shrine, Cait said, "People do leave gifts for the gods, as they do at any holy shrine. The Shelter Stone is revered by the Picts, the Scots, the Glenmuirians, the Athdarians—by all Highlanders, no matter what tribe they claim or what gods they worship. Even people from lands across the sea have traveled here to bathe in the holy water."

"I'm sure your shrine is all that you have said, madam, but I have never been there before. This is my first visit to your land."

Cait raised the flap of her purse, returning the daggers to their leathern loops. As she raised her head, he touched his throat, drawing her attention to his torque. From three ropes of silver that had been braided together hung a black enameled cross.

"You wear the cross of the Northmen," she said.

"Northmen call it the hammer. It is the sign of Thor, our god of thunder and lightning. 'Tis the

Christians who have taken our hammer symbol as theirs and called it the cross."

"You are a Northman, a sea raider?"

"Sea raider," he repeated softly. "Some would describe me as such, but I call myself Michael Langssonn, a sojourner who belongs to all the lands."

"For a sojourner, my lord, you travel with a large escort," Cait observed dryly. "A ship full of warriors, and all of them dressed for battle."

"One can never be too careful in foreign lands, lady."

"And one can never be too careful when foreigners enter one's own land unannounced," she countered.

Michael's eyes narrowed; his brow furrowed. "You and your people have nothing to fear. I am here for one purpose—to find the man who stole my betrothed from me." His voice had grown as cold as his blue eyes.

Cait shivered and was glad she was not the person for whom Michael Langssonn searched. "Is that man here in Glenmuir?"

After a pause, he said, "Nay, in Northern Scotland."

"But you have landed in Glenmuir."

Michael frowned. "We could not find the landmarks that were described to us. Are we far from our destination?"

Relieved, and wanting this man and his warriors out of Glenmuir as quickly as possible, Cait was eager to point them on their way. "About six days' journey if you ride from daybreak to sundown, moving along the marked pathways."

"Is there a shorter route?"

"Aye, one by land and another by water, but both routes are unmarked. You would need a guide."

It was true that the second land route, the quickest and easiest to travel, was not clearly marked. She chose not to tell him about it since it would take him too close to the cloister, and she was wary of him.

"Could you guide us? I would be willing to pay you well for your trouble."

"I don't know the waterway. Even if I did, I cannot. I am one of four cloister minstrels, called the Silver Daggers, and I—"

"A minstrel," he interrupted.

His lips tipped into a full smile. For the first time Cait saw the stirring of lust in his eyes. Aye, since she had been traveling as a minstrel, enough men had stared at her with the same look that she now recognized it.

She wondered what the Northman was thinking. Would he, like the majority of the men whom she had encountered during her travels, assume that a wandering female minstrel such as herself was a whore? Men often traveled as minstrels without sullying their reputations, so why not a woman? Yet a woman minstrel was always considered a woman of easy virtue.

Perhaps, in time, that would change. Cait was the first priestess of the Shelter Stone to become a cloister minstrel. Her role was distinctly different from the casual wandering minstrels, often thieves and charlatans, who roamed the countryside.

Cait had been invited to join the Silver Daggers at a moment in her life when she was looking for a new purpose. Not long before, King Ido had ruptured her betrothal to a warrior named Brieve. Humiliated, angry, and hurt, Cait had protested the king's action and begged her betrothed to do the same. But Brieve had not. He begged Cait's forgiveness, but told her they must do as the king wished. When a short time later Brieve married the king's daughter, Cait realized that Brieve had not loved her. He had loved the power and position that the king promised.

In a fit of rage, before all those who had assembled for the wedding feast, Cait had vowed that one day she would avenge her honor, that the gods would curse Ido and his entire family for the wrong they had done to her.

And then the Council of Priests had chosen her as a candidate for the Silver Daggers. Her adopted father, Sholto, had been honored but also sad. He and his two closest friends—Trevor and Blar, also priests of the shrine—had begged Cait to reconsider, warning her of the difficult role she would take on, the prejudice and condemnation she would inevitably face.

Cait had weighed their advice, but after long consideration, had chosen to become a cloister minstrel. She was happy she had. She had found that people did assume the worst about her at first, but as they benefited from her help and enjoyed the singing and feats with which she entertained them, they began to accept her as she really was.

"Learning that you are a minstrel is a pleasant surprise," Michael said now. "I had not imagined meeting one here."

"Aye, my lord. I am also a priestess."

"How is it possible that you are both?"

"Once we enter the cloister, sire, we all become warrior priests and priestesses," she explained. "A few of us go on to become ovates or bards. An even fewer number are chosen as cloister minstrels. We cannot be considered for this special honor until we have completed all our training. And then we must be chosen by the Council of Priests and approved by Sholto, our high priest and the Ancient of Nights and Days."

"You must be proud to have been singled out in such a way."

" 'Tis a great honor to be chosen, lord, since it allows us to do service for others," she confirmed. "Because we are dedicated to the gods, we travel through the land, unhindered, carrying news and learning all that we can—about medicine, bartering, sowing, reaping, politics. We share our knowledge with others, and dispense gifts to the needy. We tend to the sick and the dying."

"And you entertain," he said, his blue eyes moving boldly over her, making her glad her body was hidden behind the folds of her cloak.

"Aye, we sing and dance and juggle and do acrobatics." She paused. "And since all of us are blade masters, we perform feats with the dagger."

She deliberately omitted telling him about her ability to wield the whip. If he was a dishonorable man, the knowledge could play to his advantage.

"I am exceedingly fond of minstrels," he said. "During my travels I have seen and heard many."

She said nothing. Perhaps the Northman was unlike the others and did not assume all women minstrels were whores.

But his next words belied that notion. His voice heavy with innuendo, he said, "It has been my experience that of all performers, women minstrels are the most entertaining. . . ."

Nay, she realized, he *was* like all the others.

"I said minstrel, lord, and that is what I meant. No more. No less."

"I know what a minstrel is, madam. I know what she does."

He smiled, drawing Cait's attention to his mouth. His lips, like everything else about him, were hard and masculine, yet also sensuous. His eyes shone with amusement, as if he knew she was intrigued by him. Embarrassed, she wanted to turn from him, but couldn't. He held her entranced.

"I am not a whore, sire."

"Nay," he drawled softly, "none of the women minstrels I have known were . . . whores. They were bards and dancers and . . . entertainers."

The mockery in his eyes and the sarcasm in his voice stole the sincerity from his words.

"What is your name, lass?"

"Cait nea Sholto."

"Cait daughter of Sholto," he repeated, and laughed softly. "The pure one."

"Aye."

"You claim to be one of a group of wandering minstrels, madam, but I have searched the area and found no evidence of a large group having passed through here."

"You found no evidence of *my* passing through here either," Cait retorted.

He arched a thick brow in question.

"As members of the cloister, all of us have been taught to move through the forest without leaving a trace of our presence, my lord. We are followed only if we wish to be followed."

"Yet I found you."

Cait looked at the huge silver wolf who lay docilely at his master's side. "Nay, lord, your beast found me. He followed my scent."

The warrior acquiesced with a crooked smile and

a shrug. "He is exceptionally smart, madam, and has a nose for only beautiful women."

"Then I must thank him for the compliment."

" 'Twas I who taught him to track beautiful women." The blue eyes glittered, and Cait's heart skipped a beat. "Why not thank me?"

"Thank you."

Michael brushed a tendril of hair from her cheek. He tucked it behind her ear, his finger touching the sensitive lobe. He stoked the fire that he had already ignited in her, and it took residence in her lower stomach, burning hot and heavy. She drew in a deep breath.

"I would like more than words, madam."

" 'Tis all you're getting, my lord."

Her fear rising again, Cait stared into his darkened countenance. "Truly, lord, my friends travel ahead of me. I lingered so that I could gather herbs for my father. As the high priest of the Shelter Stone Shrine, he needs many sacred roots and herbs with which to prepare medicines for those who are ill and potions for the cloister sacrifices. He is too old and infirm to travel and must depend on others to gather the plants that do not grow close to the cloister."

Michael had crossed his arms over his massive chest. His expression was skeptical.

Her fear was verging on desperation, but she disciplined her errant emotions and said calmly, "I am alone now, but I do travel with others."

The warrior stepped closer. "I'm glad you lingered behind, Cait nea Sholto, else we would not have met."

While the seductive thrum of his voice and the darkening of his eyes filled Cait with apprehension, they also sparked an excitement in her that she had not experienced during her twenty winters.

"I am in need of entertainment tonight," Michael added.

She drew in a ragged breath, wondering how she could escape the warrior . . . wondering if she really wanted to escape him. "Then, my lord Michael, why don't you and your men travel to the Shelter Stone cloister and watch us entertain? 'Tis not so far that you cannot ride it in two days or sail it in one. I'm sure my adopted father would welcome you and your warriors."

"I don't want to wait for two nights," he answered, his voice sultry. "I want to be entertained . . . now."

Straining to keep the nervousness from her voice, Cait said, "I have told you that I am not a—"

He laid a finger over her mouth. "I have said nothing about your being . . . anything. I have asked only to be entertained . . . as a minstrel entertains."

Cait's heart thundered in her chest. " 'Tis better to see us performing together, sire."

"At the moment you are the only one I am interested in."

He was now standing close enough for her to see that his clothing was not black, as she had originally thought, but a deep blue, the color of the sky at midnight.

"You are a beautiful woman, Cait nea Sholto." Slowly his gaze moved over her face. He flicked the end of her single braid, which hung over one shoulder. "Unusually beautiful with your russet-colored hair and tawny gold eyes." He gazed into her eyes with such intensity that Cait felt as if he were merging with her soul. "They remind me of a cat's eyes. Provoking and alluring and mysterious."

Traitor to herself, Cait felt a tremor run through her. With words and looks this warrior was seducing her. And she was allowing it, even enjoying it. Her breath came short and wispy. Bewildered by her reaction, she tried to move away, but one of his arms gently encircled her waist, pulling her closer. Her heart beat faster. She should resist him, but she didn't want to.

He crooked his finger beneath her chin, tilting her face up.

She saw the lines and angles of his face, the texture of his skin. The misty rain formed water droplets on his forehead and cheeks. She wanted to raise her fingertips to the black beard-stubble that leant him a rugged virility.

"Normally, madam, I do not find women who are as small and short as you attractive. But you fit into my arms perfectly, and I enjoy holding you."

"I may be slender, but I'm not short," Cait said. "I measure six-and-ten hands and one half tall."

"You feel small to me, madam, and you excite me."

All her adult life Cait had heard about the intimacies between a man and a woman, but she had never experienced them herself . . . had not wanted to until today. His words, his looks, and his nearness caused her to feel new and exciting emotions and to want to feel them again . . . and again. With him.

As she stood in the circle of his arms, she felt his hardness, his strength, and remembered he was a Northland warrior. It was easy for her to think Michael Langssonn was made of the same metal as his sword, forged in the heat of the furnace and tempered until he was as dangerous as the long silver blade at his side.

But as he held her, she knew he was made of flesh and blood. His breath, warm and smelling faintly of mountain berries, blew against her flushed cheeks. Unable to help herself, Cait burrowed closer to him.

"Ah, lady, my body responds quickly to your wiggling."

Cait tensed. She felt the jutting strength of his arousal and gasped.

"You're blushing, madam. I like that." Then he bent and pressed his lips to her forehead. " 'Tis all I can do, not to take you here . . . now."

The slight movement of his lips against her skin, his threat—or was it a promise?—ensnared Cait once more. She grew still, hardly daring to breathe. He lifted his head and gazed into her face. His lips were curled into a beautiful, seductive smile. They hovered above hers.

"But that would not bring the greatest pleasure to either of us, would it?" he murmured.

She felt his breath on her face; it became her breath. He framed her face with his hands. His leather gloves were soft and smooth against her skin. The musky scents of leather and of man filled her nostrils. His fingers once more lit a fire that spread through her body and burned in her secret parts.

Softly, ever so softly, he said, "Ah, little minstrel, I do have need of your entertainment tonight. The kind that only you can provide."

The wind blew silken strands of his hair against her face as he bent and placed his mouth on hers. The touch ignited an instant explosion in Cait. Her blood pumped through her veins. Simultaneously he frightened and excited her, stirring a deep yearning.

He raised his lips slightly. "Have you ever enjoyed carnal pleasure before, Cait nea Sholto?"

"Nay."

"I can give you that pleasure." He brushed kisses over her mouth.

"Aye, lord, I'm sure you think you can. Every man I meet boasts that he is better in bed than the next one."

Michael lifted his head.

Cait moved out of his slackened embrace.

"I don't *think* I can give you pleasure, madam. I *know* I can."

His voice was smooth and soft, but Cait sensed his anger.

She wished things could be different between them. She liked it when he held her in his arms and pressed his body against hers. She loved the feelings he evoked. She had never felt so alive. Her body tingled with a new awareness of herself as a desirable woman, of the man who held her as a desirable male.

"Would you have me believe that you are not on fire with wanting for me, madam?"

Without touching her, he held her captive with his eyes, his voice, the warmth and vibrancy of his body. Cait was frightened by the invisible bond she felt with him, yet she could not deny its presence.

"Nay, lord, 'twould be a lie. I am on fire for you."

Chapter 2

Cait's admission was as much a surprise to her as it was evidently a pleasure to him. He smiled broadly, and his eyes sparkled with triumph.

"Come with me to my camp." He caught her hand and tugged.

"Nay, lord." Pulling from his clasp, she stepped back.

"Nay?" His voice hardened, his lips thinned. "Do you tease, lady?"

"I said I want you, but I did not say I would bed you."

His irritation turned to puzzlement. "If this is a game of seduction you have learned during your travels, I don't like it."

"Nay, lord, 'tis the truth plainly told."

Leaning back, he gazed thoughtfully into her eyes. "Why won't you bed with me? Do you think I lie about giving you pleasure?"

"I think you tell the truth so far as you see it," she answered. "But I will not bed you because we do not know each other."

His sudden smile disarmed her. "My lady, there is no better way to become acquainted . . ."

She sighed. "Nay. A carnal coupling such as this, lord, is not to my liking."

He studied her. "Has a man hurt you before, during the mating?"

"Nay."

"Then you are frightened . . . of me?" When she nodded, he said gently, "Don't be, lady. I won't hurt you."

But he could hurt her. Not because he wanted or intended to, but because he made her vulnerable. Though a virgin, she knew about the sexual intimacies between a man and a woman, about the pleasure and the danger.

She had not been without suitors during her twenty winters—in fact, she had been betrothed to one of Glenmuir's most valiant warriors—but she had not felt about any of them as she did this stranger.

Aye, she was frightened. Of herself. She was attracted to this stranger and she had no desire to rebuff him. But she must . . . she must.

Michael reached out to touch her braid.

She dodged her head. "Don't . . . please."

"You remind me of a kitten, madam, a frightened kitten in need of stroking and petting."

To be likened to a cat was a compliment among Highlanders. Cait wondered if the silver warrior knew this . . . She doubted it.

"Mayhap I am a full-grown cat, my lord."

His mocking gaze said he didn't believe her.

"I have been accused of being wild and unruly like the Highland mountain cat."

"Whether you are a cat or a kitten, my lady, I find you exciting. And if you are wild and unruly, I should like to be the one who tames you."

"Have you been around cats before, my lord?"

Michael shook his head.

"Then you have much to learn about them. They

may be captured and caged, but they will not be tamed."

"Ah, my lady, I have seen far too many of them domesticated into lap pets to agree with you."

"Nay, lord, cats are not domesticated by people. *They* domesticate *people*. If a cat chooses to love someone, it gentles that person."

"Is that the way it is with you, my wild and spirited Cait nea Sholto?"

"I don't know. I have sung about men and the pleasure they give women, but I have no knowledge of love or of gentling between a man and a woman." She plumbed the depths of his eyes. "Do you, sire?"

He shook his head. "Nay. But I have found passion to be a pleasurable substitute for love. Surely, my lady, if you are a wandering minstrel, you must have discovered the same."

"Nay, I have not."

"If you have not yet experienced the gentling that comes with carnal pleasure," Michael said, "you have missed out on much, my lady. I can teach you."

As if he had stripped the cloak from her and she stood naked before him, he looked slowly down her body, then back up again with the same thoroughness. His visual caress was as potent as his touch and left a scorching heat in its wake.

"If you'll let me, lady, I can make you purr with satisfaction. I'll make mating a new and wonderful experience for you." She heard the teasing laughter in his voice when he added, "And I'll gladly let you make me growl."

"I suspect, lord, that I shall only make you growl in anger . . . not in satisfaction. I also suspect, my lord, that I will hiss and scratch more than I shall purr."

He laughed. "Hissing and scratching sounds much more exciting than purring. I had not dared to hope for such passion, but I would want no less from a Highland mountain cat."

"My lord, nothing you say will make me change my mind. No matter how much I may want to bed you, I shall not."

"Nay?"

"Nay."

The Northman pushed back on his heels and stared at her.

"Michael!" a masculine voice shouted in Norse. "Where are you?"

"Over here, Kolby," Michael answered in his native tongue.

As a bard, Cait had been educated to speak several different languages, Norse among them. She understood what the two warriors were saying.

"My lord Michael," Cait said in Gaelic, "my friends will be waiting for me. If I don't join them by—by—"

He hiked a brow, but she couldn't allow him to daunt her.

"If I don't join them shortly, they shall come searching for me."

Actually they wouldn't be expecting her until tomorrow evening. Glenmuir was a peaceful kingdom and had been for hundreds of years. As she had told Michael, all Highlanders, no matter what tribe they belonged to, no matter what gods they worshiped, revered the Shelter Stone Shrine and considered Glenmuir hallowed ground. None would dare fight there. Nay, Cait thought, the Silver Daggers would not be unduly concerned if she didn't arrive for several days. They would think she was still gathering herbs and roots for her father.

Michael grinned. "Are you threatening me with a few minstrels?"

"Four warriors," Cait corrected him.

Another Northman as big and powerful-looking as Michael pushed through the brush and rounded one of the huge oak trees. He stopped short when he saw Cait. Although this warrior seemed to be as dark and forbidding as Michael, his hair and eyes were golden brown. He said in Norse, "Where did you find her?"

"The wolf found her," Michael answered, then reverted to Gaelic. "My lady Cait nea Sholto, I would like to introduce you to my headman, Kolby Ingerssonn."

Ignoring the introduction, Kolby said, " 'Tis time to leave the wench behind and to cease playing games, Michael. Lang is ready to set out."

"I'm not playing a game, my friend." The teasing glint had gone from Michael's eyes. "And I don't propose to leave her behind. She was spying on us, and I fear she will report what she has seen to others. The fewer who know about our presence here, the better. We came to these shores to avenge a wrong, not to do battle with innocent people."

Cait listened attentively as Michael and his friend spoke. She wanted to learn as much about them as she could. Not realizing that she understood their language, they would speak candidly to each other.

Michael glanced over his shoulder at Cait. She gazed back with what she hoped was an innocent expression.

"This woman could spread unfounded rumors that would disturb the people," Michael continued.

"They might force us into unwanted battle and hinder us from accomplishing our goals."

"If you don't want to leave her," Kolby said, "you have only two choices: kill her or take her." The Northman's brow furrowed, and he shook his head. "Nay, Michael, you cannot take her with you."

Michael grinned.

"Michael, you cannot!"

Cait's heart skipped a beat. Inside she shouted, *Nay, you can't!* But she said nothing aloud.

"She's a minstrel, Kolby."

Cait didn't like Michael's inference.

"A wandering minstrel," Michael clarified.

Feeling Kolby's gaze as it raked over her body, Cait was glad for a second time that the mantle hid her from his leer.

"We have been without women for a long time," Michael said.

The wolf tensed, raised his ears, and looked around. He growled low in his throat.

"Quiet, Ulf," Michael commanded.

"Aye, we have," Kolby reluctantly agreed, "but—"

Growling again, Ulf rose.

"Sit!" Michael snapped.

Obedient, the wolf hunkered down, but continued to growl softly.

"She's a whore, Kolby. Why shouldn't we take her with us?"

"Whore!" Cait exploded, her role as eavesdropper exposed. She didn't care if they knew she spoke their language. Michael Langssonn had not believed a word she had said.

Surprised, both men stared at her.

She reverted to Norse. "I don't care what language you speak, Michael Langssonn, I am not a whore in any of them! And I will not be treated as one."

"Nay, lord," a young male voice said, "she is not. Cait is a virgin dedicated to the gods Night and Day and to the Shelter Stone Cloister."

"Rob!" Cait looked beyond the two Northland warriors to the young man who pushed his way past a clump of dense brush. Twigs and leaves snapped beneath his boots.

Still growling, his hackles raised, Ulf assumed a menacing stance.

"Sit!" Michael ordered.

The wolf obeyed but kept his gaze on the advancing warrior.

His sword drawn, Rob came forward until he stood between Cait and the two Northmen. His short blond hair was a mass of curls, and he had tied a plaid headband around his forehead. He wore baggy trousers, the legs stuffed into knee-high boots. Over his long-sleeved wool shirt he wore a leather vest.

Rob laughed. "I have taken you by surprise, have I not, stranger?"

"'Tis a little early in the game to be laughing, lad," Michael warned.

Cait joined her cousin in soft laughter. "My lord Northman, you should have listened to the beast. He tried to warn you."

"Aye, lady, I should have." Michael's blue eyes fixed on hers, he asked, "Did you know your friends were nearby?"

"Nay, lord," she said, then added, "Some claim that we are invisible, because we can move through the forest without making a sound or leaving a trail. None can see us unless we wish to be seen."

"I am beginning to believe you, lady."

"After we spied your ship sailing into this little-used cove," Rob said, "we doubled back to find Cait."

"Put your weapon away," Michael said. "You cannot begin to compete with two seasoned warriors like Kolby and me, and I have no wish to take your life."

"Mayhap you are right, lord," Rob answered, his gaze never wavering, "but I shall fight to the death for my cousin's honor."

Michael's hand rested on the hilt of his sword. "You are so convinced of her honor, lad, that you would lay down your life to defend it?"

"Aye, lord, I am and I would."

"Please, my lord Michael," Cait said, "this is Rob, my young cousin and a Silver Dagger. He has seen only seven-and-ten winters."

Michael shot her a scathing gaze. "You travel through the land with a band of children?"

"I may be young, sire, but I am an honorable warrior worthy of respect."

Michael gave Rob a measured look. "Aye," he agreed, "you have proved that this day."

Another masculine voice came from the forest to the right of Michael. "Rob is the youngest in the troupe of minstrels, sire, and Cait is his cousin. It is his right and choice to fight for her honor." All turned to see an older man, huge and burly, step from behind a tree. "I am Dettra, and I also travel with the Silver Daggers. Make no mistake, sire, I am neither a lad nor an unseasoned warrior."

"Nor I." Another large warrior emerged. "I am called Bhaltair."

Michael, rocking back on his heels, gazed at the three Silver Daggers who fanned out in front of him and Kolby.

"How does it feel to be threatened by *minstrels*, my lord?" she taunted.

"I suppose the other Silver Dagger is also lurking about?" Michael guessed.

"Nay, lord," Dettra answered. "When we spied your ship this morn, I sent Fagan to the cloister to inform the high priest of your presence."

"Michael—" Kolby leaned close to his warlord "—they are a threat to us. We must do away with all of them."

As if his headman had not spoken, Michael said to Dettra, "If we release Cait, will the four of you be gone and leave us to our business?"

"Release her!" Kolby exclaimed. "Nay, Michael, we must ensure our safety—"

Michael waved Kolby to silence.

"That depends on your business," Dettra said.

"I search for the man who stole my betrothed from me," Michael said. "I have no quarrel with anyone but him. I must avenge the shame he has brought on my name and honor. Surely, warriors and minstrels of the Shelter Stone, you understand this."

All warriors lived by the law of revenge, no matter what their loyalty or their kingdom. One of the most heinous crimes was the theft of a man's betrothed or bride.

"You are going to fight this man to the death?" Dettra asked.

"Aye."

"Let him go his way, Dettra, and leave our kingdom," Cait said.

The three warriors looked at her.

"Glenmuir has never known blood letting. Let us not be the first to shed it."

Sighing, Dettra nodded and lowered his sword. "Go quickly, Northman."

"Nay," Rob said, "we have our own quarrel to settle with this man. He insulted Cait by calling her a whore."

"Most women who travel in the company of minstrels are whores, Rob," Cait pointed out, hoping to soothe the boy.

"But the Silver Daggers are different."

"Aye, we know that, but the stranger didn't." Cait turned to Michael. "My lord, thank you for releasing me. The Silver Daggers and I shall travel on to the Shelter Stone cloister. To reach the kingdom of Northern Scotland, travel northwest. Two days shall see us at the cloister, and three shall have you across the border of Glenmuir into Athdara."

"What about the minstrel who was sent ahead to the cloister?" Michael asked.

Dettra answered for Cait. "Fagan will tell Sholto that we saw a dragon ship sailing into the cove. Sholto is to await further word from us before he takes action."

"Will he not warn the king of the arrival of strangers?"

"Because many people make pilgrimages to the Shelter Stone Shrine, Glenmuir sees more strangers than most kingdoms," Cait answered. "Sholto is a wise man, not given to hasty decisions. Not wanting to worry King Ido unnecessarily, Fagan will wait for our report." She paused, then added, "Besides, my lord, the cloister is more than half a day's ride from the king's village."

Cait gave Michael her assurance that he would be safely out of Glenmuir by the time warriors could be gathered to pursue him and his men.

She spoke again to give him directions that

would hasten his journey. "When you find the three oaks that twine together in such a manner that you think they are one, you have crossed into Athdara territory. From there, you will turn to the east and travel for three days. Athdara is a wild country and scarcely populated, so you will encounter few people. When you come to the river, look for a double mound of stones. Cross over at that point, and you will be in Northern Scotland. One more day's journey will carry you to the king's village."

"My lord," Dettra said, "I am not a seafarer, but if you are interested, mayhap I can guide you another way by water. It would slow your journey because you must retrace your steps before you can begin in the correct direction, but it would hasten your leaving. When you have completed your mission, you will reach your ship in one day and be able to sail straight out to the sea, saving yourself several days of land travel through Athdara and Glenmuir."

Aye, Cait thought, praising Dettra for his quick thinking, if the Northman took that route, he would not come back through Glenmuir at all.

"Return to the sea the way you came," Dettra said. "Then sail south until you reach the first river. 'Tis a narrow one, but if your captain is careful, he can navigate it. When he becomes landlocked, you will be at the border between Athdara and Northern Scotland."

"Thank you," Michael said.

"Will you go by land or sea, my lord?" Cait asked.

"I have not yet decided."

Cait held out her hand to him. Although she was relieved that he was going, she was also sad that she wouldn't get to know him better or see him again. "Good-bye, my lord. May the gods prosper you."

He took her hand, his leather glove soft to her touch. "How long shall you be at the cloister before you begin your travels anew?"

"One moon."

Michael raised her hand. His lips grazed the tips of her fingers, sending a shiver of pleasure through her body. "Mayhap, my lady, when my business is finished in Northern Scotland, I shall return to the Shelter Stone Cloister and see you perform after all."

"Mayhap, lord, your business in Northern Scotland shall finish you."

"You think so, my lady?"

"I say the man who stole your betrothed was the better warrior."

Michael's eyes narrowed to blue-gray slits. "That is yet to be proved, my lady." Lowering his voice so only she could hear, he added, "Be watching for me, Cait nea Sholto. I shall return."

He turned and strode away, the silver wolf trotting at his heels.

"Come," Dettra said, "we must hurry. A storm approaches."

A single thread of lightning streaked the sky; thunder followed. A gust of wind billowed the midnight blue mantle around Michael before the mist completely enveloped him, his head man, and the wolf.

Nay, Cait thought as she stared at his retreating figure, *the storm is already here.*

Chapter 3

Michael gazed at the blackened sky. "A storm comes. We must make haste."

"You've made a mistake you're going to regret," Kolby replied.

"Perhaps." They walked farther before Michael said, "But we know where we are and where we should be going."

"If you can trust the woman."

"Aye."

"If you hadn't been so enamored of her, you would have known—"

"I knew the Silver Daggers were there. Remember I trained in blind fighting with you." Pushing wet hair from his face, Michael looked at Kolby. "Did you know they were there?"

Grinning, Kolby shook his head. "I was distracted by your announcement that you intended to take the woman with us."

Michael laughed.

"You were jesting about that, were you not?"

"About taking Cait with me?"

Kolby nodded.

"Nay, she intrigues me."

An older warrior, as massive and muscular as Michael, stepped out of the mist.

"Ah, Michael," Kolby drawled, " 'tis your father,

and he looks angry. I'm glad it will be you facing him and not me."

Lang's dark hair, silver at the temples, hung loosely to his shoulders. He also had a dark beard. He was attired in a light-colored shirt and oiled trousers that tightly fit his muscular hips and legs. His mantle hung from his shoulders as if he were unaffected by the chill.

" 'Tis time you returned," Lang called. "What kept you so long?"

"A woman," Kolby answered.

"Tell me the truth," the older man demanded.

" 'Tis true, my father." Michael knelt and took the wolf's face in his hands, scratching behind his ears. "I found a maiden—rather, Ulf found a maiden—hiding in the bushes, spying on us."

"By Thor's hammer!" Lang swore. "This trip has been cursed from the beginning. We got our landmarks confused. We don't know where we are or—"

Rising, laughing softly, Michael clapped an arm around his father's shoulders. "Don't get upset, Lang. Thanks to the woman, I now know where we are. Glenmuir. And I know what direction to take to reach Northern Scotland."

"What did you do with her?"

"Sent her on her way."

Lang gaped in surprise.

"Aye, Lang," Kolby drawled. "He's taken leave of his senses."

Michael playfully cuffed his friend. "She's a bard priestess at a cloister called the Shelter Stone. According to her, all Highlanders consider the shrine holy and this kingdom hallowed. 'Twas best to let her go."

Still Michael could not get the Highland beauty

off his mind. Her mantle had concealed her body from him, but he would never forget her vibrant, russet-colored hair and her tawny gold eyes. Even now he remembered the melodious lilt of her laughter. When he held her in his arms, she had been soft and pliant, and had smelled clean and feminine. Even now, the subtle fragrance of her herbal scent lingered in his mind. But he could not allow himself to be distracted with thoughts of the woman. He needed a clear head to accomplish his mission.

Returning his attention to more immediate matters, Michael said, "We're about six days' ride from the kingdom of Northern Scotland."

"And from Malcolm mac Duncan," Lang added.

"Aye," Michael agreed. "Soon, my father, I shall have settled our debt and restored honor to the House of the Wolves."

"And we can leave these Highlands."

"Aye."

As Michael stood on the bank of the Scottish river gazing into the aquamarine water, he thought of the irony that it was he who must avenge his father's honor. Michael himself had not even known his betrothed, Lady Jarvia of Southerland. He had been a-viking when Lang and the woman's dying husband had drawn up two contracts—one for the betrothal and the other for the marriage. After Jarvia's husband died, Lang had fulfilled his part of the first agreement. By proxy he had betrothed Michael to the widow.

Then Lady Jarvia had requested an honorable rupturing of the betrothal so that she could marry Highland warlord Malcolm mac Duncan. Lang, knowing that Michael had no personal interest in the marriage, had agreed. In accordance with custom and law, he had also stipulated the amount of gold and silver that Jarvia and Malcolm must pay for an honorable rupturing of the betrothal.

From all accounts Malcolm mac Duncan had magnanimously supplied the rupture-endowment, but it had never reached Northland. Not long after Lang's ship, filled with treasure, had departed from the coast of Northern Scotland for its return trip home, Malcolm's warriors had attacked it. They robbed the men of their personal wealth and stole the rupture-endowment, then left for dead all of Lang's warriors. Only one survived. He was subsequently rescued and lived long enough to tell the gruesome details of the raid and to identify the man who had led the attack: Lachlann mac Niall, Malcolm's best-man.

When Michael returned from his journey and learned about the raid and massacre, he swore a blood-oath to Thor that he would kill the man who had brought dishonor on Lang of the Wolves. And he would. Michael prided himself on being a man of his word.

"Lord Lang."

The shout from a young warrior jarred Michael from his ruminations.

The youth, wearing mail but carrying his helmet in his hand, ran up to Michael and his father. "My lords, shall we begin unloading our equipment?" he asked.

"Aye," Michael said. "Have the men prepare their mounts. We shall be riding shortly."

"Why not take the water route?" Kolby asked.

"We will do both," Michael answered. "See to the unloading, Kolby. Father, come with me. I want to speak with the captain."

Brisk steps carried father and son to Michael's

ship, the *Sea Wolf*, where the captain stood talking to another warrior. Lang and Michael joined them. Michael went to his seaman's trunk and extracted a large satchel made of hardened leather. He withdrew several thin sheets of wood, which he laid flat on the deck. With a slender, sharp-pointed cylinder of iron, he began to make indentations into the wood. Lang and the captain hunkered down beside him.

"This," Michael said to the captain, pointing at a curved line, "is the loch where we are now. You are to take the ship with the small crew that I leave aboard and retrace our journey. You will end up here." He pointed to several other indentations in the sheet of wood. "My father and I shall lead the rest of the men through these two territories, ending up here in Northern Scotland. If what the minstrels have said is true, on our return trip we shall meet with you here."

The captain nodded. "This is good. 'Twill take us longer to get there because we will have to double back, but 'twill be shorter when we leave."

"Aye. Once you arrive at your destination," Michael said, "keep the ship hidden and all of you out of sight. Do not stir up any trouble. Expect us back at the ship after ten risings of the sun."

"And then?"

"We will return home."

As Michael walked away, a young lad sidled up to the captain. "Do you think he will return in that length of time, sire?"

"Aye." The captain tugged lightly at his beard.

"Lad," Lang said, "if Michael Langssonn is anything, he is a man of his word. When he says something, he means it."

Lang watched Michael as he strode off the ship.

Although Lang was a tall, burly man himself, his son was taller and more formidable. Since childhood Michael had been obstinate and opinionated, always one to do what he wanted, not caring what other people thought about him.

He had also been unusually gifted with a strength and wisdom that surpassed those of most children his age. He had excelled in physical contests, in endurance and agility, in might. But Lang, being a simple man, could not appreciate his son's intellectual curiosity and endless search for knowledge.

Despite Lang's disapproval, Michael had educated himself. He had learned to read and to write the runes, and he enjoyed recording his journeys to strange lands. During his travels he had learned to speak and write in several languages.

To Lang's joy, Michael had proved himself a mighty warrior as well. Aye, Lang was proud of his son. Truly Michael was the next chief of the House of the Wolf.

Michael walked off, and Lang turned to watch the Northmen transfer their personal belongings from their sea trunks into their leathern satchels. Knowing he must do the same, he crossed the deck and joined the men.

Soon the ponies and pack animals were ready for the overland journey. Michael disembarked from the ship and went to his steed, a magnificent white stallion. Lang, astride his black, rode over to Michael's side.

"Northmen," Michael shouted to the twenty men he had chosen to accompany them, "we ride to Northern Scotland, where I shall avenge the dishonor brought on the House of the Wolves."

Pulling his sword from its sheath and holding the hilt in both hands, he raised it to the sky. The long, thick blade gleamed silver in the eerie, storm-colored light.

"Thor, God of thunder and lightning, and Keeper of the Oaths, hear me this day. I shall keep the oath that I have sworn to you. Death to the man who brought dishonor on my father and on our name."

As if Thor himself acknowledged Michael's vow, thunder clapped loudly. Lightning chased across the darkened sky and seemed to touch the tip of the sword, filling Michael with its bright, deadly current.

"Death to Malcolm mac Duncan," the Northmen shouted, clanging their weapons together in the *vápnatak*, a vote of agreement among Northmen and a show of support for their chief and warlord.

All at once, rain pelted down in torrential fury. Truly his son was rightly named, Lang thought. Elemental, avenging, Michael Langsson was indeed the Lord of Thunder.

The storm had passed, and the sun was shining brightly, casting the Shelter Stone Bridge in gold. The warmth of the sunshine took away the bite of the brisk autumn wind. Exhausted, Cait was glad to be home. At Dettra's insistence, the Silver Daggers had traveled the remainder of yesterday, all night, and the majority of today, stopping at intervals for a few hours of rest. So much had happened that Cait could hardly believe that only yesterday afternoon she had been talking with Michael Langssonn.

He had occupied a lot of her thoughts during her journey home. She was still plagued by the idea that she had seen him somewhere before. Dettra also thought he looked familiar, but he quickly dismissed the idea that he knew Michael. He figured that Michael reminded them of someone they had met during their travels. He confessed that this had happened to him so frequently that he had grown accustomed to it.

Cait was also preoccupied with the emotions that Michael had awakened in her. Before she had met him, she had only heard about desire and passion, and she had wondered if she would ever experience them herself. With Michael she had felt them. During the short time she had spent with him, he had infused her with an awareness of life that she had been lacking.

Cait knew that as a warrior, Michael was a hard man. All the same she was attracted to him, and she wanted to see him again. She wanted to become better acquainted with him. As she remembered his words, *There is no better way for a man and a woman to become acquainted*, warmth filled her and she smiled. Aye, she had wanted to mate with him. He had promised that he would visit her at the cloister. She hoped he would come.

"Cait, watch where you're going," Rob grumbled when she bumped into him. "You've been walking around as if you were in a fog."

"I'm sorry," she apologized, and immediately moved to her side of the pathway.

Ahead, she saw the wondrous beauty of the snow-capped mountains in the background and the thick forests that surrounded the Shelter Stone Cloister. In the far distance the Shelter Stone River—now a blue line—ran down the mountain. Looming up and connecting two foothills just ahead of her was the Shelter Stone Bridge.

"We're home," Cait murmured, drinking in the beauty of the shrine.

"Aye," Rob said. "At last."

The cloister had been Cait's and Rob's home for

the past two-and-ten winters, since both their parents had been killed by brigands and they had been orphaned. Cait loved it. As she and the other Silver Daggers topped the foothill, they saw the full magnificence of the Shelter Stone Shrine. A natural rock bridge hewn out of the mountain by time and the elements, it spanned the Shelter Stone River and waterfall that plunged down the mountain into a deep, richly blue pool of water.

A thick forest, like guardian sentinels, surrounded the connecting maze of deep underground caverns. The Shelter Chamber was the first and largest of these caverns. Through years of usage the rock floor had been worn smooth and shiny. Windows lined the front of the room, letting in the sunlight and offering the guests a breathtaking view of the Highland mountains and the valley far below where the cloister village, surrounded by a stone wall, was nestled in the foothills.

The weary travelers picked up their pace down the incline. As they neared the small village associated with the cloister, Cait saw a tall, slender, robed figure.

"Father!" she called.

A smile burst across his face. "Cait!"

She ran into his outstretched arms.

"I have been worried about all of you, my daughter."

She pulled back to look at him. "We're tired, but fine."

"And Rob?" he asked.

"He did well. He's growing into a fine warrior, Father."

"I know he'll be a fine warrior—if he lives long enough. I've been concerned ever since Fagan arrived home with the news that you had seen a dragon ship."

Cait laughed softly. "Dettra was also worried about the strangers, so we hurried home."

By this time all the Silver Daggers had gathered around the high priest. They shook hands and exchanged greetings. Then, in answer to Sholto's question, they launched into a full report about the Northman, his ship, his crew, and his reason for being in Northern Scotland. After they had satisfied Sholto's curiosity, they excused themselves. They each wanted to take a bath, eat a good meal, and rest.

When Cait and Sholto were alone again, she patted the pouch that hung at her side. "I brought you some sacred plants."

He smiled and placed an arm around her shoulders. " 'Tis good to have you home, my daughter. I miss you when you're gone."

"I missed you, Father. I enjoy traveling, but I am glad to be home."

As Cait described her journey, she and Sholto walked down the pathway and through the open gates into the cloister village. The Great Hall, an imposing rectangular building, was where Sholto and Cait resided. On either side of the Great Hall were two smaller stone buildings, the residences of the two guardian priests, Blar and Trevor. They were Sholto's assistants and his closest friends and advisors.

Completely encircling the three stone buildings were many small, round, one-room structures made of wattle with thatched roofs. Some of these were the individual houses for the cloister priests and priestesses. Others were workshops for cloister weavers, bakers, tanners, and smiths.

"Cait!" called guardian priest Trevor as he emerged from his house. A puff of wind blew the cowl from his head. Holding out his arms, he moved toward Cait. "You are home!"

"Aye, Trevor." She smiled and gave him a brief hug.

Unlike Sholto, Trevor was a tall, muscular man, but his features were angular and solemn, his hair thinning and white. He was kindly and spoke softly. He was the one to whom Cait generally went with her troubles. He was never too busy to listen or give advice.

"Where is Blar?" she asked.

"He had to lead the retreat this year," Trevor said. "He'll be home on the morrow."

"Let us go inside," Sholto said. "Although the sun shines brightly, the day is cold. I need the warmth of the fire."

Trevor and Cait followed Sholto into the Great Hall, and soon both priests and Cait were seated in cushioned chairs in front of the fire pit. The door of the Great Hall opened and a mammoth man strode into the room.

"Cait," he called, holding out his arms.

"Blar." Cait leaped to her feet and ran to greet her friend.

Blar, a strapping man with a booming voice and effusive personality, caught her in his arms and swung her around. " 'Tis good to see you, lass."

To Cait it seemed he was always laughing, always able to see the good side of life. A man of strong emotion, he was never indifferent, and a person never felt indifferent about him. Although he was close to fifty, he had the physique of a man who had seen only thirty winters. His thick hair was white, cut short and brushed back from his face.

"Ah, Cait, I miss your smile and your laughter when you're gone from the cloister."

He set her down and she gazed into his twinkling blue eyes. She was reminded of Michael's eyes, except his were a deeper and purer blue. Confusion swept over her with such strength, she thought she might cry. She had met men before, had been attracted to them, but she had never been as overwhelmed by them as she was with the Northman. Would she ever stop thinking about him?

"Is something wrong, Cait?" Blar asked.

"Nay, I'm just glad to be home."

"Not as glad as we are to have you here." The guardian priest looked at her for a long time before he guided her back to her chair. As he moved a chair closer to the fire, he greeted Sholto and Trevor.

"You're home early," Sholto said.

"Aye, I wanted to be here when the seafarer comes to pick up the gold to transport it to the Cloister in the Grove."

" 'Tis good you remembered," Sholto said. "I had forgotten."

As Sholto ordered a servant to prepare heather tea and informed Blar of all that had happened during his absence, Cait gazed fondly about her. Colorful embroidered tapestries interspersed with wrought-iron lamps decorated the walls. An especially large tapestry hung behind the dais of the High Seat. Plaid tartans were draped over the closed windows to keep out the drafts. There were several trestle-tables, one laid with linen and set with dishes. Servants moved in and out of the room, serving the guests and preparing the evening meal.

"Now, Cait, tell Blar and Trevor about the Northmen and the dragon ship," Sholto requested.

The three priests listened as she described her meeting with the chieftain of the dragon ship—excluding the most intimate details. By the time she was finished, the other Silver Daggers had joined them. All circled the fire and sipped from large cups of hot heather tea.

Finally Cait settled back in her chair and listened as Rob and the others regaled Blar and Trevor with other stories of their journey. They laughed and talked for several hours. Then all of them walked over to the Shelter Chamber to look at the gifts the people had sent through the Silver Daggers for the gods of the Shelter Stone Shrine.

"Trevor," Sholto said, "make a record of the items received."

"Shall I transfer them to the Gift Chamber?"

"Nay, we'll do that on the morrow," Sholto said. "Let everyone have a chance to see and enjoy the newest gifts of the gods." He turned to Cait. "Come with me, daughter. I want to show you something."

When they had entered another cavern, Sholto pulled a cloth bag from his purse. "I have something to show you, but I need to blindfold you with this."

"What is it?"

"I prefer to surprise you."

She nodded and waited as he slipped the covering over her head and pulled the drawstring around her neck.

"One moment," he said. "Let me get a torch."

She heard him walk away. When he returned, she smelled the smoke and felt the heat of the flame as he passed in front of her. Holding her hand, he guided her through a maze that carried them deeper into the bowels of the earth. Finally, after so many twists and turns that Cait had lost her bearings, they stopped.

Sholto took the bag from her head, and she saw that they were in a large room. He pushed on a panel and a huge rock slid to one side, leaving a doorlike opening.

Waving his hand, he said, "This is the Gift Chamber."

The chamber she had heard so much about but had never thought she would see, this was the secret chamber where the riches of the shrine were hidden. Only the Ancient of Nights and Days and the Council of Priests knew the location. Over the years Sholto had often allowed Cait to help him catalog the gifts in the Shelter Chamber, but he had never allowed her inside this room.

"The Gift Chamber," she murmured.

He nodded. "I want you to see all the gifts of the gods."

Still carrying a lighted torch, he entered first. Cait followed. Entranced, she gasped as she stared about her. She had heard about the vast treasure that had accumulated here over the years, but she had never imagined such wealth. The room was filled with gold and silver and precious gems that glittered in the torchlight. Sholto walked across the room and lit other torches. Soon golden light flickered brightly all around them. Cait moved through the room, running her hands lightly over the gifts. Finally she stopped in front of a huge, open chest.

"Look, Father," she cried, and picked up a helmet. It was gold and silver and bronze, inlaid with precious gems. She had never beheld such a magnificent helmet. She could imagine it upon a valiant warrior's head.

As she leaned back and closed her eyes, the first valiant warrior who came to mind was Michael Langssonn. She tried to imagine him in this helmet, but she couldn't. This one looked like the swirling radiance of the sun. It was golden fire. Michael was strong, bold lines and sharp angles. Silver and black, he was the misty rain, the thunder, the lightning. He was silver fire.

Cait recalled him as clearly as if she were still looking at him. His cheeks and chin were shadowed with beard stubble, and the wind was blowing his hair, the long black strands flying about his shoulders. Even through memory she could see the lines and texture of his face. She could inhale his herbal scent. She could hear his deep voice.

Then she was ensnared by his blue eyes ... by the glitter in them when he teased her, by the sultry darkness when he blatantly revealed his desire to mate with her.

Again Cait was hit by a longing for him so intense that she felt the bite of tears. She opened her eyes and clutched the helmet tightly to her chest. She had met Michael Langssonn only yesterday, and only for a brief time, but he fascinated her. She felt as if she knew him with her heart and soul. She missed him ... wanted him.

Cait was shocked by the intensity of her attraction to this man.

"There's a sword that matches the helmet," she heard her father say. "It should be here somewhere." He began to dig through some of the chests. " 'Tis a beautiful sword."

Aye, Cait thought, the sword that matched the helmet she was holding.

"Come, Cait," Sholto called. "Help me search."

Abandoning her fantasies of the Northman, Cait

looked through the chests until she found the weapon. Sitting on the floor, she studied both the sword and the helmet.

"Aye, the design on both is similar," she said.

She ran her hand over the hilt, but again she wasn't seeing the one she held. She was seeing a silver and black-enameled sword that belonged to the Northman.

The Northman! He was gone, and she probably would never see him again, but he possessed her as clearly as if he had abducted her and mated with her.

Hope swelled up with her. Michael had promised that he would visit the cloister when he returned from Northern Scotland. Perhaps he would. As quickly, hope turned to disappointment. If he returned from Northern Scotland, he would have defeated the man who stole his betrothed . . . and he might be bringing his betrothed home with him. He would have no thoughts for Cait . . . or if he did, they would be less than honorable.

Like a bolt of lighting, jealousy seared through Cait and her hand tightened around the hilt of the sword. She didn't know the woman to whom Michael had been betrothed, but already she disliked her.

"What's wrong, child?" Sholto asked.

Cait looked up at him.

"You seem—" he paused, then shrugged "—preoccupied."

Blar had spoken the same words to her earlier, when she had been thinking about Michael.

Cait gripped the sword hilt so tightly that her knuckles turned white. Pushing thoughts of the Northman away for a second time, relaxing her hand, Cait smiled. "Nay, I'm just a wee bit tired."

She made a pretense of studying the sword. "Who gave these weapons to the gods, Father? A king?"

"I don't know," Sholto answered. "One season they were not here, and the next they were." He laughed softly. "'Tis a sign that I am getting old, my daughter, when I can't remember who gives the gods such a gift." He waved his hand to the *ogham* marker that hung on the wall. "All the gifts and their donors have been listed, except for the contents of these trunks over here."

Cait moved from one trunk to the other, looking at the riches, admiring the beauty of design and craftsmanship. A long time later she stood on the other side of the room in front of a large table over which a blue linen had been draped. Lying there was a beautiful golden sickle sword inlaid with silver.

"Our symbol," Cait whispered, and reverently touched the handle. "Given to us by the gods of Night and Day."

Sholto moved to stand behind her. "Nay, the gods gave us the world—the sun and the moon, the skies and the earth—and they gave us intelligence. 'Twas we who gave the gods their names and created their legends and their symbols. We had to, my daughter. Unlike the gods, we are visible and deal with a visible world. These tales and these symbols form the foundation of our faith and help us to face life."

"The sickle sword belonged to the god Night," Cait said.

"Aye, and the shield to Day."

"'Tis said that the person who possesses both the sickle sword and the shield will be the ruler of all the Highlands," Cait said.

"Aye," Sholto said. "According to the legend of

our people, Father Creator gave the high seat of the seasons to his identical twin sons, Night and Day. Before they could assume their seats of rulership, however, they had to fight Chaos. During the great struggle between good and evil, Chaos stripped the young gods of their magical weapons."

Sholto picked up the ancient sword and studied it as he continued. "The sickle sword and the shield fell into the pool below. Although the twins were victorious, the cost was high. Both were wounded and would have died if their mother, Lunar Goddess, had not come to earth and bathed each of them in the sacred pool of the Shelter Stone. They recuperated, but they never found their weapons. Since then, Highlanders have believed that the man who possesses both the sickle sword and the shield will have the powers of the gods and will rule over all of the Highlands."

"What would happen if a golden shield bearing the same inscription as the ones on this sickle sword was found in the Shelter Stone Pool?"

"I have thought of that possibility," Sholto said. " 'Tis not uncommon for a warrior to have his weaponry crafted by the same smith, and for all of it to carry the same design."

He ran the pad of his thumb over the sharpened side of the blade. "Glenmuir would no longer be a peaceful kingdom. Greedy and power-hungry people from all around would fight to own both the sword and the shield." Replacing the sword, Sholto turned to Cait. "I promise you, my daughter, that as long as I am the Ancient of Nights and Days, no golden shield that bears ancient inscriptions similar to those on the sickle sword will be found in the Shelter Stone Pool."

Cait looked into her father's gaunt face, the torchlight flickering shadows over it. His gray eyes pierced hers.

"The shield must never be found, Cait. Never. Do you understand?"

She nodded.

He sat down on one of the carved stone benches and motioned for her to sit beside him. "You have heard of the Cloister Breastpins?"

"Aye, ever since I came here," she answered. "The Lydian Stone and the Bloodstone. They are the key to finding the Gift Chamber and are hidden in a large gold brooch."

"Only one—the Lydian Stone—is hidden in the brooch," Sholto corrected. From the leathern purse he wore about his waist, he extracted an extremely large gold brooch. "I took this out of hiding today because I wanted to talk to you about the sacred pins."

Holding the brooch firmly in one hand, he took his dagger from its sheath and ran the point around the piece of jewelry until it caught. Then he twisted, and the top of the brooch sprang open. Inside lay a beautiful amulet. Sholto lifted the oval medallion out of the brooch case and dangled it from his hand by the chain.

"The Lydian Stone Breastpin."

"But it looks like a necklace," Cait said.

"It can be worn either as a necklace or as a breastpin. Its design is part of its mystery."

"Did you design them?"

"In a way I did."

Cait looked questioningly at him.

"Each new Ancient of Nights and Days may choose to have new Cloister Breastpins designed and crafted, but for a long, long time no change was made. When I decided to do so, I came up with this concept, and had the gifted high priestess of the Dryad Cloister of the Grove do it for me."

"The Cloister of the Grove," Cait murmured as she gazed at the medallion that spun about on the chain. "That is the cloister of women priestesses who have taken a vow of silence and refuse to be seen by or mate with men."

"Aye."

"Then she knows the secret of the Gift Chamber," Cait said.

"Nay, only I, my daughter. She did all the engraving except the *ogham* inscriptions on the inside of each amulet. I did those myself."

Cait touched a finger to the oval amulet. "I still can't quite comprehend that this is a breastpin," she murmured. "It is not at all as I imagined."

"Breastpins, no matter what their shape or size, signify a certain kind of jewelry to us," Sholto explained. "Thus, through the years, people have grown accustomed to thinking of the Cloister Breastpins in those terms. No one would expect them to look as simple as an amulet." He handed the sacred piece of jewelry to her and pointed. "Run your finger over this, and you'll find the pin."

Following his directions, Cait released the latch that held the pin in place and formed the hook that held the chain.

"If you look closely," Sholto said, "you will find that it has a secret latchet." He ran his nail around the base of the two black Lydian stones that were inset in the top of the medallion. The amulet opened. "*Ogham* inscriptions give directions for locating the second amulet—the Bloodstone Breastpin. On it are engraved directions for finding the Gift Chamber. And the Secret Chamber."

"I haven't heard about a second secret hiding place for the treasure," Cait said.

"Nay, no one knows about it."

"Not even Trevor and Blar?"

Sholto shook his head. "Only me. It is the chamber where the Ancient of Nights and Days is instructed to hide the treasure if he feels it is threatened by remaining in the Gift Chamber. Unlike the Gift Chamber's location, which is known by the Council of the Priests as well as the Ancient of Nights and Days, the location of this room is known only to him."

A feeling of foreboding enveloped Cait. "Why are you telling me this, Father?"

"Of all the people in the world," Sholto said, "you are the one whom I trust most. Recently I have had the premonition that someone is searching for the treasure." He paused. "Perhaps someone has a healthy curiosity to see the gifts of the gods, or . . . perhaps it is greed."

"Nay, Father," Cait exclaimed, "surely not."

"Aye," Sholto insisted. "That is why I wanted to show you the chamber and to tell you the secret of the sacred Breastpins. At all costs, Cait, the treasure must be protected. It doesn't belong to us, but to the gods. We are merely guardians who ensure that the will of the gods is carried out. We pray for the people and return the bounty of the gods to them. This shrine and its riches must not fall into the wrong hands."

"That is a heavy responsibility, my father," Cait murmured. "It takes a strong person to be the high priest and the Ancient of Nights and Days."

"Aye, and the Council has been considering their selection of the next high priest of the cloister."

Sholto turned to her. "Cait, the Council is considering you."

Sholto's announcement stunned Cait. "What about Blar or Trevor?"

"Both are good men and dedicated priests. I trained both of them, and I believe one of them should be chosen. But the Council is debating whether or not the cloister needs a younger high priest, someone with a new vision."

"Do Blar and Trevor know about this?"

"Aye. Blar is angry," Sholto said. "In the beginning Trevor was upset, but now he claims to see the wisdom of the Council's thinking."

"This takes me by surprise," she said. "I must think about it."

"Aye, that is why I told you. You have plenty of time in which to consider it." He rose and picked up the head covering once more. "Now we must be going."

After they returned to the Great Hall, Cait sat quietly eating her dinner and thinking about what her father had told her. When it came time for the Silver Daggers to perform, Cait pleaded exhaustion and retired to her sleeping chamber. She opened the window, letting the brisk autumn air blow against her face as she stared into the black night.

Finally she took off her clothing, washed, and slipped into her night tunic. She lay on the bed, looking out the window and pondering what her father had told her.

In the distance she saw a small streak of lightning and thought about the Northman . . . about the hammer he wore around his neck, the symbol of his thunder and lightning god. His words haunted her. *Be watching for me, Cait nea Sholto. I shall return.*

Chapter 4

"**A** rider is coming."

The watchman's shout awakened Cait.

" 'Tis Dacy, and he rides as if the hounds of hell are after him."

Cait bolted out of bed and grabbed her tunic, slipping it over her head. She entered the Great Hall as the door was flung open and a young warrior strode into the building. His boots echoed on the plank floor as he approached the three priests and Rob, who sat in front of the fire.

"Dacy!" Cait exclaimed, welcoming her childhood friend.

Dacy was older than she and Rob, and had left the borderlands to become a warrior of the king long before the brigands attacked their families, killing the parents of all three children. After the attack, Cait and Rob had set out to find Dacy in the king's village. He, in turn, had brought the two youngsters to the cloister, where they had been ever since.

"Dacy!" Rob also shouted, and leaped to his feet.

"Cait, Rob, I have grave news." Dacy brushed windswept hair out of his eyes. His mantle flared out to reveal his green shirt and brown trousers— the livery of King Ido of Glenmuir.

51

"What brings one of the king's men to the cloister at such speed?" Sholto asked, his face somber.

"Northland sea raiders attacked the king's village at early morn," the young warrior announced.

Nay! Cait thought. It could not be! Michael could not have betrayed her.

"King Ido and all his family are dead!"

Sholto rose. "Dead! Ido and all his family?"

"Aye," Dacy said. "We were taken unawares."

"Glenmuir has no king," Sholto murmured.

Trevor, standing also, paced in front of the fire pit.

Blar closed his hands in front of himself. "Northland sea raiders," he muttered, dazed, "This is incomprehensible!"

Cait blamed herself. She had been naive in believing Michael's peaceful intentions. If only she had not become so enamored of the barbarian. If only she had not succumbed to his blatant virility.

But she reminded herself that she had not given him directions to the cloister. She had not revealed any of the cloister secrets. Instead, she had pointed him toward Athdara and Northern Scotland. And the Northmen had clearly outnumbered the Silver Daggers.

"We should have fought them when we had the chance—" Rob began.

Cait spun around. "I did what I thought was right. Besides, Rob, we don't know that these invaders are the same men."

It couldn't be the same man, Cait thought. Not Michael Langssonn.

"Come, Cait," her cousin said sarcastically. "You have to admit it cannot be a mere coincidence that Glenmuir is attacked the day after we saw the dragon ship in the cove."

"You saw a dragon ship?" Dacy swung around. "And you didn't send word to the king?"

Sholto raised his hands for silence. "Stop these senseless accusations. Whatever has happened has happened. We must take care of the present. What else have you to report, Dacy?"

"High Councilman Conn sent me to tell you that fighting is still going on in the king's village, but some of the raiders may be headed here."

"How far behind are they?" Sholto asked.

"Half a day and better. I cut across Hag's Field."

Hag's Field was a large plot of ground between the king's village and the cloister. It had once belonged to an old widow whose fields were the most fertile in Glenmuir. Her vegetables and fruits tasted like none other in the kingdom. King Ido, growing jealous of the woman's produce, had had his warriors remove her from the land so he could live on it himself. But before she died, she cursed the land, and ever since, it had been barren. Soon after, Ido's wife gave birth to their first son. He was stillborn. Declaring the land accursed and forbidding any man to own it, Ido moved again. People rarely set foot on Hag's Field now.

"Cutting across the field was wise," Blar said, "but what is to stop the raiders from also crossing it?"

"Nay, they won't," Dacy said. " 'Tis a blighted plot of land that would frighten away even warriors who knew nothing of the Hag."

"Have you more to report?" Sholto asked.

"We captured one of the sea raiders." Dacy paused, as if reluctant to go on.

"Well, what is it?" Sholto demanded.

"He ... he accused Cait of conspiring with them."

"Nay!" she and Rob cried out together.

"Cait spoke to the Northmen," Rob went on, "but you know she would not betray us."

"I have conspired with no one."

"The prisoner called you by name, Cait, and identified you as one of the Silver Daggers," Dacy said. "He accused you of whoring with his lord, of enticing him to attack by promising him the delights of your body and the riches of the Shelter Stone."

"He lies!" Cait said. "I have lain with no man, and certainly not a Northland sea raider."

But you wanted to, a small inner voice nagged, *and you still want to. If Rob and Dettra and Bhaltair had not shown up when they did, Cait, you might have lain with the chieftain of the Northmen.* He had threatened to take her with him, and Cait had railed against him. But in her heart she knew that a part of her had wanted to go with him.

Still, even now, Cait was not convinced that it was Michael and his warriors who had attacked the village.

"A champion called Gilbert and his warriors have chased the invaders out of the village, though not out of the kingdom," Dacy continued. "The High Council has asked him to act as the provisional king of Glenmuir until they find another heir to the High Seat."

"How dare they take such authority upon themselves," Blar shouted. "They know they must confer with the Ancient of Nights and Days and the Council of Priests before making such a decision."

"High Councilman Conn told me to tell you that they had no time to call a formal meeting, lord. Fighting is still going on, and they need a man to lead the scattered warriors against the invaders and to drive them back into the sea. In light of the emergency, they felt that appointing Gilbert interim-king would calm the people and settle their fears."

"Gilbert. Who is this Gilbert?" Sholto muttered, looking from Blar to Trevor. "Have you ever heard of him?"

Both men shook their heads.

"None of us knows him, lord," Dacy said. "He rode into the village in the heat of the battle after the king and all his family had been killed. He fought against the raiders, and now he is called a hero."

"How fortuitous that this man came along when he did," Trevor murmured sarcastically.

"Aye," Sholto said, "my thoughts also."

"Perhaps, my friends," Blar said softly, "we are misjudging events and should indeed be grateful that this Gilbert was here to save us."

"Gilbert, with the High Council's approval, has declared that Cait is a conspirator and murderer of the king's household," Dacy said. "He has put a price on her head."

"Why would I betray the gods and my kingdom?" Cait demanded, stunned. "If I wanted the treasures of the Shelter Stone, I wouldn't need Northland sea raiders to take it."

"No one has accused you of wanting the kingdom or the treasures of the Shelter Stone for yourself, Cait," Dacy said. "The informer said you boasted to his warlord that you would have your revenge against the king."

"Revenge against King Ido?" The announcement staggered Cait.

"Oh, Cait," Blar said, "don't act the innocent! Everyone in the kingdom knows that two seasons past, Ido ruptured your betrothal to Brieve and married the warrior to his own daughter. You announced in front of all who had assembled for the wedding that one day you would avenge your honor, that the gods would curse Ido and his entire family."

"Don't speak to her in such a tone, Blar," Trevor snapped, his fury so unusual that everyone turned to look at him. "She had a right to be angry and to promise revenge."

"Of course she had a right," Blar agreed, "but she must know that it is no secret she cried out for revenge."

Cait had never dreamed that her fit of outrage would have such dire repercussions, that it could be so perverted and used against her.

"Aye, Cait," Rob said. "You had quite a tantrum."

"No matter what this man says about my wanting revenge against King Ido because he ruptured my betrothal," Cait said, "he is lying about my having conspired with the Northland warlord. This is all wrong, Father. I talked with the Northman, and he assured me that he and his men were headed for Northern Scotland to settle a debt of honor."

"That was yesterday afternoon," Trevor murmured. "If the Northmen sailed off at the same time that you and the Silver Daggers left, they could have sailed on to the king's harbor and landed there by morning."

"Perhaps another woman conspired with him," Rob said.

"Aye," Cait said, "it must have been another woman."

"Still, the informer called you by name," Dacy pointed out.

"The Northman may be seeking revenge against Cait," Rob said. "He thought she was a whore and—"

Sholto spun around and moved closer to her. "You did not tell me this, Cait!"

"I didn't think it mattered, Father. When I told him I was a minstrel, he thought ... well, he thought ..." She shrugged. "He thought I was a whore."

"You told him nothing about the cloister or its riches?" Trevor asked.

"Nay," Cait answered. "He had already heard of them."

"What are we going to do?" Trevor demanded.

"Call the Council of Priests together," Sholto said.

" 'Twill take time," Blar said.

"Send Fagan after them," Sholto ordered. "He's our best rider. Rob, you and the other Silver Daggers, help Trevor and Blar move all in the cloister village who are unable to fight into the inner caverns. We must protect them from these invading Northmen." Whereas before Sholto had seemed quiet and unimposing, he was now a commanding figure. "Cait, you will come with me. Dacy, get something to eat and drink. I'll send for you later."

"Sholto, what about the Breastpins?" Trevor asked. "Is the brooch case in a safe place?"

"It is safe."

"Perhaps we want more than your word," Blar said.

The two men glared at each other.

"My word is all you're getting, Blar," Sholto said. "I shall meet with you and the Council in the Shelter Chamber and let you know how I intend to protect us all from the invaders."

Sholto waited until they were gone, then said in a low voice, "Cait, as soon as we have finished one last task, I want you and the Silver Daggers to leave for Northern Scotland. You are to go to High King

Fergus and ask for sanctuary. Report to him all that you have seen and heard."

"Let the others go, Father," Cait said. "I want to stay here with you."

"No matter who else goes, my daughter," Sholto said, "you must go with them. You are the one who has been unjustly accused. You are the one with a price on your head, and you are the one whom I trust implicitly. I want you to take the Lydian Stone Breastpin with you. 'Twill be a dangerous journey, but I shall show you a route that is little used."

When Cait nodded, he pulled the brooch from his purse. "Swear before the gods that you will guard the pin with your life."

"As a priestess-bard of the Shelter Stone Shrine, and as a servant dedicated to the gods Night and Day, I promise to guard this sacred Breastpin with my life."

He handed her the brooch. "Now, let us get Rob, Dettra, and Bhaltair. We shall need their help."

"With what?" Cait answered.

"We must move the treasure to the Secret Chamber. Too many know where it is now," Sholto answered. "The raiders may try to torture the secret out of one of us, but if only I know how to find the treasure, there is less chance they will find out."

"What about us?"

"If all of you are blindfolded, I have no doubt that you will become so confused in the maze of underground caverns that you could not find your way back to the chamber. Not so with the priests, who are more familiar with the passages. Even blindfolded, one of them might recognize something that would serve as a landmark. As it is, only I shall carry the burden of shame and dishonor should I betray the gods by revealing the location of the Secret Chamber."

"Father—"

He shook his head. " 'Tis part of my responsibility as the Ancient of Nights and Days."

Several hours later, the four minstrels finished moving the cloister riches from the Gift Chamber into the Secret Chamber. Now only Sholto knew the hiding place. As soon as they had finished their task, Sholto once more blindfolded and led them to the surface. He then sent Rob, Dettra, and Bhaltair to join the other warrior priests who awaited the raiders. He and Cait headed toward the Shelter Chamber.

Sholto's face was grim, saddened by the day's events, as he told Cait which route to take into Northern Scotland. He described the landmarks where she was to leave messages for him. The two of them agreed upon the code that Cait would use.

Part of Cait's education had involved learning to read and write the *ogham*, and to use body signals for silent communication. So fluent and versed in this language were the keepers of the Shelter Stone Shrine that they could carry on two conversations at the same time—one aloud and one silently. So competent were they that no one knew when they were speaking the silent language. They were also trained to leave coded messages for fellow bards along the trails they traveled. These messages might consist of one stone, a mound of stones, broken twigs, or branches of particular kinds of trees and bushes. The common traveler would never notice them.

"I'll have Dacy ride part of the way with you," Sholto said. "The two of you are to separate when you reach the twin foothills. You must head on to-ward the Athdarian border. Dacy will go on to Hag's Tree and leave ponies and supplies there in case any of us should need them."

He caught her by the shoulders with sudden urgency.

"The two of you must leave as soon as possible." Sholto hugged her tightly. "Be careful, my daughter. I shall worry about you until I know you are safe with High King Fergus."

"Don't worry, Father," Cait said. "I'll make it."

"I pray to the gods that you do, Cait."

Cait and Sholto parted. He went to the Shelter Chamber, she to her sleeping chamber, where she hastily changed into a shirt and trousers, thinking about the sacred amulet Breastpin that had been en-trusted to her safekeeping.

She opened the brooch case that held the Cloister Breastpin and removed the sacred amulet. After delving through the contents of a large trunk beside her bed, she withdrew a smaller casket in which she kept her jewelry. She searched until she found one of her personal amulets—one that was inset with two black stones and looked similar to the sacred Breastpin in shape and design. Dropping her own necklace into the brooch case, she snapped it shut and hid it in a secret compartment in one of her leathern girdles. She slipped the sacred amulet around her neck.

She would guard the sacred Breastpin with her life.

"All of us will hide in the secret chambers of the caverns until the invaders have left," Sholto said. He stood on the dais in front of a long trestle-table around which were seated the seven other members of the Council of Priests. "That is what I propose for those who are unable to fight. But we, the guardian priests of the shrine, cannot remain hidden forever. This is a shrine to the gods Night and Day. We have taken a sacred oath to protect it from blasphemers and desecrators. And that is what we must do."

"Aye," the members of the Council agreed.

"I don't like it, Sholto," Blar said. He rose and walked to stand before the Ancient of Nights and Days.

"Neither do I," Trevor agreed, pushing back in his chair. "You have put Cait's life in danger."

"I didn't," Sholto answered. "Gilbert and the High Council did. Besides, she is a cloister minstrel, one chosen to take messages through the land."

"Why a woman? Why not one of us?" Trevor asked.

"Why *not* a woman? She's the best person for the task. She has taken the same vow that all of us have taken," Sholto said. "I didn't send one of the other minstrels because they chose to stay and protect us. I didn't choose one of us because we're too old, Trevor, and we are needed here."

"Still, Sholto," Blar said, "what if Cait is captured? We stand to lose the Lydian Stone Breastpin."

"We would take the same chance if we had kept it," Sholto said. "I believe it will be safer with her, out of Glenmuir. I have chosen the quickest and safest route for Cait's escape. None but cloister members know of its existence, and only I know which route she is taking. I also instructed her to leave messages for me at specific places along the route."

"Since she is gone, Sholto, there is nothing we can do now but wait," Blar said. He splayed his hands over the fire flames. "At least, we can rest assured that the treasure is safely hidden in the Gift Chamber."

Sholto smiled. "Aye, Blar, we can rest assured that the cloister treasure is safely hidden."

"None of us will ever divulge the treasure's location," Trevor promised.

Sholto looked at each of the priests who sat around the large hall. "Nay," he agreed, "none of you will. As I said, the cloister treasure is safe, my friends, because I have hidden it in the Secret Chamber."

Two men hid in a stand of trees, away from the moonlight that spilled over the clearing and pathway.

"Gone." Gilbert curled his hand into a fist and glared through the silvered shadows at his companion, a priest of the Shelter Stone Shrine. "What do you mean she's gone?"

"Sholto sent her away from the cloister several hours ago with the Cloister Breastpin. You must send your men after her immediately."

"You know which way she went?"

"Sholto didn't tell us, but he would have directed her on one of two possible routes. If you send riders out on both of them, you'll find her."

"And the cloister pin?" Gilbert said, staring into the fathomless blackness that concealed his companion's face.

"I don't know if you'll find the pin. Cait is a smart woman, and she'll die protecting the cloister treasure."

" 'Twas an ingenious plan of yours to blame Cait for the invasion. It was easy to convince the High Council that she was a traitor and a murderer," Gilbert said. After a pause, he asked, "You believe the high priest suspects that the raiders and I are accomplices?"

"Aye."

"That could hinder us," Gilbert said. He walked to the edge of the trees and gazed over the clearing. Finally he said, "You know the sea raiders are going to have to torture you until you divulge the secret of the Gift Chamber?"

"That was our plan," the priest said, "but not any longer. Sholto has emptied the chamber."

"*What?*" Gilbert whirled around.

"Lower your voice!"

"Don't speak to me in that tone!"

"Then be quiet. You need me, Gilbert, and you're going to need me even more." The priest laughed softly. "You may come to rue the day that you had your men hide your riches among those of the cloister."

"I already do."

Gilbert's treasure was the rupture-endowment that Malcolm mac Duncan had sent to Lord Lang of Northland. It had never reached the Northman. Gilbert—then known as Ghaltair—had seen to that. In an effort to discredit Malcolm mac Duncan, Gilbert and his warriors had disguised themselves as Malcolm's men and had stolen the treasure from Lord Lang's warriors as they returned to Northland. Word reached Malcolm that the rupture-endowment had never reached Lord Lang, that the Northman believed Malcolm had stolen it, and that Lang considered the betrothal dishonorably ruptured. Lang's son Michael Langssonn had sworn vengeance.

No one knew who had stolen the treasure. They certainly didn't suspect Gilbert. Later, Gilbert had been declared a traitor for conspiring against High

King Fergus, and had been banished from Northern Scotland. He had left, taking his stolen hoard with him. Several of his faithful warriors, among them one called Ardac, had joined him, finding shelter in the wilderness of Athdara.

At one time Ardac had been seriously wounded and had gone to the infirmary at the Shelter Stone Cloister for treatment. During his recuperation, he had worked as a keeper of the grounds and discovered the Shelter Chamber. He had sent word to Gilbert about the huge treasure room. Working clandestinely, they had transferred all their treasure to the Shelter Chamber of the cloister.

Later, when Gilbert gave the order to retrieve his goods, Ardac learned that they had been moved. A quiet investigation revealed that gifts and offerings were received in the Shelter Chamber and later removed to the secret Gift Chamber.

"You'll never find that treasure without me," the priest now said. " 'Twas your good fortune that it was I who found your warrior Ardac searching through the caverns."

Gilbert nodded.

"I'm keeping my part of our agreement," the priest said. "You wanted to retrieve your treasure and to become king of Glenmuir. Already you are the king."

"The provisional king," Gilbert reminded him. "It would have been different if my accomplices had not accidentally killed the princess. If she were living, I would now be wed to her and would be the true king of Glenmuir."

"Once you learned she was dead," the priest said, "you had the foresight to kill all the king's household and known heirs. If you are a good ruler, the Council will end its search for a blood relative and proclaim you king." The priest paused, then said, "And as soon as you find the treasure of the cloister, the sea raiders, under your orders, are to kill Sholto and the other members of the Council of Priests. Then you will rule Glenmuir absolutely, and I shall be the high priest and the Ancient of Nights and Days of the Shelter Stone." He laid a hand on Gilbert's shoulder. "But you must have patience. Do not act rashly."

"All of this planning seems to be for nothing!" Gilbert exclaimed. "Why has that old fool emptied the Gift Chamber?"

"Sholto is not a fool. Do not underestimate him. When he learned that the raiders were on their way to the cloister, he knew he must protect the treasure at all costs. Now only Sholto knows where the treasure lies."

"By the gods!" Gilbert swore. "I shall show that old man who he's dealing with. I'll make him watch as I torture each of his priests in turn."

" 'Twould do you no good. Sholto has sworn a blood-oath to the gods. He will never divulge the secret of the hiding place."

"Not even if we threaten his daughter's life?"

Several seconds passed before the priest spoke. "I wouldn't think so, but . . ." He ended with a shrug. "We will have a better chance of finding the treasure if we can capture Cait and the Breastpin. They give directions to the Gift Chamber and perhaps to the alternate secret room as well."

His hands twined together behind his back, Gilbert paced back and forth. "You are sure that no one knows you and I are working together?"

"Nay," the priest answered. "And as far as I can tell, Sholto is the only one who may think the sea raiders are your accomplices. The majority think that the invaders are the Northmen who landed on our shores two days ago."

His interest piqued, Gilbert stepped closer. "I've heard nothing about a Northman."

"Aye, a warrior by the name of Michael Langssonn. He was headed for Northern Scotland, seeking a man who stole his betrothed from him."

"Ah," Gilbert drawled, recognition dawning. "He wants to avenge his honor. I hope he finds the man he is seeking."

Gilbert did not reveal that he knew the name Michael Langssonn very well, or that he realized who Michael sought: Malcolm mac Duncan.

Gilbert hated Malcolm. It was Malcolm who had discovered that Gilbert had conspired against High King Fergus in an effort to topple the newly established kingdom. It was Malcolm who had banished Gilbert from the kingdom.

Aye, Gilbert hated Malcolm, and had spent the last six seasons planning the warlord's fall. Soon, with Michael's help, his own revenge against the Highland warriors would be complete.

"What are you going to do about Cait?" the priest demanded.

"Tell me the routes she may have taken, and I shall send my best warriors after her," Gilbert said. "Also describe this brooch case in which the Breastpin is hidden. My men need to know what they are looking for."

Unable to sleep, Michael leaned against a tree and gazed out over the moonlit camp of sleeping warriors. All his life he had felt that something was missing in his life, and he had spent his adult years searching for it. He had sailed the world over, seeking but never finding what he sought . . .

He had come to this land for one reason—to kill Malcolm mac Duncan because of a woman Michael had never met. For a woman who had chosen Malcolm mac Duncan instead of Michael to be her husband.

Until Michael had met Cait, he hadn't thought beyond this goal. Now he did. After he killed Malcolm in a duel to the death, by custom the woman Jarvia would once more be his. What would he do with her? He didn't know if he even wanted her.

All he could think about was the russet-haired Highlander. She was a desirable and innocent woman who had set him afire with longing. He would have soon forgotten any other woman, but he hadn't forgotten Cait nea Sholto. And the more he thought about her, the more he wanted her . . . almost to the exclusion of everything else.

Michael's preoccupation with Cait angered and frustrated him. He had always been a single-minded man, a man who decided what he wanted and went after it. He had never allowed himself to get so involved with a woman that she distracted him. Or . . . he had never found the woman he wanted to become so involved with. Right now he had no time to explore what she might mean to him. He must focus on his blood-oath to Thor. Then he could consider Cait, and satisfy his desire for her.

Aye, he thought, pushing away from the tree, he had done a lot of traveling in his life, but there was one more trip that he would take, no matter what. When he had settled his score with Malcolm mac Duncan, he would make his first religious pilgrimage, to the Cloister of the Shelter Stone Shrine. Aye, 'twas time he paid homage to the gods. And he wanted to hear Cait sing . . . for him.

Smiling, he went to his pallet, the wolf Ulf trotting beside him, and opened the flap of his satchel. Taking out his flute, he moved to the other side of the camp and sat down on a boulder. Ulf lay down at his feet.

Thinking about Cait, Michael began to play a soft melody. It was a song about a warrior who had been a-viking for two years. During his trip he had been badly wounded from a sword blow to the side of his head, which had taken one eye and left him badly disfigured. As he sailed home, he wondered how his young bride would greet him.

Closing his eyes and giving himself up to the music, Michael imagined himself as the warrior, Cait as the young bride, dressed in a long, flowing tunic, running to the dock to greet the returning warriors. Her husband moved slowly toward her, and she gazed up at his face. She touched the long scar that ran from his forehead across his cheek. She touched the black leathern patch over his eye.

Tears running down her cheeks, she threw her arms around her husband and murmured words of love to him. She caught his face between her soft hands and spread kisses over his cheeks and forehead, and finally around the leathern eye patch. Then she kissed him fully on the mouth—a long, passionate kiss. She caught him by the hand and let him to the sleeping chamber in their longhouse.

Michael could see himself lying on the bed, Cait standing in front of a blazing fire. Piece by piece she stripped off her clothing until she was clad only in her sheer undertunic. The firelight at her back outlined her beautiful body.

"So you're thinking about the woman, Michael."

Kolby's sleep-gruff voice shattered Michael's fantasy. He lowered the flute.

"What woman?"

Kolby, lying on his pallet nearby, pushed up on one elbow and ran his other hand through his hair. "You know as well as I do. The minstrel bard."

"You don't know that I'm thinking of her."

Kolby plumped the blanket he was using for his head cushion and lay back down. "You forget, my friend, that I know you better than anyone else, except your father. Anytime you play that melody, I know you are thinking of a woman. And it must be that bard."

Michael feigned his indifference and began to play again.

"I knew she was going to be trouble," Kolby grumbled.

Chapter 5

As dawn lightened the horizon, the wind, cold and cutting, bit into Cait's face. It whipped against her as the pony raced along the mountain trail in a desperate effort to outrun the five men who were chasing her . . . who had been chasing her throughout the night. The mare galloped fast, but not fast enough.

Cait didn't know who was pursuing her, but she suspected they were either sea raiders or Gilbert's men. Who else could they be? She also suspected that someone at the cloister had betrayed her. Only priests and priestesses knew of the two routes she could be traveling, and only they would guess she would head to northern Scotland.

On and on she traveled. At the bottom of a foothill, she glanced over her shoulder. Three men topped the incline. Only three. Before there had been five. Evidently they had separated.

Cait leaned down and urged the faithful mare to a faster pace, but the exhausted animal had no more to give. Pony and rider moved through the maze of rocks up the next, steeper foothill. Another glance over her shoulder showed that they were closing in on her.

Earlier, sure she was being followed, she had debated taking time to stop and hide the sacred pin.

She had decided to pause at one of the designated message points—the spear boulder. She had hidden the Breastpin at its base and left a coded message for Sholto. Now, as the riders closed in on her, she was glad she had had such forethought.

A horn sounded. The three behind her were sure they had captured their prey and were signaling for the other two to join them.

"Halt!" The shout came from in front of her. They had surrounded her.

The pony stumbled, snorted, and twisted its head. It fell to the ground, rolling down the incline and taking Cait with her. Stunned, Cait lay at the bottom of the hill on the damp ground, her clothing no barrier against the cold. Beside her lay the dead mare, a lance through its chest.

By the time she pushed to her feet, her pursuers had formed a circle around her. They dismounted and walked toward her. The older one, a puffy scar running down his cheek, stepped closest, looking first at Cait, then at the dead pony.

"Who are you?" she demanded. "Why are you chasing me?"

"I am Ardac," the man answered, kicking the mare. "We serve Lord Gilbert, the king of Glenmuir."

"Glenmuir has no king," Cait said. "Ido and his entire family were killed by Northland sea raiders."

"Aye, Glenmuir has a king. His name is Gilbert. 'Twill serve you well to remember that, Cait nea Sholto." The warrior smirked. "You should also remember that you are the one who brought about the king's death. You and your obsession for revenge."

"I had nothing to do with the attack or the massacre. The captured sea raider lied."

Ardac laughed mockingly.

"But you know that," Cait said.

Still smirking, he said, "But the High Council doesn't."

"Does Gilbert?"

"Aye."

Cait remembered Trevor's words about Gilbert's fortuitous arrival in the king's village. "This is all Gilbert's doing," she said. "Are the sea raiders his accomplices?"

"Aye."

"Why are you being so forthcoming? When we return, I shall appeal to the High Council of Glenmuir for a hearing."

"You won't," Ardac replied. "Gilbert sent me to find you because I am his most valiant warrior, the master of his men. I've been instructed to take you directly to him. He won't let you speak with anyone else. In fact, Cait nea Sholto, no one will know that you have been captured and are his prisoner . . . except your father, the two guardian priests, and your cousin."

"What have you done with Sholto and Rob?"

Ardac laughed and turned from her. Cait caught him by the shoulder and pulled him around.

"What has happened to my father and Rob?"

Ardac brushed her hand from his arm. "All are prisoners and will remain so until your father takes Gilbert to the treasure room."

Cait scoffed. "Gilbert comes up against an enemy of a different caliber when he fights my father. The riches of the cloister belong to the gods, and my father and the other cloister members will die before they give such sacred treasure to Gilbert."

"If your father doesn't reveal the whereabouts of the treasure," Ardac said, "the cloister members will be joining their gods sooner than they expected."

A chill ran down Cait's spine. She turned slightly and gazed at the forest to her right. As a silvery mist settled around them, the massive trees with their widespread branches and mammoth roots looked more and more like huge warriors towering toward the heavens. Cait only wished they were, and that they would come to her rescue.

Ardac waved his hand, and two of his warriors approached her. One held her, while another tied her hands behind her back with slender leathern thongs that cut into her flesh.

"Search her," Ardac commanded. "She has the brooch."

How could they know about the brooch? Only cloister members knew that the amulet Breastpin was hidden in a brooch case. Earlier she had suspected that someone in the cloister had betrayed her. Now she was sure.

Gilbert's warriors stripped the clothing off her piece by piece. Her mantle. Her girdle. Her overtunic. They cut them into shreds and threw them on the ground. When she stood in nothing but her long, sleeveless undertunic, one of them callously ran his hand over her body.

"Nay," he said. "She wears no jewelry."

Ardac drew his brows together. "You're certain, Ern?"

"Aye," the man said. "If she had it, Ardac, she must have gotten rid of it before we captured her."

Ardac paced restlessly, his gaze on the ground. "If she hid it," he muttered, "it could be anywhere." He raised his head. "Search the satchels on the pony."

Cait watched . . . and prayed . . . as they tore

through her belongings, cutting and tearing them into shreds. One pulled out the leathern girdle in which she had hidden the brooch case that contained her personal amulet. She tensed. Muttering obscenities, he cut into the leather.

His face suddenly lit up. "Ardac!" He waved the brooch case in the air.

The men closed around him. Ardac unsheathed his dagger as he took the piece of jewelry the man held out. A frown of concentration on his face, he moved the tip of the blade around the edge of the large medallion. Abruptly he smiled, then laughed.

Cait strove to hide her satisfaction. Mayhap the gods were blessing her today.

Ardac exerted pressure, and the piece of jewelry popped open. Cait's necklace, an oval gold medallion inset with black stones, fell to the ground. Ardac picked it up by the gold chain. He examined it. Then, satisfied, he dropped it into the leathern pouch at his waist. He looked at Cait, grinning smugly.

"Who told you?" Cait asked, feigning defeat.

"Lord Gilbert has a friend in the cloister who tells us all that happens there."

Now Cait knew how Gilbert had entrapped her. The cloister traitor had informed him of her ruptured betrothal, her subsequent fit of anger, and shout of revenge. The two of them had used this humiliating event for their own purposes.

"The informer told us what path you were traveling," Ardac continued, "and what to search for when we captured you."

Ardac moved closer to her. He ran his leering gaze over her body, beginning at her feet and working slowly upward. Cait straightened her back and glared into his ugly face.

"You're beautiful. Aye, even in your tattered garments, you're a beautiful woman." His lips curved in an ugly, mocking smile. " 'Tis easy to see why the High Council so quickly believed that men had bartered their souls for you, had killed and destroyed a kingdom for you."

Grabbing her arm, Ardac jerked her close and cupped one of her breasts in his hand. Cait spat in his face. He slapped her, the blow jarring her head so hard that her neck cracked. Pain racked her body. She fell.

"Gilbert has warned us that your soul is dark. So is your magic," he bellowed, "else my men and I would take your body, *traitor*."

He bent, grabbed her by the hair, and jerked her to her feet. She nearly fainted from the pain. The glen spun around her. He dragged her across the ground toward a fallen tree. Twigs and sharp rocks dug into her flesh, ripping her tunic. Muttering imprecations, he pushed her facedown on the rough trunk. Splinters pricked her cheek; she cried out.

"I'll teach you to have respect for the king's men, *whore*."

Above her head she heard the whine of an ax blade. Fear struck her heart. They were going to behead her!

The ax thudded against the tree trunk. She seemed to feel the cold metal slice through her neck, but she was still alive! Her body convulsed. Gilbert's men laughed. They were teasing her. She heard a thump in front of her and saw her russet-colored braid fall to the ground.

"We shall get a good price for this," Ardac observed.

They had cut off her hair! Cait squinted to hold back hot tears. She drew in a deep breath. *They had cut her hair off!* Sheared hair was a public sign of shame and disgrace. Gilbert's men had stripped her of her integrity. She felt her control slipping away. Inside she trembled. Tears threatened.

Still, she would not give in to hysterics. She would not.

" 'Tis thick and long," Ardac continued. " 'Twill make a woman a fine wig. She will be willing to barter *anything* to have it."

The autumn wind howled mournfully through the forest. Leaves fluttered to the ground, landing at Cait's feet to form a red, gold, and yellow carpet. Her short hair swirled across her face, and her undertunic hugged her body.

Again the executioner swung his ax. She heard it cut through the air. Once. Her heart beat, erratically. Twice. Her entire body was covered in perspiration.

"Halt!" The disembodied masculine voice, deep and authoritative, came from far off to the right, at the edge of the clearing.

Momentarily hope pushed aside Cait's fear. She stiffened and gazed into the forest, still cloaked in the early morning fog. The sun had begun its ascent, and rays of light cut through the haze, coloring it a silvery white. Perhaps the gods had come to rescue her, and the trees *were* warriors.

Ardac cursed and brought down his arms. She saw the glint of the ax blade. She heard the whoosh and felt the burning graze of the flying metal as it shaved the tree trunk and wedged into the earth inches from her face. Frozen with fear, Cait did not move. She did not breathe. She didn't know if her heart was still beating. Then her lungs felt as if they were going to burst. Air painfully invaded her chest. With a gasp she wilted to the ground.

"Who goes there?" Ardac called.

Gilbert's men, poised to fight, tightened their hands on the hilts of their swords and battle-axes. Sweat beaded their faces. Their eyes rolled as they sought the source of the commanding voice.

"Who goes there?" Ardac raised his voice to call a second time.

"Michael Langssonn."

The Northman took form out of the mist.

He stood at the forest's edge—much like the first time Cait had seen him. Only now he wore a black-enameled and silver helmet. Its visor and nasal, protecting his eyes and nose, disguised his features and lent him a sinister appearance. The wind blew tendrils of raven black hair against his shoulders and about his exposed lower face. When the mantle billowed open, Cait saw that he was dressed in dark clothing, wearing his silver chain mail. His dagger and sword were strapped about his waist.

"Who are you?" Ardac demanded.

"A sojourner."

Michael and his warriors had arrived in time to hear the man accuse Cait of being a whore and a traitor, to see them chop off her hair. Sadly he looked at the long, thick braid lying on the ground, then glanced at her to see the short, russet-colored hair flying about her face. She gazed at him with soulful eyes, conveying to him her sorrow and shame.

Michael looked at the man who held the ax. "Who are you, executioner?"

"Ardac. I serve King Gilbert of Glenmuir. Why have you come to our kingdom, stranger?"

Always a cautious man, one who had been taught to keep his own counsel, Michael said, "I am but passing through. I'm on my way to Northern Scotland."

"Travel in peace. We will do you no harm."
Ardac's eyes narrowed, and he ran a finger down
the scar on his cheek. "If you continue on this trail,
sire, there is the possibility you may be attacked by
Athdarian border bandits."

Michael fixed his gaze on Cait. She had lied to
him about who she was and how to travel safely to
Northern Scotland.

"There's another route you can travel, sire. 'Tis a
little longer, but it's safer and easier to travel and
will get you to your destination quicker."

"Is this route clearly marked so that a sojourner
would be able to travel it?" he asked.

"Aye, fairly so, especially if you know which
signs to look for."

As the warrior described the landmarks, Michael
listened attentively. As soon as Ardac had finished,
Michael recited them to make sure he had memorized them correctly.

After Ardac nodded, Michael said, "Since the
woman is of no use to you, I will barter for her."

Openmouthed, Cait stared at him. Also astounded, Gilbert's men looked at one another.

"Nay, we cannot," Ardac said.

"Why? You mean to behead her, do you not?"

"This matter does not concern you, stranger,"
Ardac said. "Be gone."

Michael did not move.

Ardac leaned his ax against the tree trunk and
drew out his sword, then stepped away. "I've given
you permission to travel through our kingdom in
peace. Now, leave before I change my mind and behead you."

"Nay," Michael said, "you won't be taking my
head. I'm not as easily defeated as a defenseless
woman." He lifted his gloved hand, and ten war-

riors, like apparitions, materialized from the hazy forest and surrounded Gilbert's men.

"Ulf," Michael commanded, and the wolf tore out of the forest and bounded up to Ardac. The animal bared sharp, dangerous teeth and growled low in its throat.

"I could kill him with one blow," Ardac bragged.

"Try it."

Ardac swiped an arm over his forehead. He started to step back. Growling louder, the wolf crouched, ready to spring. As if frozen, the warrior halted.

"Now, executioner, shall we barter?" Michael said. "As I told you, I am a sojourner here and have no wish to loiter longer than I must. Nor do I wish to end our discussion with battle." Michael paused. "As you can see, my men and I easily outnumber you, and the victory would be ours. The woman would be mine." Again he paused to let Ardac ponder his words. "But fighting is not in our best interests. So I am willing to settle our differences with a fair amount of gold and silver."

Out of the corner of his eyes, Michael kept watch on Cait, who was bracing her shoulder against the tree trunk and pushing to her feet. He trusted her no more than he trusted the warrior who stood before him.

"My lord," Ardac said, "the king's village is only a few hours' journey from here. You can get all sorts of women there."

"I don't want all sorts of women," Michael replied. "I want this woman."

Aye, he wanted her. She intrigued him as none other ever had. He had dreamed about her for the past two nights. Her smile, her tawny gold eyes, her laughter, everything about her haunted him. He should have taken her when they first met. Once he had had his fill of her lovely body, he would be rid of her.

Not only did he burn with lust for her, he burned with anger. She had deceived him. She had lied to him about the pathway, telling him that it was unclearly marked. Deliberately she had instructed him to take the route that was most dangerous for him and his men.

"My lord," Ardac said, "the woman is evil, her soul dark. Her whoring and perfidy have brought a curse on our land."

"Her whoring and perfidy," Michael said quietly, his opinion of her confirmed.

"Nay, lord," Cait cried.

"Aye," Ardac answered. "She conspired with Northland sea raiders to have the king and all his family killed. They sailed into the harbor yesterday morning and attacked the king's village. This woman bartered her body to the chieftain of the sea raiders, sire. In exchange he killed the former king, Ido."

"Why did she wish to have the king killed?" Michael spoke to Ardac, but he looked at Cait.

"I didn't," she exclaimed.

She was bedraggled, cut, and bruised, and her mass of lovely hair was shorn. But she stood proudly, her back straight, her shoulders squared.

"They claim I did because four seasons past, King Ido dishonorably ruptured my betrothal to a warrior named Brieve."

"And wed him to his own daughter," Ardac added. "Our new king Gilbert and the High Council of Glenmuir have declared her a traitor and put a bounty on her head."

"How much?"

Michael felt Kolby's disapproving gaze on his back, but he did not turn to look at his friend. He was also glad that his father was not here. Yesterday Lang had insisted that they split into two groups to spy out the land. He did not trust the information Cait and her friends had given them. He wanted to search for better trails in case something should go wrong and they should have to return through Glenmuir rather than by sea. The better they knew the terrain, the quicker and easier their departure would be.

"Gilbert has promised us a pound of gold," Ardac answered.

"Then I shall give you two measures."

Gilbert's men looked at Ardac, their greedy expressions giving him permission to barter.

"Two pounds, Ardac!" another of the king's men emphasized.

"I cannot," Ardac finally said. "Lord Gilbert commanded me to—"

"*Ardac!*" one of the other men shouted, and strode to his leader. "One moment. I wish to speak to you privately."

Nodding, murmuring among themselves, the others pressed into a tight circle around their leader.

Waiting patiently, Michael continued to watch Cait. The helmet he wore was heavy, hot and uncomfortable, but it allowed him to observe people without their realizing it. Michael watched Cait cautiously wiggle her way back to her mare. He couldn't see what she was doing, but he knew she was up to no good.

Ardac moved out of the circle and once again faced Michael.

"What is your answer?" Michael demanded.

"Three pounds of gold and you shall have her without a fight."

Michael wasn't surprised. "You're getting greedy, executioner."

"The risk is great," Ardac replied. "By releasing her, we shall be returning without proof of her death."

"Aye, but you can sell her to me for three pounds of gold, steal her back later, and still collect your one pound from Gilbert. That, executioner, would give you four pounds in all."

When Ardac's warriors began to fidget, Michael knew he had guessed their plan.

"Whatever you think, sire," Ardac continued, "my lord demands her head. Since I am the master of Gilbert's men, I am putting my life in danger. I want more for my risk. One measure more."

Tensely all awaited the stranger's reply.

"Luck is with you this day, executioner. I shall give you three measures of gold."

"Agreed, lord. She is yours." Ardac rubbed his palms together.

"Luck will be against you," Michael warned, "if I should see you or your men again."

"Nay, sire," Ardac promised with a shake of his head, "you won't. When we leave here, we intend . . ."

Michael heard the rumble of words, but at the moment he was more interested in what Cait was up to. She toppled over, but when she pushed herself upright again, Michael was fairly sure she had managed to get one of her knives from her saddle bags and had cut through the ropes. She was free.

She sat for a moment, looking around. So did Michael. He saw the lone horse—it belonged to one of Gilbert's warriors—standing close to her. Michael walked over to her, grabbed her by the shoulder, and yanked her to him. A dagger slid out of her hand and landed with a thud at their feet. Cait looked into his face.

Speaking in an undertone, he said, "Nay, lady, you shall not escape me a second time."

She glared at him. "I am not chattel, nor am I a whore that you can barter for me."

"Aye, she is a whore," Ardac shouted, "else she wouldn't be a traveling minstrel."

"He lies, my lord," Cait said.

"So do you, madam," Michael replied. "I choose to believe the warrior since I have need of a whore, not a lady. My loins are swollen and in need of release. I have not had a woman in several moons. So you see, a whore is worth three measures of gold to me. A lady is worth nothing."

"Sire . . ." Cait directed her beautiful tawny gold eyes on him, and he felt desire spear through his body. He also felt compassion for her, but he was not going to allow her to deceive him now as she had done the day before yesterday.

"Please believe me," she said. "My adopted father and all the other cloister members are in danger. A ruthless man, who I am convinced is responsible for the massacre of the king and his family, has placed himself upon the high seat of authority. I am on my way to . . . to seek sanctuary and help."

"Do you have proof of this treachery, madam?" Michael asked.

Cait stared at Ardac, then at Michael. She opened her mouth as if to speak, then closed it. Finally she sighed. "Nay."

"Nay, lord, is correct," Ardac said. "The woman lies and deceives. Gilbert is a hero. It was the High

Council who asked him to be the provisional ruler
of Glenmuir."

Michael gazed solemnly at both Ardac and Cait.
He knew not which one lied, or if both did. And he
didn't care. He wanted Cait, and fully intended to
have her.

"Not only is the woman a lair and a deceiver,
sire, she is also a thief," Ardac continued. "King
Gilbert thwarted the sea raiders in their attempt to
steal sacred statuaries from the shrine. He believes
that she has stolen one of the most sacred objects
and is taking it out of the kingdom."

"I know you don't believe me," Cait said, "but I
am innocent of these charges. Please, give this man
three measures of gold to release me."

Michael curbed his smile. Cait nea Sholto was a
fighter, and he admired her for that.

"Then escort me to Athdara, where I may take
sanctuary. I shall repay you for your trouble." When
Michael did not reply, she added, "I will give you
six measures of gold. Three to repay you and three
as a prize for you and your warriors."

She waited. "My father will also give you a handsome reward for escorting me to safety in Athdara."

"When would I receive the payment, madam?"

"Not until—"

Michael started to laugh softly.

"Please, sire," Cait begged.

"Madam, you are convincing, but I am accustomed to the antics of whores. I have no intention
of giving this man three pounds of gold to set you
free, then escort you to Athdara only to learn that
you have lied to me." He lowered his voice and
trailed an index finger down her neck. "Besides, I
want you for myself."

She jerked away from him. "I would rather have

my head chopped off than service your *carnal needs.*"

He crooked a gloved finger beneath her chin. Softly, ever so softly, he said, "Then, madam, perhaps I can service yours."

"Then I should chop off your rod."

"You're feisty. I like that." He grinned and touched his finger to the racing pulse at her neck. "The man asks for three measures of gold. Much more than any piece of chattel is worth. Do you think you're worth it?"

"I'm worth far more than that." Her voice was husky. "So much, *my lord,* that you or any other man does not have enough to buy me."

"Then, *my lady,* I am getting a bargain."

"It might seem so." She gave him a brilliant smile.

But he knew she was frightened. He could see it in her eyes, which had turned a deep shade of russet.

"You're getting trouble, sire, much more than three measures worth. That, I promise you."

"I like trouble, madam." Never taking his gaze from her, Michael called out in Gaelic, "Kolby, bring my bartering trunk."

Three helmeted warriors moved out of the forest. Kolby led the way; the other two carried a chest between them. When they stood before Michael, they halted.

Reverting to Norse, Kolby said, "Are you sure what you are doing is wise? Already this woman has slowed us down."

His voice hard, Michael said, "Give me no argument, Kolby."

They stared at each other for a second before Kolby nodded and stepped back. Michael waved to one of the other warriors who stood beside the trunk. At the silent command, the man knelt, unfastened the lid, and lifted it. Michael leaned down and rummaged through the contents until he found a silver torque inset with obsidians.

Straightening, he ran a finger over the design. "Good," he murmured. "My name is engraved on it." He looked at her. "You will wear this, madam."

Cait shook her head and licked her dry lips. "I have my own jewelry."

"From now on you will wear only what I allow you to wear."

She shook her head.

" 'Tis a command, madam, not a request. At the first opportunity, I shall have this soldered about your neck."

"Nay!" she exclaimed, gazing at him with large, fear-darkened eyes. "I do not wish to wear jewelry that I cannot remove. That torque with your name engraved on it will mark me as your property."

"That is the intent, madam."

Chapter 6

Cait stared at the silver torque that would shackle her to Michael Langssonn.

Gilbert's men had dishonored her by shearing her hair. The Northland warlord would enslave her. She had escaped one punishment only to be caught in a worse one.

"Do you want it soldered about the woman's neck now?" Kolby asked.

"Nay, we shall wait until we stop for the night," Michael answered. "Measure out the man's gold."

Lost in her own thoughts, Cait watched Kolby set up the scale. She had asked Michael to take her to Athdara instead of Northern Scotland because she didn't trust him or Gilbert's men. If she escaped, she was praying that Ardac would report that she had requested to go to Athdara. Perhaps Gilbert and the traitor priest would suppose that's where Sholto would ultimately contact her.

Kolby selected pieces of gold jewelry and dishes and piled them on the scales. Ardac and his warriors, all eyeing the riches greedily, pressed closer. One pound. Kolby emptied it into a large leathern bag. Two. Three. The bag bulged. The Northman tied it off, rose, and turned to Michael.

"Your three measures," Michael announced. "Take it and be gone."

Two of Gilbert's men carried the bag between them. As they fastened it to one of their ponies, the two Northland warriors who had brought the trunk to Michael closed it and secured the straps. They stood and moved to Michael's side.

Beneath the gaze of the vigilant Northmen, Ardac and his men mounted their ponies and rode across the clearing toward the farthest edge of the forest. When they reached an outcropping of rocks, Ardac stopped the men, turned, and looked back.

Morning had fully arrived, and golden sunlight had dissipated the fog so that Cait could see them well. Ardac looked forward, motioned, and the men began to ride again. Soon they were mere dark shadows moving farther and farther away. They rounded a foothill and were gone. She was alone with Michael and his warriors.

"We have not seen the last of them," Kolby predicted.

"Nay," Michael agreed. "They are a greedy lot."

The wind picked up momentum and swirled coldly around Cait. She began to shake both from the cold and fright. She hugged herself tightly. Michael unfastened the brooch on his shoulder, took off his mantle, and draped it over her. She welcomed its furry warmth and was glad that his hands cupped her shoulders. Still she trembled.

As if she were a child, Michael pulled the cloak closer about her shoulders and held her against himself for a long time. He seemed to give her his warmth and strength. When she no longer shook, when she felt desire begin to flow through her, she slid her hands up his chest and pushed him away.

He kept her locked against his lower body, though he pulled back his head. She gazed between the metal slits of his helmet into his dark and fathomless eyes. She wanted to jerk the helmet off, to see his face, feel the texture of his skin, know the angles and planes that comprised his visage.

His eyes seemed to darken and she felt his body growing hard. For a moment longer she gazed at him, then, unable to come to grips with the emotions that flowed through her—and which she sensed also flowed through him—she lowered her head. This dark warrior frightened her, but not as Gilbert's men had. They could take her life. This man would take her body. She knew and accepted that, but she also sensed that this would not satisfy him and he would take her soul. Aye, he would consider that he owned that, too. She feared he would not turn her loose until he had destroyed that which made her Cait nea Sholto.

As Michael had done only moments ago, he tucked a finger beneath her chin and raised her head. "Does your face hurt?"

At first Cait didn't comprehend. Then she remembered. The scratches. She shook her head.

He moved his hand from her chin and touched a gentle finger to her cheek. "They are not deep and will not scar."

"Nay." Cait averted her gaze and saw her dagger lying on the ground where it had fallen when Michael wrested it from her. If only . . .

Michael moved his boot onto the hilt of the knife. He looked down to see the silver blade extending from beneath his foot. He looked back at Cait. "Don't do anything foolish, madam."

"You don't know what I was planning to do."

"Aye, I know." Softly he called, "Here, Ulf. Sit."

The wolf trotted to Cait's side, making her its prisoner. Today she was too exhausted to be frightened of him.

"You can stop me from escaping," she said to Michael, "but you cannot stop me from thinking about it."

She had to escape, had to retrieve the amulet Breastpin. Sholto had entrusted it to her.

"I would say, sire, that you will fare better if you kill me and be done with it."

He studied her for a long while before he sighed. "Aye, Cait nea Sholto, you're probably right." He pinned his mantle about her with his brooch, then captured her hands in his. "But I want you, despite all your warnings. I shall make sure you don't escape."

Cait's breath lodged in her chest when he twined his fingers between hers. The clasp was warm and firm . . . and totally possessive. Confused by these new feelings, frightened by the turn of events, Cait twisted her hand from Michael's clasp.

He made no attempt to hold her again, but gazed thoughtfully at her. He touched his fingers to his chin. He looked puzzled, held out his hand, and looked at the dark stains on his glove. He caught Cait's hand and raised it.

His voice oddly gentle, he said, "You're bleeding."

Cait looked self-consciously at the red welts and cuts on her wrists. Before she knew what was happening, he motioned and called out, "Veld, bring the physician's pouch."

"I don't need a physician." Uncomfortable with his gentleness, Cait spoke more gruffly than she intended. "The cuts are not deep. Besides, I have a knowledge of herbs."

As she spoke, ten of Michael's warriors led their ponies into the clearing.

"Where are the others?" Cait asked.

"With my father," he replied. "We decided to travel in two groups so that we could study the land."

"You didn't trust me," she said.

"I did, but my father didn't," Michael replied, looking up at her. "And it seems that he showed better judgment than I did. You lied to me."

"Nay, lord, I didn't outrightly lie."

His eyes narrowed.

"I was frightened of you and your men, and I directed you to the route that was farthest from the cloister. I was protecting my home, sire, the same as you would have done, had it been you."

By now the majority of Michael's warriors had fanned out into small groups, talking quietly . . . and watching. One, slipping a leathern strap over his head, approached Michael and handed him a pouch.

"Sit down," Michael commanded Cait. He shucked off his gloves and tucked them into his girdle.

When she did not immediately obey, Michael nodded at Kolby. He clasped Cait by the shoulders and firmly guided her to the ground. Michael knelt beside her.

He took her hand in his and probed the swelling flesh around the rope burns. For the first time she saw his fingers without gloves. Michael's hands were clean, his nails cut short. She felt the calluses at the base of his fingers; she felt his strength tempered with unexpected gentleness.

Touched by Michael's concern, Cait said, "The burns are not serious."

"Not now," he said, "but if they become infected, they could be."

"The worst that can come of this is a few scars."

"Aye," Michael said, "and I don't want that."

"This is kind of you, lord."

"Not kindness, madam." He looked up as he took off his helmet and brushed a hand through his hair. "Practicality. I value my property and take care of it."

For a brief moment Cait looked into his eyes. Then he lowered his head again and she stared at thick, raven hair.

" 'Twas foolish of you to let Gilbert's men see how much wealth you carry with you," she said.

"Perhaps."

"They didn't intend to behead me. They were playing with me, having their fun."

Sunlight burnished his hair to a blue-black sheen. Strands blew against Cait's arm, the darkness a contrast to her fair skin. She wanted to touch his hair, to splay her fingers and let the silky strands slide through. In an effort to resist the temptation, she clasped her hands together in her lap.

"Ardac and his men would have returned whether they saw the filled treasure trunk or not. They are greedy and deceitful men," Michael said as he set out a small bowl, the inside of which was lined for measurements. "The only other way to get you was to fight. That would have put my men at risk."

He arranged more bowls, along with spoons and vials, before him.

"When the booty is to be shared, we all take the risk," he said, "but for the present I want you for myself. Dispensing with a little gold seemed the most practical and expedient way to settle the matter."

He pulled stoppers out of several vials, set them

in a line, and meticulously measured small amounts of powders and liquids into the bowl.

"I doubt you will think that when you meet them again. This time you had the advantage. The next time they will."

He laughed. "Even if that group put all of their thinking matter into one head, they would still be lacking." He recapped one of the flagons. "Time is on our side, woman. At present they are too few in number to risk an attack on us, and they have the extra burden of their ill-gained loot. So do not be concerned."

"Ardac lied about me."

"So you say." He held out a mixing bowl. "Veld, pour water to the first line."

Cait's gaze went to Michael's hands. They were beautiful, she reluctantly admitted. His long fingers were clever and deft. She stared at the silver ring on his little finger, but the position of his hand prevented her from distinguishing the design. He took the bowl from Veld and stirred the mixture until he had made a soft paste.

Opening another vial, he dipped a reed into it. Placing his thumb over the end, he withdrew the reed and held it over the mixing bowl. By carefully lifting his thumb, he began to measure drops into the paste.

"Why are you—"

"Quiet, woman!"

Cait flinched from the harshness of his voice. Kolby squatted next to her and bent his head close. " 'Tis a difficult mixture," he explained softly. "If it's handled properly, it brings about healing. If not, it's deadly."

A chill shook Cait. "What is it?"

"We call it the laughing root," Kolby answered.

Cait drew back in alarm. "The smile of death."

"Aye," Kolby said. "You have heard of it."

Cait nodded and swallowed, hoping to dislodge the fear that knotted in her throat. " 'Tis said that those who take it die quickly with a smile on their faces."

"But I have no desire to kill you," Michael said. "I am preparing an ointment that will hasten the healing of your wounds." He smiled—a full, deep smile that touched his face and settled in his eyes. "I have better plans for you, madam, than a funeral pyre. I want you to burn, but only for me."

Already Cait burned. Her entire body felt inflamed, and Michael had only spoken words of letching to her. What would happen when he actually touched her? When he mated with her?

She had no doubt that this time Michael would bed her.

Without anyone telling her, she knew that he would be as gentle in mating as he was in doctoring. She intuited this would not be from any tenderness he felt for her but out of pride of ownership. And she was his possession. He had paid three pounds of gold for her.

Michael set the reed aside, recapped the vial, and replaced it in the leathern pouch. He pulled out a large piece of white cloth that brushed against Cait's arm. The soft, transparent material caressed her. Using a pair of scissors, Michael cut off several long strips.

"Why are you doing this rather than your physician?" Cait asked.

"I am the physician."

Cait's eyes went to the sword and the dagger at his waist.

"Aye, I am also a warrior," he explained. "Hold out your arms."

She did, and he gently applied the ointment to her cuts. "It is an ugly salve," he said, "and it stinks, but it brings about a fast healing." He wrapped her arms with the strips of fabric and tied them off.

"I have never seen a male physician," Cait said, "but you are truly a good one, sire."

Michael laughed softly. "Soon, madam, you shall know that I tend to other ... er ... needs with the same proficiency."

Cait's cheeks blazed.

Michael moved away from her and began to search through his bag again.

"My lord," she said as he opened a small pouch and extracted a root, "I think perhaps you are too gentle a man to be a good warrior. Perhaps you should be a priest and physician."

The muted sounds of the warriors talking ceased, and Cait felt all their attention center on her.

In a cold voice, devoid of all emotion, Michael said, "Madam, for the second and last time, I remind you that I am neither kind nor gentle. I do whatever is necessary to accomplish my goals. Never make the mistake of thinking I am less a warrior because I am a physician. I learned the art of doctoring so that I could take care of my men. Sick or suffering, they are no use to me or anyone else."

Aye, she thought, she should have known. He was concerned only with himself. He would not want to be burdened with ailing warriors.

With a proficiency she had seldom seen, he unsheathed his dagger and held it in the same hand that only moments ago had mixed powders and treated cuts. Yet subtly his hand had changed. It was no longer the physician's hand; it was the warrior's. No longer to be trusted, rather to be feared. He cut a lump out of the root and handed it to her.

"Chew this and swallow the juice," he ordered. "It will cause you to feel less pain."

Cait winced away from him. "I can do without herbs."

"Chew it!"

"Nay!"

Michael clasped her face in one hand and forced her mouth open. Although his hand pressed into her cheeks, he did not grind her flesh against her teeth. He shoved the root into her mouth and held it and her nose closed until she had chewed and swallowed as much of the juice as he deemed necessary. He released her. Gasping for breath, she spat out the pulverized root.

"Do you have any other clothes?" he asked.

"Scattered around my dear mare."

"Veld, fetch Cait's clothing."

"I am called *Lady* Cait."

"I am called many things, also. Some are true, the majority are not."

Anger boiled within Cait. Rising, Michael held out his hand to her. She slapped it away and rose without assistance. Veld returned with the satchel—the few pieces of her clothing that had not been shredded stuffed into it—and her purse. Michael took the leathern purse, flipped it open, and studied the silver daggers that were precisely arranged there.

"Twenty," she said in answer to his unspoken question.

"Only nine-and-ten now."

"Aye," she murmured.

Kolby and Veld pushed closer to see.

"Can you really use them?" Veld asked.

"Aye, she is a blade master," Michael answered. "I suppose as a minstrel, you find it necessary to protect yourself."

"As a woman, I must know how to protect myself," Cait retorted.

Michael closed the pouch flap and refastened it. "Kolby, do away with this."

"Nay!" Cait cried. "Not my purse."

Of all her possessions, the purse was the one she valued most. She had owned it since she was a lass of eight winters. It was the last gift her mother had made for her before bandits attacked their farmstead. They killed Cait's parents and all the animals; they burned the crops and buildings. They would have killed Cait and her younger cousin, Rob, too, if they had not been out hunting.

"I don't think it would be wise to let you have access to your daggers, lady. Remember, I have seen you demonstrate your skill."

"I'm not talking about my daggers," Cait said. "My purse. Do not throw it away, my lord. Please. My mother made it for me. The last gift she gave me before brigands killed her and my father."

Michael was quiet for a long while. Finally he said, "Put it with the rest of her belongings, Kolby, but keep it out of her reach."

"Aye." Kolby looped the purse over his shoulder.

Michael rummaged through the satchel and pulled out several items of clothing. Draping them over his arm, he took his mantle off her shoulders and handed it to Veld. Then he held up Cait's overtunic. With efficient motions, he turned it right side out and slipped it over her head . . . as if he had done so many times before.

"I can dress myself," Cait snapped, displeased with the idea that he had probably dressed and undressed many women during his lifetime—about thirty winters, she guessed.

"Aye," Michael answered, "but it would be a trifle painful."

He secured her girdle about her waist. The brush of his fingers, even through two layers of fabric, sent a rush of heat through her body, reminding her that he was a man who stirred her desire as well as her anger and frustration.

"I've suffered worse than this," Cait muttered, though she wasn't sure when.

"No doubt."

Taking her mantle from Veld, Michael threw it around her shoulders.

"Where is your brooch?"

"I—they—" Cait had forgotten about her mantle brooch. "They took it when they . . . stripped my clothing from me earlier as they . . . searched me."

To Cait's surprise, Michael, Kolby, and Veld laughed.

" 'Tis the first time I've heard it called *searching*," Kolby quipped.

"It was searching," Cait spat. "Brutal searching. They had no interest in my body when they ripped my clothing from it. They looked for—for—" Almost she had betrayed Sholto's confidence and her vows to the gods of the Shelter Stone.

"One of the sacred objects of the sanctuary," Michael finished.

"Aye." *One of the most sacred.*

"Kolby," Michael said, "hand me a brooch out of the trunk."

As the warrior walked away, Cait lapsed into silence, contemplating how she could get away from the Northlander and retrieve her sacred charge.

Kolby returned to Michael with a brooch. "She has no pony. She's going to slow us down, Michael."

"A little."

Slow us down! No pony! But Cait knew where to find one for riding, and others packed with supplies. Knowing that other Silver Daggers would escape the cloister if they could, she had instructed Dacy to bring their satchels with their weapons. And perhaps there was a way she could get back to the spear boulder to retrieve the sacred Breastpin.

"My lord," Cait said, "I know where I can get a pony. The friend who helped me escape hid both riding and pack ponies there with supplies in case others in the cloister should need them."

Both men turned in her direction.

"It isn't far, lord." Cait had already decided to double back to get the amulet first. "And the place is isolated. None go there because it's close to Hag's Tree—an old blackthorn tree that is supposed to be cursed."

Michael waved his hand, and his warriors rose. Veld led a huge, silver-gray stallion to Michael.

"Which way, madam?" Michael asked.

Cait pointed in the direction that the king's men had ridden.

"By the gods, Michael!" Kolby exploded. "The woman lied to you about the path we should take. She could be lying again."

Michael turned to Cait. "Is this another of your lies, lady?"

Cait shook her head. "There is no reason for me to lie, sire. I want a pony to ride, since I don't relish walking or running beside you and your warriors."

She thought the corners of Michael's mouth twitched, but she couldn't be sure.

"So be it," he announced.

"You know as well as I do that those warriors intend to circle back and attack us," Kolby exclaimed. "By following them, we will be playing right into their hands. And what is Lang going to think? We promised that we would meet him by dark tonight."

"Aye, Kolby, you are telling me things I already know, but I have made my decision," Michael said, looking his headman and best friend straight in the eye. "If you or any of the other men do not wish to ride with me, you may leave."

"Nay, Michael," Kolby answered quietly. "I'll ride with you to the death."

Michael nodded curtly, and another motion from him set his men to mounting. Then Michael mounted.

"Help her up," he ordered.

Kolby caught her around the waist and hoisted her up.

"Up front," Michael instructed. "I can handle her better here."

Cait did not like being nestled so closely to his warm, hard strength. One arm banded her waist, and he pulled her even closer. She felt bonded to him.

"Ulf," Michael commanded.

The wolf moved to stand beside the stallion.

"Northmen," Michael called out when all were mounted, "I have claimed the woman as mine. She will bring trouble, no doubt. Women always do. Do you wish to continue to ride with me?"

"Is there more booty for the trouble?" one asked.

"Nay. When I have found the rupture-endowment

that the Scot warlord stole from my father, I shall divide that evenly among you. That is the only promise of booty I make. If we should find more, you will receive your equal parts. You know I am a fair man."

"How about sharing the woman with us?" another shouted.

Cait stiffened; her breath caught. Michael's arm tightened around her. He leaned closer, and she felt the solid wall of his shoulders behind her. His breath fanned against her neck. Oddly, he seemed to be reassuring her.

"Nay, she is mine," he answered.

"What about when you tire of her?" the man pressed.

Michael shrugged. "An answer, Northmen. Do we ride together?"

"Aye!" Drawing their swords, they clanged them together in the *vápnatak*—a vote of agreement.

"Lead us to the place where the ponies are hidden, madam," Michael instructed.

With Michael in front and Cait guiding, the Northmen moved out of the Highland forest over the mountain trail. After an hour of traveling a narrow, circuitous route, they reached the place where Cait had hidden the amulet.

During the ride she was quiet as she devised a plan of sorts. She would tell them the truth—as much of it as she could. The spear-shaped rock was one of the landmarks where traveling Druids left messages for one another. This is where Dacy would leave her instructions for finding the ponies. While she pretended to search for a sign, she would slip out the sacred amulet.

"We must stop here, lord," she said. "I seek a sign."

She felt Michael tense and saw Kolby glance at him.

"What kind of sign?" Michael asked.

He didn't believe her. Not wanting to lie to him, but also afraid to tell him the truth, Cait sat there. Ulf trotted to the base of the boulder and began to sniff. In a little while he began to scratch.

"Madam, I am waiting," Michael said, clearly impatient.

" 'Tis a pile of rocks," she answered.

"Tell my man what to look for, madam, and he will describe to you what he finds, and you can interpret the message," Michael said, adding, "Kolby, dismount and follow her instructions."

"Nay," Cait said, before Kolby moved.

Silence such as Cait had never experienced descended upon them.

"My lord," Cait said, "I know where Dacy would have taken the ponies, but—"

"There is no sign!" Kolby exclaimed angrily.

"Is there, Cait?" Michael spoke in a dangerously soft voice.

"Aye. It is one that I left when I hid my talisman here. I didn't want Gilbert's men to steal it from me. 'Tis blessed, lord, and was—"

"Given to you by your mother before she was killed by brigands," Michael curtly finished for her.

"Nay, by my adopted father."

Michael's warriors, rumbling their discontent, looked at one another.

"Michael, this woman has endangered the mission and all of our lives," Kolby said.

"Aye," one of the warriors agreed. "Let us be rid of her."

Cait felt Michael's chest rise and fall against her.

"Madam, in the future when you want me to do something, ask me."

Ulf trotted back to Michael and whined.

"Would you have brought me here, had I asked?" When he didn't answer, she said, "I thought not. So I did what I had to do."

The wolf whined again. Michael paid him no attention. Ulf reared up, planting a front paw on Michael's thigh, the other on Cait's. She jumped with fear. This was the closest the wolf had ever been to her.

Then she gasped and laughed. Dangling from the wolf's mouth by the chain was the amulet Breastpin. Tears of joy ran down her cheeks.

"The talisman," Michael murmured.

The warriors' anger was appeased when they saw the medallion spinning from the golden chain. All knew and understood the importance of blessed talismans.

Forgetting her fear of the wolf, Cait reached out and tugged on the gold medallion. Ulf's silver-blue gaze stayed on her for a long time before he opened his mouth and released the chain. Still he did not move.

"Thank him," Michael commanded softly.

She turned to look at the Northman as if he were dim-witted.

"Reward him," Michael ordered.

She looked at the silver beast who was panting in her face. "Thank you, wolf."

"Nay, lady." She heard the laughter in Michael's voice. "Rub his head."

Again Cait stared at the animal for a long time before she tentatively reached out and touched him. Taking advantage of the attention, Ulf pushed his head against her palm and nuzzled her. Cait's hand slipped, and her fingers dug into the bristly hair behind his ears. When he growled and twisted his head for more petting, Cait jerked back and Michael laughed.

"Down, Ulf. You've had enough thanks for the time being." Michael caught the amulet from Cait and slipped the chain over her head. "Now, madam, keep this on. I won't go out of my way to get it a second time."

"Aye, my lord." Cait clasped the medallion tightly in her hand, and looked down at the silver beast who sat cockily beside Michael's stallion.

"Now, lady," Michael said, "take us to the ponies."

Her heart lighter than it had been since she had hidden the cloister pin, Cait headed toward Hag's Field. But an hour later, the company of warriors pulled to a halt in an empty plot of land.

"Michael," Kolby said, "the woman played you for a fool the day before yesterday, and she is doing the same today."

"Kill her," one of the warriors shouted.

Others clanged their weapons together.

Cait turned on the stallion, pressing against Michael as she looked into his face. "Lord, I haven't deceived you. This is the place."

"Pray that it is, madam, or I cannot protect you." Michael slid from the stallion, then swung Cait to the ground. She followed him as he studied the area for signs.

He straightened. "There have been no ponies here."

Wildly Cait looked around. Something must have happened to Dacy.

"Which way would your friend have taken from the cloister?" Michael asked.

She pointed.

"Let's search there."

A wave from Michael sent several of the warriors fanning out in the general direction she had indicated. For big men, they walked quickly, their steps light. Farther and farther they moved, pushing bushes aside, examining, and searching.

Michael knelt. "Kolby."

The head-man hunkered down beside him.

"Do you see it?" Michael asked.

"Aye." Kolby scooted around, scrutinizing the plants and trail.

"Several ponies have ridden through here," another warrior called. He kicked through the brush, knelt, and rose. "Michael, I've found something." He held out a piece of green and yellow cloth.

Michael took it from him. "Do you recognize this, madam?"

She shook her head.

"Yellow and green," Michael muttered, brushing the material between his fingers.

"Yellow and green," Cait mused. " 'Tis the king's colors, and Dacy—he is a king's man."

"Mayhap we are riding into a trap," Michael snarled.

Frightened, Cait backed away. "Nay, Dacy and I grew up together in the border country, lord. The same brigands who killed my family killed his. He is a king's man, not Gilbert's man. He would not betray me."

"What is this man to you?" Michael asked. "Did you barter your body for his help?"

Cait had the urge to slap him. "I gave him nothing for his help. I didn't have to. He did it because he loves me as a friend."

Michael lowered his hand, letting the wolf sniff

the fabric. His head down, his nose to the ground, the animal began a thorough investigation. Then he darted into the woods.

"Come, Kolby, he's picked up the scent." To the others, Michael called, "Wait here, but be prepared. We don't know what we're going to find."

The two Northmen ran after the wolf. Cait followed. She could have taken the opportunity to run away, but if there was any possibility that the fabric remnant belonged to Dacy or that Dacy was in trouble, she had to help him.

The wolf stopped and turned around in circles. He sniffed the ground, then moved slowly to a clump of bushes. He sat down beside them. Michael nodded to Kolby. Winded, Cait rushed up. Their swords drawn, the Northmen edged closer. Cait stepped on something and stopped. She looked down to see a small dagger. The dagger she had given Dacy.

She picked it up, then caught Michael by the shoulder. Silently she pleaded with him to let her handle the matter. He stepped back.

Cait inched closer to the bushes. "Dacy," she said, "it's Cait."

Nothing.

"Dacy?"

She heard a rustling. "Caity?"

"Aye."

"You're— Why aren't you gone?"

"Gilbert's men found me."

"How?"

"Someone in the cloister told Gilbert what pathway I would be using for my escape."

She caught one of the broken limbs and dragged it away.

"Who . . . who . . ." The voice was weak. "Who are you with?"

"The warriors who saved me," she answered, speaking the truth as far as was possible. "They have bound my wounds. We—We came back to search for the ponies."

"I didn't make it to the tree with the ponies." His breathing was labored, and he spoke haltingly.

"You're hurt," Cait said.

Disregarding her injured wrists, she began clawing through the limbs. Michael nudged her aside. While he removed the brush, Dacy talked, his voice weak and halting.

"After I helped you escape . . . I went back to the cloister. The raiders had already been there and searched for the treasure."

"Did they find it?"

"Nay. Soon afterwards Gilbert and his men arrived. They took Rob and the other Silver Daggers prisoners." He coughed.

"Why?"

"He claims that they might have been involved in the conspiracy with you . . . especially Rob."

"What about Sholto?"

"Gilbert . . . left . . . men to guard . . . cloister." He licked his lips. "All are . . . kept separate."

"Aye," Cait said. "They fear our silent hand communication."

Dacy laughed weakly. "They have a right to. You frighten me with it also. I never—" he coughed again "—know if you're rubbing your nose because it . . . itches or if it's one of your secret signals.

"Fagan . . . escaped." Dacy's voice grew weaker, his words coming slower. "He was waiting here . . . at the tree when . . . I rode up with the ponies. Five of Gilbert's men surprised us." He took a long, quivering breath.

"Ardac?" Cait asked.

"Aye," he murmured. "I think one of them was called that."

"He was the one who chased me." Cait rocked back on her knees. "He was probably circling to set up an ambush for us when he spied you and Fagan."

"We set the ponies loose," Dacy said. "Fagan . . . rode off in one direction . . . I in another. They got me with a lance."

"Don't talk anymore," Cait said, tears running down her cheeks. "We're going to take care of you."

Michael finally exposed the wounded man, who lay on his side, his back to them. His clothing was saturated with blood, and a lance protruded from his shoulder. He clutched his sword in his bloody hand.

"I crawled here to die," Dacy said. "Ardac would have beheaded me. Couldn't roam the earth as a lost spirit forever, not with my fighting hand ruined."

"Nay," Cait said.

"Kill me," he said. " 'Tis painful. I'm ready to go now."

Kneeling, Michael pulled his dagger from the scabbard at his waist and cut through the material of Dacy's shirt. He studied the entry of the lance, then leaned over and examined his chest.

" 'Tis a death wound," Dacy said.

"Aye." Michael leaned back, and Cait saw the ugly lance head with its small curved and spiked barbs—ingeniously constructed to render the greatest amount of pain and damage possible. "Perhaps I can save you."

"How?" Dacy asked.

"The lance was thrown with such force that the majority of the barbs have pushed through to the outside of your chest."

"Aye," Dacy said, "it chewed up my shoulder."

"If you can live through the pain, I can try to push the lance on through."

Cait cringed at the thought.

"I've lost a lot of blood."

"Aye," Michael answered.

"If I survive, I shall have a gaping wound," Dacy continued. "And will be unable to use my right hand or arm."

Cait looked at the swollen, ragged flesh around the lance shaft.

"Mayhap I can keep that from happening," Michael said.

Dacy laughed mockingly. "Are you a god come to save me, sire?"

As the question slipped past the warrior's lips, a chill raced over Cait's body. Michael Langssonn was silver and black, like the god of night, like the ruler of the autumn and winter tides, of lightning and thunder.

"Nay." The Northman laughed also. "I'm a mortal, but I have knowledge of surgery. I have traveled in the land of the Far East."

"Aye," Dacy nodded. "I have been there and know what they can do. You can do this also?"

"Aye."

"I am a warrior," Dacy said, "one of the king's men. If I live through this and am unable to use my sword arm, I will be dishonored."

"Aye," Michael answered.

Cait leaned closer. "He has with him an herb from the land of Léon, Dacy. The smiling death."

As he grew weaker from exertion, Dacy's eyes began to droop.

"I want an answer," Michael said. "Night comes early in autumn, and I will need all the daylight I can have."

"Aye," Dacy whispered. He drew in a deep, labored breath. "If I live and do not regain use of my arm, will you give me the herb to take?"

"I have the herb," Michael said.

"Please, Dacy," Cait said. She moved closer and caught his unwounded hand in hers.

Cait looked at Dacy, but she felt the heat of Michael's gaze on hers and Dacy's hands.

Dacy nodded. "I'm ready."

A tear slipped from between Cait's tightly shut lids.

"Cait."

She looked at her friend.

He whispered in a border dialect that only they understood, "Gilbert didn't get the—"

"No, I still have it."

"You must protect it," Dacy said.

"I will."

Dacy's head rolled and he lapsed into unconsciousness.

"What did he say?" Michael demanded.

" 'Twas a private conversation between two friends, sire."

Michael caught her face in his hand, his thumb pressing into one cheek, his fingers into the other. "He can be your friend, but you belong to me. I, and only I, will be your lover."

Chapter 7

"Northmen," Michael said, "the man is badly wounded. His only chance of living lies in me performing surgery on him immediately. We'll set up camp here for the night."

The men looked at the barren land that surrounded them.

"Here?" one of them asked.

"What about Ardac's men?" another questioned.

"We're safe here," Cait said. "Ardac and his men won't venture close to Hag's Field. Many people think it is cursed."

Again the Northmen warily surveyed the wasteland.

"It may be cursed to the Glenmuirians," Michael said, "but not to us. We are Northmen and serve the gods of Asgard. They are stronger than the gods of the Highlanders."

"Also," Cait said, "I am a bard and have great magic. I shall build a sacred fire of rowan wood. That will keep away evil in any form."

Michael gave her a cursory nod.

"Lang shall be worried when we don't meet him tonight as we planned," Kolby said.

"He'll wait," Michael replied, "just as we would if he were late meeting us."

The Northmen spoke among themselves, their voices a gruff rumble.

Michael began to bark out orders.

"Kolby, erect my tent first. See that a stretcher is made, and set up camp. Sven, round up the loose ponies that the wounded man was bringing here. Veld, you and Cait will help me."

Veld, holding the physician's satchel, stood next to Michael. The other nine Northmen glared at their leader.

"Make haste," Michael ordered. "Look. Storm clouds are gathering, and we have little daylight left."

By the time the premature darkness settled around them, the men had quietly, but disapprovingly, set up camp. Sven had returned with the scattered ponies and pack animals and had enclosed them safely in a makeshift corral. Michael had completed the surgery. Dacy lay beneath the shelter of an oiled, water-resistant pavilion, one of several that jutted gray against the shadowed sky. A central fire burned low.

Although Cait had assured the Northmen that no one would disturb their camp, they maintained all the usual precautions. Two men guarded the ponies while others kept watch over the entire encampment. Wearing their weapons and staying outside their tents as long as possible, the warriors pulled their mantles close about them, some sleeping, others watching. All expected Ardac and his men to attack.

The wind slapped ruthlessly against the yellow and white pavilion where Michael and Cait sat with Dacy. It whipped the entrance flap, which had been pegged to the ground. Shivering and leaning closer to the central fire, Cait ran her hands over the soft, worked leather that formed the floor of the shelter. It was smooth and shiny and had been treated so that it was water-repellent like the tent material.

Light from the small fire and several soapstone lamps illuminated the interior and flickered golden shadows over Michael, who sat opposite Dacy. He still wore his mail, but he had stripped off his weapons and helmet and had tied his hair back with a leathern thong. His face was drawn, the skin dark beneath his eyes. Cait could tell he was exhausted. He had ordered Veld to get some rest so that he could sit up with Dacy later during the night, but Michael himself refused to leave.

"Your warriors are angry because we have tarried here," she said.

When Cait had gone out earlier to get fresh water, she had felt the tension and anger that permeated the camp.

"Aye, they have a right to be angry," Michael replied. He massaged the back of his neck. "By staying here, I have jeopardized their safety."

"Nay, lord," Cait said, "as I told you earlier, Hag's Field—"

"But we cannot spend the rest of our lives here."

Cait bent her legs and pulled them up to her chest. She wrapped her arms about them and rested her chin on her knees. "But we're not going to stay that long. Only until Dacy is fit to travel."

"We leave before dawn in the morning."

Cait straightened. "We cannot, lord! Dacy cannot travel on the morrow."

Michael stared at her, and Cait knew.

"Do you think that—that—" She couldn't put the thought into words.

Michael caught her hand in his and squeezed

gently. "Only Odin in all his wisdom knows who is to live and who is to die, madam."

Two tears rolled down Cait's cheek.

"You really care for this man?" Michael brushed his other hand gently beneath her eyes.

"Aye. I was sad when his father fostered him to a warrior in the king's village, and he left. When I saw how his mother grieved his leaving, I promised myself that I would never leave and hurt my mother like that."

Dacy muttered and tried to twist his shoulder. He grunted, then grimaced with pain. Cait looked at the large bandage wrapped around Dacy's chest and shoulder. Blood was beginning to seep through.

After Michael had completed the surgery, he had taken care to see that Dacy did not further damage his injured shoulder during his delirium. He and Veld had crisscrossed wide leathern thongs down Dacy's body from his chest to his ankles, strapping him onto the stretcher. The binding was tight enough about his body to keep him from thrashing about, but not so tight that it hurt him.

At first, Cait had thought kindly of Michael. Then she had remembered. Kindness did not prompt his actions. He was a practical man driven by reason.

"Yet you did leave the land of your childhood," Michael said.

"Aye, but only after my parents were killed." Although two-and-ten years had passed and dimmed the memories, they still hurt.

"At the hands of brigands?"

"Aye. Rob and I were out hunting. When we returned, we found first the bodies of my parents, then his. Later we found Dacy's parents. If Rob had not been so young and in need of care, I would have gone searching for the murderers."

"How old were you at the time?"

"I had seen the passing of eight winters. Rob had seen only five." Remembering the events as if they had happened only yesterday, Cait said, "Rob and I buried our families first, then we gathered what food had not been stolen or ruined and stuffed it into a leathern bag. Since we lived close to the border of Glenmuir and far from the king's village, travelers often stayed the night with us. They bartered many goods with my father for food and bed. My father owned one of the best hunting lances in the kingdom. I got it and his dagger, then Rob and I set out to find Dacy at the king's village."

"You were a brave lass."

"Nay, lord, a frightened one."

Cait glanced at the trunk next to Michael. Clustered on top and around the low-burning soapstone lamp were flagons, beakers, vials, and bowls, filled with liquids and pastes and powders.

"Rob and I must have made a strange sight as we marched toward the king's village. My father's lance was longer than both of us were tall."

"It took courage to drag the weapons with you," Michael pointed out. "Did you know how to use them?"

"Aye. My father had already fashioned a dagger and lance for me in proportion to my size. He also taught me how to use them . . . and I had to protect both Rob and myself. I had to be brave for Rob. I was all the family he had left in the world."

"A little mountain cat protecting her cub," Michael said. "Now I understand more fully why you hiss and scratch rather than purr."

Cat smiled. "Rob and I were ragged, but not dirty, when we finally found Dacy. And we were not empty-handed when he brought us to the cloister. As a gift to the gods, I gave them my father's dagger and lance."

"I would have expected no less from you, lass."

"Please don't call me lass," Cait said. "*Madam* and *woman* are closer to the truth. I have not been a lass, lord, since the day I discovered the dead bodies of my family."

Lost in her thoughts, reliving the deaths of her family and the subsequent journey to sanctuary, Cait was silent. She would never forget how Sholto had given refuge to her and Rob, how he had adopted them both. Cait loved the cloister. Sholto, Blar, and Trevor had become her family. The three priests were such generous and loving people that Cait had gladly taken her vows to be a bard of the Shelter Stone Cloister.

" 'Tis a shame that you and Rob were deprived of your innocence, first by the bandits, then by this shrine . . . What do you call it? The Shelter Stone?"

Cait bristled. "The bandits may have stolen our innocence, but the cloister did not. Sholto has been a wonderful father to us."

"So wonderful that he allowed you to become a wandering minstrel."

"It wasn't his fault. He tried to talk me out of it, but it was something I wanted to do."

"Have you ever regretted your decision?"

"Nay, lord. I love bringing laughter to people. And I also enjoy discussing new cures for old ailments. Or hearing about a better way to plow a field. Or giving someone a gift they have long wanted. The Shelter Stone Cloister is the grandest place on earth, lord, one of the most beautiful in all the Highlands."

Cait saw no harm in talking about the shrine with Michael as long as she did not reveal the secret of the Breastpins. "Shall I tell you about the Shelter Stone?"

"Why not?" Michael's eyes twinkled kindly. "You are an entertainer, so entertain me."

Momentarily Cait was disconcerted. His eyes were warm, genuinely warm, and he had lowered his guard. He smiled, and she did so too. She settled more comfortably on the folded blanket beside Dacy. Some of the grief and heaviness she had felt since they found her friend now lifted.

"The Shelter Stone is a natural rock bridge formed over a mountain stream where the stream becomes a waterfall. Below is a beautiful pool of crystal-clear water."

"This bridge is so important that all the Highland people revere it," Michael said. "Why?"

Forgetting the biting cold and wind that slapped against the tent, Cait tucked the covers around Dacy and began to tell Michael the legend of the Shelter Stone.

"At the beginning of time, the Lunar Goddess and Father Creator gave birth to twin gods, Night and Day. The Creator divided the world equally between his sons. Night ruled supreme during autumn and winter, Day during summer and spring. Before the twins could take over their kingdoms, they had to overcome the forces of Chaos.

"The Father Spirit allowed his wife to create one magical weapon for each son. For Night she crafted a sickle sword. The hilt was silver to represent the luminescent splendor of the moon. It was also magical and could be disconnected from the blade to become a silver lance. The Lunar Goddess called this the Silver Beam. For Day she crafted a shield that was golden fire—inlaid with silver rays to also symbolize the full moon. She called this the Golden Ray.

On each she put magical writings, sun rays and moonbeams.

"Chaos became jealous of the twins and began to pursue them relentlessly. Although the twins were young, unproven warriors, the Creator parents had to step aside to let their sons prove themselves worthy to rule the world. The twins fought valiantly, but were too inexperienced to defeat the forces of Chaos."

She paused for a moment, thinking of all that had happened to her and wondering if the gods had abandoned her. Sholto had entrusted the Cloister Breastpins with her. No matter how kind Michael might be treating her at the moment, she had to escape him.

Cait's greatest concern was getting the Cloister Breastpin safely out of Glenmuir. As long as she traveled with Michael, she would be compelled to travel the route he chose. Even if it was the one she pointed out, the one that Sholto had instructed her to take, she would not be free to leave messages along the way. She could travel much faster by herself and could reach High King Fergus's village much sooner.

Aye, she must escape the Northman. He considered her his slave and would take her in lust. She had to protect her integrity.

"Is that all the tale?" Michael asked as he spread another blanket over Dacy.

Jarred out of her thoughts, she said, "Nay. Night and Day managed to kill all of Chaos's army except Chaos himself. Wounded, both on the verge of death, they made their last stand against Chaos beside a mountain stream. Chaos descended. Night was ready to hurl his silver sword; Day defended them with his golden shield.

"So great was the struggle among Night, Day, and Chaos that they hewed a natural rock bridge out of the mountain. Finally the twins killed Chaos. During the battle, however, they dropped their magical shield and lance into the mountain stream. Mortally wounded, the twins crawled to the eastern side of the stream and took shelter beneath the bridge they had created."

"Hence its name, Shelter Stone Shrine," Michael said.

"Aye. When it looked as if her sons were going to die, the Lunar Goddess intervened. She carried Night to the stream every evening and bathed his wounds; she did the same to Day every morning. When they were fully recovered, they searched for their shield and lance but never found them. After they returned to their high seats, people discovered the miraculous healing powers of the water."

"This is a beautiful legend, lady. Similar to our story of the gods of night and day. But I can't say that I believe it even though my father had a sickle ring crafted for me."

"You wear a sickle ring?" Cait exclaimed. "Let me see it, lord."

Cait held his hand as she studied the silver band on the little finger of his right hand. "Aye, lord, the band itself is silver, and the crescent is gold. Just like ours."

She pulled up the long sleeve of her overtunic. "See, lord, I have a sickle tattoo."

Michael brushed the tip of his finger over her upper arm, sending fire through her.

"Those of us who become members of the cloister receive it." She laughed softly. "My lord, do you think it is a sign from the gods that you and I both wear the holy symbol of the gods Night and Day?"

Michael shrugged. "You may believe it if you want to, Cait, but I think it's just a coincidence."

"As my adopted father says, belief is up to the individual. So you must judge for yourself." She was quiet for a few minutes, then said, "Those who believe in the gods of the Shelter Stone do so from faith. The only evidence of Night and Day's recuperation at the Shelter Stone is a stone monument with ancient writings that tells the story of the twins' victory over Chaos and the loss of their sacred shield and lance."

"It is yet standing?" Michael asked.

"Aye, but it is so old, lord, that the markings are no longer distinguishable. But the pool of water is holy," Cait said. "All who make a specific request as they bathe in its waters at sunrise during the Summer Solstice and at moon rise during the Winter Solstice receive an answer. Because all Highlanders revere the Shelter Stone as holy, the kingdom of Glenmuir has lived in peace with its neighbors." Her voice trailed off. "Until now."

"Why, madam, after all these years of peace, would someone attack your kingdom and shrine?"

"As I see it, sire, there are only two reasons why men go to war. Greed or revenge."

"Has your kingdom done something to inspire another's revenge?"

"Not that I know of."

"Then it must be greed."

"Aye, it must be."

Dacy cried out and rolled his head. Cait looked down to see his face twisted in pain. He grunted and tried to raise his shoulders. More blood seeped into the bandage, the stain growing larger and darker.

"Be still, Dacy," Cait ordered softly.

Dacy lifted his lids and gazed at Cait, his eyes glazed with fever and pain.

She brushed a lock of hair from his face. "Michael has erected a tent for you, and he and I are sitting with you."

Dacy showed no signs of having heard her.

"Dacy . . ."

He gave a small nod.

"Michael has . . . he has finished with the surgery."

Again Dacy nodded. Then he closed his eyes and drifted off to sleep.

A short while later, Kolby called from outside, "Michael, what do you want me to do with the torque?"

The torque! Cait had forgotten about it.

Michael sighed. "We'll solder it on her later."

"Aye," Kolby answered, and Cait heard him walk away.

The past hour she had enjoyed talking with Michael so much that she had forgotten she was his slave. She watched as he mixed more medicine. She had been with him for only hours, yet already he had become an integral part of her life. She owed him her survival. So would Dacy . . . if he made it.

Aye, she admitted, Michael had done this for his own reasons, but he had done it. With every action he was binding her to him, making her his. No matter how attentive he might be, or tender or interested, she was nothing more than his possession. To him she was no more than his dirk or sword or stallion. Perhaps she didn't even mean as much as those things did. But she belonged to him, and he intended to brand her so that all would know.

Suddenly her breathing was constricted. She rubbed her hand around her neck. She could hardly bear the thought of a permanent metal band secured around her throat.

His. His. The words kept running through her mind.

"Why don't you rest, lady?" Michael said, his soft, caring tone belying the stark reality. "I know you must be weary, and we have done all we can. I'll send for you if his condition worsens."

"I'm tired," Cait admitted, "but surely not as exhausted as you are. You have done surgery, yet still you care for him."

" 'Tis my duty."

" 'Tis mine to be with him also."

"How so?"

"One of my duties as a bard/priestess is to help prepare the way into the other world. We do this through songs and poetry. The last rite for the dying is the singing of their death song."

"Then, lady, I shall let you stay close to him."

Cait nodded. Leaning over, she lifted one of the flagons of medicine from the trunk and held it to the lamp, watching the light filter through the muddy liquid.

"Ugh." She made a face. "This looks terrible."

Michael smiled. "It's a powerful herb. It induces deep sleep."

Cait returned the flagon to the trunk and leaned back. Michael stood and flexed his shoulders. Then he stretched out his legs several times.

They heard a pony gallop into camp.

"One of my spies," Michael said. "I shall go talk with him. I shall be back soon."

Cait nodded.

He caught her hand in his and held it warmly, protectively. "You know what to do while I'm gone?"

"Aye." Cait did not understand the contradictory emotions that coursed through her. One moment she thought she hated the man, the next she was burning with desire for him.

He leaned closer and kissed her softly. Sighing, Cait closed her eyes and gave herself over to the sweet warmth of his lips on hers.

Lifting his mouth slightly away from hers, he whispered, "Later, my little minstrel, we shall finish what we have begun."

"We . . . haven't begun anything."

His laugh was as evocative as his kiss had been. "Aye, but we have, Cait. We started in the day Ulf found you lurking in the bushes."

Michael rose and quickly belted on his sword and dagger and bent for his helmet. He tucked it under his arm, then moved to the tent exit. When he unpegged the flap, the wind tore into the shelter. The small fire sputtered. Then the flap fell into place and was repegged.

Michael was gone.

Dacy shivered. Scooting closer to him, Cait stretched out beneath the blanket beside him, sharing the warmth of her body, willing him to live. Until that moment she had not realized how exhausted she was. She closed her eyes.

"Madam," she heard Kolby say.

The cold wind swirled around her, and she opened her eyes to see him standing in the entrance of the pavilion.

Without fully entering the shelter, he said, "Michael rode out with one of the men. Veld is on his way over here to look after Dacy so you can eat and rest. There's a cave behind the big boulder to the back of the camp where you and Michael will sleep tonight. He had me put out a basin of water and herbs. He thought you might want to bathe."

"I will later," Cait answered wearily. She was exhausted and worried and cold. She wished Kolby would either come in or leave and secure the flap. She was also frustrated with herself. She felt that she must do something for Dacy, for herself, for the cloister pin, but wasn't sure what or how. " 'Tis cold, but I'll take a quick bath in the brook."

"Nay," Kolby said. "My orders were to see that you take a basin bath in the cave."

Cait pushed up and tucked Dacy's blankets more tightly about him. "You'll personally carry out those orders?"

"Aye. If you bathe in the brook, you'll get your bandages wet, and Michael will not want to change them tonight." The Northman cast her a withering look. "Have you not caused him enough trouble for one day?"

Cait drew herself up imperiously. "Thank you for the explanation, Kolby, but regardless of what Michael has ordered, I shall take a full bath if I so choose."

"I think not," Kolby replied. "Once Michael has given me an order, madam, I follow it to the death."

"I never knew my taking a full bath could be considered a challenge to the death," Cait said dryly.

"In this instance it could be. Michael is strongly attracted to you and will do anything to keep you to himself. You'll be protected at the cave. You won't be if you bathe in the brook."

"Hail, Kolby," Veld called from outside the tent. Kolby withdrew and dropped the entrance flap in place. Cait stared at the swaying material. Again she had been reminded of her status.

Veld's head appeared in the opening. "Hail, Cait."

She smiled and greeted him.

Veld entered the tent to sit beside Cait.

"I am willing to sit with Dacy," she said.

"Aye, Michael knows that, but he wants you to eat and to rest, and he knows that you worry about your friend." Veld covered one of Cait's hands with his and pressed reassuringly. "I am well trained. Why don't you get some sleep while you can? I'll send for you if his condition changes."

Dacy woke up, his eyes wide. "Cait."

"Aye, I'm here."

"Cait," he called again.

"I'm here, Dacy." Cait leaned closer, and he smiled at her.

In border dialect, he said, "I want to talk to you."

Happily she realized that he was clearheaded. He whispered to her in their childhood language. "You must leave as soon as you can. Get ... to ... Fergus."

"Nay, Dacy, I'll not leave you."

"Must." He breathed deeply and winced. "What if Fagan did not make it?"

He had voiced Cait's own fear.

"Some of Ardac's men chased him," Dacy reminded her. "Mayhap ... he's lying somewhere with a lance through him. Remember ... traitor ... in ... cloister. Fergus ... must know ... of Glenmuir's plight. You must go, Caity."

"Nay."

"You're the only one who can save Glenmuir." Dacy's voice was growing fainter, his lids drooping.

She was losing him to unconsciousness again.

"You're my friend," she said. "I want to stay with you."

"You're always mothering someone or something, Cait." Dacy tried to smile. "Remember, this is one reason why Sholto didn't want you to join the minstrels."

"Aye."

Dacy coughed. "He said you were not tough enough, that you had the maternal instinct that would render you a useless warrior."

"I'm tough enough."

He closed his eyes. "Then at your first opportunity, you must escape and go to Fergus."

"I don't know what will happen to you, Dacy."

"I am not your responsibility."

"But you are." She moved the blanket aside and gripped the hand of his uninjured arm. "Dacy, you may need me—"

"Nay, Cait, I need you now." His clasp on her hand tightened, and he seemed to have rallied his strength. His voice was stronger, his eyes more alert. "Sing my song, Cait."

"Dacy—"

"Sing my song, Cait, and give me my sword," he repeated, "and I shall go to sleep. If I should cross over tonight, I shall be at peace."

Cait placed Dacy's sword in his right hand and held on to the left one. Softly she began to sing, unmindful of the tears that ran down her cheeks. Since she had become a bard of the Shelter Stone, she had fulfilled her responsibilities and done her duty. No matter how worried she was about her friend, as a servant of the Shelter Stone, she must leave him tonight.

"He's sleeping peacefully," Veld said later. "Perhaps you should eat."

Cait nodded. She released Dacy's hand and leaned over to kiss him lightly on the forehead.

Then she rose and walked to the campfire, already planning her escape. She filled her bowl with the thick, aromatic vegetable stew and found a quiet place to sit while she ate. She looked all around her, memorizing the placement of people and animals, of pallets and tents, of the guards. When she had finished eating, she rinsed out her bowl. Then she headed toward the ponies.

"Where are you going?" Kolby materialized out of the darkness, frightening her.

"To get my clothing. I want to take a bath," she answered. "One of my satchels should be among those Dacy was bringing to Hag's Tree for the Silver Daggers."

"I ordered the animals unpacked and groomed," Kolby said, and pointed in the opposite direction. "The baggage is over there."

Without a word, Cait turned and walked toward the pile of bundles. Kolby followed her. She rummaged through the bags until she found the satchel containing her clothes—and her whip. Kolby took the satchel from her.

She feared he would search it as Michael had done earlier today. Her hands were clammy; her heartbeat accelerated. She felt a fine sheen of nervous perspiration all over her body. He dangled the satchel from his hand as if measuring its weight. Inwardly she smiled. He was checking for silver daggers, not for a whip. When he seemed satisfied, he slung the satchel over his shoulder. Cait breathed easier.

He led her through the camp to the entrance of the cave shelter. Laying down the leathern case, he said, "If you need anything, call me. I'll be sitting on the other side of the boulder."

Two more warriors stood on either side of the

cave in the shadows. Close by she heard the nicker of a pony, mayhap two. "Are all of you going to be watching as I take my bath?"

"As long as you remain in the cave, you'll have privacy. We're here to keep an eye on you when you leave."

"Will they stay on guard all night?" Cait asked, wondering what would happen if she didn't escape and she and Michael did spend the night together. She flushed with embarrassment at the thought of these strange warriors being privy to what would happen between them.

"Nay, they'll leave as soon as Michael joins you."

"They figure he can watch me then," she said.

"They don't figure anything," Kolby answered. "They only obey Michael's orders."

She met his gaze, taking in his unspoken warning. "Good night, Kolby."

"Good night." He turned, his footsteps fading away.

Stepping beyond the small fire at the opening of the cave, Cait circled the interior. In one of the darkened corners she found a rock large enough to crouch behind as she bathed. She opened her satchel and pulled out her whip. She hid it behind another, smaller rock, then loosely stacked several more rocks on top of it. Then she laid out fresh clothes. When they were spread on the boulder, she ducked behind it and undressed. Fearful that Michael would return before she completed her bath, she hurriedly washed off as much grime as she could.

She lathered her shorn hair, and biting back tears and ignoring the cold, worked her fingers through the short strands. They felt so strange to her. After she had rinsed it and dried off, she slipped into her clean clothes: a russet tunic and brown trousers, and a darker brown leathern girdle fastened with russet laces.

She smiled and looked over to where she had concealed her whip. If only she had her purse of daggers . . . But she did not. She would have to make do. Aye, she would be ready when the opportunity came to make a dash for freedom.

She combed her hair, and moving closer to the fire, looked at her reflection on a piece of polished metal. She was unaccustomed to having hair hang loosely about her face and brush against her shoulders. Although it branded her as a dishonored woman, it did not look as bad as it might have, she thought. Ardac might have cropped it close to the scalp. After she repacked her belongings, she returned to the central campfire. She did not want to be in the cave when Michael returned. Her presence there would speak of an intimacy she wished to avoid as long as possible.

Chapter 8

Cait watched Michael ride into camp, the wolf prancing alongside him. She knew him as a warrior and a physician ... Soon she would know him as a lover. She would not submit willingly to him, but she knew he would not hesitate to steal her innocence.

The midnight blue mantle, billowing in the wind, revealed that he still wore his mail. The visor of his helmet covered his eyes and nose, the night shadows making his face appear fearsome.

He dismounted and led his stallion to the corral. As he stood beneath the fluttering torchlight, talking with the guard, Michael took off his helmet and looped it over a fence post. The guard disappeared into the darkness, and Michael squatted and called to Ulf. He caught the animal's face in his hands and scratched behind his ears. He laughed and talked softly to him. The wolf responded with whimpers and low growls.

For a moment Cait was jealous ... of a wolf. He was receiving caring attention from his master. Pets and strokes and soft words of ... love and affection.

When Michael entered the pen to tend to his stallion, Ulf lay down outside the fence. Cait rose, moved to the corral, and in the torchlight watched Michael brush the stallion. As if he sensed he was being watched, he lifted his head and stared through the shadows at her.

" 'Tis I, lord," she called out.

"Aye, lady, I know. The torchlight gleams on you. 'Tis hard to know which is more vibrant, the fire or your hair."

Pleasure ripped through Cait with such force that she caught her breath. "I was worried about you," she said. "You have been gone a long time."

"Aye, Sven and I rode a long way. We wanted to make sure the camp would sleep this night in relative quiet."

"And will we, lord?"

Without breaking their held gaze, Michael crossed the corral, the ponies whinnying and nickering as they moved out of his way. A gust of wind swept his hair about his shoulders. He stopped before her, the fence between them. He tweaked her curls.

"Some will sleep. Others will find more pleasurable ways to spend the night, my lady."

Cait lowered her eyes and gazed at the cross, the Thor's hammer, around his neck. Enameled in black, it stood out against the silver mail.

"Did Kolby tell you about the cave?" he asked.

"Aye."

His gloved fingers brushed through her hair.

"You have posted guards to watch me."

"Aye."

He was so close, Cait was trembling. She had never known another individual who had such an effect on her. The tips of his fingers brushing against the base of her neck sent shards of fire burning through her.

"Surely, lord," she said, "you are exhausted."

He laughed softly. "Not too exhausted for a pleasurable romp with a beautiful woman."

He moved away from her, opened the gate and walked through, then shut it. She turned to face him as he closed the distance between them. She felt his breath on her face. Again the wind blew strands of his hair across his face. He shucked off his gloves and tucked them into his girdle.

"Sometimes, my lady," he said, "long hair is a nuisance." He caught his hair with his hand and pulled it to the nape of his neck.

"You had it tied back earlier with a thong," she said.

"It must have come undone when I was riding."

Cait nodded. "My hair often gets—" She stopped talking as she remembered her short hair. She shrugged.

"Even short, madam, your hair is beautiful. It is russet, the color of fire." Again he put his hand to her head, his fingers pressing pleasurably into her scalp. "Aye, it is fire."

Staring at his shining black hair, Cait said, "Your hair is beautiful too, lord."

She touched it, as she had wanted to do early this morning. She ran her hands through the length of it. "I'm glad you don't wash it in lime like many of our warriors do."

"What is the benefit of the lime wash?"

She splayed her hand, the silken strands flowing through her fingers. As she had imagined, his hair was soft and silky.

"It causes the warrior's hair to stiffen out in the back like spikes, making it look thick and wild, but it also discolors the hair. All of this tends to frighten our enemies."

With the tips of her fingers she massaged his scalp.

"Ah, madam, your touch is gentle and welcome to a head that has worn a helmet for so long."

She kneaded her fingers more deeply. Michael stood quietly, his eyes closed, then he caught her hand in his. It felt warm and big and strong. He lifted his lids, and Cait stared into eyes that burned with a fire brighter and hotter than that of the overhead torch.

"This should be done in a more private and comfortable place, madam."

Cait shivered with anticipation, apprehension.

"You're cold?"

" 'Tis a brisk night," she replied, not willing to reveal how strongly he affected her.

Michael moved to unfasten his brooch.

"One mantle is enough, lord. I can do without yours."

The temperatures dropped; the wind blew around them; lightning flashed and thunder boomed intermittently. A storm gathered, but Cait was aware of nothing but the man standing in front of her. She was ashamed that her body should respond so completely, so quickly, to him ... even when she knew what he thought of her, what he planned to do to her.

"I am glad you are with me, Cait," Michael said. "I have thought of you a great deal since I first met you." He tucked a strand of her hair behind her ear. "Have you thought of me too?"

"Aye."

He cocked a brow in question. "Just 'aye'?"

"My attraction to you has never been a secret. My concern is your intention to mate with me without my consent."

"I will not need to force you," Michael returned, leaning forward and placing soft kisses over her forehead and the tip of her nose.

"You will elicit a response from my body," Cait said, "but that is not consent, lord."

"Aye, lady, but it can be wonderful."

He slipped his hands beneath the folds of the mantle, and she felt their warmth at her waist. She sucked in her breath. Her nipples crested and strained against her shirt.

"Even through your clothing your body feels lovely," he said. "I want to see it, Cait."

"You—You saw it this morning when you brought me from Ardac."

"You wore the sleeveless undergarment. I want to see you naked." His hands glided up her abdomen, resting beneath her breasts. "I want to feel your nakedness."

Heat boiled through her, leaving her weak. He rubbed his thumbs over the sensitized tips of her breasts.

"And you will consent for me to do so, Cait. That's a promise." He lowered his head and captured her lips in a warm, sweet kiss.

His words, his promise, sent pleasure through Cait's body and warmth to her cheeks.

"But this is not the time or the place. Our mating will be special. That also is a promise."

He released her, and suddenly Cait felt cold and alone. She wanted to grab him, hold him close. He reached over her shoulder and lifted his helmet from the fence post.

When he went to slip it over his hand, she caught his wrist. "Must you, lord?"

Golden shadows flickered across his face. His voice was sultry when he said, "For now, madam, I must. I have no thong with which to bind my hair, and I find it irritating to have the wind blowing it in my eyes and mouth."

"I shall bind your hair for you, lord." She pulled a russet lace from her girdle. "Turn around."

Michael stood with his back to her. She finger-combed his hair as she brought it back to his nape and tied it with the lace.

"Mayhap, lord, you would wait awhile before mating with me."

"Nay, lady, I am weary with waiting."

"Let us meet with more people of the Highlands, others who recognize the holy sign on my arm. They will testify that I am not the whore that Ardac claims."

Michael turned to look at her, but his back was to the torch, and she saw only shadows.

"Cait, there shall be no more discussion on the matter. You are mine, and I shall have you tonight." He smiled grimly. "My men think I have taken leave of my senses as it is, lady. They would know it for a fact if I did not stake my claim on you."

Stake his claim! No physical blow had ever hit Cait as hard as those words.

"Come," he said. "I am hungry."

Holding the helmet under his arm, he stepped away from her. She followed. So did the wolf. When they were close to where the men had laid their pallets and the fire, Kolby waved.

"Michael!" he called. " 'Tis time you returned. We were worried."

"All is fine, Kolby. I'll be along in a little while."

Walking beside Michael, Cait asked, "Why didn't you take Kolby with you this evening?"

"He is my head man. If something had happened to me, Kolby would have carried out my orders."

"Is it true, lord, that you would have punished Kolby to the death if I had taken a proper bath in the brook that is close by?"

Michael stopped and looked at her strangely. "Kolby told you that?"

"Aye."

"My men know to obey my orders, madam." He sighed. "Now, cease your prattle. Already you have distracted me enough for one day. I must eat, then spend some time with my maps before I forget the markings."

"Your maps?" Cait asked, surprised to learn about this new facet of the Northman.

"Aye," he answered, "I draw maps to show the areas I have visited and explored. I have found several natural encampments I wish to record."

"Do you have your maps with you?"

"Aye."

"May I see them sometime?"

"Mayhap."

Several warriors—Cait supposed these were the spies Michael had dispatched earlier—looked up when he approached the fire.

After he had exchanged greetings with them, Michael said, "Let me look in on Dacy. Then I shall meet with you."

Catching Cait's hand, Michael walked past his warriors and into the pavilion where Veld sat with Dacy.

"How is he?" Michael asked the youth.

"He's been resting peacefully."

Michael pulled back the covers, unfastened the thongs, and removed the bandages. After he had examined the wound and applied more salve, he put on fresh bandages.

"Stay with him through the night, Veld. Get me if you need me."

"Aye, Michael."

"Let me stay with him," Cait pleaded.

"Nay, lady," Michael replied. "He is resting well and has no need of you. I do."

Clasping her elbow, he guided her from the tent. The wolf rose and trotted alongside them toward the fire.

"Are you hungry?" Cait asked.

"Aye."

"I'll prepare your meal."

Michael and the wolf joined the men, who moved to make room for them. Cait knelt in front of the huge caldron and dished out Michael's food. When she handed him the bowlful of stew and the chunk of bread, he smiled at her.

"Get one of those blankets to sit on." He pointed to a pile of them.

Cait picked up one and moved to the other side of the fire away from Michael and his men.

Michael looked up. "Nay, lady, I want you closer than that." He pointed between his legs. "Here. Sit in front of me."

For a long time Cait stared at him over the dancing flames.

"Here, lady."

"Aye."

She stepped around the fire and laid out the blanket. She sat stiffly, her legs tucked beneath her to one side, and listened as the men reported to Michael all they had observed on their ride.

After he had finished his food and set the empty bowl aside, he caught Cait's shoulders and drew her closer into the curve of his legs. She nestled against him, enjoying the warmth of his body and the gentle kneading of his hands on her shoulders.

Cait yawned, and Michael leaned over. "It won't be long, lady. I, too, am ready for bed."

She could not understand Michael Langssonn. He had rescued her because he needed a woman, he said. Yet he could have gotten a whore at any of the villages throughout the kingdom. He had paid a great price for her, yet he refused to believe she was not a woman of easy virtue. At times he treated her kindly, but always he reverted to treating her like a whore. The thought rankled her, but she could do nothing about it.

Cait felt something brush against her legs. Then she felt a warm weight. She looked over to see the wolf pushing in between her and Michael. She eased over, allowing him room.

As she glanced at him, she realized that she could not escape with him around. He would protect Michael with his dying breath. She couldn't cage him for the night; she hadn't the heart to maim or kill him. The longer she pondered what to do, the more elusive the answer seemed and the more exasperated she became. If only he were a deep sleeper, she thought. *Sleep!* The word leaped out at her. The sleeping draft Michael had concocted for Dacy.

Turning, she laid her hand on Michael's thigh. "Lord, before all of us go to sleep, Veld probably needs to get out of the tent for a while and stretch his legs. While you're talking to the men, let me sit with Dacy."

Michael laid his hand over hers.

"You shall have me the rest of the night," she assured him.

He inhaled deeply. "Go ahead."

"Thank you, lord." Before she could rise, Michael

caught her close, his lips capturing hers in a long kiss. When he lifted his lips from hers, he gazed into her eyes. "I leave you with this and a promise of more, lady."

Trembling, Cait rose cautiously and moved around the wolf. She hastened over to the tent, unfastened the flap, and entered. Veld look up.

"Michael said I could sit with Dacy while you go outside and stretch." She smiled. "Michael has work to do before we go to bed."

Veld nodded and rose, quickly leaving the tent. As soon as he was gone, she plundered the physician's chest until she found an empty vial. Holding it, she poured it half-full of the sleeping tincture. She recapped the vial and slipped it into her girdle, then waited for Veld.

When he returned, she said good night and left. Walking over to the fire, Cait spoke to the cook. "If you don't mind, I'll gather some food for Michael's wolf."

"He's already eaten."

"He's a big animal," Cait said. "I'm sure he will want more."

"Aye," Michael said, "he will."

Working quickly, Cait filled a bowl with leftover food. Then, her back to Michael, she mixed the sleeping draft and water in with the solids. She hoped ... nay, prayed ... that the wolf would eat every bite, then have a deep and restful sleep. If not, she didn't know what she would do.

When she set the bowl in front of the wolf, Michael said, "I'm sure he thanks you, madam."

Ulf sniffed, then seemed to inhale the morsels in one breath.

"Aye, he thanks you."

Cait smiled and sat back down on the blanket

close to Michael. As he drank a tankard of ale, he opened his leathern satchel and withdrew several thin sheets of wood. He laid one flat on the ground in front of him. Using a thin cylinder of iron with a sharpened point, he began to make indentations in the wood. With a hammer and another instrument, he began to shave off a finer layer of the wood, turning the flat surface into hills and valleys and riverbeds. Cait watched in fascination.

Sitting down closer to her, Kolby asked, "Are all the Silver Daggers wandering minstrels?"

"All of us are wanderers and blade masters," Cait said, "but I am the only musician. All of us perform feats with the daggers. We also juggle, dance, and do acrobatics."

Remaining at her side, Kolby lapsed into silence as Cait continued to watch Michael.

The wind blew sharply. Sparks from the fire sputtered in the blackened sky above Michael's head. He reached for his satchel and reinserted the thin sheet of wood on which he had been working. Cait lifted her face to the biting cold and let her hair swirl around her head. Again she thought about the strangeness of her short hair.

But she couldn't sit around feeling sorry for herself. She touched her hand to her breast to reassure herself that the amulet was there and to remind herself of her vow. She had to escape. But she needed more than her whip as a weapon. She needed her daggers. First she had to get to her satchels. Then the idea came to her.

She looked up at Michael. "Would you like me to entertain you?"

"Nay," Michael said. "We should get some sleep."

" 'Tis not sleep you're thinking about this night," Kolby teased.

"Aye," went up in unison among the men, and they all laughed.

"We will get little rest when the rains start," Michael continued as if Kolby had not spoken.

"Let her sing," Kolby said. "One song. We have rescued her for you and understand that her body is yours. Let us have the pleasure of hearing her voice. One song, Michael, to bid us good night and sweet dreams."

Michael sighed and waved his permission. Rising, Cait walked over to the baggage. She unfastened the largest satchel and rummaged through it until she found the purse containing her blades. She retrieved four of them—all she could safely conceal in her girdle. Leaving her purse where it was, she found a leathern thong and laced her girdle. Next she pulled out a small lyre.

When she returned, Michael was sitting beside one of the scraggly trees, the wolf beside him. She sat down next to the fire and plucked the strings, soft music winging through the brisk mountain air. As she strummed and sang, she closed her eyes and recalled another day when she had played the same song for her family—a song her birth father had taught her, one he had learned on his travels through the Northland.

It was the story of a beautiful young maiden whose husband had to go to battle on their wedding day. He was gone for weeks and months and years. When he finally returned home, he was badly disfigured from wounds he had received.

The warrior, afraid that his wife would no longer love him, returned a bitter and hostile man. He treated his wife coldly and gave her a bill of divorcement. But the wife had not accepted it. She saw beyond the battle scars to the man whom she had married. Refusing to leave him, she fought her husband's anger and hostility and bitterness until he was able to admit his love for her once more.

When Cait finished the song, someone threw more wood on the fire. The flames danced into the air. Mesmerized by their glowing beauty, their freedom to climb the sky, Cait rose. In answer to the men's plea for one more song, she held the lyre close and began to walk among them. She sang again, a haunting Highland melody of a warrior who traveled far over the sea to find his lost lady-love.

She could not see Michael, but she felt his gaze on her. She moved closer to where he sat. He stood. She halted and stopped singing. Like a spirit of the night, dark and forbidding, he beckoned to her. He held out his hand.

"Come, Cait. 'Tis time."

She could hardly see, but she answered his call.

Lightning flashed; thunder drummed.

Aye, 'twas time.

Chapter 9

Autumn leaves—red, gold, and russet like flames—swirled around Cait as she lowered her lyre.

Aye, Michael thought, Cait nea Sholto was fire and passion, and much more. He had told the truth this morning when he said he had been without a woman for a long time. He had lied when he said he had need of a whore. He wanted Cait, and Cait alone.

When Ardac had pretended to chop off her head, taking the braid instead, she had not whimpered. Her body had convulsed, but she had faced Gilbert's men proudly. She had more courage than all five of her adversaries put together.

And her voice was one of the most beautiful Michael had ever heard. Both husky and melodic, it had so moved him that he had easily envisioned the maimed warrior returning to his lovely young bride. Aye, Cait had touched cords in Michael that had not been touched in a long time . . .

He took the lyre from her, holding it in one hand and clasping her hand in the other. He led her away from the warmth and glow of the campfire, away from his warriors to the interior of the shallow cave. Ulf, moving lethargically, followed and lay down in front of the fire just outside the entrance.

143

Michael unfastened the brooch that secured her mantle.

"Your hair has dried." He sniffed it. "It smells good."

"I smell clean," she replied lightly. "While you were gone, I took a basin bath."

"Ah, lady, I wish I had been here to see the sight."

He swept the mantle from her. Holding the russet and gold material in his hands, he gazed at her with the same intensity and thoroughness with which Ardac had regarded her earlier in the day. But his gaze did not disgust Cait. Instead, it filled her with breathless excitement. She felt as if she were balanced on one foot at the edge of a cliff.

"You changed clothes, madam."

"Aye." She forced herself to breathe deeply, slowly. "Riding is much easier in trousers than in the tunic."

"Trousers also reveal more of the female anatomy."

"To your displeasure?"

"Nay, madam, to my *pleasure*."

He set the lyre on the ground, next to a pile of firewood. He turned to her; her gaze was fixed on the pallet. Beside it, glittering silver in the faint light of the outside fire, lay his mail and his helmet.

"I laid the pallet earlier," he said. "It is not as comfortable as a bed, madam, but much better than the hard ground."

Cait clutched the neckline of her shirt.

"Nay," he said. "I want to undress you. 'Twill be a new experience for me."

"You've never undressed a woman before?"

"Not one wearing trousers."

"I have never been undressed by a man before."

" 'Tis part of mating. Most women find it pleasurable. I think you will, too." Michael smiled.

"You are a strange person," Cait said. "I am your slave. Why do you care whether I receive pleasure from our relationship? When most men want to mate with a woman, they take her whether she is willing or not."

"I am not most men, madam, and I have learned that one never truly possesses what one takes. Always one fears someone will take it back. Generally it requires little to make another person happy."

"If you make me happy," Cait said, "then I shall make you happy."

He nodded. "You will decide that life with me is better than life away from me."

Once more Michael had changed, Cait reflected. While she would never again consider him kind or gentle, neither was he harsh. He seemed to be genuinely concerned about her.

"What will happen when you cease letching for me?" she asked.

"I will help you find a good home, madam, and a man whom you can respect and who will do the same for you."

"As I said, my lord, you are strange. I find it difficult to believe that you are a warlord. You are more like an ovate."

"An ovate?"

"A scholar and philosopher."

"I *am* a scholar, madam. I have traveled the world over in my search for knowledge." He smiled in response to her obvious surprise. "My father taught me that respect must be earned and equally shared. If my men respect me, they will follow me to the ends of the earth."

"Have you been to the ends of the world?"

"Almost." He unfastened his brooch. "Have you?"

"Nay, I haven't been a wandering minstrel for long."

"But you enjoy traveling?"

She nodded.

"Soon, my lady, I shall take you on a journey you have only dreamed about."

He slipped the mantle from his shoulders, and sparks from the fire spewed into the air.

" 'Tis time to begin our journey."

He dropped the mantle next to the pallet. He unfastened the buckles on his weapon belts, then laid dagger and sword beside the mail—within arm's reach. He unbuttoned his tunic and tugged it loose from his trousers. Crossing his arms over his chest, catching the tail of the tunic in both hands, he began to tug it over his head.

"Aye," she said, and he heard the smile in her voice, " 'tis time to begin our journey."

His hands above his head, bound in the shirt, Michael heard the swish of material. Something twisted around his ankles, binding his feet, tripping him. A painful blow struck his stomach. He bent double in agony. She struck him across the shoulders. He grunted and fell sprawled on the cave floor.

"If you're wondering why your wolf is not protecting you," Cait said, grunting with effort, "I gave him some of Dacy's sleeping herbs."

The wind knocked out of him, pain slivering throughout his body, Michael lay stunned and tangled in his clothing. Again the swish of material alerted him to her movements about the cave. He pushed to his knees and lunged toward the sound. His stomach struck the cudgel a second time. He toppled but didn't fall. The toe of her boot kicked him over.

He fought to free himself from the shirt, but she must have tied his sleeves together over his head. She secured the binding about his ankles, then caught the material above his right shoulder and fastened it to the ground; she did the same to the left. He shouted for Kolby, but the sound was muffled and garbled by his tunic banded tightly across his mouth.

"That should hold you for a while, *my lord*." She laughed again. "Trussed in your own clothing, winded by a piece of your firewood, and ensnared by your own letching."

Michael heard her footfalls crunching on the rocky ground as she ran away. He jerked up with his shoulders—once, twice, three times. The material ripped. He freed himself but could not divest himself of the torn shirt. He straightened it. In the distance he heard a pony galloping away. As he listened, calculating the direction she had taken, he glanced at the ground and saw firelight glinting off the blades of two small daggers.

He curled his hands into fists, furious with himself. In his infatuation with the woman, he had lowered his guard and allowed her to outmaneuver him. She had fastened him to the ground with her daggers. Using one of them, he slit the leathern thong that bound his ankles, then grabbed his weapons and fastened them about his waist. Angry, humiliated, he left his helmet and mail and grabbed his mantle. He fastened it about his neck, pausing at the cave entrance long enough to make sure Ulf was only sleeping. Then he marched out of the cave.

"Michael," Kolby called out, "what has happened?"

"The woman has escaped. What fool left his pony outside the cave?" Michael ran toward the corral.

"The only fool was the man who bought himself a slave and underestimated her cleverness. You're much too preoccupied with this woman, Michael. 'Tis not good."

"Mayhap what you say is true," Michael said, "but when I relieved the men from guard duty, they should have taken their pony with them. That, head-man, was their mistake, and one of them shall answer for it."

"How did she get past the wolf?"

"She gave him a sleeping draft."

Kolby laughed. "So our little wandering minstrel has outsmarted the wolves?"

"You're not amusing, Kolby." Michael glared at him.

"I'm not trying to be. All along I've known the woman would cause trouble. You're too attracted to her, Michael, and because of this, you're making decisions that imperil us."

"Watch your tongue, Kolby. You are too impudent. One of these days it shall land you in trouble. Mayhap a duel to the death," he added dryly.

"As you can see," Kolby returned, his tone unrepentant, "one has to take drastic measures with her. She is far too spirited and quick-witted."

"Lower your voice, Kolby. You'll wake the entire camp."

"Few are asleep, and soon all will know of their lord's folly. Shall I go with you?"

"Nay. She escaped because I underestimated her. I shall find her myself." Michael entered the makeshift corral. "While I'm gone, deal with the one who left his pony outside the cave."

Kolby laughed.

" 'Tis a laughing matter to you now, my friend, because Cait is merely a bedmate and not a dangerous enemy. We cannot allow our warriors to be so careless. Our lives, rather than my pride, could be at stake."

"Aye, Michael."

Michael swung onto his huge stallion.

There was an explosion of lightning and a rumble of thunder, and suddenly the sky opened up in a violent downpour. Unminded of the deluge, Michael urged the stallion into a fast gallop heading in the direction he thought she had taken.

The gray mare stumbled badly, tossing Cait to the ground, and galloped away. Fighting the wind and rain, she raked hair out of her face and scrambled to her feet. For the second time in a few hours, she crouched behind a huge boulder. To escape the Northman, she must have another pony. Now the only one available was his. He was following her. She knew it.

The coils of the whip slid down her arm. She was glad she had retrieved it earlier. It and the two daggers were her only weapons.

She heard the thud of the stallion's hooves. She waited. The rider moved from behind an outcropping of rocks. In the flash of lightning she saw that it was the Silver Warrior. He wore no helmet or mail, and his mantle billowed from his body. She bit back her smile when she saw the jagged tears at each shoulder of his shirt.

Cait knew what she must do. As he drew near, she lifted her arm. The whip moved out like a long snake, back, back, then looped up into the air and traveled swiftly. The long leathern lash flicked past the stallion's head, never touching the animal, then licked down and coiled its deadly fang around the rider. She heard Michael grunt, then swear. A stream of Norse words she didn't know spewed from his mouth. Pulling in the whip, she dragged him from his horse. His body landed on the hard ground with a loud thump.

She dropped her whip and raced to the stallion. She had grabbed its mane and was about to swing onto its back when hard hands grasped her waist, biting into her flesh.

"Not with the help of all the gods of Asgard," he raged. He jerked her to the ground. "You told me you would make me growl in anger, but I had not figured you for a dimwit."

"I was desperate." She panted. "I must save Glenmuir and the Shelter Stone."

They rolled and tumbled on the ground, each grunting and swearing, their sounds primitive and guttural. Cait reached for her knife, but Michael, on top of her, caught her failing arms and pulled them above her head.

"My wrists," she cried out.

"I'm sorry," he murmured, loosening his grip only slightly, imprisoning her body with his.

Storm shadows cast his face in an eerie silver mask. She was frightened of him as she had never been before.

"Please, sire, I beg—"

"Aye, madam, it's time you begged. I also want an apology."

"An apology?" she repeated.

"You could have easily broken my ribs."

"I wish I had. Then you wouldn't have come after me so soon."

"I should have come after you sooner!"

"Don't do this, lord. You'll regret it, I promise."

"I shall regret it if I don't."

Michael removed his hands from her arms, and slid down the length of her body, his hand cupping her chin. He pressed his mouth against hers in a hard, hot kiss. Cait clenched her mouth shut, refusing the angry, possessive touch. His fingers bit into her cheek, applying just enough pressure to force her mouth open. Before his tongue could seek entrance, Cait bit his lips.

"Damnation!" He jerked his head back.

Taking advantage of the diversion, Cait crammed her fists between their bodies and pushed him off her. She rolled away, leaped to her feet, and ran beneath a high rock plate that jutted from the side of the mountain. Grateful for the respite from the rain, she ran beneath and along the shelf, hoping she could find either one of the ponies. Then she saw Michael moving toward her. His stance was predatory. Aye, he was dangerous.

"You cannot get away, madam. I have bought you. You are mine."

His voice was soft against the howl of the wind, but Cait had no difficulty hearing him. Dark. Strong. Dangerous. This was Michael Langssonn, and according to all the laws of the land, she belonged to him.

For a moment Cait stared defiantly at him. The wind whipped his mantle about his body, and his wet, dark hair framed his shadowed face. Rivulets of water ran down his face and neck through the thick mat of hair revealed in the opening of his tunic.

"When I first saw you I knew you were an impassioned creature," he said.

"Only because I'm frightened."

"Nay, because you truly understand the fury of passion. Because you understand the carnal beast that lives within the warrior. This merry chase you have led me on ... the whip—"

"Escape. Protection."

"Fire. Passion."

"Let me go, lord so that I may help my people. I must reach Athdara." Not trusting him, she dared not tell him of her intention to go to Northern Scotland.

"Nay, I need you." He stepped closer.

Cait brushed dripping hair out of her face and laughed bitterly. "Any woman would do, lord. You said yourself that I am a small woman, not at all to your liking."

She heard his soft laughter. "I said you were smaller than most, but I am very much attracted to you, Cait nea Sholto."

He stood with his hands on his hips, his chest rising and falling with his heavy breathing. With a start Cait realized her own breathing was timed with his, slow and deep. It seemed as if the rain were washing away her purpose, her resolve, replacing them with flames of yearning. She felt desire settling through her, a slow fire building in her lower regions.

"I have wanted you since I first set eyes on you."

Michael's water-drenched clothing stuck to his muscular physique. His stance was filled with the fury of unleashed passion in its most primitive state. He took a step forward. She pulled a third blade from her girdle.

"Don't come any closer," she warned.

"Or?"

"I shall be forced to hurt you."

Michael laughed. "Killing me is the only way you'll stop me."

He stared at Cait. Lightning illuminated her in explosive bursts. Her eyes were large and round. Her mouth was parted.

His gaze lowered to her breasts, to the nipples straining against the wet material that molded their fullness. He wiped his wrist over his mouth. He imagined he could feel the creamy texture of her skin, could taste the honeyed sweetness. His nostrils were filled with her strawberry water scent. Down his gaze wandered to linger at the juncture of her thighs and hips, where the material of her soaked trousers clung enticingly.

Michael's gaze was hot and lustful; it fed the already raging fire within Cait. She could hardly stay where she was or keep her hands to herself. For the first time in her life, she wanted to run to a man and press herself against his chest. He took another step forward, jarring her out of her trance, and she bolted.

She spun around, tripped, fell, and dropped her dagger. She was crawling away from Michael when he landed beside her.

"Nay." His hand tangled in her hair. "You won't get away from me again."

The rain pounded down upon them in torrential fury. He pressed her into the ground and covered her mouth with his in a hot, demanding kiss.

"My mountain cat," he murmured. "Hissing and scratching. Playing your mating games. Pretending you do not want me, but all the while leading me on a merry chase."

Cait hissed and scratched. She forgot about her

wounds as she fought. She twisted her face away from his. "Have you so soon forgotten your words, lord?"

A new curtain of rain sluiced down on them.

"Any man can take by force," she reminded him.

"Aye, that is true," Michael said. After a short pause, he added, "I have never been a man of extreme emotion. But you, woman, push me to the edge." He brushed his hand over her face, touching her brows, her nose, her mouth. "At times you act as if you are an experienced woman of the world. At others you seem innocent. You project a mystery that attracts me."

"I *am* an innocent."

"I doubt it, madam, but if you want to play that game, then so shall I. Let us pretend that you are a frightened kitten." His voice had become low, sultry, stroking away all her resolve. "I want you to purr for me, to rub against me, to sit in my lap . . . because you want to. I shall be gentle with you, little wild cat, and tame you."

" 'Tis possible I shall tame *you*, lord," she murmured.

His laughter became their kiss as he laid his mouth on hers. But this time he didn't take or demand. He swept his hands down her body, his lips repeatedly seeking hers. His giving was Cait's undoing. She trembled and curled closer to him. The tip of his tongue ran along the seam of her quivering lips. Cait gasped and stiffened. She was tempted to open her mouth to receive him but did not.

"From your reaction, madam—" his voice was deep and warm "—I would say that you are pretending you haven't been kissed before."

"I have."

She had, if one counted the tentative pecks she had received.

"You aren't responding to my kisses. Do you like them?"

"Aye."

Michael lifted his head and brushed wet tendrils of hair from her face. In the darkness she couldn't see his expression, but she could feel his smile. "Aye, what, madam?"

"I like them."

"Good," he murmured, his hands still caressing her face. "Soon, madam, your entire body shall be singing with pleasure ... at my touch."

"I would like that, lord," Cait said. "As I told you when I met you in the forest in Glenmuir, I have sung all my life about men and the pleasure they give women, but I have never sung from that pleasure myself."

"Never?"

"Never."

"Then I shall be the first for you in many ways."

In all ways.

The tip of his finger traced the outline of her bottom lip, then stroked the fullness. She sighed with pleasure. His mouth over hers, he caught the soft rush of her breath. Slowly, gently, he increased the pressure of his kiss until her lips parted. This time when his tongue demanded entrance, she welcomed him. He dipped in deeper to taste the inner softness of her lips with a new intimacy.

The penetration of his tongue both shocked and pleased Cait. She pressed her palm against his chest and felt the thudding of his heart. He was as affected as she was. Slowly he withdrew his tongue. She cried out. Loneliness assailed her. Quickly he penetrated even deeper. Cait moaned.

"Aye, madam, purr for me."

Michael's body tightened. He teased and caressed; he enticed; he seduced until Cait heard only the thunder of her desire and knew only the taste of that same emotion in Michael. It licked through her like fire during times of drought. She slid her hands around his neck, pulling him closer. His arms circled her in return, gathering her against his chest.

Cait's breasts swelled. She trembled. The pressure of Michael's hands increased as he arched her more fully into his embrace. Cait moaned again.

Her sensuality seared through Michael, shaking him. He had known many and varied women. He knew the art of making love according to many cultures. But this was the first time a woman had responded so completely—so honestly—to his kiss.

He had wanted Cait, but he had never dreamed what intense passion she would stir in him, what response she would demand in return. The more he had of her, the more he wanted.

Michael forgot everything but Cait. His hands moved from her back to her hips, ravishing and cherishing her in long strokes. His tongue mated with hers in wild, seething silence. He slid his fingers between her legs and wished she were unclothed so that he could feel the naked fire of her.

Cait stiffened in shock. Reflexively she struggled, clamping her legs together. She caught his hand and tried to push him away.

"Nay!" she cried.

Although she was desperately hungry for the barbarian's touch, she could not accept him within her body.

"Nay?" he said thickly. He levered up and looked down into her face. His voice harsher, he repeated, "Nay, madam?"

"Please, my lord," Cait said, "do not take me like this."

Michael was breathing deeply. "Why not? You admitted that you enjoy my kisses, and you are the one who has driven us into the wilds."

"Aye," she whispered, feeling humiliation heat her cheeks, "I did enjoy it, but I—I have never lain with a man before."

"The time for pretense is over! I have tired of it."

Knowing it was futile to struggle against a man who was so much stronger than she, or to argue with one who had already judged her, Cait said, more for effect than with the conviction of truth, "I have allowed you liberties with my body, sire, but I—I am frightened. And cold."

Immediately Michael threw his mantle over both of them, and Cait burrowed closer to him.

Stalling for time, she said, "I apologize for having run away, and for having hit you with the firewood, and for having put Ulf to sleep. Please take me back with you and let the taking be more gentle. Let us return to your pallet in the cave."

Lying half over her, Michael pinned Cait to the ground with his weight. "Why should I do that?"

Knowing that escape would be impossible, she said, "You would get more pleasure, and you are a practical man."

Michael laughed in spite of himself. "You are right. This is not the best place for us to mate. We shall return to the cave. First we must find the ponies."

He rose and held out a hand to assist her. As she stood, water cascaded from her clothing. He inspected the bandages around her wrists. "I'm going to have to change these again, after all."

"Aye."

"Also, madam, remember when we reach the cave, I shall accept no more excuses for delay." He caught her chin and raised her face to his. "Do you understand?"

"Aye." Soaking wet and cold, she shivered.

Michael sighed, unpinned his mantle, and threw it around her. "Am I always going to be rescuing you?"

"There is no call for you to give me your cloak," she answered, but gratefully burrowed deeper into the thickness.

"It is fur-lined, warm and dry."

"You will need it yourself."

"I shall take the blanket off Silver Prince," he said. "It will keep the worst of the rain and chill off me until we reach the cave."

"I would feel better, lord, if—"

"Nay. I want to keep you as dry as possible. I said I will accept no excuses when we arrive back at camp."

Michael pulled the mantle higher about her neck and repinned it.

Cait sighed as a measure of warmth seeped into her body. "Why isn't it wet on the inside?"

"We Northmen are sons and daughters of the sea, and of the icy Northlands. We oil many of our skins to make them water-resistant."

"Like the pavilion," Cait said. "You shall have to teach me this technique."

"Aye," Michael answered, "I shall." After a moment he added, his voice warm, "You will be the first woman besides my mother and my aunt who will have fashioned clothing for me."

"I hadn't meant that I would be making clothing for you! I was thinking about making mantles for the Silver Daggers."

"Then you had better redirect your thinking. You shall be taking care of me in the future, not the Silver Daggers. They shall have to learn to do things for themselves. Now we shall hunt the ponies."

As he had done earlier that day, he twined their hands together, careful of her wrists, and the two of them walked through the rain in search of their mounts. Eventually they found the stallion but not the mare.

"Your foolishness has caused us to lose a good animal," Michael said. He took the blanket from the stallion's back and threw it around his shoulders.

Weary, the events of the day having caught up with her, Cait said, "Are we going to ride double, sire?"

"Nay," he said. "My stallion is tired. He has been sorely ridden. He shall carry no more than one tonight."

Cait sighed and nodded. She understood the warrior's code. The lord rode; the lady walked. Michael's hands banded around her waist. She gasped as he swung her onto the back of the silver-coated steed.

"I want you on the stallion because I fully intend to avail myself of your body when we return, and I do not wish you to be so exhausted from walking that you pass out on me."

Aye, she thought, *the stranger is a practical man, one who always sees to his own interests.*

Yet excitement raced through Cait. In protecting his own interests, he was providing her with another opportunity for escape. She pressed her knees to the sides of the stallion. Mayhap she would still taste freedom this night.

As if he had read her mind, Michael said, "My patience is at an end, madam. A second attempt to escape will result in dire consequences. As soon as we reach camp, I shall have the torque soldered around your neck."

Cait quailed at the thought. "It really isn't necessary as long as I have short hair, lord."

"Your short hair marks you as a dishonorable woman. The torque will mark you as my property."

Cait swallowed her disappointment. She finally accepted that she now stood a better chance of reaching Northern Scotland if she traveled with Michael.

"I do not contest that you have bought me from Gilbert's men and that you consider me your property, but I do ask one favor. Don't take me in lust, sire, and don't solder your torque about my neck until after we reach Northern Scotland."

Michael stopped and turned. "What about your plans for going to Athdara?"

Without revealing more than she had to, Cait answered honestly, "I will seek the help I need from the people of Northern Scotland. There are those there who will testify that I am a bard of the Shelter Stone, not the traitor or the whore that Ardac claimed. I must persuade them to help us in Glenmuir. From there I shall return to Athdara." When he did not respond, she added, "I can lead you along a shorter route that will get you there in three days rather than four days."

After a moment, Michael said, "If I wait to put my torque around your neck and do not mate with you until we reach Northern Scotland, will you give me your word that you will not try anything so foolhardy as escape again?"

"I promise." Relief washed through her. "Oh, my lord, thank you. High Queen Muireall of Northern

Scotland knows me. She has visited the Shelter Stone Shrine many times."

Cait realized she was rambling, but she was too happy to care.

"The queen's last visit was only a few moons ago. She and her daughter-in-law, Princess Jarvia, made the pilgrimage. When I spoke with the princess later, she expressed regret that her husband, Malcolm mac Duncan, could not make the journey with her."

"Malcolm mac Duncan," Michael said. "Do you know him?"

"I have seen him only once, lord, and that was six winters ago. But I know of him. He is the fostered son of High King Fergus. He is also one of the most valiant warriors in all the Highlands."

"High King Fergus is the one who will grant you sanctuary?"

"Aye. Will you take me to his village?"

"Aye, Cait," Michael said. "I shall. Then he will direct me to the man I am looking for."

"Or if he can't, one of the clan chieftains will," Cait said. "Everyone shall be gathered at Fergus's village to celebrate the autumn feast." Relaxing more than she had for days, Cait smiled. "My lord, you will not regret this. For a verity, it is a prayer answered."

Cait looked down to see Michael's hand close forcefully over the black-enameled Thor's hammer he wore around his neck.

"Aye, madam," he said, "for both of us."

Chapter 10

The dark clouds dissipated for a time, leaving only a spidery veil to cover the luminescent crescent in the sky. For one magical moment the glen was awash in a shimmering wonder of silvery blue and black. Soon the moon would disappear. More rain would come. But for now the worst of the storm was over.

As Michael and Cait rode into camp, all was quiet and dark, except for several tents that glowed dimly, illuminated by small fires inside.

"The rain has driven the men to seek shelters," Cait said. "Look how many more tents they have erected since we left." She noticed a blue and white one in particular. "Aren't those your colors?"

"Aye," Michael answered dryly, "my father has arrived."

Michael halted Silver Prince outside the corral, dismounted, then opened the gate.

"I thought we were going to meet him," Cait said.

"I thought so too."

A deep voice boomed, "What happened?" as Michael's father emerged from the darkness.

"I was detained," Michael said, then added dryly, "As I am sure Kolby and the others have already told you."

Michael pushed his hands beneath the mantle, caught Cait around the waist, and swung her down. He settled her on her feet, then led the stallion into the corral.

"When I insisted that we separate, Michael, I meant for us to go forward toward Northern Scotland, not farther back into Glemnuir." Lang glanced at Cait, and in the blue wash of moonlight she saw disapproval on his bearded face.

"I suppose Kolby has given you a full report," Michael said.

"Aye, and I only hope the whore is worth all the trouble."

Cait fumed, but Michael flashed his father a grin. "I have yet to find out, and probably won't, any time soon."

"Nay," Lang returned, "there are not many more hours left in which to rest at all. Kolby tells me you are planning to leave before dawn?"

"Aye, but I have been thinking that we might pull out now." Michael slung the reins and halter over the fence, then the sodden blanket he had wrapped around his shoulders. "The rain would wash away our tracks."

Lang rubbed a hand through his dark beard, which was streaked with silver. "Unless you're being followed, that should be no concern to you."

"At present we are not, but the warriors from whom I bought Cait are a greedy lot. They will be back to steal her so they can collect a second reward."

"Bartering for her was foolish."

"I wanted her. My mistake was in letting them live to tell the story."

Although Cait did not relish the idea of belonging

to the Northman, she was glad that Michael did not apologize for having bought her.

Kolby, a burning torch in hand, walked up to them. "So our warlord and wandering minstrel have returned." He looked them both over. "No great damage to either, I see."

Michael frowned. "Take care of Silver Prince for me."

Kolby chuckled. "Aye, my lord." He attached the torch to a corral post.

"How is Dacy doing?" Michael asked.

"Fevered. Delirious," Kolby answered. "Veld is delirious also. He's out of medicine and thinks you have deserted him and the patient."

Lang stepped into the glow of the torchlight. " 'Tis unlike Michael to be so remiss in his duties."

Michael swore.

Lang was close enough that Cait could see him better. He was indeed a massive man. Dark hair, sprinkled with silver at the temples, hung loose to his shoulders. He wore a light-colored shirt and dark trousers, and his mantle was draped carelessly over one shoulder.

"Was your trip without mishap, Lang?" Michael asked.

"Aye, and would have been better had you traveled farther today. We would be out of Glenmuir."

"I didn't, and we aren't," Michael said, "and that is that, Father."

As Kolby moved among the ponies, they began to whinny. One of them darted past the fencing where Cait stood and caught her attention. It was familiar. She moved closer to the corral.

"That pony!" she exclaimed, pointing. "It's one of ours."

"Of course it is," Michael answered impatiently.

"Not yours. See the mark on it? It belongs to the Silver Daggers. It may be the one Fagan was riding."

Michael moved to her side. "Fagan?"

"Fagan is our fastest runner and rider. He was on his way to Northern Scotland to let High King Fergus know that Glenmuir had been attacked."

Even as she said Fagan's name and remembered his agile body flipping through the air in feats of stunning acrobatics, the possibility that he had been captured . . . or killed . . . brought the prick of tears to Cait's eyes. The last night the Silver Daggers had camped together, they had been so happy and eager to be home. Tonight they were scattered . . . in danger.

"We found the pony when we doubled back to look for you," Lang told Michael. "We also found the decapitated body of a warrior nearby. A barbed lance had pierced his heart."

"Perhaps it is not your friend," Michael said to Cait, then of his father, he asked, "Can you describe him?"

When Lang was finished, Cait said grimly, " 'Twas Fagan. Gilbert's men killed him." She clutched the corral railing with both hands and forced back her tears. Although she and Dacy had feared for their friend, Cait had clung to the hope that Fagan had arrived safely and that warriors of Northern Scotland were even now on their way to Glenmuir.

"What did he mean to her?" Lang asked, turning to Michael.

Cait knew Lang was referring to her and Fagan, but his manner of talking as if she did not exist angered her. She spun around and glared at the old man.

"My lord, I have ears with which to hear and a mouth with which to speak. If you want to know something about me, ask me. Fagan was my friend, one of the minstrels I traveled with."

"Your slave is impudent, Michael. You need to teach her respect."

"Aye." Michael grinned. Clasping Cait's shoulders, he tugged her gently. " 'Tis time you changed out of your wet clothing and we started our lessons."

"Aye." But Cait did not feel the cold. Grief and despair over her friend's death had encased her in numbness. Fagan was dead. Dacy was wounded, perhaps fatally. Gilbert had virtually imprisoned her adopted father, the cloister priests and priestesses, and the Silver Daggers. And she was Michael's slave.

Once more Cait felt Lang's gaze on her. She turned to find him glowering at Michael's oiled-skin mantle, which she wore.

"I think it is time for you to change clothes also, Michael." Lang barked the words.

Cait felt Michael tense, but he kept walking.

"The night air is brisk, and you have no cloak," Lang continued. "You are wet to the bone."

"That I am," Michael agreed, "and cold. The best way for a man to get warm when he's both cold and wet is to lie with a woman."

Lang snorted.

Michael laughed. "You were the one who gave me the advice."

"Then here's more advice, since you're inclined to listen. There is a time and place for all things. This is not the time or place for *her*."

"Let's have no more bickering this night, Father," Michael said, his voice soft but firm. "I'm weary."

"Michael—"

"No more, Lang." Over his shoulder, Michael called out to Kolby, "We'll be on our way before dawn. A mere three or four hours."

"Aye."

Guiding Cait, Michael headed toward camp. Lang fell into step beside them.

"Don't forget why you are here, Michael."

A heavy pause, then: "I haven't."

Cait felt the tension between father and son. Still Michael offered no apology for his actions. Nor did Lang retreat or desist. Cait gathered that father and son were alike—headstrong and accustomed to having their own way.

"The sooner we complete our business and leave, the better it shall be for us all," Lang said. "Mayhap we can return home before the rivers begin to freeze."

"Aye," Michael said.

Lang stopped at the blue and white tent. "When shall we talk?"

"Tonight," Michael replied. "I'll be back after I've changed into dry clothes and looked in on Dacy."

"Let's look in on Dacy first, lord. He may need you," Cait implored.

"I'll be waiting," Lang replied.

Michael and Cait walked on toward the pavilion that sheltered Dacy.

"Michael," Lang called out.

He turned and looked at his father.

"Where's the wolf? I didn't see him with you."

"Asleep."

With a grunt Lang disappeared into his shelter, and Michael guided Cait through the camp to the yellow and white pavilion.

"I'm sorry about the death of your friend," he said.

"Aye." She composed herself. "I am worried, lord. I fear the worst has happened to my adopted father and my cousin."

"For your sake, I hope not."

"Rob's so young," Cait said. "It's difficult for me to realize that he has seen only ten-and-seven winters."

"Maturity, madam, has nothing to do with the passing of the seasons," Michael said. "It is the result of our experiences."

He lifted the flap of the pavilion. Veld rose hastily.

"Michael!" he exclaimed, his face brightening. "I'm glad you have returned. He has taken a turn for the worst."

Cait dropped to her knees on one side of Dacy, Michael on the other. He pulled the covers down, unlaced the leathern thongs, and unwrapped the bandages.

"Dacy," Cait whispered, darting a quick glance at the red and swollen wound. She focused on Dacy's pale and hollow face. She knew he was dying, but she wouldn't let him go. "It's me, Cait. I'm all right. The Northman has agreed to take us to Northern Scotland with him. He'll protect us."

"Cait—" Michael warned.

"You're going to be better by morning, Dacy. You really are." Tears rushed down her cheeks and fell on the blanket.

"Cait—" Michael said a second time.

"We're going to be up early, and—"

Michael moved around Dacy and caught her in his arms. He pressed her cheek against his chest. " 'Tis time to sing to him, Cait."

"Nay, lord." She sagged against him. She had lost Fagan. Now she was losing Dacy. She would never see him again, never speak to him in their childhood dialect.

"Sing, Cait," Michael ordered softly.

"I've already sung to him."

"Then sing again." He seemed to growl the words at her.

She looked up at him.

"Now."

An inner calmness and strength flowed through her. She pushed away from Michael and caught Dacy's hand. She twined their fingers together and began to sing. Through the lyrics of the song, she escorted him through the Highland mountains and glens, across brooks and rivers into a bright, sunshiny world.

Dacy began to breathe deeply. He caught his breath, held it, then faintly coughed. He breathed no more.

Cait continued to sing. She couldn't stop.

Michael wrapped his arms around her and held her tightly. She slid her arms beneath his mantle and circled his waist, not caring that both of them were wet. Her fingers dug into his back. Needing his strength and warmth, needing a friend, she pressed against him. Finally, after gently putting Cait away from him, Michael pulled her up with him.

"Veld, see to the burial."

"Nay, lord," Cait said, "I'll—"

"You sang his song and escorted him to the other world," Michael said softly but firmly. "We can bury him. See to it, Veld."

The youth nodded.

"I'm going to take Cait to the cave."

Michael swept the grief-stricken woman off her feet and into his arms and walked out of the tent into the biting chill of the autumn night. Long strides carried him through the camp. When they reached the cave, he sat down on a boulder and held her close.

All Michael wanted to hear, all he did hear, was the sweetness of Cait's voice as she had sung to her friend. The beauty and simplicity of the ritual touched him in ways he had never dreamed possible. He could not remember when words, tone, and rhythm had moved him so deeply.

"Dacy's in the other world now, my lord."

Michael brushed his hand through her wet hair, down her shoulders to the small of her back. He wanted to take her sorrow into himself, to wipe her tears away.

"Everything I ever loved has been taken from me," she murmured. "My family. Fagan. Dacy. And I don't know what has happened to Rob and Sholto."

"My little bard," he said softly, "we have no news that anything bad has happened to either of them. Don't let imaginary fears haunt you."

Cait cried harder. "Something has happened to them, I know it."

Gazing into the fire pit, where only embers glowed, Michael stood Cait on her feet.

"You need to undress," he said.

She was so cold, her body was shaking, but still she stood there and cried. Michael unfastened the brooch and jerked the mantle from her, tossing it to the ground. He quickly stripped her clothing from her body, thinking only of her health. As soon as she was naked, he laid her on the pallet and covered her with a fur-lined blanket.

As quickly, he shed his own clothing, for the first time pushing his mail carelessly across the floor. For one of the few times in his life, he disregarded his fighting gear for something he considered more important. Through the enveloping shadows, he returned to the pallet, scooted between the covers, and caught her in his arms.

She was a delicate woman. He smiled as he remembered her defiance when she told him that she measured nearly seven-and-ten hands high. He pressed his face against her head, loving the feel of the silken strands. Rather than stirring his passion at that moment, her softness, her feminity, seemed to bring a gentling and a peace to his spirit.

"Dacy was my closest friend, lord," she said in a hollow voice, her palm resting against his chest.

She turned and burrowed her cheek into his chest, and Michael enjoyed the pressure and warmth against him.

"We used to play together. We never dreamed that it would end like this." After a long pause, she added, "He died helping me escape."

Fresh tears wet Michael's chest, but he only held her more tightly. She began to talk about her childhood with Dacy, and he listened. Although she spoke only of her friend, Michael knew that she mourned all her losses.

He held her, stroking his hand over her head and through her hair. He pressed a comforting kiss to the crown of her head. Finally the tears . . . and the talk . . . subsided. Every so often she sniffled.

Cait liked the feel of his hand in her hair, the tantalizing brush of his fingertips along her scalp. Closing her eyes, she relaxed against him. At the moment she didn't care who he was or what he had done. She needed and wanted his strength and protectiveness. With a reverberating boom that vibrated the earth, thunder heralded the return of the storm. Rain pelted down.

Above the sound, Cait heard the strong beating of Michael's heart beneath her ear, rhythmic and powerful. Michael Langssonn was alive, and she needed life . . . mayhap more now than ever before.

"Thank you for holding me, lord," she whispered with a teary laugh. "I know you don't like me to accuse you of being kind, but right now, let me believe it. Please."

"Believe what you like."

She smiled. "I was so frightened the first time I saw you."

"Were you?"

He felt the brush of her cheek against his chest as she nodded. "I thought you were the storm. Lightning and thunder rolled into one."

"Mayhap I am." He moved a little away from her.

"I don't think so. Storms leave destruction in their wake. But you are a healer, lord."

Michael reminded himself that he was the avenger . . . not the healer. He had come to Northern Scotland to kill Malcolm mac Duncan. And he would. Cait was leading him directly to the man. Yet inside Michael burned with a desire to heal people, to bring peace instead of war, to barter for possessions instead of taking them by force.

He was Lang's son—heir to the Clan of the Wolves. His father had instilled in him since babyhood his duties and responsibilities as a leader, as a warlord. Only as long as Michael had fulfilled his obligations as a warrior had his father reluctantly allowed him to pursue his separate callings as a physician and a scholar. At times the inner conflict was so great, Michael felt as if several different men inhabited his body.

He pushed down the covers.

"Don't!" Cait cried, then she saw his naked body.

"If I come back, lady," he said, "comforting will give way to lust. Already my body is growing hard at the thought of your sweetness."

Inside Cait cried for him to return to her arms. But outwardly she said nothing, unable to give herself to him when he did not trust her, did not respect her.

Moments ago he had been warm and caring. Now he was once again powerful, controlled, remote . . . and lustful. She shivered.

He rose from the pallet and quickly piled wood on the glowing embers. Soon a fire blazed.

He hunkered over the sleeping wolf.

Worried, Cait asked, "Is he all right? I didn't mean to hurt him. I—"

"You haven't," Michael answered. "He'll be fine when he finally awakens." He rose, and without looking at her, added, "The night is cold. You need to put on more clothes even for sleeping."

"You're . . . not coming back to bed?"

"Nay." His voice was gruff. "Get moving, woman, before I change my mind and forget my promise to you."

Wrapping herself in the blanket, Cait scooted behind the boulder in the far corner and searched through the satchels for her dry clothing. She shivered again as she dropped the coverlet and slipped into leggings. She had put on her shirt and was holding her trousers when she looked up to see Michael standing naked outside the cave.

She had caught a glimpse of his nudity earlier,

but now he was fully revealed to her. The sight of him pushed all other thoughts from her mind.

Seemingly oblivious to the cold, he stood with his back to her. His head was raised, and rain sluiced down his body. She caught her breath. She had seen naked men when tending to the ill and wounded at the cloister, but none compared to Michael Langssonn. He was a glorious sight. Golden firelight played over his massive shoulders, which tapered into a slim waist and lean, muscled buttocks. He turned. Cait continued to stare. His masculinity both fascinated and excited her.

He stepped inside and picked up a drying cloth. Across the cave their gazes met. He smiled. Pressing her trousers to her burning cheeks, Cait slid down behind the boulder. He found her there moments later.

"Ah," he teased her. "Already you are dressed, and I am denied the pleasure of seeing your naked body."

He knelt and moved the trousers from her face. She stared at his chest covered with curly, dark hair. Her gaze slid slowly down to encounter the drying cloth, fastened about his waist.

"I wish I could stay with you now," he whispered, his lips brushing against her forehead, "but I cannot. And probably that is best for both of us, seeing that I have all but promised I would not take you. I go to see my father now and will return after you are asleep, when I'm too weary to do anything except sleep, and you are less provoking to me."

He touched her face but made no attempt to hold her. Mesmerized, Cait remained still under his regard. Finally he rose and moved away. Cait hastily finished dressing. By the time she had slipped into her trousers and fastened the girdle about her waist,

Michael was clothed, sitting on a smaller rock and pulling on his *cuarans*.

"You said earlier you know a shorter route to Northern Scotland?" he asked.

"Aye," she answered, moving to the pallet. "It is a safer route, because it is much rougher and fewer people travel it. It cuts across the northern tip of Glenmuir and Athdara. Even if Gilbert's men follow us, we shall soon lose them there."

"If the route is in Glenmuir, why do they not know about it?"

" 'Tis thought to be cursed."

"First you take us to an evil tree, madam, then force us to camp on blighted soil. Now you're asking us to travel a cursed trail. Mayhap you wish us ill?"

"It would be foolish of me to endanger you when, in doing so, I would be endangering myself," she said. "As before, I shall build a sacred fire of rowan wood and pray to the gods to lift the curse before we enter the pathway."

"I have pushed the patience of my warriors as far as I can," Michael said. "No matter how many sacred fires you light, if they learn that the trail has been accursed, they will not be willing to travel on it."

"I am a bard, sire, and my magic is strong. The Silver Daggers have traveled on this trail for many winters, and they have never been cursed."

Until now! She refrained from adding.

"Then, madam, perform whatever ritual you must and say nothing to my men. I shall let you guide us into Northern Scotland." Michael pulled the hood of his cloak over his head. "I shall return later."

He disappeared into the silvery curtain of rain.

* * *

"Bartering for the woman was foolish!" Lang thundered.

"I wanted her," Michael answered.

"I have never known you to think with your rod instead of your head."

Michael grinned. "There is a first time for everything, my father. I can remember when you were pushing women at me. You were afraid I would never become experienced at letching."

Lang stared at his son for a long time before he, too, laughed. "Aye, 'tis true, Michael, but it is also time for you to find a wife." He stepped closer and clapped a hand on his son's shoulder. "You are the only son I have, and I worry about you. You are my namesake. It is your duty to carry on the House of the Wolves. I care not if you letch or how many bedmates you have, but I want you to marry, Michael, and to give me a grandson."

"If it were not for Malcolm mac Duncan, I would be married now to Jarvia, his wife." Michael sat down on one of the folding stools.

Lang's hand curled into a fist, and he paced the tent. "Aye."

"I have sworn to Thor that I shall kill the man who brought dishonor on Lang of the Wolves," Michael said. "This is my first concern. Then mayhap I shall take his bride."

Lang's eyes took on a faraway look. "I have lived for the day when I shall avenge my name. Now justice is about to be done." After a moment of silence, he asked, "Does the woman know why you are here?"

"Aye, but she doesn't know for whom I search."

"Good," Lang said. "Be careful that in your passion you do not tell her too much. She might use it against you."

Michael sighed. "I letch for her, Lang, but I am not dim-witted. I doubt she'll try to escape again since I promised to take her to Northern Scotland, but if she does, she knows nothing that can harm us."

"I didn't mean to imply you were slow-witted," Lang answered. "I know for a fact, my son, that it is easy to tell your secrets to the woman who shares your bed."

Michael chuckled bitterly. "We have yet to share a bed."

Lang opened a leathern drinking pouch and poured himself and Michael each a tankard of ale.

After several long swallows, Michael said, "I'm concerned that Gilbert's men have not returned."

"For the woman?"

"For her and for booty."

"When we found the dead man," Lang said, "we searched the area and found six different sets of pony prints. The minstrel's and five others. Could these be the same men you encountered?"

Michael nodded. "They were led by a man called Ardac."

"They were headed toward the northwest. Away from us."

"Back to the king's village in Glenmuir," Michael guessed. "I wonder why? I was so sure they would double back."

"Perhaps they decided to concoct a story to tell their king and save themselves further trouble with you," Lang suggested. He refilled his tankard. "What do you know about the woman?"

"She claims to be a bard of the Shelter Stone Shrine in Glenmuir," Michael said, "but Ardac says she is a whore and traitor, that she conspired with sea raiders to have the king and his family killed and to steal all the riches of the Shelter Stone Cloister."

"Did she?"

"She says she's innocent."

"Were all the riches taken from the shrine?"

Michael shook his head. "Nay, Ardac says that Gilbert and his men thwarted the sea raiders."

"So," Lang mused, rubbing his hand over his beard, "the treasure is still there."

"Once we have killed Malcolm mac Duncan," Michael said, "and have retrieved the rupture-endowment, we'll consider looting the Shelter Stone."

"And you think we'll accomplish what the sea raiders were unable to do?"

"Aye, because we will know more about it than they did," Michael said. "Right now, though, we don't know enough. Neither Ardac nor Cait has told me everything. But Ardac did reveal that Cait had stolen a sacred statuary from the shrine. I'm sure they were looking for it."

Michael rose to leave. "I think, Father, that in Cait we have the missing piece of this game. No matter whether she is a whore or not, she loves both her adopted father and her cousin, and I think we can use her to help us loot the shrine."

Lang laughed heartily. "This is good for my soul, my son. Now I can overlook the risks you have taken for your lusting. I hope you enjoy the woman immensely. Tomorrow I shall tell the men that after you have killed Malcolm mac Duncan, we shall look for treasure."

"Warn them to say nothing in front of Cait," Michael urged. "She speaks many languages, ours

among them." He pulled the cowl over his head.
"Good night, Father. It is time to rest. I intend to be
on the trail by dawn."

When Michael returned to the cave, the fire had
burned out once more, leaving a bed of glowing
embers. Both Cait and the wolf were asleep. He
took off his mantle and boots, then spread the mantle over Cait. He slipped onto the pallet next to her,
curling his body around hers. She mumbled in her
sleep.

Michael's heart went out to her, and he snuggled
closer. He wanted to protect her from grief and
harm.

Cait stirred and burrowed her buttocks into Michael's body. The smell of the burning wood drifted
to him ... and something else, the faint scents of
soap and strawberry water. Before her attempt to
escape, Cait had bathed, and he had not been here
to see her. Had she taken off her clothes and stood
in the rain outside the cave as he had?

Still remembering her beautiful slender body, her
gently rounded breasts and hips, he could visualize
her standing there, water sluicing over her. Her
arms raised, her hands cupping the back of her
head. Her breasts thrust upward, as if begging for
his touch. The thought of entering into her tight
sheath sent a bolt of heat through him. He was
hardening, readying. It didn't surprise him. His ap-
petites were strong, and it had been too long since
he had satisfied them. But he had promised her.

He was unbearably conscious of the soft, wom-
anly weight of her pressing against him as he grew
in dimension. He tried to shift away; she wiggled
her buttocks against him. He was throbbing, flex-
ing, growing hotter and harder with every breath.

He wanted her. Why didn't he take her? She meant nothing to him. She was a slave. He had bartered three measures of gold for her. A whore, the king's master of arms had called her. Why should he stand on his promise not to take her until they reached Northern Scotland?

Because he had given his word, he told himself, and Michael Langssonn never went back on his word.

Chapter 11

Michael bolted upright on the pallet, his lungs silently screaming for air, his heart beating erratically, his body drenched in sweat. He had had another of the haunting dreams that had plagued him all his life. He yanked off the russet cord with which Cait had tied back his hair. Breathing raggedly, he raked his fingers through the loose strands and cradled his forehead in both hands, gradually regaining his composure. He breathed deeply . . . slowly. He despised himself for losing control.

He pushed aside the covers, careful not to waken Cait, and left the cave. The wind blowing against his damp body felt cool and refreshing.

All his life he had been blessed . . . or cursed . . . with visions and dreams. He could not recall a time when he had been free of them. Tonight his dreams had carried him to that strange other world that he often inhabited in his sleep.

At times he felt as if a part of himself were missing; other times he felt as if he were two men. Always he sensed that someone shared in his victories, in his glory . . . and in his defeats and sorrows.

As a lad, he had discussed these unusual feelings with his mother. She had told him that he was a special child, that the gods had given him to her and Lang when they had given up all hope of having children. In these dreams, she explained, the gods were talking to him. He was destined to be a magnificent ruler who would eventually take over his father's estate. He was meant to unite all the surrounding estates into one. When Michael had asked her why he was both right- and left-handed in his dreams, she could not answer him.

Michael's most powerful vision had come after he had proven himself as a warrior and was to receive the torque of heirship to the House of the Wolves. Guided through the ritual by a seer, Michael had set himself apart and fasted for days. On the tenth night he received his dream. He started out as one warrior, then became identical warriors—although his double was dressed in strange garb.

As long as he was the *double warrior*, no one could defeat him. As he stood side by side with himself, one of his forms wielded the sickle sword with the right hand, the other with the left. Both held a golden shield between them. In his vision he had vanquished all his enemies.

The next morning when he had awakened, he had felt a strength flowing through him that he had never since forgotten or doubted. The seer had explained that what Michael had experienced was the merging of himself and Thor. Michael knew the gods had chosen him, that in him ran the wisdom and the might of two warriors. From that day forward Michael had determined to fulfill his destiny.

He returned to the cave and built up the fire. As he squatted in front of it, he recalled another dream ... from last autumn. Once again he could see the hill, dark and foreboding, with smoke belching out of the entrances and twisting pathways encircling it.

In his dream he scaled the hill and ran into the tunnel, knowing it was on fire, knowing he would probably die, but driven by duty and desire to save the woman . . .

Flames scorched his palm, and Michael jerked his hand back. He stood and put on his mail. With his back to the fire, still pondering his strange dreams, he gazed at the pearl gray horizon.

"Is it time to get up?" Cait asked.

"Aye," he answered.

"Surely you must be cold standing out there. Come get your mantle."

"I'm all right." He welcomed the cold, hoping the chilled wind would drive away his haunting dreams . . . his fears. "Do you believe our dreams reveal the truth, Cait?"

She took a moment to answer, as if seriously considering his question. "Aye. Do you?"

He shrugged.

He dared not believe his dream tonight. As in so many others, he was left-handed and wore a gold torque around his neck. He was burying his father, except it wasn't his father. Why did he feel so heavy-hearted about the death of a man he didn't know? What did it all mean?

The horn sounded, and Michael slipped his black-enameled and silver helmet over his head. He waved, and two warriors stepped forward.

"I'm going down to the camp," he said. "Stay with Cait until she has packed our belongings." He turned to her. "Eat a hearty morning meal to break fast. We shall not be stopping for food until nightfall."

* * *

Gilbert leaned forward in the High Seat of the Great House of the king's village. Although the air was brisk, the windows were open and sunshine poured into the room. Gilbert glanced at his visitor, who sat on the guests' settle.

"Matters would be much simpler if my accomplices, the sea raiders, had not accidentally killed the princess when they attacked the village," Gilbert said, not for the first time since the fatal accident. "Marriage to her would have given me clear title to the High Seat, and I wouldn't be having such difficulty getting the Breastpin."

Seated in a chair close to the fire, the priest leaned back and bridged his hands in front of himself. "We must be content with what we have. At least you are the people's hero, and the High Council has allowed you to act as interim-king. In fact, they have given in to all of your requests."

"I am interim-king only until they locate a blood-heir." Gilbert curled his hands into fists. "I want clear title to the High Seat, and I want High Councilman Conn and High Priest Sholto killed."

"Don't be a fool, Gilbert," the priest hissed. "Your impulsiveness will be your undoing."

"I didn't say I would kill them. I said I want to."

Gilbert picked up his tankard and, on discovering it was empty, held it out to a servant woman, who refilled it. He looked over to see the priest fiddling with the gold amulet that had proven to be a mere talisman, not the sacred cloister pin that could lead them to the hidden treasure.

"What has Sholto done with that damned Breastpin?" Gilbert muttered.

"Not Sholto, Cait," the priest said. "She has outfoxed us all. She always was an extremely intelligent woman. Now we have lost both her and the cloister pin."

"Let's say they are temporarily misplaced, my friend. I know where she is probably headed."

"Where?"

"She is with the Northmen, headed for Northern Scotland."

"How do you know?"

"Ardac had just captured the woman and taken the brooch case when the Northland warlord and his men—evidently the ones you told me about several days ago—came upon them. Ardac claims that a bitter battle ensued. The Northmen clearly outnumbered him and stole Cait away."

Gilbert took a long drink. When he lowered the tankard, he said, "The Northman travels with ten warriors and a huge wolf. Since Ardac was outnumbered—*and outwitted, no doubt*—he planned to ambush the Northmen farther down the road. On their way to set up the ambush, he and his men came across one of the fleeing Silver Daggers and one of the king's men, a borderland warrior called Dacy. The Silver Dagger is dead. Ardac brought back his head as irrefutable proof. They pierced Dacy with a hunting lance and surmise that he, too, died.

"When Ardac made his report, he asked to gather more warriors and set out after the Northman. I denied his request. As long as we know where Cait is, and I have her father and cousin, I'm satisfied.'

"Why are you so interested in these Northmen?"

"Only one interests me—Michael Langssonn. I want him to carry out his task unhindered."

"What task?"

"He has come to the Highlands to kill Malcolm mac Duncan."

"Is that important to us?"

"At the moment, no," Gilbert replied, "but it will become critical once I am crowned king of Glenmuir."

Gilbert explained the details concerning Malcolm and Jarvia's marriage, the paying of the rupture-endowment and its subsequent theft by pirates, and Gilbert's own banishment from Northern Scotland because of his conspiracy against High King Fergus and his fostered son, Malcolm mac Duncan.

When he finished, the priest laughed. "Do I surmise correctly, Gilbert, that you were responsible for the theft of the rupture-endowment?"

Gilbert smiled. "Aye."

"And just today we received word that High King Fergus has died and Malcolm mac Duncan has been elected High King of Northern Scotland. What do you think of that?"

"I hate Malcolm," Gilbert confessed, "and am furious that he has become high king. But the higher his rise, the further he will eventually fall."

"Don't let your preoccupation with Malcolm take your attention from the matters at hand," the priest advised.

"Nay, I shall sit back and let the Northman take care of Malcolm."

A knock sounded, and a servant called out, "Lord Gilbert, High Councilman Conn is here to see you."

Gilbert laughed. "Everyone knows that you were brought to the Great Hall for questioning. Conn probably wants to see for himself if I have harmed you."

"It may work to our advantage if I am not here. Call your guards and have them take me to a storage shed."

Gilbert agreed. As the robed figure, escorted by

two men, disappeared out the far end of the hall, Gilbert called to the servant, "Show the high councilman in."

The door to the Great Hall swung open, and a man of nearly sixty winters marched down the aisle to the High Seat. "I apologize for this unannounced visit, Lord Gilbert," the high councilman said, his gaze sweeping the hall.

"If you're looking for the priest," Gilbert said, "he is being kept in the storage shed behind the Great Hall."

"He is unharmed?"

"Aye. I have him under guard while I am questioning him."

"Has he told you where the treasure is?"

"He claims that only Sholto knows."

The high councilman nodded. "Aye, that sounds reasonable."

"What is your purpose in coming to see me, Lord Conn? To see if I am mistreating the priest?"

"I wanted to see for myself that he was all right," Conn answered, "but I also want to talk with you about the cloister. The High Council met earlier, and we—"

"Without my knowledge?" Gilbert managed to hide his irritation, but he was furious that the Council had dared to convene in secret. It showed the little regard they held for him as the provisional ruler of the kingdom.

"Aye, lord," Conn answered boldly. "Thanks to you and your warriors, the sea raiders have been driven back to the sea. Our people and shrine are safe once again, and we are able to search for an heir to the High Seat."

"Aye," Gilbert said, choosing his words carefully, "all you say is true, High Councilman. For the moment we are safe. But what if others—say, the Picts to our west or the Athdarians on the east—seeing what the sea raiders have done, march against us? We must be prepared for any event. The sea raiders stole much of Glenmuir's wealth and killed many of the king's warriors.

"We must have money if we are to build an army. We have no trained warriors, and so must hire mercenaries. The only treasure remaining is that at the Shelter Stone Cloister. Surely the gods will approve of our using it for our protection."

"Aye, my lord, your argument is sound, but you cannot keep the priests and priestesses of the cloister prisoners. Even now the people are frightened because you are questioning one of them. Sholto is the Ancient of Nights and Days. As long as you hold him captive, you bring the wrath of the gods of Night and Day against us. The High Council begs you to remove your warriors from the Shelter Stone."

"My lord High Councilman," Gilbert said, "Sholto knows where lies the treasure that can save this kingdom. We must persuade him to tell us."

"The Council agrees," Conn said. "But you are creating fear among the people by keeping your warriors at the shrine. Please remove them."

"I will consider doing so, but I fear it would be a mistake."

"If you do, Lord Gilbert," Conn said, "I will try to persuade Sholto to cooperate with us."

"Thank you, High Councilman," Gilbert said. "I appreciate your efforts."

"Lord, may I visit with—"

"Aye," Gilbert said, "you may visit with him before he returns to the cloister. I shall send for you."

Conn took his leave. As soon as the door closed

behind him, Gilbert nodded to the guards to return the priest to the main hall.

When the men were alone again, Gilbert repeated his conversation with the high councilman. "One of these days, my friend, I shall kill both Sholto and Conn," he promised.

"One of these days," the priest readily agreed. "Until then, we need both of them to find the treasure."

Gilbert paced back and forth in front of the high seat.

"Are you going to release Sholto and all the others?" the priest asked.

"Aye, for the time being. But I shall have Sholto watched in case he tries to escape from Glenmuir. And I must have more warriors."

"Mercenaries?"

"Aye."

"They will cost a handsome sum."

"I have to find that secret chamber!"

"We shall," the priest promised. "Leave Sholto to me."

Two days had passed since the Northmen had resumed their journey to Northern Scotland, taking the overland route that Cait had promised would bring them there swiftly and safely. Good weather and the unsettled nature of the land through which they traveled had allowed them to cover the ground quickly.

Occasionally they had seen Highland riders at a distance—men sent by High King Fergus to patrol the borderlands, Cait had explained. Yesterday the men had ridden openly, and in greater numbers.

"I'm sure they have reported our presence to the king," Michael had said.

"Aye. Now they're watching to see what we do. We'll camp in the open tomorrow night on the Athdara side of the river and cross in the morning. When we awaken, you will no doubt see a Scottish force as great if not greater than yours waiting for us."

Today Michael and Cait had ridden out early, in advance of the other Northmen, and were now some distance ahead. Michael was pleased with this opportunity to be alone with her. He watched as she led them through a narrow pass that would eventually bring them down the mountain. A trained rider, she sat her pony well, erect yet relaxed in the saddle, moving in natural rhythm with the horse, fully aware of her surroundings and alert for the trail markers that indicated the correct path. As usual, no hood or scarf covered her head. He loved to see the play of sunlight on her hair, turning it to fire.

Cait pulled her pony to a halt and turned to him with a bright smile. "One more day, lord, and we will cross the border into Northern Scotland." As he drew his mount beside hers, she gazed appreciatively at the valley far below them. "Isn't it beautiful?"

"Aye," Michael answered, never taking his eyes off her.

"There is no sight more beautiful in all the Highlands."

"Aye, lass, I agree." Patiently Michael waited for her to realize he was flirting with her. "Hair and eyes the color of autumn leaves."

Cait turned to him with a quizzical expression.

"Skin as smooth as the petals of a flower."

As a warrior, Michael had been trained to discipline his emotions and hide his feelings. At will he could lower an invisible shield over his countenance. But these past two days and nights, he had opened himself to Cait. He wanted her to read his expressions, to plumb the depths of his soul.

He brushed an errant curl from her face, but as soon as he turned it loose, it bounced back against her cheek.

Gentle color washed her cheeks. "You said, lord, that you wouldn't—" She broke off. "You promised you wouldn't—"

"I said I wouldn't mate with you. I never promised not to touch you." He laid his gloved palm against her cheek and lightly rubbed his thumb over her bottom lip. "Or to make you want me." He caught her hand and pushed it inside his mantle over his heart. "See how my heart beats for you, lady."

"Lord . . ." Her voice was husky and tentative. "You promised."

"But you didn't." He moved the stallion closer so that his leg brushed hers. He liked having their thighs touch, but he wanted to caress her naked skin. He wanted all barriers removed so that she would receive him, and he could fill her. "You, Cait nea Sholto, can choose to release me from my promise."

Still holding her hand against his chest, Michael cupped the back of her head and pulled her close. Their lips touched, warmly at first, then the warmth turned to fire.

She parted her lips. Michael answered the invitation, slipping his tongue into the moist sweetness of her mouth. She whimpered as he filled her. Through his caress, he willed Cait to want him with the same intensity that he wanted her.

He heard the clump of pony hooves, the creak of

leather, the low rumble of talk and laughter, and knew that his men were approaching from behind them. Soon they would round the jutting ridge and the stand of trees and enter the clearing where he and Cait sat their mounts. Michael reluctantly released Cait's mouth and straightened.

Flushed, her eyes bright, she said, "One more day, lord. Then you'll know the truth about me."

"I know all the truth I need or want to know."

"My lord . . ." To his surprise, Cait caught his face in both her hands and gazed solemnly into his eyes. "I know you believe what you are saying, but when we mate—"

Michael felt himself growing hard, and it was all he could do not to swing Cait off the pony and take her there and then.

"Aye, lord," she whispered, "we will mate. As you told me before, we will finish what we began the day I spied on you."

"Cait—"

As she stroked her thumb over his lips, Michael's blood felt like hot oil seeping out of a lamp. Cait's eyes darkened from tawny gold to russet, and Michael knew that she understood her affect on him, was aware of his arousal. And she was not averse to using that knowledge to her advantage.

In a few words Cait had taken the control away from him. He felt weak, vulnerable, and didn't like it. He lowered his eyes and caught her hands in his.

"I know what you're doing," she told him softly. "When you raise your eyes, you will have lowered that invisible shield, lord, so that I won't know what you're thinking or feeling anymore. But I do know."

Michael met her gaze. She was smiling at him.

"You made me a promise, Michael Langssonn,

and now I shall make you one." She pulled her hands loose. "One of these days I shall ask you to unleash for me all the passion that runs through your body."'

"I await the word, my lady."

"That you set me afire is no secret, lord. But I promise that one day I shall reach a part of you that no one has reached before. When I do, I shall destroy that shield you hide behind."

"As always, Cait nea Sholto, you challenge and excite me. I look forward to the day when we . . ."

"Duel with your mighty sword, my lord," she boldly teased.

He laughed. "Aye, Cait, to the day when we duel with my mighty sword."

Michael stared at her for a long time, knowing that Cait had already touched a part of him that no other person had. But he was reluctant to give more of himself to her. He had watched his father suffer deeply when his mother died. Unlike many of the Northmen whom Michael knew, his father had been faithful to his wife. He had taken no other bedmates.

Pushing these thoughts aside, Michael gazed out at the distant mountains.

"Your land is indeed beautiful," he said. "When I sailed from Ulfsbaer—"

"The Wolf's Estate or Steading," Cait translated.

"Aye. My father is chief of the Clan of the Wolf."

Cait glanced down as Ulf trotted up beside them. "Hence your pet."

"Ulf rescued me a few years ago and hasn't left me since. I was deer hunting when I came upon a boar. A fight ensued, and the boar was about to kill me when a ferocious wolf pup ran out of the woods and attacked the boar, drawing its attention away from me. By the time I killed the boar, I was badly wounded. The next thing I remember is awakening with a rough wet tongue licking my cheek, and the wolf pup stretched out alongside me. I claim that I took him and the boar home with me, but my parents claim Ulf brought *me* home."

Michael's laughter filled Cait with joy. She listened avidly as he talked about his mother and father, about the Northland. The majestic mountains. The craggy bluffs and sheer cliffs. The short summers and long winters.

As they resumed their trek down the trail, Michael described his home, Ulfsbaer. She imagined the steading with its huge Great House, and the many smaller longhouses built around it that belonged to the *karls*, or freemen, who worked the estate. There was a byre for cattle, stables for ponies, a pigsty, storehouses, a forge, and a bathhouse.

He described the pits where the warriors prepared the tar from resinous woods that they used to daub ships, treat ropes, and seal roofs. The tannery where they hand-tooled their leather. The saltworks where they extracted salt from seawater.

"You love the Northland, don't you?" Cait said.

"Aye, lady, 'tis my home."

"Someday, sire, I should like to visit it."

"You will not only visit it, little bard, you will live there . . . with me."

"I—" Cait swallowed. "I only meant—"

"And I meant what I said."

As she gazed into Michael's eyes, Cait knew that she had been living in a dream since the night of the storm. Michael had promised not to put the collar on her and not to mate with her before they reached Northern Scotland, but he had not relinquished his claim upon her. She was still his slave.

"What about your betrothed?"

"She is of no concern to you."

"Aye, she is. If you win the duel, she will become yours once more."

"That is my concern, not yours, lady." His eyes narrowed until they were blue slits, sharp and cutting.

"Aye, 'tis mine if you're planning to take her back to the Northland with you."

His voice chilled her. "You, Cait nea Sholto, belong to me, and when the time comes, you *will* mate with me . . . no matter how many wives or other bedmates I have. And you will return to the Northland with me."

They glared at each other. When he was coldly angry like this, he frightened her, but she would not back down.

"Do you love her? Are you going to take her to wife?"

" 'Tis time to cease speaking, lady."

"Answer me, Michael," she demanded.

He said nothing.

"You say you want me." She dared him to refute her words. "Do you want her also? Do you want both of us?"

A grin softened Michael's face. "Are you jealous, Cait?"

"Perhaps I am," she admitted. "I don't rightly know. These feelings are new to me, and at times, most uncomfortable. I don't like that you seek me for your carnal pleasure yet also want your betrothed."

"Nay," Michael drawled. "I am seeking the man who stole her from me. The man who brought dishonor on Lang and the House of the Wolves."

They rode a way in silence before Cait said, "Will you tell me about her?"

Michael sighed. "I don't know much to tell. I have never met the woman. I was betrothed to her by proxy. I was a-viking, and my father and her husband—"

"Her husband!" Cait exclaimed in outrage.

Michael laughed. "Nay, lady, 'tis not as disreputable as it might sound. My betrothed was a young woman married to a much older man. When he realized he was dying, he sought to ensure that his wife would be well provided for and that her inheritance would revert to the House of the Wolves. Thus, he sought out a distant relative, my father, and arranged for a betrothal. When I returned from a-viking," Michael went on, "I learned that I had been betrothed and that it had been dishonorably ruptured."

"I can understand how you felt," Cait said. "I was betrothed to one of the king's men, a warrior named Brieve. King Ido decided that he wanted Brieve for his daughter instead."

"Did your betrothed challenge the king's decision to do this?"

She grazed her bottom lip with her teeth.

"I contested, lord, but Brieve sought to be released from the commitment. Through marriage to the princess, he became the next king of Glenmuir."

"He meant a lot to you, lady?"

"I liked him and wanted to marry him," Cait confessed. "When the king broke the betrothal and Brieve offered no resistance, I thought my heart was broken." She sighed. "I was so humiliated and angry that I lost my temper and swore revenge against King Ido and his entire family. I swore that Brieve would never be king of Glenmuir. 'Twas this fit of anger that has landed me in trouble. Gilbert claims that I conspired with the sea raiders in order to avenge the wrong that Ido did to me."

"Did you make a blood-oath to avenge your dishonor?"

"Nay," Cait answered. "Once I had ranted and raved, I began to realize that it was not my heart that had suffered, but my pride. In the excitement of being selected for the cloister minstrels, I forgot Brieve."

"Neither my heart nor my pride is involved in my revenge," Michael said. " 'Tis my father's. The man who married my betrothed generously agreed to pay the endowment that my father demanded for an honorable rupture of the betrothal, but it was for show only. The ship never reached Northland with the endowment because Scottish raiders boarded the ship and stole the endowment, killing all of my father's warriors. This, lady, is why I seek revenge."

At that moment the main body of the Northmen caught up with them. As the horses halted together, Lang dismounted and joined Michael and Cait, who also slid from their mounts.

"How far are we from the border of Northern Scotland?" Lang asked.

"It lies across the river yonder," Cait answered, pointing. "See the huge tree over there?"

"The three oaks twined together so that they look like one?" Michael asked.

She smiled. He had remembered her instructions.

"Aye, we shall camp on this side of the river tonight and cross on the morrow. Although we can't see them from this distance, there is no doubt an armed contingent camping there, summoned by the outriders we saw yesterday. But be assured that they will not harm us," Cait said.

"Are they so trusting of strangers?"

"Nay, but as I've told you, I wear the holy mark of the gods," she answered. "It identifies me as a priestess of the Shelter Stone Cloister and allows me to travel through all the kingdoms of the Highlands without being hindered or molested." She smiled. "Lord, you wear the same symbol on your ring. Be assured you will be invited to the king's village."

That night after dinner, Cait banked the fire and took a quick basin bath. After she had slipped into clean clothing, she crawled between the thick, fur-lined blankets on her mattress of bracken and heather, and waited for Michael to join her. He had kept his promise not to put the collar on her or to make love to her, but he slept with her each night. She was drifting off when she heard him enter the shelter and take off his boots.

She watched as he slipped out of his mail and shirt, refilled the basin with water, and washed his face and neck.

Michael's body was all beautiful sun-bronzed skin and muscle. Her breath caught in her throat as he shoved his belt and trousers down over his hips, revealing the thatch of dark pubic hair from which jutted his slightly aroused manhood. Cait's mouth went dry as she watched him move the washcloth over, around, and down his ever-enlarging shaft.

She felt a burning in her lower stomach that she could hardly endure, an ache that she knew only Michael Langssonn could assuage.

"Say the word, Cait, and I'll give pleasure as you've never experienced it before."

He was staring down at her. He had finished bathing and stood naked, hard and ready for her. The firelight touched him with gold, and she could have sworn that the god of Night had entered her pavilion.

She closed her eyes. "Nay." Her voice was so thick, she hardly recognized it as hers.

"I don't understand you, Cait," Michael said, irritation in his words. "You want to share carnal pleasure with me, yet you refuse the chance to do so, again and again."

"Aye, lord, I must."

He rummaged through his satchels until he found a clean pair of trousers and slipped into them. "Why, Cait?"

"Because, lord, you don't understand or know me."

He pulled his shirt over his head, then banked the fire and slid between the blankets curling around her.

"Do you intend to tease me until I lose control and take you?" he asked.

"Nay, lord, I want you to know who and what I am when we share the pleasure of mating."

"I could mate with you, and you wouldn't fight me."

"But that would mean going against your word."

He gazed at her for a long time before he finally laughed. Cait felt his warm, ale-scented breath against her neck.

"Cait nea Sholto, I am so glad we found each other. This trip would have been a bore without you. You drive me to distraction, push me past my limits, yet you never cease to delight me."

Cait smiled. "I like being with you too," she admitted, and burrowed against him. She drifted off to sleep with a smile lingering on her lips.

Chapter 12

The wind was cold, but the morning sun shone brightly, dispelling the lingering mist that hung over the glen. Mounted warriors, clad in mail and visored helmets, stood in lines on both sides of the river that marked the boundary between Athdara and Northern Scotland.

Cait shivered from both cold and fear as two Scottish warriors, their ponies bedecked with war accoutrements, crossed the river toward the Northmen. From atop their wrought-iron standard fluttered a red and yellow banner.

"We are kinsmen of Chief Malcolm mac Duncan of Northern Scotland," announced the first. "Who are you?"

The skald who served as both bard and interpreter for the Northmen answered in Gaelic. "My lord is Michael Langssonn of Northland."

"We have been expecting him. We shall take you to Malcolm's village."

Cait laid a hand on Michael's arm and whispered, "It would be better, sire, if you asked to see High King Fergus. He will be best able to guide you to the man you seek."

The Duncan warrior moved his head as if he had heard her, and Cait felt his piercing gaze through the eye slits of his visor.

But Michael waved away the rider and said, "I shall find the man I seek in Malcolm's village."

Puzzled, Cait could not read his expression beneath his helmet, but she did not need to see his face to know he had reverted to the cold, formidable warlord she had first met.

"I seek Malcolm mac Duncan," he told her.

Cait felt as if her insides had flowed out of her, leaving her lifeless. In a dull tone she said, "*Princess Jarvia* was your betrothed?"

"Aye."

"Why did you wait until now to tell me?"

"Your loyalty is to the Highlands, not to me. I did not trust you."

His words hurt Cait, until she realized she did not trust him either. Physical attraction was not a foundation for trust. No matter how much she and Michael desired each other, they were enemies and could have no future together. Cait was glad they had arrived in Northern Scotland. Perhaps when the king identified her as a bard-priestess, Michael would set her free. On the other hand, there was no one here who could confirm that she was not a traitor.

Cait glanced across the river at the Duncan warriors. The leader and his men began to cross the river toward Michael.

At last, halting his pony in front of the Northmen, the lead man called out, "Hail, Lord Michael Langssonn. I am Brian mac Logan, best-man to Malcolm mac Duncan. I shall take you to his village."

Duncan warriors fanned out on either side of the Northmen until they were surrounded. Brian's visored gaze seemed to rest on Cait . . . on her short hair. Self-consciously she brushed back a strand. He would think she was a slave or whore, yet she must speak out. She opened her mouth, but Michael's gloved hand closed over her arm. His fingers dug into her flesh.

"If you value your life, keep your mouth shut," he whispered.

Brian turned his pony and nudged it forward. Raising his hand, he gave the order, and the group began to move.

Slowly—too slowly for Cait—the last leg of the journey began. Earlier she had been bubbling with excitement. Now she felt confused and angry and hurt. Princess Jarvia was Michael's betrothed. Cait had seen the princess on two occasions, and she had thought her one of the kindest and most beautiful women.

This angered Cait. She wanted to hate Michael's betrothed, not like and respect her.

Still Cait took hope in the fact that soon she would be her own person again. Michael claimed to be a man of his word, and he had promised to give her the chance to clear up the misunderstandings about who and what she was. She would tell High King Fergus about the threat to Glenmuir. He would know that she couldn't have betrayed her country.

If only she could be free of this enigmatic man called Michael Langssonn. That's what she wanted, wasn't it?

Nay, she did not. Even now she remembered every line and angle of his body, the texture of his skin and the hardness of his muscles. Just the thought of him made her body burn, her lower body ache with unfulfilled need . . .

As they rode along the river, Michael admired the tall evergreens that spired into the sky, and the colorful autumn foliage of the leaf-bearing trees. Ahead he observed snowcapped mountains against a blue sky dotted with fluffy white clouds.

They had turned from the river and had ridden a long way into Duncan territory when Michael noticed a high hill in the distance. His heartbeat quickened. It was the hill he had dreamed about. Pathways circled it, crisscrossing one another as they wound from bottom to top.

He felt as if he had been here before. He broke out in a sweat. Flames seemed to engulf him. He was suffocating. He caught his throat and kneaded it.

"Michael, what's wrong?" Cait demanded.

He breathed deeply until he felt as if cool waters had doused the fire that burned at him. He lowered his hand from his throat.

"Is something wrong?" Cait persisted.

Lang looked at his son in concern.

"I've—I've dreamed about this place," Michael said.

Cait caught his hand in hers, and he gripped it tightly.

"I walked through a tunnel of fire." And he had saved a woman and a wolf, he realized.

"My hand, Michael," Cait said. "You're hurting it."

Only then did he realize how hard he was holding her. "Forgive me," he murmured, and turned her loose. Then he called out, "Man of Duncan."

The skald translated, and Brian mac Logan halted and turned around.

"Does a tunnel of fire run through that hill?" Michael asked.

"There is a chamber of fire within the tunnel,"

Brian answered. "You have heard of our Labyrinth Hill?"

"A tunnel of fire?" Lang asked, looking discomfited.

"Aye." Brian guided his pony back to them. "Inside is what we call the Chamber of Fire. 'Twas used as a place of ancient worship."

"And a place for trials by ordeal," Michael said, rather than asked.

"Aye."

"You've had one here recently, haven't you?"

"Aye," Brian said slowly. "Have you heard about it?"

"No, I was guessing." Michael did not wish to reveal how he knew.

"At the top of the hill is a pool of clear springwater that Highlanders consider holy," Brian explained. "They take offerings to Our Lady of the Lake, who is said to visit the pool once a year, during the change of the seasons. The few who have seen the Lady claim to have received a miracle from her."

As if some supernatural force had control of his eyes, Michael could not pull his gaze from the hill. He felt the insufferable heat, the fear. Dark clouds covered the sun, casting the hill in shadow. He shivered.

They rode through a meadow, onto a deeply rutted road and into the village. Cries of celebration resounded. Music unlike any Michael had heard filled the air as the company crossed the main bridge into the walled enclosure.

" 'Tis the pipes," Cait explained, her disappointment in him pushed aside by her excitement. She had begun to feel more in control of her own destiny now that she was in Northern Scotland among

friends. She didn't know how she would free herself or save the shrine, but she would. "They're
playing the Duncans' song."

The brilliance of the autumn sun added to the
gala spirit. Cheering people lined the road and
leaned out of windows. Brightly colored banners
snapped in the breeze. Lush green tree branches
had been laid across the road.

"What is the occasion?" Michael asked.

" 'Tis the coronation of Malcolm mac Duncan as
high king," Brian answered. "His father died two
moons ago."

Cait hid her shock and surprise.

"My condolences on your loss," Michael said.

"Thank you, my lord," Brian said. "We shall miss
High King Fergus, but the gods have favored
Northern Scotland with a fearless leader in Malcolm
mac Duncan."

Cait did not doubt Malcolm's ability to lead the
people, but fear constricted her. Two kings were
dead, and Michael had come to kill a third. She
wondered if the deaths were omens, a portent of
bad things to come.

"High Queen— I mean the queen mother," Cait
said. "Is she here?"

Brian laughed and nodded. "Nothing could keep
her away. She dotes on her son."

Cait breathed more easily. She gazed at the people around her. She drank in their joy.

Laughing and clasping hands, a young couple
ran toward them. "Brian!" they called simultaneously.

The best-man pulled his stallion to a halt and
smiled down at them. "Ah, Rus and Inga, is this
what I suspect it is?"

"Aye, my lord," the young man answered. "Please witness our handfasting."

"What is happening?" Michael asked.

"We call it handfasting," Cait explained. " 'Tis a trial marriage that we Highlanders have among ourselves. Rather than swear before the gods that we will live together for the remainder of our lives, we swear before the people to make a commitment for one year and a day."

Brian's voice echoed back to them as he asked the couple, "You don't want to have a formal wedding?"

"Nay, we want to be sure we'll be happy living together," Inga replied.

Brian nodded. "And both of you are willing parties to this handfasting?"

"Aye," they cried.

"You understand that in front of witnesses you have sworn yourself together for a year and a day. After that, either of you may object to further cohabitation. If a child is born of the union during this time, the objecting party receives custody of the child."

"Aye, we hear and we agree."

"Then, Rus and Inga," Brian shouted, "I declare you handfasted."

"That is all?" Michael asked.

"Aye, 'tis a simple ceremony," Cait said, "but 'tis binding. If a child is born of the union, it is both fathered and mothered."

Brian waved his hand, and the procession resumed.

The crowd forced them to move slowly, and they had not ridden far when Cait exclaimed, "Isn't the village grand?"

Michael smiled at her enthusiasm. He had seen so

many villages during his travels that they had all begun to look alike. The streets were paved and curbed with stone, the ponies' hooves clip-clopping as they pranced through the village. The main street led directly to what Michael identified as the Great Hall; other streets and pathways fed into the main street and connected the many buildings.

Behind the Great Hall stretched a tourney field. Houses were neatly arranged around it, the larger ones residences, the smaller ones outhouses. Animal pens ran along the outside walls of the village. Surrounding the outbuildings were large vegetable gardens, neatly laid out and divided with stone fencing, as were the larger fields outside the village.

To the right of the Great Hall stood several smelting furnaces. Beside them were piles of charcoal, bog ore, and wood. Close by was a large hut. Anvils, bellows, hammers, tongs, and rods of wrought iron identified it as a smith's workshop.

Brian pointed to a large rectangular building with a thatched roof. "The Small Hall. It houses Malcolm's personal warriors who are not married. Over here are the guesthouses." He waved his hand to include four large structures that flanked the Small Hall.

"The Great Hall," Brian announced, as they approached the structure.

Around it was a kiln, barn, mill, kennels, stables, and a chicken house. A knee-high wattle fence surrounded Malcolm's estate, including all the outbuildings, the guesthouses, and the Small and Great Halls.

"Duncan man," Michael called out, conversing through the skald, "who owns these ponies?"

"The Duncan himself. He breeds ponies. Sometimes, my lord, I vow Malcolm converses with the animals. He has a way with them." Brian laughed. "But I guess he would. He's from the House of the Horse."

Michael brought his steed closer to the corral and pointed to a liver-chestnut stallion with a silver mane and tail. "That one is superb."

"That's his studhorse," Brian said. "Malcolm has been offered great sums for this stallion, but he won't part with it. Golden Ray, he calls it."

Brian discussed Malcolm's interest in ponies and his successful pony-relay system by which he communicated quickly and efficiently with his subjects throughout the realm.

Then Brian turned and led them on toward the Great House. As they neared, Cait heard music coming from the main hall. The people who crowded around the Great House stared curiously at the newcomers and stepped aside to make way for them. Brian halted. Michael dismounted and beckoned his skald with a wave. Michael—Cait on one side of him, the wolf on the other—Lang, and the youth followed Brian, who pushed past those thronging the porch and the entrance of the house.

At the far end of the crowded hall, on a large stone dais, stood the king's High Seat, now vacant. Next to it was a smaller seat for the queen, and on either side were settles for guests. Behind the dais were two windows. The wooden shutters were open and the cloth shades rolled up. On the wall between the windows hung an enormous, colorful tapestry.

The hall was lined with tables, all filled with food and set with tankards, drinking horns, and pitchers, as well as spoons and knives crafted from gold and silver and inset with precious jewels. Beside them were ornately carved wooden serving and eating bowls and plates, also trimmed in jewels and precious metals.

The benches were fitted with thick cushions for comfort and decorated with bright embroidered furniture covers. Servants scurried around, and a great fire blazed in the oblong stone hearth in the center of the hall. The aroma of food permeated the room.

The music was loud, the celebrating people even louder.

Michael stood for a moment looking around, not so much getting his bearings as marveling at how familiar it all felt to him. He experienced the strange sensation that this was home, his home. Glad that he wore his helmet, he closed his eyes and breathed deeply.

He would be glad when he had fulfilled his oath to Thor and could leave this land. The strange dreams he had experienced all his life were beginning to seem real. They were haunting him, causing him to recognize places he could not know, to sense the presence of his elusive double self who could not exist.

Even now he felt as if this shadow of himself were here, in this room; that he could reach out and touch him. The idea excited Michael, but also unsettled him.

"Stay here at the door with three more warriors," Michael told Kolby. "Be prepared for anything."

Kolby nodded. Brian led the way forward, followed by Michael, Cait, the skald, and Lang. Again they had to push their way through the tightly packed crowd.

Michael noticed the beautiful young woman who sat in one of the High Seats. Her hair was the color of purest silver and hung in deep waves down her back. Without anyone telling him, Michael knew she was Princess Jarvia of Southerland, the woman he had dreamed of saving in Labyrinth Hill. She was everything that Michael had once hoped to have in a wife ... and she was to have been his wife, the future Lady of Ulfsbaer, Northland.

"Queen Jarvia," Cait murmured.

"Aye," Michael said.

Jarvia held a little girl about two winters old in her lap. Her hair was russet and her eyes were blue. She was beautiful, and could have been his. His child. The thought warmed Michael. He knew his father wanted grandchildren, but Michael also wanted children. A son he could teach to hunt, to hawk, and to sail. As Lang had loved and guided him, Michael wanted a namesake whom he could love and guide.

"The other woman, sire, is the queen mother," Cait said.

Michael watched as the handsome older woman handed the child a ring of colored beads. Smiling, the little girl clutched the toy and began to spin the beads. When one of them did not move as she thought it ought to, she made a face and muttered something. A daughter, Michael thought. Aye, he wanted a daughter.

But Malcolm mac Duncan had taken Jarvia from him. He had dishonored the name of Lang of the Wolves.

Silently Michael cursed the law of revenge, which decreed that he must take a life in order to restore the honor that had been stripped from his father. Michael wanted his father's shame avenged, but he hated the waste of life.

"Where is Malcolm mac Duncan?" Michael asked.

"I assume he's been in purification for several days," Cait answered, "and will not enter the build-

ing until he is summoned. He must do the Dance of
the Swords before he can become king."

Two lads raced down the center aisle and laid out
two swords so that they formed a cross. The blades
gleamed ... long ... sharp ... lethal.

A portly man in white robes who identified himself as the Christian high priest of Northern Scotland rose and began to talk to the people about the
meaning of the dance, the ascension of Malcolm
mac Duncan as high king, and the future of the
kingdom.

When he finished, he said, "I, Rudie, high priest
of Northern Scotland, bless High King Malcolm
mac Duncan, fostered son of Fergus, as he does the
Dance of the Sword. May God bless his reign."

More cheers followed the priest's blessing, and
the music grew louder.

"Malcolm mac Duncan!" Rudie shouted.

"I am Malcolm mac Duncan," a deep voice bellowed from the open door of the Great Hall, "and I
have come to claim the High Seat of Northern Scotland."

Michael turned to see a huge warrior, clad in gold
mail and a gold and black-enameled helmet, stride
down the center aisle. The people roared their welcome. Old people, women, and children clapped
their hands and stamped their feet. Some of the
warriors clanged their weapons together; others
beat their shields.

"Halt!" Brian shouted.

Laughter turned to surprise and bewilderment.
Cheers slowly died.

"Halt, I say!" Brian shouted again.

A discordant note was struck, and the music
ground to a halt.

"My lord, Malcolm mac Duncan," Brian said,

"chief of Clan Duncan and high king of Northern Scotland, we have a visitor. Lord Michael Langssonn of Ulfsbaer, Northland."

Michael followed Brian to the dais.

Murmurs raced through the room. People shifted; they strained to see this Northlander whom they had been expecting, whom they had hoped would never arrive. Disapproval etched in their expressions, the Highlanders glared at Michael.

Cait had never before experienced such an ominous stillness. Not a sound stirred within the Great Hall.

Then the wind howled around the Great Hall, slapping the rolled-up tartan shades at the windows. It seemed to Cait as if the north wind had cast its spell over them.

She gazed at the two helmeted warriors who faced each other. They reminded her of the most ferocious and respected of all Highland animals—the wildcat. Predators both, they radiated power.

The sun shone into the room through the open windows and cast the warlords in a golden haze, reflecting brilliantly on their helmets and mail. How similar they were, Cait thought. The same height and breadth. The same stance. Even their weapons were similar.

They could have been brothers.

Malcolm mac Duncan wore a gold and black-enameled helmet and gold mail. Around his neck hung the golden torque of leadership. Michael Langssonn wore a similar helmet of silver and black enamel. His torque was silver. One noticeable difference was that Malcolm defied custom and wore his weapons on his right side because he was left-handed. Michael was right-handed.

Outside, the wind blew with renewed fervor.

Russet, yellow, and brown oak leaves fluttered through the window and landed at the warriors' feet. Both men looked down, then up . . . at the same time.

"Nay," Cait whispered, "it cannot be oak leaves."

"Ah, my lady, but it is. The gods have spoken."

Cait looked over to see an elderly woman standing beside her.

"The oak is symbolic of fate, a prophecy that the truth about the past will be revealed," the old woman declared.

"Aye," Cait replied. "Are you a seer, good mother?"

"Aye, I am Feich."

Michael moved, his mantle swinging from his shoulders. "I am Michael Langssonn of Ulfsbaer, Northland," he said, speaking Gaelic. "I seek Malcolm mac Duncan."

"I am the one you seek," Malcolm answered in Norse.

Without taking his eyes from Michael, Malcolm lowered his left hand to the hilt of his sword. His gaze never wavering from Malcolm, Michael did the same with his right hand.

"You have dishonored Lang of the Wolves," Michael accused.

"Nay," Malcolm replied. "My wife, Princess Jarvia of Southerland, honorably ruptured her betrothal to Michael Langssonn. We sent Lord Lang the rupture-endowment he demanded."

Cait looked at Princess Jarvia, who sat in the smaller High Seat. Pale and frightened, she clutched the squirming child close to her breast. The queen mother, her face also drained of color, sat rigidly, her gaze fixed upon her son.

"You sent the rupture-endowment for all to see,"

Michael continued, "but as soon as Lang's ship sailed for Northland, you sent your warriors in secret to attack the ship. All but one was killed, and even he was left for dead. But he lived, Malcolm mac Duncan, to identify the man who carried out your orders."

"No one carried out my orders," Malcolm said, "because I gave none."

"Aye, you did. And the man who carried them out was Lachlann mac Niall."

"Nay." Brian rushed forward. "'Twas not Lachlann."

Malcolm laid a restraining hand on his bestman's shoulder. Brian stepped back.

"How do you know it was Lachlann?" Malcolm asked.

"My father's vassal lived long enough to tell the tale. Your man Lachlann boasted of his heinous deed. He thought no one would ever find out because he left all Lang's warriors to die. Lang's man recognized the helmet and sword that Lachlann wore. He described them in minute detail. The helmet and its matching sword were crafted of gold and inlaid with bronze and copper and black enamel. They were so superbly crafted that anyone who sees them never forgets them."

Cait gasped. The helmet and sword that Michael described sounded exactly like the one Sholto had shown her in the Shelter Stone Cloister.

"I don't doubt what your man saw," Malcolm said, "but I do doubt that the man wearing the helmet and sword was Lachlann."

"It is reasonable to assume that any Scots warrior—any warrior who spoke Gaelic—could have donned that particular helmet and sword," Michael conceded.

"Aye," Malcolm said.

"Then, my lord Malcolm, I ask to hear the testimony of your best-man Lachlann mac Niall."

"He is not here," Malcolm answered. "Presently Lachlann and some of his warriors are in the South negotiating with other tribes. We hope to reach an agreement with them in regards to our southern boundary. I don't know when he will return."

"Has Lachlann mac Niall worn his helmet and used his sword since he was in Southerland six seasons ago when you wed Princess Jarvia?"

"Aye."

Then it couldn't be the same helmet and sword that she had seen in the cloister, Cait thought.

"Did he ever complain about its having been stolen or taken from him?"

"Nay."

"Then, my lord, I insist that Lachlann was a party to that raid, either directly or indirectly. No one could have stolen, or borrowed, such a costly helmet, without Lachlann's awareness. Either he or someone whom he knows directed the raid."

"Since your father's warriors spoke Norse, how do they know the sea raiders spoke Gaelic?"

"There was a slave aboard ship, sire, who was a native Gaelic-speaking Scot. Thinking that he might be spared, he conversed with the assailants. Alas, they killed him also. Before the slave died, he confessed that these raiders spoke fluent Gaelic that sounded as if it was their native tongue."

"Evidence seems to point toward me," Malcolm said, "but I assure you, my lord, I and my people are innocent of such a crime. To steal the rupture-endowment from Lord Lang was not in my best interest."

"Mayhap, my lord Malcolm," Michael said, "your

best-man, Lachlann mac Niall, did this of his own accord. If so, you are as guilty of the crime as he is."

"Aye."

The two warlords stared at each other.

Again murmurs buzzed through the large room, but no one moved. Servants holding trays laden with food and drink had not taken one step since Brian had announced Michael Langssonn. The celebrants themselves had not moved. A hostile tension gripped the crowd.

"Malcolm mac Duncan, I am here this day to avenge the wrong you have done to my house. I challenge you—"

Angry shouts drowned out Michael. Warriors shook their fists in the air. Weapons were drawn. One warrior, snarling his battle cry, leaped forward. Silver arced the air. Ulf leaped up and bit into the warrior's wrist. The man cursed as his sword clattered to the floor and he fell to his knees.

"Good boy," Michael said. "Sit."

The wolf released the man and padded over to his master.

Holding his bleeding wrist in one hand, the man stumbled back.

"Pick up your sword," Malcolm commanded his man, "and be gone. See about your wound."

Malcolm raised a hand, and all quieted down. He brought his hand halfway down, indicating that he wanted the people to be seated. To show their support, their readiness to come to his aid, they remained standing. He raised his hand and lowered it partway again. This time they sat.

Michael reached up with his right hand, Malcolm with his left, so they could take off their helmets. A gasp went up throughout the hall. Cait pushed closer. Malcolm had his back to her, and she couldn't see him.

"Destiny has brought them together again," the old seer muttered.

Lang took several steps forward, then stopped. "By the gods!" he swore, and Cait turned to see his shock. She spun around to look at the warlords.

Their helmets in their hands, Michael Langssonn and Malcolm mac Duncan stared at each other face-to-face for the first time. The helmet slid from Michael's right hand, Malcolm's left, to land with dull thuds on the bracken-covered floor. As if he were gazing into a piece of polished bronze, Michael raised his right hand to his face and brushed it along the jawline. Malcolm did the same with his left one. Expressions of absolute disbelief on their faces, they stared; they scrutinized. Michael brushed his right hand through his hair. Malcolm did the same with his left.

"By the blessed mother!" Cait breathed. There were two of them! Now she knew why Michael had seemed so familiar to her. He looked just like Malcolm.

"Aye," the old woman called Feich said quietly, "there are two of them. The Wolf and the Horse. The Ancients considered them sacred signs of might. Faced with one, valiant warriors tremble in fear. Faced with both, they run like cowards."

Not speaking a word, Jarvia clutched the baby close to her breasts.

"Mother of God!" the queen mother cried out. "How can this be?"

Her face was ashen, her eyes rounded in disbelief. She pressed a hand to her breast, then began to crumple slowly to the floor.

Malcolm and Lang ran to her. The Northman reached her first, sweeping her into his arms.

"Put my mother down!" Malcolm ordered.

"I will not hurt her," Lang said. "She has fainted and needs to lie down. Please direct me to a bed."

Malcolm pointed. Long steps carried Lang down the aisle of the Great Hall to a sleeping chamber.

Now Michael understood the meaning of his dreams. He was the double warrior in that he was an identical twin. He was right-handed, his brother left-handed.

"Malcolm mac Duncan," Lang thundered from the sleeping chamber, "send someone here to help me with my lady."

His shout jarred everyone from their stupor.

"She's not your lady!" Malcolm gritted between clenched teeth. "She is my mother, the queen mother of Northern Scotland."

"I'll take care of the lady Muireall, Malcolm," Feich said. "You have matters to tend to here." As she hobbled toward the sleeping chamber, the old seer mumbled, "Aye, the Wolf and the Horse have come together. The earth trembles."

Malcolm mac Duncan was his brother, Michael thought, stunned, his identical twin brother. But he was also the man who had brought shame to the House of the Wolf. He was the man Michael had sworn a blood-oath to kill.

"Malcolm mac Duncan," Michael said, his voice strong and composed, despite the turmoil he felt within, "I challenge you to a duel to avenge the dishonor you have brought upon my father's name."

Cait rushed up to Michael and grabbed him by the arm. "My lord," she murmured in Norse for only him to understand, "you cannot do this.

Malcolm mac Duncan is your brother, your identical twin brother."

Michael jerked his arm from Cait's clasp.

"He claims he is innocent of the crime, lord," she argued, "and I think he is. Please, lord."

Michael's features were sharp and implacable, as if they had been chiseled out of ice. "This is the man who has dishonored Lang's house, the man I have sworn a blood-oath to Thor to kill."

"I accept," Malcolm said, equally dignified. "I shall appoint one of my best-men to be master of the duel."

Once more the room was filled with excited voices. Some of the women and children clapped their hands; others slapped them against the tables. The old men clanged their weapons together; the young warriors beat their shields.

"I appoint Brian mac Logan to be master of the duel."

"I appoint Kolby," Michael shouted.

Kolby moved through the crowd to stand to the right of his warlord. Brian stood to the left of Malcolm.

In a loud, clear voice Brian announced in Gaelic, "As the challenged, Malcolm chooses the weapon, the time, and the place."

In the background the translation sounded.

Brian turned to Malcolm.

"The sword. Since we are past noontide on this day, I choose to have this meeting on the morrow when the sun is highest in the sky."

"Aye, Lord of Fire," Michael taunted, "that is an appropriate time. That is when the power of the sun begins to diminish."

"Nay, Lord of the Northland, that is the time when the fire of light is most vital."

"Where?" Brian asked.

"The tourney field," Malcolm said.

More cheers went up.

"The Dance of the Sword," Brian said to Malcolm. "You must do that."

Rudie, the Christain high priest, pushed forward. "Nay."

The people quietened, and an air of expectancy hung over the building.

Rudie looked at Malcolm. "Which of you is oldest?"

The twin warlords looked at each other, then at the priest. Michael shrugged. Finally Malcolm said, "He is. Although my mother never told me that I had an identical twin brother, she did say that I had a brother who was older than me."

"Michael, by claim of the blood that flows through your birth mother into you, you are the one who inherits the High Seat of Northern Scotland. You are the one who must perform the Dance of the Sword."

Malcolm glared at his brother.

"Nay," Michael called, reading his brother's hostility. "I am a Northman. In front of all these witnesses, this day I renounce my claim to the High Seat of Northern Scotland. I bestow it on Malcolm mac Duncan."

"I want nothing from you," Malcolm shouted.

"Since your kingdom means nothing to me, Malcolm mac Duncan, consider that I am giving you nothing."

"It means everything to me," Malcolm said.

"And it should," his brother replied. " 'Tis yours."

Rudie nodded. "All these people have witnessed your words, Michael Langssonn. The High Seat goes to your younger brother, Malcolm mac Duncan."

With Cait at his side, Michael stepped away from the dais. The wolf followed.

Malcolm quietly said, "High priest Rudie, I shall do the Dance of the Sword. Musicians," he called, and walked to the swords that lay crossed in front of the dais. They began to play, the tempo slow at first, the dance steps simple.

" 'Tis fascinating, sire," Cait said to Michael, "especially at the end when the music gets very fast, since the trick is not to touch a sword with the feet but to dance only in the spaces between."

But Michael was not interested in the dance. He was interested in the man who was performing it. Malcolm mac Duncan was a big man, but at the moment he was a whirl of gold.

"The dance is a ritual that all kings in the Highlands perform before assuming the High Seat of the kingdom," Cait explained.

Malcolm shouted exuberantly and jabbed a fist into the air. The piper began to play faster. Malcolm danced faster, adding new and more complicated steps to the original ones. His feet seemed hardly to touch the ground as he nimbly moved around and over the crossed swords, never touching either one and never looking down.

"The dancer must have great dexterity and skill to perform," Cait said. "This demonstrates a warrior's agility and his ability in war. It is also an invocation to the gods for a good reign."

"What will happen if he touches them?"

"The people will be afraid that his reign will be turbulent and tragic. He will have to struggle to regain their confidence."

On and on, faster and faster, the piper played,

and Malcolm danced. Not once did he look at his feet, nor did he touch the swords. He displayed a self-confidence that seemed to border on arrogance. While Michael respected this trait in Malcolm, he also found it irritating.

When the last notes of the song died away, Malcolm stood poised on his left foot, his right foot held high over his left knee. His right hand was on his hip, his left one raised in the air.

He was winded, Michael could tell by the rapid rise and fall of his chest. His face was wet with perspiration. But the Highland warlord was in complete control of his body, and his body was that of a warrior.

Whooping, hollering, and hurrahs sounded throughout the room as everyone celebrated Malcolm's success.

A worthy opponent, Michael thought. A worthy king.

Chapter 13

Feich sat on the bed beside the queen mother. Lang stood over them, gazing down at Muireall. He had been attracted to her thirty springs ago when his father's raiding party had landed on the shores of Scotland. Through the passing of the seasons, he had wondered about her, had wished he knew her name.

She moaned softly and inhaled deeply. Then she opened her lids and gazed up at him.

"My lady Muireall," he said in Gaelic, repeating the name he had heard Feich use. He liked to say Muireall's name; he liked to hear it spoken. "You are Malcolm's mother?"

"Aye." Through blue eyes—the color of a warm summer day in the Northland—she stared at him. Her voice was tentative. "Who are you?"

"I am Lang. Michael's father."

She licked her lips.

"I did not know he was your child when I found him," Lang said. "He lay beneath the body of a woman, and I assumed she was his mother."

"My handmaid," Muireall said.

"I was the other maid," Feich said. "In the confusion we became separated. Another of the servants reported that she and the baby were killed."

"Only the woman was killed," Lang repeated.

223

"If only I had looked for myself," Fiech cried. She rose and moved away from the bed. Tears ran down her wrinkled cheeks.

"You gave birth to a lusty son, madam, who didn't wish to die," Lang told Muireall.

"You speak our language," she said.

"Aye, as does my—*our*—son. Our housewoman was a Gael. She taught us the language." He added, "I am sorry about the recent death of your husband, lady."

"Thank you, lord." She paused. "Please remove your helmet. I want to see your face."

Lang removed it and the coif and tucked them beneath his arm. He raked a hand through his hair so that it was not plastered to his head.

They stared at each other, and he saw in the depths of her eyes the glimmer of recognition.

"Can it be?" she whispered.

"Aye."

"Your hair is yet black," she murmured.

"The passing seasons have added a little silver."

"At the temples. Your beard is mostly black. But the eyes . . ." She gazed into them. "They have not changed. They are still gray. I will never forget them. I have lived with their memory for the past thirty winters."

"I have lived with the memory of you also, lady."

In his heart Lang had always carried the image of Muireall as she stood at the edge of the forest close to the Northland ponies, her child clutched protectively against her breast.

"Why did you let me go?" she asked.

"You captivated me," he admitted. "I had never beheld a woman as beautiful as you, my lady." He stopped speaking for a moment, then said, "If I had felt only lust for you, I would have taken you for my bedmate. I was sorely tempted. But you stirred my heart as well as my body." His gaze ran over the dark brown hair that was swept up in curls on the crown of her head. "What I wanted to give you, lady, I had already given to another worthy woman. I could not betray her."

Muireall pulled her handkerchief through her hands. "You allowed me to steal valuable Northland ponies."

"Aye. That day, lady, I acted from my heart. And the gods blessed me. When the battle was over, the village destroyed, and the booty being loaded aboard the ship, I made a final trip down the main street. I heard crying and searched until I found a baby lying beneath the body of a dead woman. It was a son, whom I brought home and gave to my childless wife so she would feel no more shame over her barrenness. Our son has given us great happiness."

"Camshron, my first husband, was killed during the raid, and I thought my eldest son was also," she said. "I wish Fergus could be here to see Michael, but I'm also glad that he isn't."

"He was your second husband?"

"Aye, of ten winters, but Malcolm's fostered father for his entire life. The only father he knew." She added sadly, " 'Tis not a good day, when Northmen march into Highland villages, bent on destruction."

" 'Twas not a good day when Malcolm dishonored me, lady. He has called for his own destruction. You understand the law as well as I do. Your son must answer for his crimes."

"He is not guilty, my lord Lang. This marriage was too important for him to behave irresponsibly. 'Twas not Duncan's men who stole your rupture-endowment," Muireall insisted. She leaned forward and caught Lang's arm. "Please, lord, believe me."

He sat on the edge of the bed. Age had added a depth and beauty to Muireall. She was more compelling today than she had been so long ago. But the separation between them was greater than it had been at that time.

"Of all people, lord, you will have the greatest influence on Michael. Surely you can persuade him to recant his vow."

"If anyone could persuade him," Lang answered, "it would be me, lady. But even I cannot. Michael will not go back on his word."

"My lord, you saved my son—my *sons*—long ago. Please save them again," Muireall begged. Her fingers bit into his arm. "I don't wish for either of them to die. Can we restore your honor another way?"

Lang laid his hand over hers. "This time I cannot help you, my lady Muireall. My son has sworn a blood-oath." He paused. "If he should break his oath, he will lose his soul to Hel, the goddess of the Underworld. He could never join the brave warriors in the mead hall of Valhalla."

"Aye, my lord, I understand blood-oaths."

As the people moved out of the Great Hall, Malcolm said to Michael, "You and your father are invited to stay in one of our guesthouses, and your warriors in the Small Hall."

"My men will camp outside the village," Michael said. "But my father and I accept your hospitality."

Malcolm nodded.

Brian said, "Follow me."

"I will in a moment," Michael replied. "I want to see my father first. He and I must talk."

"Aye." Malcolm growled the word. "As must my mother and I."

Michael turned and guided Cait down the aisle toward the sleeping chamber. Ulf padded behind them.

Malcolm turned, caught Jarvia by the arm as she handed the little girl to a servant woman, and the two of them followed Michael. Brian fell into step behind them.

When Michael entered the room, the queen mother was sitting on the bed, propped up by several head cushions. Lang sat beside her. The old seer stood by the window. Lang rose as Michael's gaze flickered over the room. Tapestries hung on the walls; chests were set on either side of the doorway. On a trestle-table were a large pitcher of ale and several tankards. A fire burned in the central pit.

"I believe you have something to tell us, lady," Michael said.

Muireall had been crying. Her eyes were red and swollen.

"Michael . . ." Lang said, but he ignored his father and stared at the queen mother.

"Aye, my lord Michael, I do."

Michael, keeping Cait by his side, leaned against the doorframe. Malcolm and Jarvia, walking fully into the room, stood in front of the central fire.

Drawing a deep breath, Muireall said, "Michael, you and Malcolm were born to me and Camshron thirty winters ago when I was a very young queen of West Pictland. Not long after your birth, our village was attacked by Northmen led by Lang and his father."

In precise tones, Muireall told them of the attack, of the death of Camshron, and the reported death of her oldest son. She concluded with her escape on Northland ponies given to her by Lang. When she finished, silence hung heavily in the room. For one of the few times in his life, Michael did not know how to respond.

"I knew I had a brother," Malcolm muttered, "but I thought he was dead. And you never told me that he was my identical twin."

Muireall picked at the coverlet. "Your father's brother was a greedy man who wanted your father's High Seat, and he would have done anything to get it. Many people believe that twins are evil, that the first one is of God, and the second one is of the evil spirits. Your uncle was trying to convince your father that one of you must be killed."

"Me," Malcolm said.

Muireall nodded. "I wasn't going to let him kill either one of you. Then the Northmen attacked the village, and we received word that your brother was dead. Thinking that he would not be part of our lives, I saw no reason to burden you with knowledge that you were twins." She sighed. "Perhaps I was wrong, but I did what I thought was best, Malcolm."

"Aye," Malcolm murmured.

"I have no brother," Michael declared. Yet even as he uttered the words, he knew they were foolish. He stared into the face of a man who could only be his identical twin brother.

"Aye." Feich sat in a chair drawn close to the fire. "You are brothers, born of the same mother and father on the same day. I delivered both of you."

Lang filled a beaker with ale and pressed it into Muireall's hands.

She said, "I—I am the mother of both of you."

"Nay," Michael said, his voice low and composed, "you are not mother to me. My mother was Astryd, daughter of Thorfin, a valiant North-woman, and she is dead."

The beaker Muireall held in her hands began to shake. Lang, sitting beside her on the bed, took it from her and set it on the nearby chest. Pulling her into his arms, he comforted her. Michael glared at his father. Since his mother had died—in his father's arms—he had never seen Lang hold a woman with such tenderness. And of all women for him to be interested in—Malcolm's mother! Never would she be *his* mother!

"Why did you lie to me about my birth, Lang?" Michael asked. Foremost among his churning emotions, he felt betrayal.

"I did not lie," Lang said as he gently resettled Muireall against the bolsters.

"But you did not tell me that I was adopted, stolen from the Highlands during a sea raid." Michael strode across the room to confront his father. "You allowed me to grow up believing I was a Northman. Even when I vowed to sail to Scotland to avenge our name, you did not tell me."

Lang rose and faced his son.

"People always commented on how much alike we are, Lang," Michael said, as if demanding that his father refute all that had been confessed. "Tall. Broad-shouldered. Black hair. Piercing eyes. And what about the characteristics of the warrior that I supposedly inherited from you?"

Laying a hand on Michael's arm, Lang said, "My son—"

Michael wanted to jerk his arm from Lang's grip, but he did not. He had never been prone to emotional outbursts and behavior; he would not begin now. "I am your son by virtue of my having lived with you for thirty winters, my lord, of having supped at your table and having been obedient to your teachings, but I have no blood tie to you. I am not of the House of the Wolves."

"Aye," Feich agreed, "you are a wolf, my son, as your brother is a horse. Do not be bitter or angry by what the gods have decreed."

Michael removed his arm from his father's clasp and pointed at Muireall. "I am a son to this woman by virtue of blood, but I know nothing about her or her people. I have been taught to hate them, to consider them my enemy. I have sworn a blood-oath to Thor to kill this man—my brother."

"Like you, my son," Feich said, "Malcolm is a horse by virtue of his mother's blood. He became a wolf when Fergus fostered him."

Michael turned to look at the seer. "Who are you, old woman?"

"I am the woman who delivered you from your mother's womb," she repeated, then added, "The woman who slapped your buttocks for the first time. I placed you in your father's arms, and I witnessed his acceptance of you as his firstborn child."

Pushing out of the chair, she shuffled to stand in front of Michael. "The gods have been good to you. They allowed a warrior of great valor to save you and to raise you. Now they have sent you back to your homeland. Soon they will make known their purpose to you." She moved away from Michael and left the room, mumbling, "Soon."

"Why did you not tell me this long ago, Lang?" Michael asked. "Why did you let me believe that the blood of the wolves flowed through my veins, that I was the warlord who should unite all the clans together in one kingdom?"

Lang looked at Michael as if asking for understanding. "The gods had blessed me by giving me the son that your mother and I had not had. No more did she feel the shame of barrenness, and we had a child who gave us great happiness. I had intended to tell you, but I didn't. People assumed that you were our child, and as you grew older, they remarked how much like me you were. You were the son that I had always wanted, and I did not want to think about you as anything but my birth child. And the blood of wolves does flow through your veins, my son."

"Nay, Lang, the blood of some Highlander. The blood of the horse."

"Lang and I each did what we thought was best," Muireall said, her voice dull. "But it is over and done with. Now we must deal with the present."

She slid off the bed. Lang was instantly by her side, his arm going around her shoulders to steady her.

Both Michael and Malcolm lurched forward, one to jerk his father away from the woman, the other to jerk his mother away from the man. Lang looked up at them at the same time with a smoldering glare that rocked them both back on their heels.

"Would you like to return to your cottage, my lady?" Lang asked.

"Nay, I would like to look at my eldest son." She moved out of Lang's embrace and stepped close to Michael.

He saw the tears that misted her beautiful blue eyes. He looked at Malcolm. His eyes were the same startling shade as the queen mother's. The same color as ... his! But Michael would not let himself be taken in by this woman.

"You are indeed a handsome man, my lord," she said, "and while you look like your adopted father,

Lang, you also look very much like your birth father, Camshron." Two tears slid down her cheeks. "He was a warrior of valor, my lord. You would have been proud to be his son."

She lifted her hand, but before she touched his cheek, she lowered it.

"I know your thoughts are muddled at this moment, as are mine, but do not close me out of your life altogether. I can never take the place of your first mother, but God has decreed that I am your birth mother."

"Aye, my lady," Michael said dryly, "the gods have so decreed. Sometimes I wonder about their sense of humor."

" 'Tis not humor, my lord, 'tis fate. Each of us has a destined path to walk. Please, my . . . " She paused. "Please, my lord and elder son, make the right choice."

Michael lifted his right hand and rubbed his forehead. Muireall gasped, and her eyes rounded. Grabbing his hand, she jerked him toward the firelight.

"The ring," she whispered. "Where did you get this ring?"

All moved closer to stare at Michael's little finger. The band was silver, but the design was gold.

"When I was a small child, my father had it designed and crafted for me," Michael said. "I received it when I became a warrior and have worn it ever since." Michael looked over at Jarvia as he said, "I had intended this to be the wedding ring I would give my bride, madam."

Jarvia moved out of Malcolm's embrace. "I received a golden sickle ring as my wedding ring." She held out her hand for all to see. "The story Malcolm told about this ring, my lord Michael, is very similar to yours."

"Aye," Muireall agreed. "Camshron had the ring crafted, thinking we would have the one son. I gave it to Malcolm when he became a warrior. He wore it until he gave it to Jarvia six seasons ago when they wed."

An eerie silence fell in the sleeping chamber.

Lang spoke up. "I had this ring designed and crafted because even as a baby, Michael loved the dark. He could see better in the dark than most, could navigate better, could fight better. He would spend hours outside, staring at the moon, thinking and planning.

"The seer advised Astryd and me that although Michael was named after the great thunder god, he should be dedicated to the god of Night, so that silver moonbeams would always direct him."

"The sickle," Muireall said. "What does it mean to your people?"

"The sickle is symbolic of the moon, lady. Our ships are crescent-shaped. As the moon sails the midnight sky, our *langskips* sail the blue seas. The golden sickle embodies both the sun and the moon. Our shields are round like the sun, our swords the rays that fan out from it."

" 'Tis the same for us," Muireall said. "The crescent shape is for the moon, and the color is for the fire of the sun. Two in one."

"Aye, madam, two in one. Night and Day. The dark half of the year and the light half."

"The dark half of the year is the beginning, the firstborn, the elder child."

"Aye, madam."

Muireall gazed first at the silver torque about Michael's neck, then at the gold one that Malcolm wore.

Finally Brian mac Logan broke the silence. "My

lords Michael and Malcolm, what about the duel? Does this not change the matter?"

"It changes nothing," Michael said. "I have sworn a blood-oath to Thor that I will kill the man who brought dishonor to my father's name. I could not recant that vow even if I wanted to."

All understood the fatal consequences of breaking an oath, especially one made to the gods.

"Malcolm mac Duncan and I are enemies first," Michael announced, "brothers second. The duel will proceed as planned."

"My lord Michael," Brian said, "I am speaking out of turn, and the Duncan may have my head for it, but someone must speak. I know you do not believe us, but Malcolm and Lachlann are innocent of this crime."

"Are you asking me to call off the duel?" Michael asked.

"Nay," Malcolm answered. "He speaks for himself, not for me. But I do ask for time. Now that I have heard what your vassal reported, I want to find the man who is really guilty of this perfidy." He moved closer to his brother. "Michael Langssonn, you promised to kill the man who has dishonored your house. Then be satisfied to kill him and him only. If you kill me, you will still owe your god a blood-oath."

"My lord," Muireall said to Michael, "the only evidence you have is the helmet and sword—"

"Aye, madam," Michael said dryly. "Such weaponry is not common. There can be only one of each—"

"I have seen a helmet and sword like the ones you described," Cait said, stepping forward.

"Where?" Malcolm demanded.

"At the Shelter Stone Cloister, sire. I am Cait nea Sholto, a bard of the cloister."

Malcolm peered so intently at her that Cait again felt self-conscious about her short hair. She imagined Malcolm's thoughts, but she would not be deterred.

"See the tattoo." She pulled up the sleeve of her tunic to reveal the golden sickle. "My father is the high priest and the Ancient of Nights and Days."

"Aye, Malcolm." Muireall moved closer so that she could see Cait better. "I have been so engrossed in your brother's return that I did not recognize her until now. She is the bard of the Shelter Stone Cloister. I met her when I visited the shrine last spring."

"After the passing of the four seasons, when we prepare to celebrate the return of spring," Cait said, "my father goes through the gifts that have been offered to the gods. We clean and polish them, and we make a new list. At this time, my father and the Council of Priests choose which ones are to be distributed among the needy in the kingdoms."

"State your point, madam," Malcolm snapped.

"Before I left the cloister to come here to seek sanctuary," Cait said, "I saw a helmet and sword just like the one Michael described."

"But how could it be?"

"Was Lachlann wearing his helmet last spring?" Michael asked.

Malcolm nodded.

Michael said, "Mischief is afoot."

"Aye, my lord," Cait said. "It is indeed."

Omitting any personal references, Cait told Malcolm about the sea raiders' attack on Glenmuir, the subsequent deaths of the royal household, and Gilbert's appointment as provisional ruler. She also relayed her suspicions concerning Gilbert's role in the perfidy and his desire to steal the wealth of the cloister.

"We haven't received any news of this," Malcolm said.

"Nay, Lord Gilbert does not wish for the news to get out," Cait said. "All are kept prisoners. Even now, my lord Malcolm, I fear for my father's and my cousin's lives. For the lives of all my fellow minstrels."

"Madam," Malcolm said, "according to what you have said, your king and his household were killed by marauding sea raiders, and the High Council has made Lord Gilbert provisional ruler of Glenmuir. I have received no summons for help, and I have no reason to march into the kingdom with my warriors."

"You are receiving your summons through me," Cait said. "Sholto sent me to get help."

"Why is your hair shorn?"

"Gilbert's men cut it," Cait cried out, knowing that Malcolm did not believe her. "Gilbert blames the attack on me. He has declared me an outlaw, but I am innocent."

She saw compassion in Malcolm's eyes, but she also knew he was not going to help her. Exasperated, fearful, Cait drew in a deep breath and told her own story, beginning with her arrival in Glenmuir and ending with her arrival in Malcolm's village. She omitted telling them about the Cloister Breastpins.

When she finished, Malcolm said, "All I can do now is to send a messenger to Glenmuir to inquire about Sholto and the minstrels in your company."

"My lord high king, did you not hear me? The Silver Daggers have been taken captive. One is dead. A king's man is also dead."

"The warrior is dead, madam," Malcolm pointed out, "because he helped prisoners of the king escape. I cannot fault Gilbert's men. My position remains the same."

"What about the helmet and the sword? Don't you want to see them?"

"Seeing them won't solve our problem."

His words dashed Cait's last hope.

"We must find the man who left the helmet and sword at the cloister," Michael said. "Does your father also record the name of the donor?"

"Aye."

Michael's eyes brightened.

"But he said these items were slipped in among the treasures. No donors' names were recorded."

Malcolm shrugged. "Then, Lady Cait, the matter is out of my hands."

"In light of what you have said, Lord Malcolm, and what Cait has told us about the helmet and sword," Michael said, "I shall grant you more time to investigate."

Jarvia and Muireall visibly relaxed, but Cait remained upset. She had thought that surely when she reached Northern Scotland, the high king would readily offer assistance. But he was very much like his brother—wary and obstinate.

Would no one believe her?

Cait touched her chest, her palm resting over the sacred Breastpin. At least it was safe for the moment. As long as she had it, Gilbert could not reach the inner sanctum and would probably not kill Sholto or Rob.

"We shall take our leave," Malcolm announced. "My lords, Lang and Michael, my wife and I invite you to celebrate the coronation feast with us tomorrow night."

Michael nodded. "We accept."

"Michael, since you and Cait will be sharing the same cottage," Lang said, "I shall sleep in my pavilion."

Michael nodded.

His arm around Jarvia's shoulder, Malcolm guided her out of the cottage. Brian followed.

"My lady Muireall," Lang said, "may I escort you to your quarters?"

Malcolm halted at the door and whirled around.

"Aye, my lord Lang," Muireall answered.

Michael and Malcolm glared at their parents.

Lang and Muireall ignored their sons.

Chapter 14

⌒◯◯⌒

Michael and Cait followed Brian to their lodgings, a two-room cottage away from the Great House. Ulf trotted along with them. Outwardly Michael was composed. Inwardly he was emotionally devastated.

"Would you like me to send you a servant, my lord?" Brian asked.

"Nay."

"I'll send someone to escort you to the evening meal. You will take it at the Great House with Malcolm and his family."

After Brian was gone, Michael shut the door and leaned back against it. His gaze flickered over the room, brightly lit with waning sunlight and the fire in the central pit. Chests flanked either side of the doorway.

A haunting silence had settled over the cottage when Michael pushed away from the door. Raking his hand through his already tousled hair, he walked into the sleeping chamber.

The bed was large and commodious, furnished with a thick mattress and bolsters. A large window broke up the far wall. The shutters were open, the shade rolled up. There was a large chest next to the bed and one at the foot, a table with two chairs against one wall. On it were a pitcher and tankards.

239

Ulf had already examined the room and was curled up on the floor in front of the fire.

Michael crossed to the table. He picked up the pitcher of wine and poured a tankard full. As if he were dying from thirst, he quaffed it down. He refilled the tankard and took several more long swallows.

A cold wind blew into the room, but Michael welcomed it. Perhaps it would sweep his mind of confusion. He had never felt so disoriented. He felt as if his body were one person, his soul another, and that neither belonged together.

Michael was a methodical man. He had mapped out his life with the same care and precision that he mapped out the seas he sailed, the lands he explored. He studied situations and anticipated the consequences of his behavior; then he chose his path. He set his goals and worked until he had either achieved them or decided they no longer mattered.

He had always known what he was going to do, then he had done it. When he had set sail from Northland, his purpose had been singular and clear. But once he had arrived on these shores, his purpose had become clouded and complex.

His parents were not his birth parents. He was a Highlander, not a Northman. He was of the Clan of the Horse, not of the Wolf. A woman he didn't know was his mother. His sworn enemy was his identical twin brother.

Cait, not knowing what to say or do, but sympathizing with Michael's confusion, stood quietly in the doorway. When he had emptied the tankard a second time, he held it out to her, an indication that he wanted it refilled.

"My lord," she said softly, "the wine won't ease your hurt."

"I have no hurt to ease, madam." He glared at her and stalked back to the table. He poured the wine himself.

"Aye, my lord, you do. You're full of bitterness, hatred, and anger—so much so that you don't know what you're feeling."

"I suppose you read minds?" he snapped.

"Nay, but I read hearts."

He shot her a sarcastic glance.

Cait wasn't deterred. During her years at the cloister, she had tended to many people who were ill, of the body, of the mind, and of the spirit. She understood that they directed their tongue-lashings at one when they really meant them for another . . . most times for themselves.

"I can understand some of what you must be feeling now."

"Can you, Cait?"

His voice was deceptively soft. She would have preferred that he yell or scream or kick furniture over. Anything to release the anger that he kept contained within himself beneath the false front of calmness and composure. She could handle honest emotions, openly expressed, but she sensed that Michael Langssonn was keeping his hidden, controlled.

He crossed the room to stand before her. "Do you know what it's like to believe you are the son of one set of parents, only to learn you are not? To think your mother is dead, only to find that she wasn't your mother at all? That your mother is alive and well in another land? That you are the son of your most hated enemy?" His fingers tightened around the tankard. "Tell me, Cait, have you ever experienced something similar?"

She shook her head.

"Then don't tell me you understand how I'm feeling."

Cait laid her hand on his arm. "My lord—"

"The irony of the situation, madam, is that the man I have sworn to kill, the man who has brought dishonor on my father—on Lang's—"

"Your father," Cait interrupted.

Michael stared at her.

"Your father, Michael. Lang is your father."

"Nay," Michael said. "Not by blood. Not by adoption."

"By love. By trust. By respect. Michael, fatherhood is not based on a ceremony or on a birthing."

"I agree." Michael returned to the trestle table and set his tankard down. "But it seems that Lang and I were not as bonded as I thought. Why didn't he trust me enough to tell me that I was not his son?"

"Because I always thought of you as my son," Lang said from the doorway.

Startled, Cait looked up. "You surprised me, my lord."

"You were too deep in conversation to hear me enter."

He stepped into the sleeping chamber but kept some distance between himself and Michael. "I have wronged you, my son. Greatly wronged you. I should have adopted you, and I should have told you what I knew about your true parentage."

Lang took another step forward; Michael moved a step back.

"From the moment I picked you up and held you in my arms, you were my son—the son of my heart." Lang paused. When he spoke again, his voice was gruff. "I would that you could have been the son of my loins, but the gods did not deem that. I had only my heart to give you, my son, and I gave it all." He cleared his throat. "Someday, Michael, you'll understand that being the son of any man's heart is more of a miracle than being the son of a man's loin."

Michael said nothing.

Lang strode over to the pile of baggage in the corner of the room. He picked up a large leather satchel. Several smaller ones, leaning against it, toppled to the floor. "I came to get my satchel. As I said, I shall be staying in the pavilions with the men. You and Cait may have the cottage." Long steps carried him across the room. He stopped in the doorway. His back to Michael, he said, "Whatever you may think, Michael, you *are* my son."

His father's words ringing in his ears, Michael picked up the tankard of wine.

"Nay, Michael." Lang dropped the satchel and swung around. He strode back into the room. "I won't leave with this division between us."

"I need time to think, Lang."

"Aye, you do, but there's more that I want you to think about," his father said, his voice growing loud. "You said you are not my son by blood or by adoption. I can do nothing about the blood, but if you want a ceremony, by the gods, Michael, we can still have a ceremony. If killing an ox and shedding its blood will make you any more my son, we will do it. If putting on the adoption boot will make you any more my son, we will do it."

Cait stepped back. Lang had launched an attack, and she didn't wish to be part of it. Seeing the two massive warriors confronting each other, Cait saw how much alike Lang and Michael were. She had a difficult time believing they were not blood kin.

"If ceremony is what you want, let me tell you about ceremonies that have made you my son, that have made me your father. What about the ceremony of my holding you in my arms and walking the floor with you night after night and day after day when the milk we had in Northland didn't agree with you? Warriors do not care for the young, my son. They abandon them. But I nursed you. Who taught you and Kolby to throw your spears with accuracy when you were blindfolded? Who allowed you to keep a pet wolf that would let no one get near you? Do you . . ."

Cait listened quietly as Lang listed poignant moments in their lives when each of them had made sacrifices out of love for the other.

"What about the ceremony when you made me learn to speak Gaelic so that our housewoman could converse in her own tongue? Remember, son, the time when you wouldn't leave my bed even after the healer said I wouldn't recover from the battle wound I had received, and if I did, I would never use my arm? Remember, Michael? You were the one who tended to me, who nursed me, who willed me to live."

Lang strode over to his son and clasped his shoulders. "That's the kind of ceremony that comes from the heart, Michael. These are the things that bespeak father, that bespeak son."

Tears ran down Cait's cheeks.

Michael and his father looked into each other's faces; then Michael threw his arms around his father. Father and son hugged. They pulled apart and smiled. No more words were spoken; they weren't needed. Father and son had reunited. Lang walked to the door. When he turned, it was one warrior looking at another.

"I'll see you on the morrow."

"Aye."

Michael knew the roughest obstacle was over. No matter what had happened in the past, he loved Lang, his father. His father loved him. Occasionally they would disagree, but they would always be father and son.

The wind whistled through the room, making the fire sputter. Still the blaze and the late afternoon sunlight kept the room warm and comfortable.

Cait stretched out on the bed. "If Malcolm doesn't find the person who stole the rupture-endowment, do you really intend to fight him?"

"Aye. I swore before Thor."

"Malcolm mac Duncan has the reputation of being the most renowned champion in all the Highlands, lord. He is not called the Lord of Fire for naught."

Michael smiled, truly smiled; she heard it in his voice. "Nor am I called the Lord of Thunder for naught." He sat on the edge of the bed. "I create fires and the rain that follows to douse them."

He rolled over, so that she received with pleasure the pressure of his partial weight. His lips touched hers sweetly, asking her with their gentle pressure to return the caress. "I want to create a fire in you, Caity, and I want you to receive me into that fire."

Michael's use of the diminutive of her name pleased her.

"I want that also, lord," she whispered against his mouth. "Will you mate with me?"

He grew still. Lifting his head, he looked at her with eyes that were dark blue fires.

"Aye, lord," she said, "I want you to mate with me. Now."

"You are no longer frightened of me?"

"Nay, lord."

She was frightened of many things, about her cousin and her father, about the safety of the cloister riches, but she was no longer frightened of Michael Langssonn. He claimed that he was not a kindly man, and quite possibly he wasn't. But he was an honest and sincere man, and she respected and loved him for that.

He had treated her wrists when they were injured. In an effort to save Dacy's life, Michael had defied his men by staying an extra night in Glenmuir when he could have traveled on. The night Dacy had died, Michael had unselfishly given of himself to comfort her. He had held her tenderly, soothing her and caring for her.

Nay, she was not frightened of the Northman, and tonight she would soothe and comfort him. She would give him something real to hold on to as the foundations of his life crumbled beneath him.

He had dreams and visions. She would give him reality.

"I am a Druid. A bard," Cait said. "I understand fire. Lightning. Thunder. I am one with them. I would be one with you." She cupped his head in her hand and pulled his mouth against hers. She gave him the kiss he asked for, the kiss she wanted.

"Have you ceased playing games?" he asked.

"Sholto claims that life itself is a game, my lord. If that is true, we never cease playing."

He reclaimed her lips in an even deeper kiss. When he raised his head, his hand, so big and strong, began to gently stroke the tangled hair from her face. In the fading sunlight her dark hair glistened rich and red.

"Many might consider short hair on a woman a

sign of shame," he whispered, "but on you, Cait nea Sholto, it is a badge of honor."

"If it were longer, I'd bind you in a silken web." She removed the ribbon from his hair, and it fell over her shoulders onto her breasts.

He stroked his fingertips over her cheeks, her lips. "Mayhap you have no need to bind me into a silken web, little bard. Perhaps you have already spun an invisible web around me."

So as not to frighten his little kitten, he kept his movements deliberate but unhurried. He worked the button of her shirt through the opening and pulled the material aside to reveal the upper swell of her breasts. He lowered his head and touched the satiny silk with his lips, then with his tongue. He brushed his lips down her throat, across her collar-bone, back and forth in whisper-soft motions designed to tease and torment.

Cait moaned and arched. As she thrust upwards, the material of her tunic slipped farther down on her breasts, revealing her nipples. His mouth claimed the creamy whiteness. His tongue sought the hard tip. When he felt her quiver beneath his caresses, he murmured, "Aye, little kitten, I want you to purr for me, but first we must undress you."

"Nay, lord, we will undress for each other."

Michael gazed at the woman in his arms. She looked so tender and innocent, and she stirred him more deeply than any other woman ever had.

"Aye," he said, "I will enjoy watching you undress for me."

She moved away from him and caught the hem of her shirt and pulled it over her head. Michael's breath caught as he watched the soft material slide up to reveal the smooth skin of her abdomen, then the swell of her breasts, the darkened areolas, her shoulders, then her flushed face surrounded by the wild tangle of russet hair.

While her arms were yet bound in the sleeves of her blouse and raised above her head, Michael leaned toward her. He caught her wrists in one hand and held her arms where they were. Using his body, he levered her against the mattress and bolster.

"Once you trussed me, so you could escape. Now I truss you, so you cannot flee my touch." His mouth hovered above her breast; she felt the warm moistness of his breath against her skin. "I can't wait for you to finish undressing to sample again the sweetness of your body."

"A sample is all you can have with me still partly dressed," Cait said, her voice husky as he took her into his mouth. "Undressed, you can taste me fully."

Ardac said men had bartered their lives and souls for Cait nea Sholto, Michael recalled. That they fought for and conquered kingdoms for her. He could understand why they would. She was a temptress, her body made for his lust.

He touched his mouth to the area around the small gold medallion that lay between her breasts. She shuddered beneath the strokes. He kissed up the delicate chain to her earlobe. He caught the chain to remove the amulet.

She stilled his hand. "Nay, lord. 'Tis my magical talisman. I don't wish to be without it. 'Twas made by a goldsmith who lives in a cloister grove. She is a Dryad, a woman who has dedicated her life to the gods and has vowed never to marry."

"I pity the woman who has sworn off men, little bard," Michael said, his mouth moving down the other side of the chain. "Or men who swear off women." His lips stopped their quest at the gold medallion.

"Shall I finish undressing?" she asked.

"Aye." Still his lips moved over her collarbone and shoulder, finally to rest on the golden sickle tattoo on her upper arm. "Your mark," he murmured.

"Nay, 'tis *our* mark, lord," she said.

He kissed the tattoo, and Cait shivered. A new wave of passion surged through her body. Michael released her wrists, and she lowered them, wiggling out of her shirt. He touched her breasts, and in the dim flicker of firelight, she saw the silver band on his little finger.

She rose from the bed and sat on the stool in front of the fire. Ulf opened his eyes and looked at her. She respectfully looked at him. He scratched his nose with his paw, then went back to sleep.

Silhouetted by the golden glow of fading sunlight, she bent over and removed her boots, then stood and unfastened her girdle. As the leather parted, she pulled down her trousers, then her underleggings. When she straightened, she was naked, but draped in shadows since the window was to her back.

Cait moved to stand behind the fire, and Michael saw the beautiful soft contours of her body. She raised her arms, the movement thrusting her breasts forward, the gold talisman glittering between them. Michael, hard with desire, propped himself up on one arm and held out his hand for her.

" 'Tis time for you to undress for me," she said.

"Aye."

He moved off the bed and caught her hands in his. He tugged her closer, but she moved only her head to plant a light, warm kiss to his lips. With her tongue she stroked the fullness of them. He tugged her again, but she laughed and ran back to the bed.

Cait had never mated before, had never gone so far with any man in the mating ritual, but she knew what Michael wanted her to do. As she stretched out on the bed, she felt, rather than saw, Michael's eyes grow darker. Some inner sense told her that he found her altogether desirable.

Standing beside the fire, its glow adding to the setting sun that clearly illuminated his body, Michael began to undress. Cait had known from the moment she and Michael entered the guest cottage that they would make love. She had made the choice then. She was going to mate with him because at this moment she needed Michael as much as she believed he needed her.

She would be receiving his seed of life into her body, and she accepted that she might conceive their child. She would take pleasure in having a baby from this valiant warrior. Whether the child was a boy or girl, it would be imbued with wonderful characteristics that would enable it to become a leader of people.

He took off his clothing, piece by piece, dropping them on top of hers. Finally he stood gazing down at her. His body gleaming in the firelight looked like sculpted bronze, and muscles rippled from his chest to his feet. Cait's eyes touched every feature of his face, his chest covered in the mat of crisp, black hair, his lean, hard stomach. She dropped her gaze to his aroused manhood.

For a moment a tremor of primitive female fear drove out some of her excitement. She knew with certainty that after mating with Michael Langssonn, she would not be the same again. In their coming together, she would be giving Michael a gift far more precious than her virginity. She would be laying herself open to him emotionally and spiritually. He would have a knowledge of her that no other man had ever had. She was giving him the key to unlock her inner self.

As relentlessly as she gazed at Michael, he gazed at her.

"You are beautiful, Cait."

She inhaled deeply, her breath liquid fire burning through her, settling in her lower body. "You are, too, my lord."

Michael laughed, the rich, husky sound filling the room. He walked across the room and slid into bed with her, straightening his lean body along the length of hers.

"So beautiful," she murmured. In the glorious blending of sunset and fireglow, the bronze darkness of his body was in contrast to the whiteness of hers.

He bent his head and slowly kissed the soft, vulnerable curve of her throat. She arched convulsively in reaction, twisting to get closer to him. Michael moved his hand to the curve of her hip and squeezed gently.

His soft, warm lips brushed hers. She felt his breath enter her mouth just as his closed on hers. She cupped the back of his head, holding him against her. His mouth, his tongue, caressed her. She curled her hand through his hair.

He kissed her again and again, teasing and tormenting her with light brushing strokes before he fully claimed her mouth, before he possessed it with his tongue.

His arms tightened. She arched until she felt Michael flatten his body against hers, his chest rubbing against her nipples. She played her fingers through his chest chair and found herself entranced by the hard, muscled contours of his body. He lifted his head and gazed down at her.

"The way you play with my body, little bard, I get the impression you've never seen a naked man before."

In the muted glow of the room, his eyes were the brilliance of lightning in a storm-darkened sky.

"I've seen them, lord," she confessed, thinking about the ill she had tended at the cloister. "But I have never seen a body like yours."

"I have never seen one as exquisite as yours either," Michael confessed.

Unhurriedly, with practiced expertise, Michael kept her in the circle of his arms, gently crushing her pliant, unresisting body to his. He held her, savoring the life she so willing gave to him. Time had ceased to exist. His world was Cait nea Sholto.

Cait's hands glided up his back, caressing the muscles along his spine and across his shoulders. Her fingers tangled in his hair. Complying with her every demand, following each loving injunction, Michael kissed her, each kiss growing deeper. They were hungry and devastating.

"My lord," Cait murmured thickly, "I feel as if you are lightning that has entered into my body and set me on fire."

"Not yet, little one," he murmured, "but I will be the lightning that enters into you. I promise."

Michael crushed her lips with his, and dark passion flowed through him into her to take Cait's breath away. The force of his tongue, the hard length of his body, bore into her with a fierce urgency.

Michael Langssonn was the Lord of Thunder; he was the storm. The violence of the storm exhilarated her. It drew her into a depth of feeling as primeval as his. His invasion of her mouth had the fury and majesty of the raging tempest. His tongue became a searing flash of lightning.

Her body cried for completion. As if he knew that she was ready, Michael began to taste her. He kissed her breasts, his lips forging a path between the cleavage. He kissed her midriff, his tongue drawing erotic designs all over her stomach. Then he kissed up her stomach to her breasts, capturing the nipple and sucking until she felt that he had drawn her soul into his.

Her fingers furrowed in the crisp, dark hair, and she guided his mouth back to hers, wanting to know again the sweet fierceness of his kiss, wanting every inch of her body possessed by this man.

Michael willingly complied. His mouth devoured hers. His hand traveled down her flat stomach to the triangle between her thighs. His fingers slid through the downy softness, unerringly seeking the place he hungered for.

When Cait felt his hand between her legs, she shuddered. She went hot and cold all over. Her eyes closed, soft sighs whispered through her lips.

"That's right, little one," Michael encouraged. "Purr for me. Whimper your delight."

Her head rolled from side to side in sheer pleasure. Her delight was Michael's. Intent on giving her pleasure, his whole body joined in the amorous assault. As his palm lay warmly over the mound of her femininity, his teeth grazed the fullness of her breasts to the throbbing nipples and back again.

The pleasure was so great that Cait cried aloud. Still she wanted more. *She had to have more!* The tormenting longing seared through her blood, pounded in her head, and drummed in her heart.

Her hips began to undulate in that primeval dance as old as time itself as she lifted herself against his questing hand.

"I did not know it could be so wonderful," she whispered.

"And we've only begun." Michael laughed gently in the shadows. "I promised you, little bard, that I would service your needs."

"And that I would service yours." As he leaned over her, she looked up at him and saw firelight reflected in his eyes. "Have you ever felt more than letching for a woman, my lord?"

"Letching is enough to feel." He kissed her with a deep thoroughness that left her breathless. All the while his hand stayed pressed between her thighs, moving gently against her. When she felt his finger slide slowly inside, she stopped breathing altogether. Then she inhaled sharply.

"Oh, my lord," she cried out. "I'm—I'm—"

She didn't know what was happening. She arched her body, straining against Michael's hand, her body trembling with the force of the emotions he had unleashed in her. She begged for release.

"Aye, let it happen." His voice was husky. At the same time that he slid his tongue into her mouth, he pushed a second finger into her.

Cait moaned as he stretched her slowly, opening her completely to his touch. A strange, pulsing tension built in her. She enclosed Michael in her arms, clinging to him, trying to bring all of him into her. He moved only his hand to find just the right place.

Cait writhed under his loving ministrations. At the moment when she thought she could stand the torment no longer, her blood turned to hot passion, surging madly through her veins. Her heart drummed frantically; her breath shortened. Every nerve in her body screamed for relief.

All her feeling was centered in the pleasure point under Michael's hand. Suddenly it exploded, and she arched her body as it convulsed around his probing fingers. Moans of delight escaped her parted lips. She heard herself whispering Michael's name over and over again in a breathless voice she hardly recognized as her own.

She wilted in his arms, her head rolling to the side, her breathing ragged. Michael rubbed the length of her back in a soothing movement.

"Fiery," he murmured, kissing her shoulder, to the tattoo. "But I knew you were fire the moment I first saw you."

Cait was so weak, she could hardly breathe. "That was wonderful, my lord. Indeed a journey."

"As I said, this is only the beginning. We have much farther to go."

"Aye, lord, mayhap we do." Cait stared into his darkened face. "But this was not the journey I planned. I had wanted both of us to make it together . . . if that's possible between a man and a woman."

"It is."

She searched Michael's face in the shadows.

"Mayhap you don't desire me any longer?" she asked.

She ran her hand down his chest to his stomach and lower. She touched him; he was fully aroused. She heard his intake of breath.

"You want me, lord?"

"Aye. And I shall have you, little bard, in due time."

Cait had always been aware of Michael's tight control over himself. She had marveled at it when he had challenged Ardac and his men. Only now did she realize that this discipline extended into every facet of his life. Michael was so tightly bound in reason and practicality that he must control his lust as he controlled everything else in his life.

It was clear that as much as Michael professed to want her, as wonderfully as he had brought her to fulfillment, he had no intention of allowing himself to be at the mercy of his own passion . . . or hers. It seemed that he was determined to prove to himself, and to her, that he was in complete control.

"When are we going to go on this journey . . . together?" she asked.

"Right now."

Later, after more wonderful foreplay, Michael claimed Cait. He lowered the weight of his body over hers, his knee spreading her legs apart, his hand stroking her inner thigh. She felt his hardness as it touched her maidenhood. She tensed.

He arched over her, his shoulders and the muscled contours of his back covered in a sheen of glistening sweat. Maintaining such rigid control of his emotions had not been easy for him, Cait thought. Yet unlike her, he was in complete command of himself.

Cait's gaze met his, and she felt as if her soul had been incinerated by the burning desire in his eyes. He lowered himself into her with a slow, tender thrust.

Then she received him completely within herself—at last, she was filled with him—and sensation flooded her once more.

"So tight," Michael whispered. He lay still, braced on his hands above her, as their bodies accommodated each other. "You did not lie about being a virgin."

"Nay."

"I'll be gentle with you." He pulled out slightly, then pushed back in. Again he paused. "I'm going to take you on a beautiful journey, little Cait."

"Aye, I'd like that." She hardly recognized the husky voice as hers. She could hardly believe her body had received him. She savored the fullness of him. Then she lifted her hips, carefully measuring the length and breadth of him. She tightened about him.

"Aye, I like that." His voice was thick.

Holding on to his shoulders, she pressed her hips upward against him, then she lowered them.

"Aye," he murmured, "like that."

He seemed huge and strange inside her, but she loved it. She loved the weight of him upon her, his body stroking her until she was ablaze with passion. As the flames licked hotter and hotter, she dug her fingers into his shoulders. Then she tensed.

"Aye, little bard, that's it."

She convulsed around him. Then and only then did he finally allow himself to savor his own release. She held him on top of herself for a long time. Finally he rolled over, still keeping her in his embrace.

"You are lightning and thunder wrapped up in one," he said.

Only because you are the storm, and I entered into you.

Soon he fell into an exhausted sleep.

Sometime later, he turned on his stomach, though he did not awaken. Cait sat up and looked down at him. The pale glow from the burning embers in the hearth illuminated his harsh features. His midnight dark hair spilled across the bolster.

Rubbing her fingers over the silken strands, she gazed at the man to whom she had willingly given her body. She would as willingly give her heart and soul.

Chapter 15

Cait opened her eyes, and for a moment couldn't remember where she was. She pushed up on her elbows and gazed around the room. She saw the reddish gray ashes in the fire pit, the table with the half-filled pitcher of ale. Clothing scattered the floor.

"My lord Michael," a young male voice called, "Princess Jarvia wishes me to inform you that the evening meal will be served in two hours. She also wants to know if she can do anything to make your visit more pleasant."

Michael stirred beside Cait, and she looked down at his tousled hair and darkly stubbled cheeks. She brushed her hand over his jaw, loving the abrasion against her palm.

"You're being summoned, my lord."

"Ah, my lady." Michael stretched, the covers sliding down to reveal his broad chest and his muscular abdomen. His blue eyes twinkled as he teased, "By more than one person, my lady?"

"Aye." Visually Cait traced the curly black hair that swirled from his chest down his stomach.

"Are you hungry, lady?"

"Aye."

"Then we shall eat." Michael pushed the cover down.

Cait caught him. "Not for food."

Michael paused. Then a beautiful smile that radiated from his eyes touched his lips.

"I always knew that you and I had many things in common, Cait nea Sholto, and I believe passion is one of them."

She leaned down and kissed him.

The youth called out, "Lord Michael, do you have a message for Princess Jarvia?"

"Shall we decline to attend dinner?" Michael asked.

"We cannot," Cait whispered. " 'Twould be an insult to our host."

"Aye." Michael sighed his regret. Giving Cait a quick kiss, he slid off the bed.

"Lord, will you ask for a bathing tub and a barber?" she asked.

Arching a brow, he touched her cheek. "I feel no beard stubble."

She giggled. "To trim my hair."

"Aye." He stepped into his trousers and pulled on his shirt as he entered the main room. He opened the door to see a youth standing there, holding aloft a burning torch.

"Good evening, lad. Tell your lady that we shall be delighted to dine with her and High King Malcolm. Also have her send over a bathing tub and a barber."

After the boy left, Michael stood for a moment gazing around the village. Winter's early darkness had fallen, but the night was yet young. Here and there, torchlight gleamed brightly. Loud talking and laughter sounded from the Small Hall, where the warriors gathered. Light glittered from the open windows of the Great Hall. Michael saw servants rushing about, preparing food and setting up tables.

Princess Jarvia entered the room, and Michael leaned back against the doorframe and watched her. Her hair shimmered silver in the torchlight. Tall and slender, she was one of the most beautiful women Michael had ever seen.

"She's beautiful," Cait said, joining him, putting Michael's thoughts into words.

He draped an arm about Cait and drew her against himself. "Aye, Caity, she is."

"I would like to hate her," Cait said, "but I can't. Instead I am jealous."

Michael chuckled. "At present, you have no cause to be. While I admire the princess, I do not wish to have her as my wife."

"You don't?" Cait seemed to breathe the words.

Holding her near with one arm, Michael closed the door with the other. Then he speared his hand through her hair. "Nay. An autumn-haired Highlander has me thoroughly ensnared in a silken web of desire."

Michael lowered his head, and Cait raised hers. Their lips met in warm sweetness. But neither was satisfied with that. Michael turned to take her more fully into his embrace. Cait also turned, slipping her arms about him and pressing close.

Her breasts swelled. They throbbed for the touch of his hand, of his mouth. She rubbed them against his chest.

Michael's hands slid down to her buttocks, and he nudged her more fully against his growing hardness.

The kiss deepened, their tongues entwined. Then they teased and dueled in that age-old game of mating. Each took from the other. Each also gave. They quickly ignited the flames of desire.

Michael released her mouth, but still embraced her. "Are you hurting?"

"Aye."

Michael pulled back. "I hurt you when I mated with you?" he demanded.

"Nay."

He gazed into her smiling face, into those glorious tawny gold eyes that flirted with him.

"I am hurting because I want you so much, lord."

Michael's grip tightened about her, and he buried his face in the curve of her neck.

"Caity," he murmured, "that is how I feel about you." After a moment he said, "I don't wish to be around Malcolm any more than I have to. Let us send word that we wish to spend the evening by ourselves."

Cait gently withdrew from his arms. "Nay, Michael, I won't let you use me as an excuse not to meet with your brother."

"Kolby is more like my brother than Malcolm," Michael replied, his voice going hard.

"Aye, that is natural. You grew up with Kolby. But Malcolm is your birth brother, and the gods have seen fit to reunite you. For a reason, Michael."

Striding to the hearth, Michael threw more wood on the fire, and Cait lit the lamps. Then they did the same in the sleeping chamber, so that warmth and light soon pervaded the cottage. Glancing at the baggage, Michael saw the satchels that had fallen out of place when Lang had retrieved his. Michael picked up a small pouch. It was Cait's purse, the one he had taken from her when he had rescued her from Gilbert's men. Sitting down in the chair, he unfastened it and dumped Cait's daggers on the table.

They were small, exquisitely designed knives, the

blades bright and sharp. He touched his fingertip to several of them.

"Twenty." Cait sat in the chair opposite him.

"Five-and-ten." He picked up one of the knives and studied it. "You used one to cut your bonds, and four when you trussed me up and escaped."

"What did you do with them?" she asked.

"I decided that since you had given them to me, so to speak, they now belonged to me. I packed them with my own weapons."

"They're rather small for a man," she said. "I think you called them toys, lord."

Michael laughed. "I did, until the night you trussed me with them." He turned the dagger over in his hand and rubbed the blade with the pad of his thumb. " 'Twas your mother's last gift to you."

"Aye." Cait answered, surprised that he had remembered. She laid the purse on the table and ran her hands lovingly over it. "She spent so many hours working on it. Tanning the leather. Cutting the pieces and sewing them together. She and I spent days going through our treasure chest seeking the right jewels with which to adorn the purse." She touched the pale green peridot stones.

"My mother chose these so their powers would protect me and strengthen my mind. Even my talisman has the peridots."

Michael looked up. "Nay, it has the black jasper."

Cait touched the cloister amulet that lay beneath her tunic. She had almost given away her secret. Mayhap she could correct her mistake. "Aye, this one does," she answered. "My adopted father, Sholto, gave me this one. The one my parents made for me when I was a baby had peridot stones in it."

Leaning over, Michael inserted the flat side of the

blade under the gold chain and pulled out Cait's amulet.

"May I see it closer?" he asked.

She didn't want him to, but she knew it would be better not to make too much of his request or she would risk arousing his suspicion. She slipped the chain over her head and handed it to him.

He held the medallion, studying first one side, then the other. He ran his fingers over the intricate design. Then he turned it on its side. He ran his thumbnail lightly up and down it. He leaned over and held it closer to the fire.

"It has a latch," he said.

"Aye." Cait swallowed her dismay at his discovery. "It can be worn both as a necklace and a breast-pin."

Michael slid his thumbnail between the two pieces of gold. It clicked open, and he pulled out the pin and swiveled it around.

"This is ingenious," he said. "The Dryad—" He looked at Cait. "That is what you called the gold-smith who designed it?"

She nodded.

"Her workmanship is exquisite."

Cait grew more nervous by the second. She wanted her amulet back, but she didn't dare ask for it. She didn't want Michael to become any more curious than he already was.

"She—She is the High Priestess of the Grove," Cait said, her eyes never leaving the long, dexterous fingers that so gently handled the piece of jewelry. His hands fascinated her. "She always wears her cowled robe, the hood covering her head, and allows no one to look upon her face."

"Probably no one would want to," Michael murmured. "Usually these women who turn from men and dedicate themselves to the gods are ugly and repulsive and old."

Cait grew more uneasy when Michael shifted in the chair, leaned even closer to the fire, and studied the designs on the inside of the amulet. As he concentrated, his brows came together.

"I don't know whether she is ugly or repulsive, but she isn't old," Cait said. "Sholto says she is not much older than I am."

Michael relaxed and leaned back in the chair.

"Like me," Cait said, "she was raised in a cloister."

He looked up. "Can you read the *ogham* characters?"

Cait's heart skipped a beat. "Aye."

"Have you read this?" He pointed to the inscription.

She countered with, "Do you read the *ogham* characters?"

"Aye."

Staring at her, he snapped the amulet shut and rubbed it between his fingers for a long time. "Is this the sacred object that Gilbert accused you of having stolen from the cloister and taken out of Glenmuir?"

"Aye."

"Did you steal it?"

"Nay. My father entrusted it to me for safekeeping."

"From reading the inscription, I gather there are two of these pins, a matched pair. The Lydian Stone and the Bloodstone Breastpin."

"Aye." Worried, Cait chewed her lower lip. His steady gaze made her want to squirm.

"After reading the inscription, I understand why Gilbert wanted this amulet. It's the key to the riches of the cloister. With it you can locate the second

Breastpin. When you put both of the pins together, you have directions for finding the secret treasure chamber of the cloister."

She nodded. Cait had made love with Michael, had touched him in the most intimate way, but she didn't really know him. She didn't really trust him. His knowledge of the secret amulet frightened her. He was an admitted Northland sea raider.

"Have you seen the other Breastpin?" he asked.

"Nay."

Firelight flickered across his face as he stared at her. "I wonder if you're lying to me."

She shook her head.

"Have you ever been to the Gift Chamber?"

"Aye. My father took me there when he told me about the Breastpins, but I couldn't find my way back. He blindfolded me, and twisted me around through the passages until I became disoriented."

She omitted telling him about the Secret Chamber, where the treasure had been moved.

He extended his hand, the chain looped over a finger, the medallion glinting in the light.

"Please, my lord, return it to me and say nothing. Its secret belongs to the gods."

"Is Gilbert a god?"

"Nay."

"Yet he knows about the Breastpin."

"Knowledge of the Cloister Breastpins is kept within the priesthood," Cait explained. "But only the high priest, the Ancient of Nights and Days, possesses the Lydian Stone Breastpin. Only he knows where the other is hidden. My father believes one of the priests betrayed the cloister and told Gilbert about the pins." Cait realized that she had nothing to lose now by telling Michael the whole story—except for the existence of the Secret

Chamber. "My father thinks Gilbert and the sea raiders were accomplices. They killed the king and his family and tried to loot the cloister. Only they found nothing because the riches are hidden in the Gift Chamber. In order to get the treasure, Gilbert must have this amulet or he must force my father to take him to the Gift Chamber. Four days ago . . ."

It seemed so much longer than that.

"Four days ago the other Silver Daggers and I arrived at the cloister. That afternoon Dacy also arrived with news that sea raiders had attacked the village and that some of them were on their way to the cloister. He informed us that Gilbert and the High Council had declared me a traitor and an outlaw. I was forced to leave Glenmuir immediately, fleeing for my life. My father gave me the Breastpin and instructed me to come here to seek sanctuary and help." She paused and shrugged. "You know the rest of the story."

Michael lifted his tankard and took a swallow of wine. Holding it in his mouth, he savored the taste.

"This is a valuable amulet, my lady," he finally said.

"Aye," Cait answered, "and I've sworn to protect it with my life."

"Vows." Michael's gaze fastened on hers. "All of us are bound by vows, lady. You have sworn to die for that damnable shrine, and I because my father did not receive a certain number of filled treasure chests in place of a daughter-in-law. We are bound so completely by vows that they dictate our lives."

There was a knock on the door. In one graceful stretch of muscle, Ulf was on his feet, poised to defend.

"Lord Michael, may we enter?" came the call.

"We bring you gifts from the high king and queen of Northern Scotland."

"Ulf, sit," Michael said softly. The animal returned to his place beside his master. "Enter."

Cait heard the front door open. She felt the rush of cold air. "What are you going to do with the amulet?" she whispered.

"Lord," a masculine youth called, "where shall we put the trunks?"

"In there," Michael answered.

Cait anxiously awaited his answer.

"I need to give the matter thought," he told her.

"The bathing tub, sire . . ." The lad placed a hand on either side of the doorframe and peered into the sleeping chamber. "It will have to be put in here. It's much too large to go through this door."

Michael nodded. Against the noise of water splashing as it was poured into the tub, he said to Cait, "In the meantime, madam, I shall keep the Breastpin."

"It's mine."

"Nay, madam, presently it is mine."

"Please, my lord, don't speak to anyone about it."

"I'll give your request some thought."

With a heavy heart, Cait stared at Michael. The sacred Breastpin had been entrusted to her for safekeeping. Now Michael, a Northman, had claimed it.

Cait had failed to safeguard the amulet!

Michael rose and held out his hand. "Now, madam, let us see what the high king and his lady have sent to us."

Feich puttered about the cottage. She knew she should dress for the evening meal. Malcolm had insisted that she dine with them, and if she was not there, he would send a servant to get her. Long ago he had assumed responsibility for her care.

Feich chuckled. She loved the boy as if he were her grandson, and he returned that love. But sometimes he infuriated her. He could be suffocating in his love and was very much a benevolent dictator.

Standing by the table in her small cottage and tying together her latest crop of sacred herbs, she inhaled deeply. She loved the heavy scent of herbs and plants that permeated the room. Dried foods, strung together, hung from the ceiling. Feathers, which she used for magical talismans and in sacred potions, also fluttered from the ceiling beams. Vials of opaque liquids and soapstone lamps were arranged on the table. A fire burned in the center of the room, the flames encircling a huge, black caldron.

The brackish liquid in the caldron bubbled over, spitting and sputtering as it hit the burning wood. Feich hobbled across the room, dipped a long-handled spoon into the brew, and stirred. She looked down at a basket filled with red and white berries. Sitting down on her stool, she scooped a handful of the berries into her hand.

With her other hand she selected two white mistletoe berries and held them against the fire's glow. Each was symbolic of the seed of life of the man. One for the Wolf. One for the Horse. She selected two red holly berries, symbolic of the woman's monthly flux. One for Cait. One for Jarvia.

Aye, she thought sadly, especially one for Jarvia. She and Malcolm had Catriona, their adopted daughter, but no birth child. Jarvia was older than Cait, and childbearing would be hard, if not impossible, for her. She had lost the first child she had conceived from Malcolm. Feich knew how grieved both Jarvia and Malcolm had been and still were, how desperately Jarvia wanted to give Malcolm more children, especially a son to carry on his name.

Feich dropped first a white, then a red, berry into a small, clean caldron set in front of the fireplace on a square of blue material. Twined around the base of the pot were honeysuckles vines.

She gazed into the big caldron on the fire and invoked the gods ... to grant the gift of life to the Wolf and the Horse.

"Caldron, reveal to me that which I seek," she chanted. "Great Mother, open my inner eye that I may truly see."

She stared a long time, mumbling her prayers. She leaned closer. One. She squinted, counting once more. She ran her hand over the top of the liquid, cutting through the spiral of vapor. She gazed again into the bubbling brew. One. Two.

"Great Mother, thank you for giving me the answer."

She stirred the caldron and studied the swirling liquid once more. One. Two. Aye, she had counted correctly. There would be two babies, one for the Wolf and one for the Horse.

Chapter 16

The green headband, embroidered with yellow honeysuckle, complemented the rich red luster of Cait's hair. Having been trimmed and shaped by a barber, her russet-colored tresses waved gently around her face and brushed seductively against her shoulders.

The yellow tunic itself was low-cut, revealing the upper swells of her breasts. Her cloth girdle, green like the hair ribbon and laced with yellow ties, accented her small waist and full breasts. The soft, gauzy material emphasized her slender beauty.

Michael could hardly keep his eyes off her as they walked down the aisle of the Great Hall that evening. For the first time in his life, he wanted to sweep a woman off her feet and lock her away with him. He wanted to shut out the world and create a new one with no one in it but her and him.

"Oh, lord." Cait breathed the words in awe. "Look."

The room was ablaze. Light from soapstone oil lamps on the tables and hanging from the ceiling glimmered throughout the room. Caldron lamps, supported on three-pronged metal rods four hands high at the end of each table, added their glow.

In all directions leaping flames cast dancing shadows on walls draped with brightly colored and embroidered tapestries. The heat of these lamps along with the fire in the central hearth chased away the autumn chill outside.

Light gleamed on wrought-iron poles from which fluttered the banners of the many clans that had gathered to celebrate Malcolm Mac Duncan's coronation.

"The Great Hall at night with all the fires burning is a sight to behold," Cait said.

"You, my lady," Michael said, "are the most beautiful sight to behold."

Cait turned to look at him. "Thank you, my lord."

Long, curling lashes, darkened with berry juice, framed her luminous eyes. Russet flames danced in their golden depths. Her lips, also softly colored, trembled into a smile that tugged at Michael's heart.

"Generally," she said, "when I enter into a banquet hall like this, I am one of the entertainers."

"From now on, lady, your entertaining will be for me only."

The palm of her outstretched hand lay atop his. He observed the darkness of his skin against the ivory whiteness of hers. She was soft; he was hard. Her fingers were long and slender—a musician's hands. Her fingernails were oval and colored red.

"Ah, my lord, although I have thoroughly enjoyed *entertaining* you, I look forward to clearing up the misunderstanding about my being an outcast so that I am no longer your slave, so that I can choose whom I entertain."

Tilting her head and looking up at him, Cait grinned and blinked flirtatiously. For a moment, her lashes lay like a fan against her smooth cheeks; then she raised them and stared at him fully. Her eyes sparkled with devilment.

"You are most impertinent, lady."

"Aye, my lord, and you enjoy it."

He arched a brow, and she laughed.

"Nay, lady, I only tolerate your impertinence."

He fixed his gaze on the creamy expanse of her breasts revealed by the low-cut tunic. "Instead of supping at Malcolm's table, my lady, I would like to be supping at yours."

Although Cait's cheeks had been softly shaded with roan, they now flushed a vivid red. "You have an insatiable appetite, my lord."

"Aye, and you share it," he teased.

This time Cait arched a brow, and Michael laughed.

"If I remember correctly, lady, you were the one who—"

"My lord—" her cheeks turned a rosy pink "—surely such talk should be done in private!"

"When I have you in private, my lady," Michael said, only then realizing how loud his voice sounded. He lowered it, and looked around as he finished his sentence. "My mind is on matters other than talk."

Whispering, Cait said, "The hall is suddenly quiet."

"Aye."

Both of them studied the crowd of people gathered in the Great Hall. They were sitting at the tables, their heads turning back and forth between Michael and Malcolm.

Some of the people shook their heads in confusion; others frowned; a few just stared. All contemplated. Michael understood their disbelief, their astonishment. Had he not experienced it himself?

"They look so much alike, I can't tell the difference." The whispered words reached his ears.

"And he's wearing clothes just like Malcolm's," another said.

Cait stifled a giggle, and Michael looked at her, both of them aware that he was, indeed, wearing Malcolm's clothes.

"You have given the people quite a turn," Cait said softly.

"Not nearly the turn Malcolm gave me. I should have worn my own clothing."

"Nay, my lord. You look handsome."

And he did. His dark hair was pulled back at the nape of his neck and bound with a blue ribbon. He wore a mantle of midnight blue, decorated in silver floss, with a light blue shirt and darker blue trousers. His boots were black, as was his leathern girdle and the gloves he had tucked in it.

"By the blessed mother!" someone exclaimed. "Look at Malcolm."

Cait and Michael looked toward the High Seat. Malcolm, also wearing blue, had pulled his hair back and tied it with a leathern thong. The two men could not have been more similarly dressed if they had planned it. Both were darkly handsome, their faces a study in rugged angles and planes. Though freshly shaven, their jaws were shadowed because of their heavy beards. Their eyes reflected the deep blue of night.

"Lord Michael Langssonn and Lady Cait nea Sholto," Malcolm said. He waved them to the nearby settle. "Welcome to the Great Hall and to the table of Malcolm mac Duncan. It is our honor to share the evening meal with you. Please be seated in the place of honor."

"Thank you, my lord." Michael guided Cait to the chair.

He looked around to see his father sitting at a table of honor next to Queen Mother Muireall. Then Michael swept his gaze over the Great Hall. As earlier in the day, the room and its furnishings were resplendent. The precious metals and jewels that bedecked the dishes glittered in the light. Servants scurried back and forth from the kitchen, carrying trays laden with platters of food and pitchers of ale. Smoke spiraled to the ceiling from the central hearth and escaped through the thatched roof. The aroma of cooking food permeated the room.

Brian rose. "People of Northern Scotland, today our high king, Malcolm mac Duncan, performed the Dance of the Sword without touching either of the swords."

Cheering, clapping, and stomping reverberated through the hall.

"Tomorrow evening we celebrate his acceptance of the High Seat of Northern Scotland with the coronation feast. Malcolm mac Duncan invites all of you to attend."

More cheering followed.

Finally Malcolm stood and quieted the crowd. "People of Northern Scotland, I'm sure rumors have been flying throughout the village—throughout the entire kingdom—with the news of Lord Michael Langssonn's arrival."

"Aye," many called out; others nodded.

"I knew I had an older brother, but I thought he was killed in a raid thirty winters past. Today I learned that my older brother is indeed alive and that we are identical twins." Malcolm turned to Michael. "My lord, would you stand beside me?"

Michael rose and moved to his brother's side. People craned their necks to see. Some rose and moved closer; they squinted and walked around them. They mumbled and nodded their heads. Finally they returned to their seats.

"As you can see," Malcolm said dryly, "we look very much alike."

Quietly he told them the story of his and Michael's separation at birth and the reason for Michael's presence in Northern Scotland now. As he concluded, a clan chief rose.

Malcolm acknowledged him. "Scully."

"What about the challenge between you and the Northman?"

"That has been postponed," Malcolm said.

"Because he is your brother?"

"Nay, because he has consented to give me time to find the person who stole the rupture-endowment."

"He believes you are innocent?" Scully asked.

"Lord Michael will have to answer that," Malcolm replied.

"I am willing to give Malcolm time to prove his innocence," Michael said.

Similar questions rose from all sides of the room. Malcolm and Michael listened carefully and answered calmly. Many people rose and gave verbal support of their king. Others complimented Michael on his public renunciation of heirship to the kingdom of Northern Scotland. When all were satisfied, they began to relax. The ale, mead, and wine flowed freely. Soon laughter replaced the long faces. Musicians began to entertain. The Scottish bard sang songs of valor about Malcolm mac Duncan. The Northland skald sang the same about Michael Langssonn.

As was the custom, Malcolm rose, his tankard of wine in his hand. "People of Northern Scotland—" he began, but Queen Muireall rose, interrupting.

"My lord high king, may I please have the honor of the first toast?"

Surprised, Malcolm nodded.

"My lords and ladies, all you people of Northern Scotland," the queen mother said, her deep and husky voice sounding throughout the Great Hall, "I wish to lift my glass of wine in thanks to the gods for having saved my oldest son, Michael Langssonn, and for having reunited him with his brother, High King Malcolm mac Duncan."

"Hear! Hear!" Lang rose and raised his tankard. "May the gods bless the two brothers, Lord Michael Langssonn and High King Malcolm mac Duncan."

Throughout the hall, beakers, tankards, and drinking horns were thrust into the air ... all but two. Neither Michael nor Malcolm lifted theirs. Muireall willed her sons to join in the salute. Lang scowled at them. Michael and Malcolm looked at each other.

Cait caught her breath as, once more, tension stretched across the room. Then as if by unspoken communication, both warlords reached for their tankards—one with his right hand, the other with his left—and swung them into the air. Cait and the people sighed their relief.

Toast after toast was made. Cait noticed that neither Malcolm nor Michael drank much, though each ate heartily.

Several hours later, Cait, along with everyone else, was in a festive mood. Their stomachs filled with succulent food, they freely imbibed the imported wine. Although she and Michael did not participate in the games, she enjoyed watching them. Many of the warriors arm-wrestled; others played table games, and still others were content to sit and gossip ... until the musicians struck up a

lively tune. Quickly tables and benches were
scooted to the walls, the center of the room left
open for dancing.

"We Highlanders love to dance," Cait explained
to Michael in a low voice.

Then all began clapping their hands and chanting
the same phrase over and over. The chant was unfamiliar to Michael.

"They are asking you to do the honor of opening
the dance," Cait said. " 'Tis customary for guests to
dance first."

"Nay," Michael said.

"Don't decline, lord," Cait said. " 'Twill be taken
as an insult."

"Your Highland flings are too complicated, and I
don't know the steps. I remember only too well the
steps Malcolm danced earlier in the day. You Highlanders may call it dancing, but I call it punishment."

Cait laughed as she said in an undertone, "Make
up your own dance."

"Lady—" he scowled at her "—I would probably
cut my legs off if I began to cavort around two unsheathed and sharpened swords like Malcolm did
today."

"You jest, lord."

"Aye." His expression softened. "Mayhap it is not
so dangerous, but if I were to do it, my lady, it
would be humiliating."

"They don't expect you to do our dance, lord.
Surely you Northmen have your own dances?"

"Aye, Northmen dance," Michael answered,
speaking louder than he intended, "but not I."

"Then, *older brother*," Malcolm spoke up, "I shall
do so for you."

People shouted, clapped, and stamped their feet

in approval of their king. Malcolm rose as the musicians began to play. The haunting wail of the pipes filled the room. Michael watched a second time as his brother danced.

"Michael—" Cait leaned over and whispered.

He touched his finger to his lip. "Shh."

Cait drew back and noticed that he was listening attentively to the music with his eyes closed. When the dance was finished, Jarvia flew into Malcolm's outstretched arms. He kissed her soundly, then swung her into the air. Cait felt a twinge of jealousy as she watched Jarvia and Malcolm together. They seemed so happy and in love.

Again the people filled the building with cheers, laughter, and clapping. Breathing deeply, laughing with the people, Malcolm clapped his men on the back and hugged the women as he passed them on his return to the High Seat.

"My lord Malcolm," Michael said when his brother was settled, "I understand that you Gaels appreciate your dancers."

Ayes sounded from around the room.

"Surely they ought to appreciate you, my lord Malcolm. You cut a fine figure on the dance floor." Michael stepped off the dais and walked to the musicians who sat in a cluster near Queen Muireall's table. "Are you Gaels as appreciative of your musicians?"

Another chorus of ayes rang out. Hands slapped the table; feet pounded the floor; weapons clanged.

"May I borrow your flute?" Michael asked one of the musicians.

Surprised, Cait could only stare. So did the flutist. Cait had no idea that Michael could play the flute.

Michael repeated his question, and the musician

handed the instrument to the Northman. All celebration ceased.

"Younger brother," Michael said, "I shall learn the steps to your Highland fling and soon shall be a better dancer than you."

Malcolm laughed. "Shall we make a wager?"

"Aye, I always believe in wagering on a sure thing."

"I want the wolf," Malcolm said.

"I want your studhorse."

"Done."

The flute in one hand, Michael returned to the dais. He and Malcolm slapped their hands together to seal their wager.

Malcolm and Jarvia returned to their seats; Michael remained standing. Putting the flute to his mouth, he began to play the tune to which Malcolm had recently danced. Cait was lost to the beauty of the melody and the sweetness of the tones. Michael was an accomplished musician.

Cait rose and moved to the center of the building. She bowed low, then once more giving herself up to the music, began to dance. An "ah" of astonishment and admiration hummed through the room. The other musicians began to play softly in accompaniment.

The people watched in rapt silence. When the last note died out, when Cait twirled around for the last time, there was a moment of appreciative silence before the building exploded with shouting and clapping and stomping.

Michael caught Cait's hand. "Madam, you dance beautifully."

"You play beautifully, my lord." She smiled. "As you said earlier, Michael, we have many things in common."

Michael returned her smile, then led her to the guest settle. He held the flute out to Malcolm. "Can you play the tune?"

"Nay." Malcolm frowned.

Michael smiled. "Then, younger brother, for the time being, we are even."

"Aye," Malcolm drawled, "for the time being." He rose. "Now, everyone, let's dance!"

Settling back in the guest chair, Michael watched the merrymaking. After a while, he leaned over to Cait. " 'Tis time for us to bid our host good evening."

Cait caught her yawn with her hand. "Aye, lord."

Before they could rise, one of Malcolm's warriors entered the Great Hall. Looking wild and barbaric, he wore fur trousers and a vest. A wide band tied around his forehead held his long hair in place. A thin braid fell across one shoulder. "Hail, Malcolm."

"Finn."

The man strode down the central aisle, coming to an abrupt halt when he saw Michael sitting on the guest settle. He stared at him; he stared back at Malcolm.

"My lord Michael Langssonn," Malcolm said, "may I introduce you to my master herdsman, Finn mac Duncan."

"The Northman?" the warrior asked.

"Aye. 'Tis a long story, Finn," Malcolm said. "Others shall tell you about it. Join us for the evening meal."

"Thank you, my liege, I will," Finn replied, "but first I must give you bad news. Raiders have stolen your cattle herd."

"The cattle!" Malcolm exclaimed, his angry cry echoing over the room.

Brian mac Logan leaped to his feet and joined Malcolm on the dais.

" 'Tis quite serious," Cait said to Michael. "In the Highlands wealth and might are determined by the size and health of a man's cattle herds. Sustenance depends on them, as does the favor of the gods."

"Two herdsmen are dead, another is fatally injured," Finn reported.

"Could you tell who the raiders were?"

"I think they spoke an Athdarian dialect."

"How many were there?" Malcolm asked.

" 'Twas a large raiding party, sire. No less than twenty."

"They have heard of Fergus's death," Brian said, "and are trying our strength."

"I shall take care of this, Finn," Malcolm said. "You refresh yourself."

" 'Tis dark outside, Malcolm," the herdsman said. "It might serve us well to wait until early morn before we start tracking them."

"Nay, they'll have too great a head start on us, and if they get our cattle over the border, we may never see them again." As the herdsman moved to one of the long tables, Malcolm shouted, "All of you enjoy the feast. I shall gather the cattle and return shortly. And I shall be here with our cattle to celebrate the coronation feast tomorrow night."

Ayes sounded from all sides.

All over the building, warriors were rising and moving toward the door.

"Brian," Malcolm said, "choose ten warriors to go with us."

"Ten?" the best-man questioned.

"Aye. Have you forgotten that Lachlann has many of our warriors with him, leaving us short-numbered? Besides that, our borders are too insecure, and I can't risk leaving the villagers and surrounding farmers unprotected. I shall be ready to ride—"

"Nay, Malcolm," Brian said. "Let us take care of this."

"Nay, 'tis my responsibility. I am the high king."

"That is why you shouldn't go," Brian said. "We cannot afford to lose our king."

"Malcolm must go," Michael said, "and I shall go with him."

The two warlords stared at each other.

"I have twenty warriors who will also ride with you," Michael said.

Lang rose. "Make that one-and-twenty, my son."

Muireall clasped Lang's hand.

"Father," Michael said, "it would be better if you remained here as Malcolm's best-man."

Malcolm looked from Michael to Lang, then back to Michael. Finally he nodded, "So be it."

Feich had moved to stand behind Cait. "Ah, so be it," she mumbled. "The Horse and the Wolf shall unite in brotherhood."

"Have you seen Ulf?" Michael asked as he rode the stallion close to the porch of the Great Hall where Cait stood.

"Nay," she answered. "I thought he was with you."

Michael shook his head. "I haven't seen him for a while."

"Michael," Malcolm called, "are you and your men ready?"

"Aye."

Michael leaned down, grabbed Cait around the waist, and lifted her up. "I'll be back soon, lady."

He gave her a long and thoroughly satisfying kiss, then set her down.

Cait watched him as he joined Malcolm and the men in front of the Small Hall. Although the glimmering light of the torches cast him in dark shadows and the helmet distorted his features, Cait no longer feared the Northman. He smiled, and she knew it was for her. She returned the gesture. To make sure he was looking at her, Cait tested him. She waved. He waited a moment, then waved back.

Cait stared as the army, a blending of Northmen and Scots, rode out of the village. Her heart swelled with pride as she watched Michael fade into the darkness. He was a warrior. He was a warlord. More, he was the man she loved with all her heart.

Michael looked over his shoulder one more time to see Cait, illuminated by torchlight, standing on the porch of the Great Hall. She was too far away for him to make out her features, but he recognized the color of her tunic and the blaze of short red hair that framed her face.

They were in a spill of moonlight outside the village wall when Malcolm spoke. "They have the ability to wiggle their way into our lives, then into our hearts, without our being aware of it."

Michael glanced over at him.

"Women." Malcolm answered the unasked question. "I married Jarvia to have a son in order to assure a peace agreement between us and a kingdom farther north. Before I quite realized it, I was doing things for her that I wouldn't do for any other person."

"Aye," Michael said. "I have already been doing that for Cait, and I only lust for her."

Malcolm guffawed. "I hid behind those words also. In the name of lust, Michael, I broke so many of our tribal customs that I cannot enumerate them. But one day I finally admitted that I loved Jarvia."

"Is the child hers by her prior marriage?"

"Nay, 'tis an orphan she found abandoned. We rescued and adopted her. She is Catriona, our daughter. And so far our only child."

"You and Jarvia are happy?"

"Aye," Malcolm answered. "Jarvia is my life."

"And you are hers," Michael replied. "She was willing to give her life for you when she went into the Chamber of Fire."

Malcolm nodded. "Someone told you about it?"

Michael hesitated, then said, "I dreamed about it."

"You have the dreams, too?" Malcolm asked.

"Aye. I recognized the hill when we rode past it today."

" 'Twas a painful experience."

"I felt your pain."

Malcolm said, "I often dream of being on a ship." Michael was surprised at how accurately he described the *Sea Wolf*.

"I have one recurring dream in which I am two warriors, fighting side by side," Malcolm said. "One is right-handed, the other left. Then they merge together to become one."

"Aye," Michael admitted, "I have had that same dream. All my life I have wondered how I could be both right- and left-handed. All the while we were dreaming of each other."

"Aye. Always I felt there was something missing in my life, a part of me that wasn't there."

"Today," Michael said, "when I saw you standing at the door, garbed in your mail and helmet, I felt as if I were going to merge with you, as if the dream were finally becoming reality. I had never met you, but I knew you."

"That's the way I felt when you walked up to the dais," Malcolm confessed.

As the brothers talked, they learned that they shared other common dreams. Malcolm had had a vision in which he received the silver torque as his symbol of heirship; Michael had dreamed of receiving the gold torque. Michael had dreamed about Malcolm rescuing Jarvia from the Chamber of Fire. Malcolm had dreamed about Michael's battle with the boar and his rescue by the wolf.

On and on they rode, following the herdsman several lengths ahead of them, talking about their childhoods, comparing their lives, and discovering that they had had many similar experiences. They attained warriorhood at the same age. Both of them could read and write and speak several languages. Each had been given a sickle ring. Even now, their hair was the same length and they combed it alike. Their taste in clothing was similar.

At the same moment both of them stopped talking. Malcolm ordered the company to halt. He listened, as did Michael.

"I hope this is my outrider," Malcolm said. "I sent him out as soon as Finn gave us the news."

Malcolm waved the men off the trail into the shadows of the boulders. "The moonlight is bright enough for us to see and to be seen," Malcolm said to the men. "The most important thing is to get our cattle back. Once we have them, then we can handle the Athdarians."

Tensely all awaited the return of the outrider. A small black dot in the distance grew until it became a man. Malcolm rode out to meet him. The rider came to an abrupt stop. Michael, Brian, and Kolby fanned out around him.

"Athdarians?" Malcolm asked.

Nodding, the rider said, "I think so. But it's odd. One group of about two-and-twenty are moving the cattle to the river. Two riders separated from them and took the trail above Acorn Ridge, heading northwest."

"That's one of the most remote areas of Athdara," Brian said. "No one goes that way unless they're in a hurry to reach Glenmuir."

Through the silver haze Malcolm glanced over at Michael, then said, "Brian, take the men and go after the cattle. Michael and I shall follow the two riders."

Michael and Malcolm galloped away from the rest of the men. When they reached Acorn Ridge, Malcolm guided them into a copse of trees out of moonlight. He slid off the black stallion and opened the riding satchel, from which he withdrew a wad of leathern squares. He kept half of them and gave the others to Michael.

"Fold these so they are doubly thick, then tie them around the ponies' hooves," he said. "It'll keep anyone from knowing that we're following until we're almost upon them, and it'll make our trail harder to follow. Where's that wolf of yours?" Malcolm asked. "We could make good use of him tonight."

"I don't know," Michael answered. "He was in the cottage when Cait and I left for the evening meal, but when I returned to put on my mail, he was gone."

Soon they were riding again, the clop of hooves muffled by the padding. Malcolm stopped intermittently to search for hoofprints of the riders they followed.

The last time he stopped, he said, "It seems they're staying on the trail. I don't think they have any idea that we're following them."

As they rode again, Michael said, "Brian told me about your relay system. He said your ponies are the fastest in the Highlands."

"Aye," Malcolm agreed. "And the sturdiest, with a high rate of endurance. My riders are also highly skilled. I believe that ponies will soon be an important part of our lives, in peacetime as well as in war. I'm so sure of it that I've begun specially breeding my ponies."

In low tones Malcolm talked to him about the ponies until they topped a hill and saw two riders silhouetted in the small gully below. Quickly they moved into the shadows. As they discussed the different strategies they could use to apprehend the men, Michael wished Ulf were with him. He hadn't realized how much he had come to depend on the wolf. Finally Malcolm and Michael decided that each would circle around the riders from opposite directions and meet in front of them.

Swinging wide, Michael cautiously rode through the stand of trees. In the clearing ahead he saw the two riders. They were moving at a leisurely pace, talking in low voices. Michael couldn't see Malcolm, but he felt his presence. Not revealing himself, Malcolm called out, "In the name of Malcolm, high king of Northern Scotland, I command you to halt."

The men pulled their horses to a stop.

His sword drawn, Malcolm rode out of the shadows from one side, Michael from the other.

"Who are you?" Malcolm asked.

"Glenmuirians," one of the men answered. "I'm Gerce. He's Dall."

"Who is your liege?"

"King Gilbert."

"You look familiar," Malcolm said to one of them, squinting in the moonlight. He rode closer. "I know you. You used to ride with Ghaltair."

The man kicked his pony and galloped between Michael and Malcolm. As quickly, Malcolm was after him. The other man whipped out his sword and attacked Michael.

The clash of steel sounded as Michael and the Glenmuirian fought. Michael gave him blow for blow—hard, swift, sharp—until finally he pierced the man through the chest. The wounded man screamed with pain and toppled off his pony. Michael leaped down and knelt over him.

"What were you doing here in Northern Scotland?"

The man coughed, blood dribbling from his mouth.

"Stealing cattle?" Michael asked.

"Nay. 'Twas Athdarians. We just happened upon them as we were riding toward the king's village. When we realized they had stolen the cattle, we separated from them. We wanted no part of thievery and were returning to Glenmuir." He talked falteringly. "We were looking for two outlaws who escaped from Glenmuir. We lost their trail in Athdara and thought maybe they had come here."

"Did you find them?" Michael asked.

The man shook his head.

"Would they happen to be priests?"

The man winced, coughed, then went limp. He was dead.

Malcolm had not returned, and Michael could not

see or hear him. He mounted and galloped after him. When he found him, he was standing over the second warrior. Michael dismounted and joined his brother.

"Are you all right?" he asked.

"Aye."

"How about him?"

"Dead," Malcolm said.

"The other one talked," Michael said. "They are Gilbert's men, searching for two escaped outlaws."

"This one was a friend of Ghaltair, a Scots warrior who was banished from Northern Scotland six seasons ago for conspiracy." Malcolm straightened. "Do you think the men they hunted are priests from the shrine?"

"I wondered," Michael replied.

Then Michael heard a scuffling noise behind Malcolm. Michael touched Malcolm on the shoulder and pressed a finger against his mouth for silence. An inner sense told him that someone was out there, spying on them.

He closed his eyes and concentrated as his father had taught him to when he was a child. *Be still and listen,* Lang had said when he blindfolded Michael. *An inner voice, an inner sight, will guide you.*

As if Malcolm also felt the presence, as if he knew what Michael was doing, he didn't move.

Relaxing, giving himself up to his inner spirit, Michael focused. He listened. Then he heard the faint rustle of material, of leather stepping softly on a rocky surface. Someone was moving. He knew where the person was. He waited ... calmly ... patiently, just as Lang had instructed.

"I know you're out there," Michael said quietly. "If you're a friend of Malcolm mac Duncan, show yourself. If not, I'll kill you."

Michael slid his hand into his girdle and pulled out Cait's daggers.

"Lie down flat on the ground," he whispered to Malcolm.

From the corner of his eye, Michael saw the shadow, and he threw the first dagger. He heard footfalls and an answering whine in the air. He dove, tucked, and rolled. He threw the second dagger.

Lying still, he listened. He heard nothing but the mournful soughing of the wind, the rustle of the grass and the falling leaves.

"It's over," he announced. He moved to the fire, picked up the torch, and walked to where he thought the other person lay.

The light played over a sprawled figure, a man with two daggers in his chest. Beside his hand lay his dagger. Michael squatted next to him. Malcolm stood over them.

"This is one of the men who sold Cait to me," he announced. "He's also one of Gilbert's men."

"You're good at blind fighting," Malcolm said.

"My father taught me. Kolby and I spent more time training in a blindfold than we did without. We were taught to rely on other senses besides sight."

"I'm glad you were fighting with me and not against me," Malcolm said.

"Me, too."

Michael and Malcolm wrapped the three bodies in blankets, tossed them over the stallions, and walked back to the village. They arrived early the next morning. After ordering a servant to bury the bodies, Malcolm and Michael went to the Great Hall, where Jarvia and Cait greeted them. The women listened as Michael and Malcolm told them what had happened.

"Perhaps it was two Silver Daggers who escaped," Cait said, taking hope. "Maybe Rob was one of them."

"Aye," Michael said. "I thought of that myself."

Not long afterward the other warriors returned. Brian reported that the cattle had been found and reclaimed and were now safely fenced in. The Athdarians had fled across the border.

As they good-naturedly swapped stories of their adventures, with Malcolm exclaiming over Michael's blind fighting and teasing him about his toy daggers, they all ate a hearty breakfast. When the Scots learned that Kolby was as skilled in blind fighting as Michael, they set up some jousts.

Later, Lang and Muireall joined them, and the stories were repeated.

When the Christain high priest entered the Great Hall, Michael refused to stay for a third retelling, although the stories were getting more interesting with each repetition.

"I've had an eventful night," Michael said. "Now I'm going to the cottage to sleep for a while."

Kolby grinned. "You're planning to sleep, Michael?"

Cait blushed, and Michael grinned back at his friend. "Aye, Kolby, I am going to sleep." To Cait he said, "Why don't you stay longer and visit with Jarvia and Queen Muireall."

"I would like to do that," Cait replied. "I want to know your sister-in-law and your mother better."

"Perhaps, Michael," Muireall said, "you and I can visit sometime. I would like to get better acquainted."

"Aye, my lady queen," he said. "We shall do that."

As Michael returned to the cottage, he pondered what Gilbert's men had said and hoped for Cait's sake that her cousin had escaped. Every now and then he strayed from the path as he looked for Ulf. He didn't see any signs of the wolf. When he entered the cottage, he stripped down to his trousers and fell across the bed. He lay there, still thinking about Cait.

He had feared for her safety, especially when the men had said they were looking for two outlaws. He had wondered if they were really looking for Cait.

He desired Cait and wanted her with him. Perhaps he could persuade her to leave with him when he had completed his mission. They shared a love of travel and could be together until the need for letching passed.

Then again, he wondered if perhaps he should escort her back to Glenmuir.

Dawn was but a hint of gray on the horizon as Ardac, master of Gilbert's men, paced anxiously in a copse of trees. Two of the cloister priests, Sholto and Trevor, had escaped and were making their way to Northern Scotland. The cloister informant had told Gilbert which route the priests were likely to take. Age kept both men from traveling fast, but Sholto was moving even slower. The beating he had suffered at the hands of Gilbert's men had crippled him.

Ardac and his men had had no difficulty in following them to the border between Athdara and Northern Scotland, but here on the banks of the river between the two kingdoms, they had lost them. Ardac had immediately sent four men across the river into Northern Scotland to look for signs of the priests. The men had ridden off yesterday at noon and had not returned.

Ardac was worried.

He paced some more.

Then he saw a dark blur in the distance. More daylight? He wasn't sure. But as he gazed, it seemed to be coming nearer. His men, perhaps. He took several steps and peered more intently into the waning darkness.

Aye, it was a rider. One rider. What had happened? Maybe nothing. Ern was young and always outrode the others. The blur took on a man's figure. Then features began to distinguish themselves. It was Ern.

The pony galloped across the river, and Ern came to a halt in front of Ardac. He slid to the ground. "They're dead. All of them."

"The priests? Our men? Who?"

"Ours," Ern said. "We didn't find any sign of the priests."

"What happened?"

"We encountered an Athdarian raiding party. High King Fergus has died, and his son, Malcolm mac Duncan, has become the new high king. The Athdarians decided this would be a good time to steal Scottish cattle. The four of us rode away from them, and later we separated. We agreed to meet back at a ridge close to the border.

"Ongus and I returned to the ridge first. The others were followed by two of Malcolm mac Duncan's men. The Duncan men killed both of ours. Then one of them seemed to know that Ongus and I were hidden out there. He called for us to surrender.

Ongus was going to sneak up on him in the dark, but the man—"

Ern wiped his hand down his trouser leg.

"Ardac, I swear the man can see in the dark. He whirled around, and before I knew what had happened, Ongus was dead and they were hunkering over him. They wrapped the bodies in blankets and carried them off. I stayed hidden for a long time, making sure they were gone."

Ardac rubbed his hand over the scar that slashed his cheek. "I hate to make this report to Gilbert. He'll be furious at us for letting the priests slip through our hands, especially after the cloister informant told us which trail they would be taking and where they were going."

"We don't need to worry, Ardac," Ern said. "Sholto won't live much longer. You have almost tortured him to death."

"Did you talk with any of the Duncan people?"

"Nay, most of them are in Malcolm's village. The coronation feast will take place tonight."

"So we have learned nothing of Cait or her father." Ardac turned to the younger man. "Ern, I need you to stay in Duncan Territory."

"But, Ardac, Malcolm recognized Dall. He might recognize me too."

"Nay. In the past six seasons you have changed a great deal. Besides, you'll stay away from the village. Visit the farmsteaders and the herdsmen. Keep your eyes and ears open. Learn anything you can. Ralf will stay at the king's village in Athdara. Report what you know to him, and he will send word to me."

Both men mounted. Ardac rode deeper into Athdara Territory; the younger man crossed over the river into Duncan Territory.

Chapter 17

～⌒○○⌒～

Sunlight poured into the room through the open window. Michael, lying on the bed, his eyes still closed, heard Cait humming in the other room. Pushing off the bed, he went to the door. Clad in her long undertunic, she was delving through the trunks Jarvia and Malcolm had sent to them. When she saw him, she rose.

"Did you finally decide to get up?" she asked.

He raked a hand through his hair. "Did you miss me?"

"Aye."

He moved around the bathtub and caught her in his arms. "I missed sleeping with you. Do you realize that this is the first night out of five that I haven't slept with you?"

"Aye, lord, I thought about it."

Michael gave her a quick kiss. "What have you been doing all day?"

"Helping Jarvia and your mother prepare for the coronation banquet tonight."

Michael breathed in deeply. "Aye, that's right. We have to attend."

"Aye, we do," she murmured, seeking his mouth, hungering for his kisses.

Michael's mouth slanted over hers, moving gently, his lips molding themselves to hers, his hand running down her back to cup her hips. He pulled her against him.

Passion, as hot as any liquid that ever boiled in a caldron, as potent as any medicine ever concocted, flowed through Cait's body. She wrapped her arms around Michael, wishing she could pull him into herself.

Michael's mouth gently tugged. It teased. It gave. It took.

"The bed," he said, his voice thick.

"We can't."

"Why?"

Michael rained light kisses from her mouth to her cheek, then down the slender column of her throat and back up to her ears. His tongue explored each tender curve and hollow, while his fingers blazed a hot trail down her back to her hips. Just a little pressure from his hands, a slight movement of his hips, and Cait began to arch toward him, an intense, aching need rekindled in her lower body.

"It is well past midday," she whispered.

"I like mating during the daytime. So will you."

"Festivities have already begun."

"Aye, my lady."

Cait rubbed her hands over his muscled shoulders. "We must go, Michael. Lang and Malcolm have planned for you and Kolby to entertain with your blind fighting."

Michael pulled back.

She laughed at his expression. "Aye, lord, they schemed while you slept."

Reluctantly she withdrew from his embrace. "I'll need time to find us some presentable clothing to wear, and I also have to press the wrinkles out."

"Ah," Michael drawled, "I'll have to don more of

my brother's clothes so that people can make remarks about them."

"They look good on Malcolm, I'm sure," Cait said, "but they look better on you."

He flashed her a wide grin.

Michael opened one of the trunks that was filled with men's clothing. He held up a shirt, measuring it from shoulder to shoulder. "Yesterday, Cait, you wanted to know how I felt about Jarvia."

"Aye."

"I think she is a beautiful woman and a good wife. For Malcolm. Even if I should have to fight to the death with him, and should I be the victor, I will release the lady from her betrothal to me."

Her heart thudding, happiness singing through her veins, Cait held a brown tunic against her chest. "Why, lord?"

"I am going to wed you."

Cait couldn't contain her smile. "You want to wed me, Michael?"

"Aye. Tonight after we sup, I shall rectify the disservice I have done to you," he said. "I shall announce our marriage."

Cait's happiness dissipated. She stared at him in disbelief. "Disservice," she mumbled.

"Aye, Cait," Michael said. "In a moment of weakness, I used you, and I'm prepared to offer you marriage."

Anger quickly replaced disappointment, flowing hot and heavy through her. "I'm not prepared to accept your *generous offer*, my lord."

He spoke quietly, like a parent to a child. "Cait, because of me you have lost your innocence."

His blue eyes were veiled. Last night making love to her, he had revealed a wonderful, caring side of himself. Now he had withdrawn and was hiding behind that damnable invisible shield. Cait saw no more than the beautiful color of his eyes, no more than he was willing to reveal.

She looked down at the clothing in the trunk. "You have no other reason for marrying me?" she asked.

"Is having wronged you not reason enough?"

She faced him. "Nay, my lord, for a verity, it is not. You have taken nothing from me. I mated with you because I wanted to. I freely gave myself as a gift to you. I took you into me as a gift for myself. Both of us were in equal need, my lord." Hurting deeply, Cait railed against him. "I also mated with you because ..."

"Because ...?" he prompted. Something about the steely quiet of his voice drew her eyes to his once more. Their softness and warmth were gone; they were sharp and cutting.

"I was curious about carnality shared between a man and a woman."

"I see." He turned his attention to his own clothing. After carefully folding the garments he had selected, Michael laid them over the top of the raised trunk lid. He pressed out the wrinkles. "I should not have mated with you, Cait. I shouldn't have taken your virginity. At the time I had no intention of asking you to be my wife." His voice trailed into silence. "I am a warlord, but not a man who takes a lady's virtue."

Cait could hardly compose herself. Yet she refused to let Michael see how deeply he was hurting her. "Lord, I feel no guilt over what we did. If you do, and if you feel you must absolve yourself of it, you must go to the gods. I can't do it for you. Even if I could, I wouldn't."

His voice sharpened with exasperation. "Madam,

from the very beginning your temperament has puzzled and irritated me."

"My lord, if it will make you feel better, I appreciate your wanting to marry me, but I don't need marriage. And I won't accept it under these conditions."

"Madam, you might already be with child. My child. I *will not* let you and my child be harassed because you are unwed."

"Thank you for caring, Michael," Cait said. "If I have conceived, I shall be happy. You are indeed a courageous warrior, a fitting father for my child. But you need not be concerned about me or the baby. Here in the Highlands, children are welcome. Our people do not vilify an unwed mother or her child. Our lineage is traced through the mother, because we can be sure of her bloodline."

"Lady, I do not understand your customs, but I do understand mine. In the Northland a warrior does not take his duties lightly, nor does he forsake his children."

"I care not what a warrior does. I shall marry no man out of duty."

"You will marry me out of duty, Cait nea Sholto." His voice blazed with anger.

"You may marry, my lord, but not me."

"You, if you conceive my child," he insisted. "I want it to go by my name. *My child* shall know whose blood flows through its veins."

The child. Michael wanted to marry her because of the child. While Cait appreciated that he felt such an obligation to his offspring, she felt a keen sense of loss that he did not have as intense a feeling for her.

"Lord, I esteem your sense of duty. I, too, owe such allegiance to the Shelter Stone. But when it comes to marriage, I want love. My mother and my father loved each other deeply. I won't settle for a marriage that offers less than they had." She paused. "I am honored that you wish to do what you consider the respectable thing, but I do not wish to marry you. When I decide it is time for me to wed, lord, I shall find my own husband."

Michael's face was drawn in hard, implacable lines. His eyes turned sharp. "If you are with my child, madam, you shall marry me."

Although she was inwardly shaking, Cait bent over the trunk and once more searched for a tunic to wear. She truly cared for Michael and would consider becoming his wife if he felt any tenderness for her. And at times she felt that he did care for her. But he always reverted back to the hard, cold Northland warrior.

Michael was here in the Highlands for one reason, revenge. He had mated with her for one reason, lust. Neither of these bespoke of a permanent relationship between them. Cait's loyalty was to Glenmuir; Michael's was to the people of the Northland.

She pulled out a tunic and straightened. "Lord, have you decided what you're going to do with the Breastpin?"

"There is no need to hurry a decision," he answered. "I have promised Malcolm time to investigate his claim."

Desperation surged through Cait. There *was* a need to hurry. Time was running out for Glenmuir. For Rob. For Sholto. She had explained, she had begged, but could convince no one of the seriousness of her kingdom's plight.

"My lord, please listen to me. My father . . . the kingdom . . . the cloister, all of these are in grave danger. Surely in light of what happened last night, you realize this. If you wish to atone for having taken my innocence, escort me back to Glenmuir."

"I told you once, lady, that I don't wish to become embroiled in local problems. When it is time for me to leave, I intend to go unhindered."

"But you were going to marry me."

"Aye, as my wife, you would return to the Northland with me."

"Then I am doubly glad that I am not marrying you, lord, for I don't intend to leave the Highlands. I shall be returning to Glenmuir." Dropping the tunic into the trunk, she began to search again. "I know I cannot effect much change by myself, but I shall do all I can."

"Nay, Cait, you'll not be leaving," Michael said in a dangerously low voice. "Not without my permission."

"I don't require your permission." She withdrew a beautiful green tunic. "I wear the holy tattoo. I am free to travel through the land unhindered and unmolested." She held the garment up to her shoulders. "How does it look, lord?"

"Beautiful."

"Please," she said, "why don't you and your men provide me escort to Glenmuir? If it's a prize you want, I shall make it worth your while."

"My lady, whether we go to Glenmuir or stay here in Northern Scotland, you *shall* make it worth my while." He smiled lazily. "Besides, my lady, I have the Lydian Stone Breastpin, the key to the riches of the cloister. I suspect that what you offer me ... in the way of material valuables ... would pale in comparison to the shrine treasures."

Cait's apprehension turned into fear that constricted her heart, her breathing. "That is a holy treasure, lord. The gods would curse you if you were to touch it."

"I don't believe in your gods, lady. But ... I shall give some thought to your returning to Glenmuir." He touched the amulet that hung around his neck. "Mayhap I shall give the matter *serious* thought."

Cait opened her mouth.

Michael held up his hand. "No more talk about this subject, madam. 'Tis time we bathed so that we may sup in the Great Hall."

" 'Tis time that *we* bathed," Cait repeated.

He nodded.

She looked at the huge bathtub. It was large enough to hold both of them. Bathing together suggested an intimacy that both exhilarated and unsettled Cait.

Suddenly doubts about her relationship with Michael beset her. In giving herself to him, she had allowed him to enter her soul, her being. She could not let it happen again, because it was clear he did not feel the same way about her.

"You may take a full bath in here, lord," she announced. "I shall take a basin bath in the sleeping chamber."

"Nay, lady, my head-man told me how much you resented taking a basin bath when we were traveling. Now that you may have a full bath, I shan't rob you of the pleasure."

Seeing a decided glint in his eyes, Cait backed away. He extended his hand toward her and stepped closer.

"Shall we undress each other?"

Cait shook her head.

"Are you turning shy?"

She looked at him.

"You weren't last night."

Their mating had seemed right then. It seemed wrong now.

"My lord, surely you understand that I am no longer your slave. I no longer belong to you."

"But you do," he replied softly.

"But the queen mother confirmed that I am a bard of the Shelter Stone."

"Aye, she did. But it stands to reason that if you are an outlaw, you have been stripped of your vesture and title."

"Nay," she whispered, shaking her head.

"Until we settle the matter, you belong to me."

"My lord, surely you don't mean it?"

"I do." He caught her hand and tugged her to him. "Now, are you going to undress yourself, or am I to do it for you?"

They gazed at each other.

"One way or the other, madam, it will be done."

Cait slid her hand out of his clasp, and with an aplomb she was far from feeling, she began to peel off her clothing and drop it to her feet. His arms crossed over his chest, Michael watched out of half-closed eyes. Cait continued to pretend indifference, but her hands shook. She couldn't believe he was once again treating her like a piece of property . . . or that she was thrilled and excited by the very thought of such intimacy with him.

Michael didn't begin to undress himself until she stood naked before him. As blatantly as he had stared at her, Cait stared at him. She watched him unbutton the shoulder placket of his shirt, then pull it over his head. He unfastened his girdle, letting it fall to his feet. His trousers and leggings slid down his hips to reveal his full masculinity.

Nude, he walked to her, swept her into his arms, and stepped into the tub. Slowly he set her on her feet, then tugged her down into the water with him. He spread his legs and brought her between them, her back to his chest.

"I told you last night, madam, that we had just begun our journey. Now we continue. I'm going to wash your hair."

Reaching over the rim of the tub, he scooped a handful of soft soap from a dish on the floor and rubbed it between his palms. He lathered her hair, cleansing it and massaging the scalp, kneading the tension from her neck and shoulders. Sinking into beautiful oblivion, she let his fingers carry her further and further from reality.

She slipped beneath the warm water, feeling the gentle lap against her skin. Vaguely she was aware of him lifting up the gourd dipper and using it to rinse the suds from her hair, keeping the lather out of her eyes. She felt him pour something on her hair; she inhaled the sweet fragrance of herbs. Then he massaged her scalp again. Once more he rinsed. With spread fingers, he combed out the tangles.

"Now to bathe you."

"Um-hum." She was too relaxed to care.

He moved so that he sat in front of her. She stared into his eyes, which were now a deep, rich blue, darker because the fire flickered to his back. He began to wash her face, careful to keep the suds out of her eyes. Lightly he touched her cheeks, her forehead, her chin. He brushed his hand over her arched neck, cleaned her ears, feathering his fingers in every nook and around every curve.

Gradually her warm lethargy dissipated, replaced with fiery need.

He took the small washcloth and inched slowly down over her wet, smooth breasts, every stroke starting a new fire of excitement in her body until she was ablaze all over.

He dropped the cloth into the water, then poured an amber liquid onto his palms and spread the lotion over her breasts, his touch a silky caress that Cait could hardly stand. His fingers rolled her nipples; his hands slid under and over her breasts.

He stood, pulling her to her feet. His hands glided over her shoulders, down the indentation of her back to her hips. Gently he worked the lotion over the gentle flare of her hips. As his finger tentatively touched her most sensitive spot, she moaned softly.

"Aye, my little kitten, meow," he said. "Let me know your pleasure."

His hands slid to her stomach, then lower to the russet triangle between her thighs. She swayed toward him.

He smiled. "Aye, my little bard, 'tis time to rinse you." His voice was thick.

He retrieved the dipper and filled it with water. Time and again he poured the water over her, letting it cascade down her body.

When her skin glistened clean in the muted glow of the fire, when the fragrance of the herbal lotion filled his nostrils, Michael dropped the gourd to the floor. He stared into her passion-glazed eyes.

" 'Tis time to dry you."

His tongue gently lapped the water droplets from each breast. Cait's soft moans became a husky groan. His mouth closed around one of the hardened nipples, and he gently sucked. Then his hand ... She shivered when she felt his fingers stroking her inner thighs. They went higher and higher, seeking her inner self. They whetted her hunger, reminding her of the passion they had shared last night. Weak with desire, she clutched his shoulders for support.

He pulled away and stepped out of the tub. She followed. He picked up a large cloth and began to dry her off. When he was finished, he handed her the cloth.

"Dry me now."

He was demanding that she give more of herself to him, this man who would leave shortly. She could not allow him to make further inroads into her heart.

"I want you to touch me as I have touched you," he said.

Cait took the cloth, not because she was his slave and he commanded, but because she was a woman filled with desire that she yearned to share with him.

Clutching the cloth in both hands, she began to dry his arms. Her breathing became shallow; her chest hurt; her heart beat frantically. She closed her eyes.

"Nay, Cait, look at me."

He tapped her chin, lifting her face. She opened her eyes. Dropping her vision from his dark, somber gaze, she rubbed the soft fabric over his sunbrowned body. Gently she patted the moisture off his shoulders and chest, down his stomach, gazing at the scars that decorated his body.

She touched her lips to one on his shoulders. "You were sorely wounded."

"Aye."

She dried his back, his buttocks, then knelt to dry his legs. Before she touched his ankles, he gripped her arms and lifted her.

"How about my chest and stomach, my lady?"

Her breathing growing more labored, she moved

to the front of him and drew the cloth over his chest. His nipples hardened, and he caught and held her hands against him. As she lost herself in his fiery blue gaze, she felt the rise and fall of his chest, the beating of his heart.

Placing his hands over hers, he pushed them down his stomach to the juncture of his thighs. "Dry me," he whispered.

She lowered her head, and gently—so gently—dried him off, feeling a sense of wonder when he grew beneath her touch. She dropped the cloth and touched him with soft, gentle strokes, feeling again the wonder of the masculine body, the wonder of Michael's body. She felt life pulsing strong and vibrant in him. Tenderly she cupped the swollen sacks that bore the seed of life.

The massive warrior trembled beneath her touch, and she experienced something new and exhilarating. She looked into those eyes that were glazed with passion.

"Do you like this, my lord?"

"Aye," he muttered, his voice thick. He stooped, picked her up, and carried her into the sleeping chamber. "I like that, Cait, but I also want more."

"Aye, my lord, I am ready for more."

A second time Michael took her. He was in no hurry. His hands—his lips—spoke to her of his needs and desires. They stirred the same needs and desires in her. They told her of his pleasure in touching and in loving her.

Unselfishly he gave, a new experience for him. Mating with her was different from what he had shared with other women. Mating with Cait was softer, gentler. It had true meaning. Before, he had taken. Now his utmost thought was to give—to give of himself as he never had before.

Cait's body grew taut as she reached the pinnacle of fulfillment. In that moment of explosive joy, when lovers become one, she tore her lips from his and gasped with pleasure, then moaned softly. Her body shuddered.

Her arms tightened around him. She turned her face to his chest, her teeth softly biting his heated flesh, her fingers digging into his shoulders. She felt the beads of moisture that formed on Michael's hot skin, and she rubbed her cheek against his chest, her tears of joy mingling with his perspiration.

Michael pushed up and gazed at her in concern. With a thumb he gently wiped her tears away. "Did I hurt you?"

It was the second time he had asked that question, and the answer was the same. *Aye, you have hurt me, Michael Langssonn. You thought to manacle me with a silver torque and brand me as your slave. But, in truth, I have allowed you to brand me with your touch and your passion. I want to be possessed by you. Nay, Michael Langssonn, I want to be loved by you.*

She sighed and ran her palms over his chest. "I never knew such pleasure could exist between a man and a woman." She laughed weakly. "If I had known, perhaps I would not have waited so long to try it."

"For your sake, madam," Michael said, "I am glad you did."

"For my sake?"

"Aye. 'Tis better when a woman has a good lover to teach her the ways of mating. Then she learns that mating is a pleasure, not a drudgery to be endured."

Cait chuckled. "You are arrogant, my lord, but you speak the truth. And you've succeeded. You have taught me well the ways of mating. I have found carnality to be such great pleasure that I want never to be without it again. I shall most assuredly initiate it myself."

"Madam!" Michael's voice had gone hard. "I like your brazenness, but as long as you belong to me, you are my woman and will not sleep with any other man."

"Ah, my lord, most assuredly I am not speaking of sleep. I speak of carnal pleasure."

Michael gazed at her solemnly before he said, "That being the case, my lady, I shall have to make sure that I fulfill your every need."

He rolled to his side, holding her tightly. He pushed the thick russet hair from her temples and covered her face with soft, quick caresses.

"You are so sweet, my little bard."

"You, my lord, are wonderfully masculine." She ran her fingers lightly up his inner thigh to touch him, to feel him once more respond to her caresses. "And hard . . . again."

He chuckled. "Do you know what you're asking for, my lady?"

"Aye."

"I thought mayhap you had had enough for one day."

"I don't think I shall ever get enough, my lord."

Laughing softly, Michael captured her confession with a kiss.

"My lord Lang," Kolby called from in front of Lang's pavilion. "You have a visitor."

Lang pushed up from the folding chair and strode across the tent. Brushing open the flap, he looked at the woman standing beside his son's head-man. Even with the hood of her mantle over her head, he recognized Queen Muireall. He was surprised but pleased to see her.

"My lady, what brings you here?"

"I know my presence goes against custom, my lord," she said, "but I need to talk to you."

"Please come in, my lady." Lang guided her into the tent. "Thank you, Kolby," he said over his shoulder. "I shall see the lady home."

"Aye, my lord."

"Will you be seated, my lady?" Lang swept his hand to the small portable chair.

Muireall turned, the rustle of her mantle gentle and seductive. With both hands she pushed the hood from her head. "I'm frightened, my lord."

"Aye, my lady."

Tears moistened her eyes. Unable to stop himself, Lang pulled her into his arms. He held her tightly, savoring the sweet warmth and softness of her body. He had dreamed of this woman, of holding her like this. She felt wonderful and right. He inhaled her herbal fragrance.

She nestled her cheek against his chest. He rested his chin on top of her head.

"I feel so alone," she whispered.

"I know, my lady."

"I needed to . . . talk."

She pulled away from him and looked into his face.

"Nay," he whispered, "you don't want talk."

She moistened her lips. "You're right, my lord."

"And neither do I."

He felt like a young man, strong and potent, with a need to mate.

"You shouldn't be here," he said.

"In a way you are right," Muireall murmured. "My husband, Fergus, has been dead for only a short while, and I do mourn his death." Again she lifted her face to his. "Strangely, I feel that being with you is where I should be, where I should have been for the past thirty winters."

" 'Tis the same for me," Lang said. "I, too, mourned the loss of my wife. She was a good woman, and I loved her."

Muireall nodded. "I loved Fergus, my lord. He was a good husband to me, and I shall miss him. But he never touched that secret spot in my heart that I had given to my enemy long ago."

"Madam, I cannot have you around me in such an intimate setting without my thinking intimate thoughts." Lang gently caught Muireall by the shoulders and set her away from him. "I shall walk you to your cottage."

"I don't want to be by myself." Muireall unfastened her brooch and threw her mantle from her shoulders. It floated through the air, then landed in a tangle at their feet.

"If you stay, lady, do you know what will happen?"

"Aye." She stepped away so that the fire was to her back. Her tunic flowed loose from her shoulders. Firelight reflected through it to outline her nude body.

"If we mate, lady—" his voice was thick "—'twill be for the rest of our lives."

"I would have it no other way, lord."

Chapter 18

The Great Hall swelled with revelry. All had eaten of the succulent food until they were stuffed, and still the ale, mead, and wine flowed freely. Temporarily Cait had pushed aside her worries and was enjoying the festivities. She had particularly liked watching Michael and Kolby blind-fight with swords. She marveled at her lover's skill and accuracy, at his ability to concentrate and to use his other senses.

"Now," Malcolm announced, "we have a surprise for you. Lady Cait is a cloister minstrel, as well as a blade master."

Cait looked at Michael in surprise. He grinned.

Leaning over, he whispered, "Lang and Malcolm schemed while I slept, my little minstrel. I schemed while you ate."

"Lady Cait," Malcolm called out, "will you give us a demonstration with your blades?"

"Aye, my lord Malcolm, but I must send to—"

A lad rushed down the aisle, holding out Cait's leathern blade purse. "Here they are, Lord Michael."

"Good lad." Michael flipped the boy a gold piece. "Hand them to the lady."

Rising, Cait took her purse and fastened it about her waist, amid the roar of cheers and clapping.

She held up her hands for silence. "Lord Malcolm," she said, "will you stand here in front of me?"

"Perhaps, lady," Malcolm said, "this is something I should allow my head-man to do."

"Nay, lord," Cait replied. "You shall be part of my demonstration."

Malcolm looked discomfited, but he moved to where she pointed.

Cait unfastened the flap on the purse, pulled out four knives, and held them in her hand. She closed her eyes and breathed deeply several times.

As she opened her eyes, she said, "Don't move your foot."

Before Malcolm could answer, she twirled the first dagger, which landed hilt up at the end of his boot. Murmuring their praise, the people craned their necks to see. Two, three, then four of the blades outlined the front half of Malcolm's boot.

Malcolm extracted the daggers from the planked floor and confirmed that she had not damaged his boot.

"Aye, my lady," Malcolm said, "you are indeed skilled. You did not harm the leather at all."

"Thank you, my lord."

"I can do that," one of the warriors yelled, "and I'm not considered a blade master."

"Then come do it, sire," Cait called out.

The man pushed to his feet and staggered around.

Laughing, Malcolm said, "Sit down, man. No one is going to let you toss daggers at them."

More laughter followed.

"Let's make this more interesting, my lady," another called out. "Something we can lay wagers on."

"Interesting?" Cait asked.

"Can you outline the body of a person?"

"Aye."

"Without hurting them." Raucous laughter followed.

"Aye."

"Do that."

"Come forward, sire," Cait called to her heckler, "and stand against the wall with your arms and legs spread wide. I'll outline your entire body with blades."

"Nay."

"Then, sire, don't demand for others what you are not willing to do yourself." She took a step toward her chair.

Michael rose. "I volunteer, my lady."

"Nay, lord," she whispered. "I have no intention of—"

"But you will, lady." He smiled reassuringly at her.

"I need you tied to the wall by your wrists and ankles, your arms and legs stretched out."

"You don't have to tie me."

"I would prefer that you are tied," she said. "I don't want to take the chance that you might flinch if the blade comes too close."

"I won't," Michael told her, "and I won't be tied."

He strode over to the wall and pressed his back against it, spreading his arms and legs.

"Lord," Cait said, "I would prefer that—"

"Nay, lady, I won't be tied. Proceed."

Cait wiped her palms down her tunic, then pulled her blades from the purse. She went through the ritual of closing her eyes and breathing deeply, of calming herself and focusing on what she had to do.

She opened her eyes and gazed at Michael. The blade balanced between her fingers, she drew back her arm and let the knife fly. It hit the wall above his head. Another whined through the air, thudding when it entered the wall. And another. Another. And another.

As she was poised to throw the last blade, which would land below Michael's crotch, a watchman shouted from the door. "Riders approach!"

People looked toward the door. Feet shuffled. Voices rose.

Cait lowered her arm, and sucked needed air into her lungs. She saw that Michael had not moved. He smiled and nodded. Cait wiped the perspiration from her brow and took her stance again. She marked her spot, willed the blade to land there, and let it fly from her fingers. She closed her eyes and heard the thud as it sank into the wood.

"No damage done, my lady," Michael shouted, stepping away from the wall and waving his hand at the outline of his body marked with the daggers. Everyone burst into cheers.

Michael caught Cait by the waist and swung her around. Bracing her hands on his shoulders, she gazed into his upturned face. She was so happy. Yesterday she had been envious when Malcolm had done this to Jarvia. Now Michael was doing it to her.

He lowered her slowly, letting her slide down his body. As his lips came down on hers, he said, "Lady, I don't know when I have been more frightened."

Cait's laughter became the essence of their kiss.

They had returned to their places at the high table when two men entered the hall. One of them was young and dressed as the herdsman; the other was elderly. His clothing was dirty and tattered, his white hair tangled.

"Trevor!" Cait exclaimed. She ran down the aisle. "Guardian Priest Trevor!"

"Cait nea Sholto." He caught her in a fierce embrace. "Thanks be to the gods, you escaped. We thought Gilbert had taken you prisoner."

"Thanks be to the gods that you are here, my lord."

"Aye, I escaped, as did Rob and your father."

"Both Rob and Father!" Cait shouted. Then she felt Michael behind her, his arm around her shoulder. She spun to see more warriors bringing in a second man on a stretcher.

"Father!" she cried.

They set the stretcher down in front of the king's dais.

"Cait . . ." Sholto tried to raise his head but could not.

"Sholto!" She fell to her knees.

Michael knelt beside her. Sholto's face was swollen and discolored from bruises; large cuts ran across his forehead and down one cheek. Cait wanted to embrace her father, but she dared not touch him for fear of hurting him. Tears streamed down her face.

"They've tortured you."

"A little."

"I'm a physician, sire," Michael said.

"I have need of one." The old man tried to smile.

Michael, examining the cuts and bruises, touched Sholto's cheek along the jawline and gently turned his head. Malcolm knelt on the other side.

"Gilbert told me that he had captured you, my daughter." Sholto touched his hand to her cheek. "He cut your hair."

"His men did," she said.

Sholto coughed, the sound deep and rasping. He drew in several breaths, his face contorting with pain.

"Where is Rob?" Cait asked.

"He's all right," Sholto said. "Now take me to the high king."

"I'm here, sire."

Sholto looked into Malcolm's face. "You are a high king as well as a physician."

"Nay, lord," Michael said from the other side of the stretcher, "I am the physician. I'm Michael Langssonn."

"The Northman?"

Michael nodded.

Moving only his eyes, Sholto looked at Michael, then Malcolm. He contemplated each one again. "Twins," he murmured. "Identical."

"Aye," Michael answered.

"Night and Day," he mumbled.

Michael unsheathed his dagger and cut Sholto's tunic. Cait gasped when she saw the wounds that had been inflicted on him. His chest and abdomen were darkly bruised and swollen. Michael lay his ear against the old man's chest. Sholto coughed and tensed with a spasm of pain.

"You are critically ill, good priest," Michael announced, "with an infection of the lungs. I want to put you to bed, where you can rest and I can treat you better."

Sholto's chest rose and fell rapidly.

"A moment—" Sholto began to cough, the hacking so deep, his body convulsed and his face twisted. He wrapped his long, bony fingers around Malcolm's wrist. "Trevor—tell—him."

"Duncan men," Michael shouted to the warriors

who had brought the priests into the room, "carry this man to the guest cottage where I'm staying."

"Nay, not yet," Sholto ordered, his voice sounding stronger. "Trevor!"

"Can it not wait, Sholto?" the guardian priest asked.

"Nay."

Jarvia pressed a glass of wine into Trevor's hands.

"Thank you," he mumbled, and took several swallows. Placing the glass on the table nearest him, Trevor said, "The kingdom of Glenmuir is ruled by a provisional ruler named Gilbert. Six days ago when our kingdom was attacked by sea raiders and our king was slain, Gilbert and his warriors rode into the village and drove the raiders into the sea. At least, that is what we thought when the High Council appointed Gilbert to be our provisional king until a blood-heir could be found.

"We have learned since then that Gilbert is a usurper. He hired sea raiders to attack our village, to kill our king and his entire family, and to leave Glenmuir without an heir to the High Seat. But Gilbert did not plan this alone. A cloister priest betrayed us."

Trevor took another swallow of wine.

"Several seasons past, King Ido had broken Cait's betrothal and married the warrior to his own daughter. In a fit of rage Cait vowed revenge. She cursed Ido and his entire family. When the traitor priest learned that Cait and the cloister minstrels with whom she travels had seen and spoken with Northmen, he told Gilbert about Cait's promise of revenge. Gilbert went to the High Council with the story that Cait had conspired with the sea raiders. She would give them the cloister riches and the

High Seat of Glenmuir if they would kill the king and his family."

As Cait listened to the guardian priest relate the sequence of events, she gave her father a drink of water.

"The traitor priest, however, did not contemplate what actions Sholto and Cait would take. When Cait learned that she had been outlawed as a traitor, she fled Glenmuir. Gilbert had to get her back. He needed Sholto's daughter if he was to find the Secret Chamber where the cloister riches are kept. But Cait was rescued by a Northman named Michael Langssonn and is now safe, as are Sholto and I."

"How did you and Father escape?" Cait asked.

"The High Council demanded that Gilbert remove his guards from the cloister. They did, but they imprisoned Sholto alone in one of the outer caverns of the shrine. In fact, all of us were kept in individual residences and not allowed to visit with the others."

"They feared your silent communication," Cait said.

"Aye," Trevor answered. "But one night Gilbert became frustrated and tortured Sholto. Gilbert underestimated his enemy. Sholto would have died before he betrayed the gods by telling where the treasure was."

Tears ran down Cait's cheeks as she looked at her father's beaten body.

"The night after Sholto was beaten, Gilbert feared he was dying. He had him removed to the Great Hall and for the first time allowed us to be together. In sign language Sholto told me he was hurting, but he was fully conscious. He had planned our escape. Knowing how weak and crippled he was, I tried to talk him out of it, but Sholto was determined. That evening, as soon as it became dark, I overpowered our guard. Sholto and I slipped out through the back entrance of the Great House. We found Blar in the woods behind the cloister. He claimed to have escaped, but he wouldn't come with us. He told us he would be of more help if he remained there. We let him know where we were going and what route we were taking."

"Blar?" Cait said. "You think he is the one who betrayed you?"

Trevor nodded. "Gilbert knew every move that was being made in the cloister, except those which Sholto kept to himself. Only Blar could have told Gilbert the route that Sholto and I were traveling when we escaped from the cloister. By the time we reached the border of Northern Scotland, Sholto and I realized we were being followed. Although we knew it would slow us down by a day, we changed our route. We were grateful when we came upon a farm and the herdsmen brought us here."

Trevor pressed a hand to his forehead. "We have traveled far, stopping for rest and food as infrequently as possible. I am tired and must sit down."

Malcolm pushed a chair up to him, and the old priest sank onto the cushions.

"Gilbert still has the High Council members imprisoned, and he's issued an ultimatum. By the eighteenth day of his reign, if no one has come forward to show him the location of the Secret Chamber, he will execute one member of the High Council each day, beginning with Conn. We have twelve days to save these men's lives," Trevor said.

"Help me up," Sholto ordered.

Putting his arms around the priest, Michael levered him into a sitting position.

"I want to stand."

"Sire," Michael said, "you're too weak."

"I must stand."

Gently Michael assisted Sholto to his feet. Although his hair was matted, and his clothing dirty and ragged, Sholto straightened his back. With piercing eyes, he gazed about the room.

"The usurper and the traitor priest think they killed the king and all his heirs to the High Seat," Sholto said, "but they are wrong. I alone know the identity of the rightful heir. She is here in this room, safe from Gilbert. She is Cait, my adopted daughter."

Trevor dropped the glass of wine he was holding. Cait blanched.

"Nay, Father, it cannot be."

"Aye, 'tis true. Until this moment it was my secret. When Ido's family was alive, it was not necessary for me to tell you," Sholto said. "But now, Cait, you are the heir to the High Seat of Glenmuir."

Dazed, Cait listened as her father began to recite her genealogy, tracing her back to royalty. When Sholto was finished, he said, "Trevor, do you bear witness to this genealogy?"

"Aye." He shook his head. "All this time, Sholto, and you told no one."

"Nay," the high priest replied, "I have suspected all along that someone in the cloister was betraying us. I told no one, not even Cait, because I feared the worst for her. My secrecy was her protection. I am confessing now because it is time, because here in Northern Scotland Cait can muster an army who will fight for her."

Sholto extended his hand. "Cait, stand with me."

Cait rose and stepped closer to her father.

"I, Sholto, high priest and the Ancient of Nights and Days of the Shelter Stone Shrine, do this day before all these people proclaim that Cait nea Sholto, through her blood lineage, is the rightful heir to the High Seat of Glenmuir. Is this witnessed?"

Warriors rapped their swords on their shields; others slapped their hands on the tables.

"High King Malcolm," Sholto said, "I'm asking that you give formal sanctuary to Cait, the queen of Glenmuir. Also, my lord, I'm asking that you help her establish her legitimate rule."

Malcolm bowed before Cait. "This night, Cait nea Sholto, I recognize you as queen of Glenmuir and I pledge to help you claim your rightful High Seat."

"Now, High Priest," Michael said, "I will take you to the cottage, where you can rest."

A smile touched Sholto's gaunt face. "I'm ready now."

The cottage was brightly lit with burning torches and lamps. Two caldrons, filled with boiling water, hung over the central fire. Michael set out his medical paraphernalia; Veld assisted him.

Cait knelt beside the bed and wept. She felt something cold and wet nuzzle her hand. She looked down to see Ulf lying flat on his stomach, two paws extended in front of him, two behind. He whined softly and licked her hand.

"Where have you been?" she asked, surprised that he was paying any attention to her.

He gazed at her with silvery blue eyes, and she could have sworn he was smiling at her.

"Michael," she said, "did you know Ulf has returned?"

He glanced over and said absently, "Good. I've been worried about him." Then he turned his attention back to his herbs.

"Cait." Sholto's lids lifted, and out of pain-glazed eyes he stared into her face. "Gilbert must not find you."

"I'm safe here," she assured him.

"No."

"He won't harm me, my father. High King Malcolm has given me sanctuary."

"Aye," Sholto said, "but it will not be enough. Gilbert is an evil man, Cait, and he will harm you in a way that you least expect." As a shaft of pain pierced his chest and back, he groaned. When it subsided, he said, "I pray to the gods he does not already know you are the heir." He caught a deep breath, held it, then released it with a soft groan. "He knows all that is going on in the cloister. When he finds out, Cait, he will force you to marry him ... so that he will have a legal claim to the High Seat of Glenmuir. Once you give birth to his child, he'll kill you."

"Tell me a mistake has been made. Tell me I'm not the heir to the High Seat. You are doing this to save Glenmuir, aren't you, Father?"

Sholto did not answer.

"Father." Cait laid a hand on his arm.

"He's unconscious," Michael said.

Michael spread his bowls, vials, baskets, and pouches over the table beside the bed. He and Veld measured, poured, and mixed. Ulf lay in the corner of the room, every now and then cocking open an eye to see what was happening.

Soon Michael had given Sholto a spoonful of a vile-looking tonic. He spread an ugly yellow salve over Sholto's chest and back, then wrapped him loosely in white bandages.

Horrible vapors filled the room. "If the infection

doesn't kill him," Cait said, making a face, "the odor will."

"Nay, the vapor is healing," Michael answered. He laid his hand on Sholto's forehead. "His body is still hot with fever, but he's resting better now. Sleep will do him good."

Still Michael mixed medicines.

A knock sounded.

"Lord Michael!" Trevor shouted. "Cait."

"Come," Cait called.

The door opened. The guardian priest called, "Cait."

"In here," she answered.

The door closed, footfalls sounded in the next room, then Trevor entered the sleeping chamber. He had bathed, changed clothes, and combed his hair. "Will he mend?"

"It's too soon to tell," Michael answered. "Cait, why don't you and the guardian priest move into the main hall. I'll be finished here shortly, and I want Sholto to rest in quiet."

"Of course."

Trevor followed Cait into the other room.

"I am so relieved to know that you and Rob and Sholto escaped," she said. "I have been so worried, my lord Trevor. Now, if only Sholto will improve."

"He will."

"So much has happened, my lord Trevor."

He patted her shoulders. "Aye, my child, it has."

"I can't believe that Blar is a traitor."

"Neither could your father or I," Trevor said. "But only Blar could have told them the route we would be traveling."

"Guardian Priest, please tell me that some mistake has been made and that I am not the heir to the

High Seat of Glenmuir. Sholto is telling a lie to save Glenmuir, isn't he?"

"Nay, Cait, you know Sholto would not say it if it were not true."

Shaking her head in disbelief, her hair brushing her cheeks, she asked, "Why didn't I know?"

"Because none of us knew. Only your father, and he felt no need to confide in us." Trevor sounded bitter, but then he shrugged. "Perhaps 'twas for the best. If he had revealed it sooner, the traitor would have informed Gilbert."

"I'm a bard," Cait proclaimed, more to herself than to Trevor, "not the future queen of Glenmuir."

"You, Cait," Trevor said, "are the queen of Glenmuir."

She looked over to see Michael leaning against the doorframe, his arms folded over his chest. Although the firelight flickered brightly in the room, she couldn't see Michael's features clearly. His expression was somber.

Cait felt her world crumbling beneath her feet. As if Michael understood what was happening to her, he pushed away from the door and strode toward her, his arms outstretched. She ran into them, and he caught and held her. He didn't let her fall.

"Oh, Michael," she murmured, "it cannot be."

Michael ran his hands up and down her back in comforting strokes.

"Compose yourself, my dear," Trevor said, not unkindly. "We have no time for hysterics. We have to—"

"Pour her a beaker of wine," Michael said sharply. "Can't you see that she's in shock?"

He gently set her away and led her back to the chair while Trevor went to the trestle-table. When she was seated, Michael took the wine the returning priest handed him and held the tankard to her lips.

"Drink," he said. Then: "Again."

When she had composed herself, she smiled tentatively at him. "Thank you," she murmured. "I'm all right now."

He rose to stand behind her, his hands curled around the back of the chair. She breathed a little easier.

"As my father said, Gilbert will want to marry me so he can have free claim to Glenmuir. That, I shall not allow. If we are to save Glenmuir, I must return and claim the High Seat."

"Aye, as queen," Trevor said.

As queen, Cait thought. She took another sip of wine. Michael had spoken yesterday of the gods' misplaced sense of humor. She had to agree with him. She had grown up thinking she was a peasant; she had been adopted into a wealthy and noble family that had elevated her to the position of lady. Tonight she had learned that all along, she had been royalty itself.

"I can rule as queen without a consort?" she asked.

"You can be seated as queen without a husband," Trevor explained, "but you must marry and be with child within a year and a day of your coronation. If this doesn't happen, you will have to abdicate the High Seat to the next closest heir. If there is none closer than you, the High Council will choose the next king."

"Then I need not concern myself about an immediate marriage and can concentrate my attention on regaining the High Seat."

"While 'tis true that you must focus your immediate attention on reclaiming your High Seat, you do need to think about a future king. 'Twill be to your advantage to have a husband who can impregnate you immediately, who is strong enough to fight Gilbert and his men. I shall speak to High King Malcolm about the matter. Surely he has such a man among his warriors to whom you can become betrothed."

"Nay, my lord," Cait said.

"Why not?" the guardian priest demanded, his tone testy. "We must settle this matter so we can return to Glenmuir. A betrothal is as binding as marriage. Your betrothed will be compelled to fight for your kingdom. If, after you regain your kingdom, you don't wish to marry him, we may honorably rupture the betrothal."

After we use him and no longer have any use of him, Cait thought.

"Thank you for your advice," Cait said, "but the decision is mine to make. I shall have to think on it."

Trevor looked puzzled. "My lady—"

"My lord," Michael said, again speaking in that soft voice that Cait recognized only too well. He was sitting, his elbows resting on the arms of the chair, and his chin on his bridged hands. "Cait has told you that she must think on the matter. Let's leave it at that."

Trevor looked startled.

"My lord, you are interfering with matters that are not your concern."

"Aye, lord priest, Cait is my concern," Michael answered. With a leisurely grace that did not fool Cait, Michael rose from the chair. "I am her lover."

Cait gasped. Whatever she had expected from Michael, it was not this confession. How dare he humiliate her in front of the guardian priest of the cloister!

Trevor swallowed, his larynx bobbing noticeably. "Her—Her betrothed?"

"Nay, Guardian Priest, her lover. An injustice I have done to her that I will soon rectify. Cait and I are to be wed."

Chapter 19

"**P**erhaps you *were* going to marry Cait—" Trevor spoke bluntly, emphasizing his words "—but you *will* not take to wife the queen of Glenmuir."

"I am lover to the *woman*," Michael said, his voice never rising, "not to the bard or the princess. 'Tis the woman whom I shall marry."

"My lords," Cait said, holding up a hand for silence. She had always despised being talked about as if she were not present. "Whom I wed is a matter that I, and I alone, shall decide. And, Lord Trevor, if I so choose, I shall marry this man."

"Nay!" Trevor exclaimed. "You are the queen of Glenmuir. Marriage to him would not be in the best interests of your kingdom."

"My lord—" Cait spoke more sharply "—remember to whom you are speaking."

Mouth agape, Trevor stared at her.

"As you have pointed out repeatedly since you stepped foot in this cottage, I am the queen of Glenmuir."

Cait hadn't asked to be queen, but if she was, then she would be treated as one. And why not? She had been looked down upon like chattel. Now she would be respected like royalty.

From the corner of her eye, she saw Michael's

mouth twitch in a smile. *Don't gloat, my lord Michael Langssonn. Once I've made sure that Trevor understands his position in relationship to mine, I shall make yours clear to you.*

"Aye, you are the queen." Trevor seemed to wilt before her, though he smiled. "I apologize. I keep thinking of you as our little Cait, and it is our little Cait whom I am worried about."

"Thank you, my lord Trevor." Cait returned the priest's smile and accepted his apology.

"Is your cousin, Rob, also an heir to the High Seat?" Michael asked.

Cait shook her head. "Nay, he is my father's nephew."

A knock sounded, and High Queen Jarvia called: "Lord Michael."

"Enter," Michael called.

The door opened, ushering in a gust of cold wind. The flames skittered about in the central hearth. Malcolm and Jarvia, followed by Lang and Muireall, entered the cottage.

"Please pardon all of us for coming at one time." Jarvia stepped forward, pushing the hood from her face. "But we were concerned about the high priest of the Shelter Stone and wanted to see how he is doing."

"It's a little early to tell," Michael answered. "But he's resting."

Standing before the fire, Cait watched the exchange between Michael and Jarvia. They were a handsome couple, his darkness complementing her fairness. In the firelight Jarvia's hair, hanging softly around her face and down her back, glimmered like the purest silver. Her lips and cheeks were rosy; her eyes, framed by long, dark lashes, sparkled.

Malcolm looked down at his wife with a tender

expression of love. Aye, there was passion, too, but it was that which went hand in hand with love. Cait had the passion from Michael . . . Well, she had Michael's controlled passion. But she wanted more. She wanted his love. And she wanted him to give free reign to his emotions where she was concerned.

As Cait watched Malcolm and Jarvia together, she felt a twinge of jealousy. High Queen Jarvia was a beautiful woman, and Cait could understand why any man would want her for his wife.

"I have instructed my cook to prepare a healing broth," Jarvia said. "She will bring it along shortly. Also, my lord Michael, I am learned in the use of herbs and medicines. May I be of any assistance to you?"

Malcolm stepped forward and held out a large chest.

"My physician's chest," Jarvia said. "I thought perhaps you may find some of the herbs of use. When you have time, lord, I shall show them to you. If there are some here with which you are unfamiliar, I shall explain them to you."

"Thank you, madam."

"May I see Sholto?" she asked. "I won't disturb him."

"Aye." Michael took the chest from Malcolm. "My man Veld is with him." As he led her into the sleeping chamber, the wolf rose and walked over to them. He sniffed Jarvia.

"Don't be frightened, my lady queen," Michael said. "He won't harm you unless—"

"I know, my lord, I own a wolf also." She laughed softly. "Malcolm and I rescued her on the journey to Northern Scotland after our marriage."

"I think, madam," Malcolm said dryly, "you alone rescued her."

Briefly Jarvia explained how she had found the baby Catriona, whom they later adopted, abandoned with the wolf. The animal had been badly beaten and was almost dead, but it had protected the babe.

"Jarvia rescued both," Malcolm said, regarding his wife with love.

Jarvia smiled at him. "Now Magda—the wolf—and Catriona are inseparable."

"Much like Michael and his wolf," Lang said. "That wolf was a pup when he found and saved Michael."

Michael and Jarvia went into the sleeping chamber, leaving the others to share stories.

After Lang had finished talking, Malcolm asked Cait, "Has Sholto been able to talk?"

"Nay."

Muireall, having slipped out of her mantle, caught Cait's hands in hers and squeezed gently. "I'm so sorry this has happened, my dear. But you are fortunate that your father and your cousin have escaped."

Cait nodded. "I'm grateful to the gods, my lady queen."

Lang, having gone into the sleeping chamber for extra chairs, arranged them around the fire. Tapping Muireall on the shoulder, he silently motioned for her to be seated. The others followed her example.

Malcolm looked at the priest. "Lord Trevor, are you refreshed yourself from your journey?"

"Somewhat, my lord king," he answered. "Thank you for the repast. I would have stayed in my quarters to sleep or await further word from you, but I was worried about Sholto. I wanted to inquire personally about his condition."

"Aye," Malcolm said, "that is understandable."

Cait sat in front of the fire, but she felt cold all over. She was thankful that both her adopted father and cousin had escaped Gilbert's clutches. Yet she worried about them, about Sholto's wounds, about how Rob would survive now that he was free.

She was troubled about being queen of Glenmuir. She had never dreamed that one day she would rule over her country. She remembered what Michael had said earlier about the two of them being tangled up in vows. With the announcement that she was heir to the High Seat of Glenmuir, she was tightly bound by another vow—one she could not escape. The gods had ordained that she be queen of Glenmuir. And she *would* be.

She looked at the people in the room. Lord Lang sat next to the queen mother, the two of them smiling tenderly at each other every now and then. Lord Trevor sat off by himself, fidgeting in the chair and rubbing his chin. His hands locked behind his head, Malcolm had stretched out his legs, warming his feet in front of the fire.

Jarvia returned and sat in the vacant chair next to her husband. Cait turned to look for Michael. He leaned against the wall by the inner door. They gazed at each other, but Cait couldn't read his expression. She didn't know what he was thinking, and she was worried about what he planned to do. His revelation to the guardian priest that they were lovers had astounded her. The longer she thought about it, the more unsettled she became. Michael Langssonn was an enigma to her, one she doubted she would ever understand.

"My lord Trevor," Malcolm said, "now that you are somewhat refreshed and rested, why don't you explain to us again what has happened in Glenmuir."

Trevor sighed and nodded. "Ah, my lord high king, so much . . . so very much has happened." Settling more comfortably in his chair, he began to describe in greater detail what he had told them earlier. He finished with, "But the sea raiders didn't find the bulk of the cloister treasure. It's hidden in a secret underground chamber, sire, of which only the Ancient of Nights and Days has knowledge."

"And who else?" Malcolm asked.

"Who else?" Trevor stared blankly.

"Aye, in case something should happen to the ancient one who knows the whereabouts of the Secret Chamber," Michael said from behind them.

"You, Lord Trevor, since you are the guardian priest?" Malcolm asked.

"I know the location of the Gift Chamber," Trevor admitted, "but Sholto entrusted the location of the alternate to no one."

"When my father learned that the raiders were marching toward the shrine," Cait said, "he blindfolded me and several other of the Silver Daggers and led us to the Gift Chamber. We moved all the treasures to another room deeper in the caverns."

Cait saw the hurt of betrayal reflected in Trevor's face.

"It wasn't because he didn't trust you," she said softly. "He did it because he feared one of the High Council might be tortured into revealing the location of the Gift Chamber."

"But he did entrust the cloister pins to you," Trevor charged.

"Aye," Cait answered. After she explained about the two Cloister Breastpins, she said, "When my father learned that Gilbert knew about the sacred pins, he suspected there was a traitor among the members of the cloister. Fearing the worst from Gilbert, Sholto decided to trust me with the secret. He wanted me to transport the Lydian Stone Breastpin out of Glenmuir for safety."

"Which she did," Trevor said. "As I see it, my lord high king Malcolm, Cait must return to Glenmuir posthaste with a military escort. Gilbert will not readily give up the High Seat. I suggest you send a messenger to Glenmuir immediately to let the people know that Cait is the heir to the High Seat and that she will be returning soon."

Michael placed both hands on Cait's shoulders. "Cait has been in grave danger since she left Glenmuir. Once Gilbert receives this message, she will be in even graver danger."

Malcolm agreed. "That's one of the reasons why Sholto did not reveal her lineage. He was frightened that Gilbert would learn who she was."

"All Gilbert wants right now are the Breastpins," Michael reminded them. "When he learns that Cait is the heir, he will want her as well. Through her, he would have permanent access to the High Seat." He paused. "Cait must have a champion."

"Aye, she must," Trevor agreed. He looked at Malcolm. "Surely, my lord, you have one to give to her, a man to whom she can become betrothed."

"One man is not enough," Michael said. "She must have a champion who is loyal to her, with warriors who are loyal to him."

Malcolm shook his head. "I wish all my warriors and I could march into Glenmuir with her, but we cannot. With my father's recent death, our borders are insecure. Many of the tribes are raiding into our territory."

"If only Sholto were well enough to advise us."

The guardian priest rose, walked to the door of the sleeping chamber, and looked in on his friend. He returned to the trestle-table under the window. With trembling hands, he filled a tankard with ale. "I fear for Cait, for Glenmuir," he lamented.

"I fear for Glenmuir also," Cait said. "I fear that other kings, stronger and possibly more greedy than Gilbert, will follow his example if he goes unpunished."

"That is possible," Trevor said. "Before the massacre, our kingdom was stable with a strong king. Now we are ripe for the plucking." Trevor quaffed the ale and lowered the tankard.

"I shall stop Gilbert and any other person who tries to take Glenmuir away from its people," Cait said. "With or without help."

"My lady," Trevor said, "it would not be in your or Glenmuir's best interests for you to return home without warriors. Why can't we wait until Malcolm's warriors have—"

"Nay," Cait said, "I dare not. Time is not on our side."

"That's true," Michael agreed. "The longer you wait, the more entrenched Gilbert and his allies will become. My warriors and I shall escort you to Glenmuir."

Trevor opened his mouth to speak to Michael, then turned to Cait. "My lady, we cannot accept the services of this Northman. It was sea raiders from Northland who originally invaded our village. It might have been him and his men."

"It wasn't, priest," Michael said. "Had it been Michael or Lang of the Clan of the Wolves, you would have known it. We would have found the cloister treasure."

"Aye," Lang agreed.

Although Cait knew that Michael was baiting the guardian priest, cold chills ran down her spine. She had given him the Lydian Stone Breastpin. At any time he and his men might loot the cloister treasures. And now he offered to escort her to Glenmuir to fight for her. But did he want to fight for her or for himself?

"My lord Michael," Cait said, "I thank you for offering to help me, but while the guardian priest is less than tactful, he speaks the truth. I cannot return home in the escort of Northmen. Sea raiders are our enemies. I fear that you would drive my people away from me and into pledging their support for Gilbert. What queen would bring home an escort that would strike fear into the hearts of her people?"

"What queen would return home without a man who could strike fear into her enemy and assure that she was crowned queen?"

Cait tried to read Michael's eyes, wishing that he trusted her enough to let down his guard. But as always, the invisible shield was in place.

"Or, madam, do you not care that you might end up married to Gilbert?"

Of course she minded, but she was not going to let him provoke her.

"I have spoken, my lord." Cait turned to Malcolm. "My lord high king, I should be grateful for any escort *you* can provide. Please put out the word that I shall be willing to pay mercenaries—"

"Nay!" Michael bellowed. "Mercenaries fight for the booty alone, Cait."

She turned from him. He caught her arm and whirled her to face him.

"You are in need of a man who has a vested interest in fighting for your kingdom. Gilbert will not relinquish the High Seat without a fight."

"Thank you for offering your services as a champion, lord—"

"Not as a champion only, madam, but as a husband. You are in need of a husband who can successfully fight Gilbert and his men."

And a man to impregnate you, he left unsaid.

"If Cait wishes to inherit the High Seat of Glenmuir, she must marry a Highlander of noble blood!" the guardian priest exclaimed, then added hastily, "I know you are the birth brother of High King Malcolm, but surely, my lord, you can understand the ramifications of a marriage between you and Cait." He shook his head and appealed to Cait. "It can't be done, my lady."

"My lord Michael," Cait said softly, and stepped away from him, "I cannot. As you said earlier this evening, all of us are bound by vows. I must think of my people. You are a Highlander by birth, a Northman by upbringing. My enemies would use your ties against us."

"This is your decision, my lady?" Michael asked.

"Aye."

In two steps he was beside her. He caught her hand. "I want to speak to you privately, Cait."

His clasp was tight, and Cait didn't wish to make a scene. She followed him to the other side of the room.

"I have offered you marriage and protection, Cait, but you have turned both down. Now I'm telling you that if you wish to protect the riches of the Shelter Stone, you must marry me."

His eyes pierced hers.

"Who am I protecting them for?" Cait asked. "You?"

"If you don't marry me, my warriors and I can march into Glenmuir and defeat Gilbert, and I can establish myself as king without you. At any time, my lady, I can rob your shrine."

He caught the chain around his neck and pulled out the sacred amulet.

"Only through marriage to me, Cait, can you save your kingdom."

"Yet through marriage to you, Michael, I risk losing my kingdom."

" 'Tis a chance you must take."

"I have no choice, do I? Very well, Michael, we shall be betrothed."

He shook his head. "We shall be handfasted."

"Nay."

"Aye."

They returned to the others, and Michael raised their clasped hands. "My lords and ladies, with you as my witnesses," he said, "I, Michael, birth son of Camshron mac Duncan and Queen Muireall of Northern Scotland, and also a birth son of the Highlands, do this day handfast myself to Cait nea Sholto in marriage to be binding for a year and a day."

Michael's hand was big and warm, but it felt like a shackle binding her to him. He had used her to get to Northern Scotland and to Malcolm mac Duncan. Now he was using her again . . . to get to the riches of the cloister and to gain another kingdom.

"After the year and one day, either party of this wedding shall be free to go his own way," Michael continued. "If at that time one party disagrees with the marriage, that party takes any child born of the marriage with him . . . or her."

Now Cait knew the full implications of what he was doing. She had worried when he purchased her from Gilbert's men that he would not be satisfied with only her body, that he would think he had bought her soul. Her misgivings now proved to have substance.

According to the laws of Glenmuir, she had one year and a day in which to become impregnated if she wished to retain the High Seat. Michael had bound them together for that same period of time, excluding the possibility that any other man could be her husband, the father of her child, or her consort on the High Seat of Glenmuir. Any child she bore Michael, he could legally claim as his heir . . . and as the heir to the High Seat of Glenmuir.

The enslavement Cait felt when Michael had bought her from Ardac paled in comparison to what she felt now. Through the birth of their child, he would bind her to his side permanently . . . unless she objected to the marriage with him first. And she knew that was doubtful. A king, immediately upon receiving his babe while his wife was yet in the birthing bed, would carry the child into the Great Hall and, before all his subjects, would baptize, name, and proclaim it his heir. At the same time, Michael Langssonn could also rupture the handfasting.

Frowning, Lang rose. "Michael—"

Muireall caught his hand. " 'Twill work itself out, my lord."

Trevor looked horrified. "Let us announce your betrothal to this Northman, Cait, not a handfasting," he begged. "A betrothal can be honorably ruptured at any time, my lady. The handfasting is binding . . ."

"Aye, Guardian Priest," Michael said, " 'twas the reason for the handfasting. To make it binding."

To the kingdom. To the riches. To the child. But not to Cait.

"For the handfast to be binding," Trevor exclaimed, "both parties must be willing!"

Michael squeezed Cait's hand so tightly that she flinched. "Cait is willing. If she seems hesitant, it's because she is reluctant to see me put myself in such danger for her."

Cait's eyes widened. He reached up and touched the gold chain that hung around his neck.

"Cait understands that this marriage is in the best interests of Glenmuir ... and the cloister, which she has vowed to protect with her life." Michael looked into her angry russet-colored eyes. "Isn't that so, madam?"

"Aye, my lord Michael." Forcing herself to smile, Cait held their hands high for all to see. "I, Cait nea Sholto, do handfast myself to Michael Langssonn mac Duncan in marriage for one year and the day."

"Nay!" Trevor shouted. "I do not bear witness. I will not have this, nor will Sholto."

"Neither you nor Sholto have a voice in what we've done," Michael replied. "The handfast is binding."

"Aye," Malcolm answered, "the handfast is binding. It requires only their consent, Guardian Priest, not that of witnesses."

"She was not willing," Trevor said. "Somehow he has forced her into this marriage."

"This is my choice, Guardian Priest Trevor," Cait said quietly.

Michael pulled the ring from his little finger. "My lady wife ..."

Such beautiful words, Cait thought, but even more she yearned to hear him call her his *ladylove*.

"I want you to wear my ring of marriage."

Cait gazed at the silver band with the gold crescent. Her mark, the symbol of the gods Night and Day and of their Shelter Stone. Michael's mark also. Did this man blaspheme when he gave her his ring with the same symbol? Would he desecrate the temple she was sworn to protect with her life? She curled her fingers into a fist. Michael uncurled them and slipped the ring onto her fourth finger.

"This ring marks you as mine, my lady Cait," he said.

He had promised to brand her. She had thought it would be a band soldered about her neck. Instead it was a band around her finger—a ring of marriage. In a way the torque would have been more honorable, more honest. As a slave, she had known what he wanted and expected from her. As his wife, she didn't fully understand his purpose, but she feared it boded ill for her and Glenmuir.

"My father Lang," Michael said, "I shall send out the war arrow tonight. To your warriors as well as mine."

"My warriors and I shall be glad to ride with you," Lang replied.

"I want you and your warriors to travel to the ship," Michael said. "Make ready to sail to Glenmuir when my warriors and I arrive."

Lang nodded.

Michael spoke to his brother. "Malcolm, I request as many of your warriors as you can spare." To the guardian priest, he added, "I want you to meet with me and my headmen tonight. Since you have recently been in Glenmuir, I need you to describe how Gilbert is using his warriors."

Trevor glared at Michael, but finally inclined his head.

"Lang," Michael said, "I need to know about the harbor."

"What are you planning, my lord?" Cait asked.

"I have several ideas," Michael answered. "But I need to learn more about the situation before I choose my strategy."

"My lady Jarvia," called a woman from outside the cottage, "I have the broth you wanted for the ailing priest."

Cait rose and opened the door. An elderly woman bustled into the room. A man followed, holding a hot caldron by a handle wrapped in a thick cloth to protect his hand.

"Take it into the sleeping chamber," Cait said.

"My lady wife," Michael said, " 'tis time for you and the women to retire."

"Do you not think I ought—"

Michael shook his head.

"I am the queen of Glenmuir, and I—"

"I am the king of Glenmuir, and I have given you an order." His eyes were blue and hard.

Cait spun around.

"My lord Michael," Jarvia called from the doorway, "with your permission I shall stay to tend Cait's father."

"Thank you, my lady queen," Michael said to her. Then he spoke to Malcolm. "I need my headmen."

Malcolm nodded. "Clete," he called to the male servant, "tell Brian that he is to gather all the bestmen, both of the Duncan and of Langssonn, and meet with us here."

The Horse and the Wolf were joining forces!

Chapter 20

Michael Langssonn and Malcolm mac Duncan—brothers by birth and enemies by upbringing—were now comrades-in-arms by necessity, planning for the coming battle with Gilbert.

Ulf had abandoned the women to join his master in the main room. Cait sat in a chair she had dragged close to the bed and watched her father as he slept feverishly. Across the room Muireall sat in a chair next to the table. In the light of the soapstone lamps, she worked on embroidery that she had sent a servant to fetch. Jarvia sat on a stool beside the bed, tending to Sholto.

" 'Tis a dangerous journey you're embarking on, Cait," Jarvia said softly as she brushed a moist cloth over Sholto's face.

"Aye," Cait answered, thinking more of her distrust of Michael than what she faced with Gilbert.

"But you are returning to your homeland with a husband and a king who will help you."

"Aye, my lady queen, I am." Cait looked down at the ring she wore, her wedding band. Already Michael acted as if Glenmuir belonged to him rather than to her. Or perhaps it was the cloister that he felt belonged to him. Even as his wife, Cait felt like one of his possessions.

The people of Glenmuir would not see Michael as

an avenging Highlander. In light of the recent attack and massacre of the king's family, they would fear him as a Northman set on plundering and usurping their kingdom. His presence could drive them to support Gilbert. No matter that Gilbert was a stranger, he was a Highlander. And as far as Cait knew, the majority of the people might yet support him.

In the main room the wolf barked, startling Cait.

"Ulf," Michael called, his voice carrying into the sleeping chamber. "Who goes there?"

"The Ancient of Nights and Days is here, and no one sent for me," Feich shouted angrily from the other side of the door.

"You aren't needed," Michael answered.

"That I am. The gods sent me."

Smiling, Cait crossed to the door. Before she could open it, the seer rushed into the room.

"Why was I not called?" Feich demanded, her mantle swirling about her spindly body.

"My lord Michael was tending to him." Jarvia's soft voice carried from the bed. "I wanted to let you rest."

Feich grunted as she laid several leathern pouches and an assortment of baskets on the floor next to the fire. She straightened, then pulled off her hood, her wiry hair standing out in all directions.

Michael glared at her. "My lady wife, see that—"

"I'll take care of the matter, my lord." Cait swung the door to close it.

But it bounced back open with a snap, Michael's palm flattened against it. He stared into her upturned face. "My lord what?" he said.

Cait debated not answering, but her defiance would serve no good purpose. "My lord . . . husband."

Michael inclined his head and shut the door.

"Your husband," the seer murmured.

"Aye, we handfasted ourselves tonight," Cait replied.

Feich smiled and moved farther into the room. "That is good, madam. Very good."

"I'm not so sure about it."

"Aye, but it'll be good." She limped over to the bed and knelt beside Sholto. "You have been tending him, my lady queen?"

"As has Lord Michael," Jarvia answered.

Feich lightly laid her ear against Sholto's chest and listened.

"Ah, the rattle is not so deep, no longer life-threatening . . . now." She raised her head and gently pulled off the bandages to look at Sholto's bruised chest, covered with the brownish salve. "Michael did this?"

Jarvia nodded.

Feich cackled. "The boy did well, Muireall."

"The boy?" Cait repeated, surprised by the lack of respect, by the idea that this old woman regarded the dark warrior as a child.

"The gods have given him a gift. By rights, the priest should not have lived." Feich lifted a soapstone lamp and held it closely over the table of medications. One by one she picked up the vials, studied them, and set them back down. She lifted the spoons in the bowls of pastes and powders. She sniffed; she tasted; she rubbed daubs between her thumb and index finger. When she had examined everything to her satisfaction, she returned the lamp to the table and rose from where she knelt.

"He will recover, my lady, but will be extremely weak and will need constant care."

"I shall need help, seer," Cait said. "We're leaving for Glenmuir as soon as we can raise an army."

"Aye, Sholto should stay here in Malcolm's village until the weather is warmer. I will tend him while you are gone. My lady queen, move the priest to my cottage."

"When the men are finished with their battle plans, I shall have it done," Jarvia answered. "If Cait is willing."

"Aye," Cait answered.

The room grew quiet, and Cait listened to the wind howling around the cottage. She knew she and Michael must begin their journey to Glenmuir, but she also knew it would be a hard one at this time of year. They must hurry to beat the autumn snows. And they must fight a battle when they arrived.

"The north wind continues to blow," Feich observed.

"Aye," Muireall murmured. "But I also feel the east wind."

Feich set a stool in front of the hearth. She banked the fire, then opened the leathern pouch about her waist and pulled out objects, which she dropped into the boiling water.

She moved to the table beside the bed and picked up several vials. Returning, she held them in her hands, closed her eyes, and chanted over them. She added several drops to the caldron from each container. When a thick steam rose from the brew, she dipped a long-handled spoon into the caldron and stirred.

The door opened and Malcolm entered. "My lady wife," he said, " 'tis time for us to retire."

"Have you finished with your men's business?" Muireall asked.

"Aye," Malcolm answered. "How is the priest?"

"Better," Feich answered.

Jarvia rose and moved to her husband.

"My queen Muireall," Lang said, standing in the doorway behind Malcolm, "if you are ready, I shall escort you to your cottage."

"Aye, my lord." Muireall straightened and folded up her embroidery, tucking it into her sewing basket.

Glancing down at Feich, Malcolm asked, "What do you see in the water, old mother?"

By now Michael had joined Malcolm. Lang remained in the doorway.

"Come closer to the fire, Northman," Feich said.

Michael looked at his father.

"You, Michael," Feich added. "The spirits are speaking to me. I would read the waters for you."

The wolf padding beside him, Michael crossed over to where the old woman sat. "What do the spirits say, old woman?"

Feich reached into a basket and selected several nuts. With a wooden hammer she tried to crack the nuts against the rocks that circled the fire pit, but her hands were too stiff. The nuts kept rolling away from her.

"Will I ruin your magic if I help you?" Michael asked.

"Nay, 'twill be good," Feich said.

Michael squatted beside her and quickly cracked five of the hazelnuts.

"You know the magical number?" she mumbled.

"Nay, I just selected that many. I knew if I didn't have the correct number, you would tell me."

Feich took them from him and dropped both the meat and the shells into the caldron. She stirred and studied the contents. "You are destined to rule a powerful kingdom, lord."

"Aye, my father's estate."

"One of the largest in the Highlands."

Michael smiled. "Nay, in Northland."

"Mayhap," Feich mumbled. "The waters are not clear." She lifted a dipper of liquid from the caldron and slowly poured it back in. "Before you rule over this kingdom, you will honor your vow to the gods."

"Aye," Michael said. "I shall kill the man who dishonored my father's name."

"You will do that."

Michael smiled. "Thank you, madam, but I did not need the spirits to tell me that."

"My lord Michael," Trevor called from the main hall, "one more question, a question of import."

When Michael started to rise, Feich caught his arm. Ulf growled and raised his hackles. Michael eased his arm over the wolf's neck and calmed him.

"I see a dark time, Michael," Feich said. "A very dark time. You will need help from the gods."

He leaned over and looked into the caldron with her.

"Remember you are the Lord of Thunder, the ruler of darkness, king of the dark time of the year." The old woman drew him closer. "You, Michael, can see in your darkness. Do not forget." She turned him loose, but kept mumbling, "Do not forget. You can see in the darkness."

"My lord Michael," Trevor called again.

A worried frown on his face, Michael left the room. Malcolm and Lang followed.

An ominous silence descended. No matter what Cait's doubts concerning Michael, she loved him and wanted nothing evil to befall him.

"Woman of sight," Jarvia said, "is Malcolm the one whom Michael kills?"

"The spirits do not show me the face of the man,"

Feich replied. "They speak to me only of what will happen."

"Is there no magic you can perform to ensure their safety?"

"Nay, the gods have decreed the future. No mortal can change it."

Jarvia knelt by Feich and laid her hands on the old woman's lap. "Please, old mother, find a way."

Feich brushed her hand through Jarvia's hair. "I shall do my best, my daughter, but this is the dark time of the year, and Night reigns supreme."

"I'm glad that Michael is traveling to Glenmuir with you, Cait," Jarvia said. "Mayhap that will give Malcolm time to learn who did raid Lord Lang's ship. Mayhap it will save an innocent man from being killed."

Michael, Cait thought.

Malcolm, Jarvia thought.

Feich rose. "Now, my lady, 'tis time for us to move the high priest to my cottage so that I may tend to him."

Once more, Cait and Michael were alone in the cottage. The wind blew with greater fury, but a warm fire blazed in the center hearth. Cait stood in front of the flames, twisting Michael's ring on her finger. It felt strange on her hand. "Why did you handfast with me?" she asked.

He pulled his shirt over his head and laid it on the back of the chair closest to the bed. "You need my help, and would not accept it otherwise."

"How will you benefit from the marriage?"

He untied the thongs that bound his boots about his legs. "I will have you."

"You had me without marriage."

"Now I have the queen of Glenmuir."

"Aye, my lord, that is what concerns me. What does the queen have that you desire?"

He took off his right boot, then his left.

"Her kingdom?" Cait asked. "Her cloister?"

"Both came to me when I wed you," Michael answered.

"Do you plan on remaining in Glenmuir once Gilbert has been vanquished and my throne has been secured?"

"Nay," he answered. "When I bought you from the king's men, I told them—and you—that I was a sojourner of the world. I have no desire to rule a Highland kingdom. I handfasted with you because we can help each other." He rose and began to unfasten the latchets on his girdle.

She gazed at the Cloister Breastpin that rested in the crisp black hair on his chest. The amulet that had been entrusted to her for safekeeping.

"You need a consort in order to claim your High Seat," he said.

"I could have found another consort."

"But not a champion to fight the usurper Gilbert, or marauding sea raiders, or anyone else who tries to take your kingdom. You said that a helmet and sword similar to the one I described was among the cloister treasures. If Lachlann is not guilty of stealing the rupture-endowment, I believe the man who is guilty may be in Glenmuir. As king, I have the right and freedom to search for him."

"Will you return the Cloister Breastpin to me?"

"Nay, I shall keep it." Michael removed his girdle and laid it on the table.

"Michael—"

"I have said all I intend to say." He smiled and waved toward the bed. "Now, my lady, it is time for the marriage bed."

"We are handfasted before the people," Cait said, "but it shall be a marriage in name only, Michael. We shall use each other to gain our ends, but you will not use my body."

His eyes narrowed. "I never have. I have treasured your body, have given and received pleasure from you."

What Michael said was true, but Cait was determined not to be used by him.

"I shall sleep in the Small Hall."

"Nay, lady, you will sleep with me. I did not buy you from Ardac and handfast with you so that I could sleep alone."

" 'Tis because you forced me to handfast with you that you shall sleep alone."

"Lady, you have one year and a day to conceive a child. That alone should be motive enough for your sleeping with me." He walked to stand before her. "Cait, let's be reasonable."

Reasonable! Cait thought.

"We are handfasted. Let's make the best of the situation."

He caught her hands and held them loosely. His eyes, framed by long, dark lashes, looked warmly into hers. They pleaded as eloquently as his soft voice.

"We enjoy mating with each other," he said.

"Aye, lord," she confessed, "I do enjoy the carnal pleasure that we share, but surely more pleasure is to be gained from it when both parties consent to it."

"You have consented before."

"Aye, my lord, but I thought then that I would be freed from my bondage to you. Now I see no freedom. I truly belong to you, and if we have a child, it will also belong to you."

He gazed into her eyes. "What if during this year another heir was found, one who is closer in lineage to the queen than you are?" he asked. "Would you not be free to give the High Seat to this person and to return to your former way of life?"

"Was that your reasoning when you handfasted yourself to me?"

"I had given the matter fleeting thought," he admitted.

" 'Twould be too disruptive to the kingdom, sire, for us to change rulers so soon. Once I am crowned queen of Glenmuir, I shall be queen. My eldest child will be the next ruler of the kingdom."

She withdrew her hands from his and looked down as his fingers grazed her wedding band. He hesitated and rubbed his thumb over the golden crescent.

"The only way I shall sleep with you," Cait said, "is if you force me."

"That, I won't do," Michael replied. "But you will sleep in this room in this bed with me. For all purposes, for your welfare, you will make this look like a real marriage."

"Thank you, my lord, for understanding and for helping me," Cait said. "I know this will be difficult for you—"

"Don't thank me," he said. "I am keeping you in my bed for selfish reasons, lady. You are a fiery woman by nature and have tasted the pleasure of letching. You will want more. Soon you'll be begging me to make love to you."

"You are insufferable!"

"So I have been told many times, lady."

Michael shucked off his trousers and leggings and faced her, almost daring her to look away from his naked body. She looked at him. The broad chest covered with crisp, dark hair. The flat stomach. The pelt of dark pubic hair that surrounded his semi-aroused manhood. Cait wanted him. She would continue to want him.

No matter how difficult the task ahead of her, she would not relent. She had lost her heart to the Northman, but she would not lose her kingdom and the Shelter Stone to him as well.

Michael moved to the bed, lay down, and stretched out. He seemed to be flaunting his masculinity, daring her to refuse the passion that blazed between them. She strode across the room, as always, giving wide berth to the wolf, and opened one of the trunks, digging through it for extra blankets.

"It's cold and wet outside, Cait," Michael said. "And we have few hours for sleep. I want to see Lang off. He and his warriors are leaving on the morrow." He patted the mattress. "Sleep here. I'm not going to touch you."

Cait looked at him. *I don't have to force you*, the blue eyes said. *You'll come to me soon enough.* She almost gasped. For the first time he had allowed her to read his eyes.

"Aye, Cait, I want to mate with you, and you want it also. But I won't, not until you come to me."

"Then, my lord, you shall never have me." She began to unfasten her girdle, her fingers trembling. "Not because I do not want it. I do. But I shall not give in to my lust. And as soon as the year and the day have passed, I shall object to our marriage."

"That's the beauty of the handfasting," Michael said. "Either party can ask for its end without recrimination."

"Also know this, Michael. If I have already conceived from you and a child is born of this marriage, it is mine. I don't care if you announce your objection to the handfasting first, *the child is mine.* Any child I bear, Michael Langssonn, is my child, and I shall part with it only through death."

"Unless you have already conceived, madam," Michael said, "I don't see how such a situation will arise . . . since we are to have a marriage of convenience."

Cait started to pull her tunic over her head, intending to flaunt her naked body as he had done, but she thought better of it. He made no secret of wanting to bed her. She was the one who objected. Still clothed, she pulled a sleeping tunic from her satchel. Moving to a shadowed corner of the room, she quickly changed into the gown. It fit closely about her neck, had long sleeves, and hung to the floor. She returned to the bed, scooted beneath the covers, and turned her back to Michael.

"Ah, my lady wife," he murmured, flipping over and cradling her body with his. "Just holding you is a pleasure."

Cait felt his warm breath against her neck. He laid his arm over her and tucked his fingers beneath her waist and the mattress. She shivered, and knew that she loved Michael Langssonn. How hard it would be to keep him from her body when he occupied her heart.

"Your hair," he murmured. "It's tickling my face."

They shifted and settled back down, his hand once more around her waist.

"Were you trying to bind me in a silken web, madam?"

"Nay," she murmured. "There is no need. You have already bound me as tightly as it is possible to bind another person."

She had tied herself to him because she could not turn her back on the Shelter Stone or her people.

But how much longer could she turn her back on her love?

Only four nights passed, but with each one, Cait found it more difficult to keep her vow to Michael. No matter that he had coerced her into marriage, she loved him. And she wanted him. Her body ached for the fulfillment that only he could give.

Michael had also been true to his promise. He slept with Cait every night, hugging her tightly to him, but he did not try to make love. When she awakened in the morning, he was gone and she would not see him until the evening meal, which they always took in the Great Hall.

Cait spent most of her time in the seer's cottage visiting with her father, who was growing steadily stronger. Not wanting to add to his worries, she did not tell him that Michael had the Cloister Breastpin. When Sholto went to sleep, she returned to the guesthouse.

She was walking on the pathway when she spied Ulf dashing between storehouses. She followed him and found him lying beside one of the storehouses behind the Great Hall. She stepped closer and peeked around the corner of the building. There lay another wolf, a female.

"Like your master, Lord Wolf," Cait said, "you have found a mate."

Ulf leaped up, pranced around, and barked.

"Now I know where you have been going, and I have a feeling I know what will be happening in the near future." She resumed her walk and called over her shoulder, "Enjoy your lady while you can."

She returned to the cottage and took out her mending. She was preparing her own and Michael's clothes for the journey to Glenmuir. Days were passing. Time was running out. They had only nine days in which to save the people whom Gilbert had imprisoned. And generally with the best of traveling conditions and the strongest of animals, the trip took seven full days. If they ran into any kind of trouble, bandits or inclement weather, they could be held up for a long time.

She fretted that Michael was not organizing the army quickly enough. They had received no word from Glenmuir since her father and Trevor had arrived. She wondered what was happening there.

Hearing voices, Cait set her mending aside and went to the door. Michael and Malcolm were walking up the lane toward her. During the past few days, they had developed a mutual respect, and were on the way to establishing a true friendship.

She marveled that they looked so much alike. Although they were identical, Cait was convinced that Michael stood out from all other men, his brother included. Always when she looked at him, her heart beat faster and she felt light and happy. He was her love.

"Good afternoon, my husband. I have news for you. Your wolf has a female companion. I found them visiting today behind the Great Hall."

"So that's where he's been slipping off to."

Malcolm shook his head. "I'm sure Jarvia is going to want to keep the entire litter."

"Since we're grandparents of sorts," Cait said, "I think we have a say in that, my lord."

They laughed, and Michael pulled Cait into his arms and kissed her.

"I also have good news for you, my lady wife. We shall be able to depart for Glenmuir on the morrow."

"That *is* good news! Does my father know?"

"Nay, I just learned it myself."

"I received word from one of my outriders," Malcolm said. "Lachlann and his men are returning home. They should be here by evening. With Lachlann remaining behind to protect the kingdom, I shall be able to travel with you and Michael."

"Thank you, my lord," Cait said. "My father and I appreciate your support."

"I'm doing it because I pledged an oath to your father," Malcolm said, "but I'm also going because Michael and I are curious about the helmet and sword that you saw among the cloister treasures. I've wondered if perhaps an old enemy of mine, Ghaltair, is in Glenmuir. The man I killed the other night was his friend, and it stands to reason that they might still be riding together. Perhaps Ghaltair is also one of Gilbert's men. He would ride with a man like Gilbert."

"I feel that the answer to clearing Malcolm's name lies in Glenmuir," Michael said. "Also, his alliance with us carries weight. When others see that the strongest high king in this part of the Highlands supports you, they will hesitate to side with Gilbert."

"My lord Malcolm," Cait said, "would you join Michael and me for a biscuit and a glass of ale?"

"Aye, madam, I will."

As they entered the cottage and sat down, Cait said, "My lord, I'm so glad that we're leaving. I've been worried, sitting here unable to do anything while you organize your warriors."

"The task ahead of us is a difficult one," Michael said. "We must ride early and hard. Once we get to the ship, the men and horses will have some respite."

" 'Twould be good if we had the element of surprise on our side," Malcolm said.

Michael nodded. "I'm hoping we may have, brother. Traveling by river will save us several days' time."

Cait smiled to herself as she lifted the biscuits from the basket into the serving dish. This was the first time she had heard the endearment slip off Michael's tongue so easily, and evidently unnoticed by either man.

"Since the king's village is built in the fork of the rivers," Malcolm said, "Gilbert will have watchmen posted."

"We'll land to the south of the village," Michael said, "and move the rest of the way by pony."

As they ate their biscuits, the brothers discussed different strategies for taking the village. Cait, returning to her mending, joined in the conversation. When she heard a bark outside, she laid aside the garment she was sewing and let Ulf in.

"So, my friend," Michael said, "you have found yourself a woman."

Ulf nuzzled Michael's hand, twisting his head and growling playfully until Michael scratched him behind the ears.

Malcolm rose. " 'Tis time for me to go."

"Have you forgotten our wager?" Michael said.

"Nay, brother. You dance and I pipe."

Michael laughed. "Already the studhorse is mine, little brother. I think I shall learn to dance much sooner than you shall learn to pipe." He paused, then added seriously, "But first we must vanquish Gilbert."

Chapter 21

"'Tis time to leave Glenmuir, Gilbert,"
Ardac said. He stood in front of the
dais in the Great Hall. "Both Sholto and Trever are
alive. Ern talked with the herdsmen who carried
them to Malcolm's village. Sholto announced in
front of witnesses, including High King Malcolm
and Trevor, that Cait is the heir. He quoted her
genealogy, tracing her back to the royal family."

His face glum, his shoulders drooping, Gilbert
slumped in the High Seat.

"Ern also learned that Cait is handfasted to the
Northman, Michael Langssonn, and that he and
Malcolm mac Duncan have joined forces. Together
they have sixty warriors," Ardac continued. "They
were planning to begin their journey yesterday."

Gilbert pushed out of the chair and shuffled to
the fire, but the flames did not warm him. He felt
old and used and cold. He picked up one of the
metal fire tongs and pushed the burning logs. Embers sputtered; smoke fogged up the room. Holding
the tongs in front of him, he stared at the glowing
tip.

"Did you hear me, Gilbert? The combined army
is large and well trained. We may be equal in
number, but we're not as strong as they are, and we
cannot count on the loyalty of our men."

"I won't leave without my treasure," Gilbert declared. "I stole the rupture-endowment from Malcolm, and it's mine."

"Gilbert, you're not making sense," Ardac said. "You don't have the Breastpin or Cait or Sholto. Since you've taken the High Council members prisoners, the people of Glenmuir are no longer loyal to you, and we don't have the booty to hire mercenaries to fight for us. Too much is against us. 'Tis time to leave."

Gilbert shook his head. "I'll not leave before I have my treasure out of that cloister. It belongs to me, not to the Shelter Stone." Gilbert laid down the tongs. "It's strange that no messenger has arrived with news that Cait is the queen on her way to claim her throne."

"They have not had time," Ardac answered. "Ern rode day and night, stopping along the way only to change ponies."

"Nay," Gilbert said, "I don't think it has to do with time, Ardac. I believe they are deliberately keeping this news secret because they don't want me to know."

Ardac looked skeptical.

"We shall ambush them and capture Cait," Gilbert said, "and I shall marry her at the shrine." He laughed. "I shall have Blar bless the union and pronounce me king of Glenmuir. Then, Ardac, we will have won."

"What about the executions?" Ardac asked.

"They shall proceed as planned."

"Lang isn't here, and my ship is gone!" Michael exclaimed in disbelief.

He stared at the raging river that separated Duncan Territory from Athdara. Rain had pelted down for two days and nights. The river was turbulent and swollen. It would rise even more. Time was passing, and soon Gilbert would begin the executions.

The swollen river was barely contained by its banks. Ulf, his wet fur plastered to his sleek body, ran up and down the bank.

"We need to look for the ship," Michael said. "The storm may have forced Lang to move it."

"This is the safest place to cross over," Malcolm said.

"We'll cross over," Michael said, "and I'll look for the ship along that shoreline. If we don't find it, we'll travel by land. Kolby, do you have your bow?"

"Aye."

Since Northmen preferred swords and battle-axes as weapons, they infrequently used the bow. During their travels, however, Kolby had bartered for one, and had become proficient in its use.

Both men stared across the river.

"Can you do it?" Michael asked.

"Swim across and shoot the line back over here?" Michael nodded.

Kolby grinned. "Aye, I'm your strongest swimmer and best bowman."

Michael grinned and clapped his friend on the shoulder. "You are the strongest swimmer and the *only* bowman."

After stripping off his clothing, Kolby slipped the bow and quiver of arrows over his shoulders. All watched as he battled the raging waters, the whirlpools, and the floating debris. Finally he crawled ashore, kneeling on hands and knees as he caught his breath. Then he rose and quickly secured the rope around a large oak tree. He attached the other end of the rope to the arrow, nocked it, and let it fly. The arrow sailed, sure and fast, to land in front of Michael's boots. Michael looked down, then across the shore at Kolby. Both men laughed.

Soon equipment, ponies, and warriors were moving cautiously across the gushing water. Only Cait, the guardian priest, Michael, and Malcolm . . . and the wolf . . . remained.

"Guardian Priest, are you a strong swimmer?" Michael asked.

"Aye, my lord."

"Then I shall let you go now. Cait will follow."

Trevor nodded and slipped out of his mantle. Cait dropped it into a satchel. When he went to loop the strap over his shoulder, Michael took it from him.

"I'll carry it for you."

The wind blew, and Cait shivered.

The guardian priest patted her shoulder. " 'Tis cold and will be even colder in the water, but we have a kingdom and a shrine to save. Our people are depending on us."

He turned, caught hold of the rope, and began to cross.

"Now, Cait," Michael said, " 'tis time for you to go."

"Aye." She slipped out of her mantle and dropped it into her satchel. She threw the strap over her shoulder, but Michael also pulled this one from her and slipped his arm through the strap.

"I'll bring it over," he said. "I don't want you weighted down either."

He reached for her purse, but she clamped her arm down, imprisoning the pouch. "Nay, lord, I shall carry it. 'Tis my good-luck talisman."

"I'll be right behind you, lady."

"I want to carry it."

They gazed into each other's eyes. Rain fell on them. Water sluiced down their faces. Michael's hair was tied back at the neck, but strands had escaped the thong to lie against his forehead and cheeks. He had not taken the time to shave, and beard stubble darkened his jaws and chin.

Remembering Feich's prophecy, Cait thought Michael did look like the storm, like the Lord of Thunder, the ruler of the night and the dark time of the year. And this man was her husband.

"Please, Michael," she said. "I know you're trying to help me, but I want the purse with me."

Michael nodded, but caught her hands in his. "Be careful, my lady wife." He leaned over and placed his lips against hers. Briefly, sweetly, they kissed. Then he stepped back. "May the gods protect you."

"May they protect you, my . . . husband."

With a last look at Michael, Cait stepped into the river. As the cold water rushed around her, she sucked in her breath. Her teeth chattered. Michael stepped in behind her. Only now did Ulf leap into the water, using his powerful body to struggle against the surging current.

Ahead, the priest had stopped. A small tree branch had hit him, and he was looking wildly about as he clung to the line.

"Cait," he shouted. "Where are you?"

"I'm here," she answered.

On the rope behind Cait, Michael called out, "Don't be frightened, priest. Pull with your arms and push with your legs."

"The gods are angry," Trevor shouted. "Look. They curse us."

Cait turned to see a tree trunk sailing down the river toward them.

"Move, old man!" Michael thundered.

"Move, my lord," Cait screamed.

The tree hit a boulder, bounced back and across the river. A huge wave hit the three of them full force. Trevor gasped, screamed, and lost his grip on the rope. He flailed his arms, kicked, and splashed in the water, then managed to catch the lifeline with one hand.

"Help me!" he cried. "Someone help me!"

"Hang on!" Cait shouted back.

Her eyes burning, strands of hair stuck to her face, she battled the current. She pulled with her arms. She pushed with her legs. At last she grabbed the priest's robe in her fist. Her purse strap slipped off her shoulder.

"Grab the rope," she ordered.

Trevor caught her.

"Not me. The rope, Trevor."

"Cait," Michael called. "I'm coming."

"Grab the rope," Cait kept yelling as she fought Trevor with one hand and hung on to the line with the other. Her purse fell into the water.

"My purse!" she screamed. A surge of water hit her and Trevor. The rope cut into her fingers; it burned her palm, but she held on. She felt as if her arms would be jerked out at the sockets.

Trevor fought. He kicked and swung his arms.

Then Michael was there, one arm around both of them. He jammed a fist into the priest's face. With a groan Trevor sunk into oblivion. Michael caught him in one arm, the rope with the other.

"Are you all right, Cait?" he called.

"Aye." Breathing deeply, she held on to the rope with both hands.

She looked down the river. Her purse bobbed up and down. The purse her mother had made for her.

Her good magic. Her blades. Her heart ached at the thought of losing her magical talisman.

Ulf crawled ashore, rested a moment, then stood and shook himself wildly. He danced around, and looked across the river as if searching for Michael.

"Cait," Michael called again.

"Take Trevor on over," she said between gasps. "I'm all right."

"I'll take both of you." Michael held the priest with one hand, the rope with the other.

"Nay." She sucked precious air into her lungs. "I can make it. I need time to rest."

"Take the priest over," Malcolm shouted, moving across the line. "I'll help her."

Nodding, Michael slowly crossed the river with his burden. When he reached the other side, he looked back at Cait.

"I'm all right," she called. "I can make it."

Malcolm was right behind her.

Michael pulled himself and the priest ashore. Ulf raced to him and licked his face. Laughing, coughing, spitting out water, Michael circled an arm around the animal and hugged him tightly.

Hanging on to the rope, moving slowly toward shore, Cait gazed at her purse. It was momentarily wedged against a rock.

Michael, drawn by the imaginary line of her vision, also looked downstream. He saw the brown leather bobbing in the water. Cait's purse. He saw the dismay on her face and leaped into the water.

"No, Michael!" she screamed.

"No, Michael!" Kolby shouted.

Michael was a strong swimmer, but he was exhausted after his bout with the priest, and the current was stronger than he was. He fought. The water fought back. It was cold and numbing. It tried to catch him in its whirlpools and suck him under. His arms hurt, his chest. He could hardly breathe. He pushed on. Cait's family had been brutally taken from her, as had her two friends. He wouldn't let her lose her purse.

He saw it. He reached out. It bobbed against the end of his fingers. It danced away. The river tormented him. With a burst of energy, a groan, he surged forward and clasped the strap. It slipped away; he caught it again. He had it. He relaxed, sank under the water, and swirled around.

Then he pushed up and out. Shaking hair from his eyes, he looked around to get his bearings. He saw all of them waiting for him, running down the shore calling to him. He saw the tree limb that Malcolm and Kolby extended into the water.

Tired. He was too tired to move. His eyes closed. The river goddess called to him.

"Michael!" Cait shouted. "My lord, please don't die. Grab hold of the branch."

Michael opened his eyes. Drenched, her clothing plastered to her body, her russet hair tangled around her face, Cait knelt on the shore, holding her hands out to him. Ulf barked frantically. Michael didn't swim toward the branch. He swam to her, to his little bard. But he couldn't lift his arms. His legs were a dead weight on his body, pulling him down ... down.

Then he felt something grip his shirt. He heard the snarl and knew it was Ulf. "Go back," Michael said, but he was too tired to make it a command.

The wolf tugged.

In the far distance Michael heard Cait's voice. "Michael, don't die!"

"Sing," he whispered. "Sing ..." *Sing my song as*

I cross over, he thought, his mind slipping into oblivion.

Then something pricked his face. He opened his eyes and cursed. The tree limb. Somehow he had collided into it. He didn't so much clasp it as become entangled in it. But he held on, and Ulf held on to him. Michael wilted as he allowed the two warriors to drag him in.

"By the gods, Michael!" Kolby swore angrily. "If you do something foolish like this again, I'll let you die and take your chances with the gods."

Michael grinned. Ulf flopped down beside him, laying his head across his master's thigh. Michael rubbed the animal's muzzle.

Sitting on the wet ground, Cait cradled Michael's head in her lap. "Oh, Michael," she whispered, pushing wet strands of hair from his eyes. Her tears and kisses mingled with rain on his face.

When he finally sat up, he handed her the purse. "Madam, I don't think I shall do this again."

Cait laughed shakily. "Nay, lord."

Michael pushed to his feet, tugging the shivering woman with him. "My lady Cait—" He stopped and looked into her eyes, swollen from tears. Then he gathered her into his arms and hugged her tightly, warmly. "My lady wife, you have no mantle."

From between chattering teeth, she said, "And you don't have one to give me, my lord . . . husband."

Within minutes Kolby and Malcolm had thrown dry mantles around them.

"Are we going to move on today," Kolby asked, "or stop here?"

"If we can find shelter," Michael said, "we'll camp for the night. If not, we'll move on."

"There's a cavern some distance over there."

Malcolm pointed. " 'Tis large enough to shelter some of us. We have enough daylight to build some shelters for the animals."

"Lead us to it, brother."

Malcolm in the lead, the procession resumed. It was dusk by the time they arrived at the cave. Without much talking, the warriors began to set up camp. Soon one large fire was burning in the center of the cavern, and the warriors were cutting branches for lean-to shelters against the rocks and scattered trees. Once they had laced the branches together with thongs, they stuffed the cracks with heather and bracken. It was enough to keep them relatively dry.

To give Cait and Michael privacy, the warriors stacked more branches in front of the cave. Michael helped her out of her sodden clothing. He dried her off with firm, brisk strokes, trying to bring warmth to her body, color to her skin. When she was clad in a dry shirt and trousers, she snuggled beneath the covers. Ulf also snuggled on an old blanket that Michael spread for him between their pallet and the fire. Michael changed quickly, spread their clothes on satchels in front of the fire to dry, and was soon beside her, holding her.

"My lord," she murmured, her face pressed against his massive chest, "I was so frightened. I thought you were . . ." She shuddered, thinking about him drowning.

His embrace tightened. "Don't cry anymore," he whispered. "I didn't drown, and I retrieved your purse."

She gazed into the face of the man she loved more than life itself. "The purse is one of my most treasured possessions, Michael, but it is not worth your life." *You mean more to me than any material thing.*

Lying close to her, he stroked her back until she fell asleep.

Michael did not sleep. He felt different about Cait. For a reason he hadn't yet identified—or wasn't willing to acknowledge—he hadn't wanted her to make the journey to Glenmuir without first marrying him. He felt that her safety lay in his hands, not as her champion but as her husband. Her father loved her, Trevor cared for her, but Gilbert posed a threat to her that only he, Michael, could destroy.

Besides, he told himself, there was no reason for him not to accompany her. The duel between him and Malcolm had been postponed . . . and he hoped to find evidence that would make a duel unnecessary.

Michael also admitted he hadn't liked the idea of Cait looking for another husband. Their problems and goals were becoming so interwoven, it was hard to tell them apart.

As unsettling as the thought was, her future had become his also.

Chapter 22

Michael was dreaming. He knew it, but he couldn't wake up. He was drowning.

"Michael!"

He heard Cait call his name. He saw her on the shore. But the current was sucking him under the water.

"Michael!"

He couldn't get to her.

"Wake up, Michael."

She clutched both shoulders and shook him. He felt as if she were pulling him out of the water. Wet with perspiration, he opened his eyes and stared up into Cait's face, illuminated by fireglow. His breathing was labored, his heartbeat accelerated. He dragged air into his lungs.

"Michael—" Kolby's voice came from the other side of the rocks "—did you call?"

"Nay, my lord Kolby," Cait answered. "He was—we were—"

Kolby laughed softly. "I apologize, my lady, I only—"

"Think nothing of it, headman," she said. "All is well."

"Aye, madam, all is well."

Grateful to Cait for hiding his distress, Michael sat up. He brushed his hands through his hair.

Grabbing the tail of his shirt, he whipped it over his head and slung it to the side of the pallet. Just as quickly, he stripped out of his damp trousers, pulling the covers over his legs and hips.

She sat up beside him. "Another one of your dreams?"

"Aye." Michael breathed deeply, welcoming the cooling breeze. He considered his dreams and visions a weakness, and had not discussed them with anyone ... until he had seen Labyrinth Hill. Then he had confided a little to Cait, and more fully to Malcolm because Malcolm also had dreams. He understood.

Tonight his dream haunted him as none of the others had.

"Malcolm and I were drowning," he said. "Each of us was calling to the other, but it was dark and we couldn't see. I tried to reach him, but I couldn't find him."

The wind grew brisker, and Michael slid down on the pallet, sinking into the warmth of the covers and the softness of his wife. Cait snuggled up to him, and he enfolded her in his arms. He listened to the river rushing outside the cave. In his dream he was on the side of a mountain. Somehow he pulled Malcolm over, and both of them fell into the river.

Michael wasn't frightened for himself. He was a strong swimmer and had swum in cold water all his life. But he was frightened for Malcolm.

"I believe in dreams," Cait told him, "but oftentimes, my lord, the meaning is different from the actual events." She brushed her fingers through his hair. "Mayhap you dreamed this tonight because of all that happened today."

"Some of it may have been caused by today's events," Michael admitted, "but not all of it, Cait. It was real." He was quiet for a long time. Then he said, "It's going to happen."

"Everything will be all right." She wanted to add, *my love.*

Michael had not yet come to grips with his feelings for Malcolm. Never having had a brother, he wasn't sure what he should be feeling. But he didn't want Malcolm to die—not like in the dream and not by his hand.

"I have a feeling that Malcolm is telling the truth when he says he knows nothing of the theft of the rupture-endowment," Michael said. "I hope we find the man who stole it."

Cait continued to hold him in her arms. She felt that he needed her comfort. More, she wanted his closeness.

"For the first time in my life, I am beginning to understand my dreams and visions. I always thought I was seeing myself, but I was dreaming about Malcolm. His father. His torque." Michael paused. "At first I was shocked to learn that I was not Lang's birth son. But now I feel a completeness that I never have before." Michael laughed. "My mother told me that when the time came, I would understand. Now I do."

He breathed deeply and lay still. His hands began to move down Cait's back.

"At times I'm almost sure I know what Malcolm's thinking. I know what he's going to say."

They lapsed into a companionable silence, cuddling each other.

She brushed her hand over the amulet on his chest. "Michael?"

"Umm." He lowered his head.

Cait lifted her face at the same time, and their lips brushed together. As desire flowed hotly through her, she forgot about the cloister pin. She slid her palms up his chest.

"Cait?"

She knew what he was asking. She had told him she wouldn't give in to temptation, but this was Michael Langssonn, the man she loved, the man who had risked his life to save her most prized possession.

"Aye."

She sat up, pushing the covers aside, and stripped out of her clothing. Then she snuggled against him, reveling in the fire they sparked when their naked bodies touched.

Even if Michael hadn't saved the purse, she would have answered the same way. She wanted no other husband or lover. He was her man, and she had a year and a day to convince him that he belonged to the Highlands and to her.

The moment his lips touched hers, the quick rush of passion lapped through her veins. Michael strewed kisses across her collarbone as his hands explored her body, thrilling her with their fevered search. He captured her whimpers of delight with his kisses.

When he raised his mouth from hers, he ran his hand through her hair.

"Thank you for saving my purse," she whispered.

"This isn't a thank you for that, is it?" he asked.

"Nay," she answered. "I want to mate with you."

"And we shall."

His finger touched her soft mouth. She parted her lips and took it into her mouth. She grazed it with her teeth and brushed it with her tongue, up one side, down the other. She sucked on it, running her tongue over and around the tip.

He withdrew his hand and ran his damp finger

over her breasts, circling the areolas. Then he shifted his weight, slipping both hands beneath her breasts. He delighted in the feel of the satin-smooth weight in his palms. He kissed the gentle swells until he reached a tempting crest. His lips closed over it, and he suckled. Desire flooded through her body.

"No one else," he murmured, his breath touching the damp skin and whetting her desire to an ever higher pitch.

"No one else what?" she muttered, awash in a torrent of passion.

"I don't want anyone else loving your body as I do, lady."

"Are you talking about suckling my breasts?" she asked.

She felt the tantalizing brush of his mouth against her highly sensitized flesh as he nodded.

"A babe will someday, my lord."

He released her and raised his head. "Aye, my lady wife, a baby will. Our baby."

Our baby. Aye, she would have his baby.

Michael's head lowered, and his lips touched the tip of her nose. "I think I should be jealous of the wee little thing."

His words sent pleasure rippling through Cait.

"Nestled against your body and supping on your breasts."

"Nay, my lord, the goddesses have given a woman a special body. She gives her body to her warrior in love and receives his seed of life. She holds it within her body as it grows into a babe, and her heart holds more than enough love for her warrior and his babes."

He laid his palm on her flat stomach. "Here, my little bard, is the caldron wherein she holds the seed of life."

She caught his hand and guided it lower. "Here is where she receives her warrior into the caldron, lord."

Michael's fingers gently curled into her as he captured her lips again, urgently, demandingly. Cait writhed beneath the love strokes, her stomach contracting with the sweet ache of desire. As if it were the first time they had mated, Cait caught her breath and moaned softly. She arched, thrusting more fully against his hand.

"Oh, my husband," Cait whimpered, "you make me feel like the river outside our cave."

"How so, my lady?"

"Desire for you rages through my body. You are the thunder, the lightning, the rain."

As the lightning and thunder went together, so did she and Michael. Because of him, Cait knew the joy of perfect communion between man and woman.

She tangled her hands in his hair and brought his face to hers. Her lips captured his, and she pulled his body over hers. His hair-matted chest touched her throbbing breasts; the muscle-corded stomach rubbed against her softer one.

He wedged his knee between her thighs, carefully spreading her legs. As carefully he lowered himself, his hardness pressed against her softness. She was ready. He knew.

"My lady wife." With his hand he gently prepared her for entry. His lips closed on hers.

Simultaneously she received his tongue into her mouth and his manhood into her femininity. They kissed. Wild. Urgent. Demanding. Her hands stroked as she gave pleasure to him. Her hips swayed with his motion, heightening his anticipation.

He began to move faster. Her arms closed around his body, and her fingers dug into his back. She arched to receive him deeper; she withdrew, then arched again ... and again. She wanted no gentle coupling. She truly wanted to become one with the raging storm that was her husband. The deeper he thrust, the higher Cait soared. Like a bolt of lightning, pleasure burned through her to set her ablaze in the core of her being. She gasped; he tensed.

They reached fulfillment together, their cries becoming the essence of their kiss.

They lay in the peaceful afterglow, hardly moving, barely breathing, not daring to break the spell that bound them together. They reveled in their moment of oneness, a moment that no one, nothing, could take from them.

They fell into a sated sleep in each other's arms.

The woman's hair, gleaming like spun gold, hung down her back in a long, thick braid. Her red mantle fell to her ankles and swirled around her tall, slender body. Her soft laughter danced on the wind.

The morning had dawned brisk and sunny, and Cait lay alone on her pallet in the cave, basking as much in the afterglow of her and Michael's lovemaking as she did in the warmth of the fire. She stared at the woman who stood talking with her husband.

Cait didn't know who the stranger was, but she was a strikingly beautiful woman. Wide-set eyes. Full lips. Oval face. Golden hair. It was the combination of these features that gave her an appearance men found alluring.

Although a storm had been raging around them, this woman was the essence of summer—warm and cheerful and bright.

A gust of wind billowed the red mantle aside, and Cait saw that the stranger wore a shirt, trousers, and boots. About her waist was strapped a sword and a dirk. She was also a lady of war.

Glad for the warmth of the fire, Cait shoved down the covers, quickly dressed, and put on her boots. As soon as she had combed her hair, she was on her feet, throwing her mantle over her shoulders. She ran out of the cave.

In the distance Brian and Kolby barked orders as warriors loaded their gear and ponies aboard a ship. Michael's ship! Cait looked again. Evidently Lang had arrived during the night.

Ulf frisked about, running up and down the banks and on and off the boat. As long as the men accorded him the respect and space he demanded, he ignored them.

"Your ship, my lord," Cait called gleefully as she joined Michael. "You found your ship."

"Nay, lady, it isn't mine." Michael draped an arm around Cait. "This one belongs to Lady Gwynneth. Lady Gwynneth, let me present you to Cait nea Sholto."

The woman looked at Cait with twinkling gray eyes. "Do you realize, my lady, that you are worth five pounds of gold if I bring you into Glenmuir and present you alive and well to Gilbert?"

Cait laughed softly. "My value has gone up. When I left Glenmuir, Gilbert thought I was worth only a pound. His men paid three. Now it's five." She laughed again. "If I live long enough, my worth will be quite high."

"Lady Gwynneth—" Michael began.

"Wynne," the woman corrected him, her full lips curving into a luminous smile. "When I chose to be a seafarer, my lord, I ceased being called a lady. I am known only as Wynne the Seafarer."

"A seafarer," Cait said.

"A Highlander seafarer, my lady, not a sea raider," Wynne explained. "Neither I nor my men were party to the raid on your village. Today, because I am a friend of your cousin, Rob, I am here to help you claim the High Seat."

Surprised, Cait said, "You know?"

"Aye, I trade with the Athdarians. As I sailed up and down the river, I saw the Northman's ship hidden in a cove. I told Rob—"

"Rob!" Cait exclaimed.

"Aye, your cousin."

"I told him and his two friends about the ship, and they thought it might be the sea raiders who had attacked the village. I set my men to watching. Finally Lord Lang arrived and we had a long talk. I've been waiting for you." Wynne laughed. "I am going to transport you to Glenmuir aboard my ship."

"Where is Lang?" Cait asked.

"He's gone on ahead," Wynne explained. "Since I know the waterways better than he, I sent him on the easiest route." Her gray eyes twinkled. "And I sent along Rob and two of his friends as navigators."

"Dettra and Bhaltair. The Silver Daggers," Cait cried. "They are free."

"Aye, and I'm sure when they see you, they'll have a story about a daring escape to tell you," she teased kindly. "They are guiding Lang and his warriors up to the Shelter Stone. We're going to sail up the Treacherous River."

Fear sent chill bumps over Cait's body. "Lady Gwynneth," she said, "those who have lived in the village all their lives and know the waterways don't venture on the Treacherous River."

"Aye, that is why we will," Wynne answered. "You and Michael shall surround the village. Michael and Malcolm will come by land, Lang and I by water."

"You're fighting with us?"

"Aye. Normally I don't involve myself with such matters," Wynne said, "but I don't like Gilbert, and I don't like what he's done to Glenmuir."

Two Northland warriors, lugging Michael's treasure chest between them, arrived at that moment. One unfastened the straps and lifted the lid. Soon he had set up the scales. As he measured out gold and silver, the other warrior filled several bags. When the transaction was completed, Cait noted that Michael's chest was empty.

"Thank you, my lord." Wynne smiled at Michael. The brilliancy of her smile transformed her from an ordinary woman into sunshine itself.

" 'Tis the least I can do to repay you for all your help," Michael said.

Although he and the woman were not flirting, a jolt of jealousy hit Cait as she witnessed the exchange between her husband and the lady of summer. It reinforced her feeling of uncertainty where Michael was concerned. She knew he lusted for her, but otherwise she wasn't sure of his feelings or his motives. He had handfasted himself to her, but theirs was a temporary marriage.

Last night they had mated. Cait had wanted to chase Michael's demons away as much as satisfy her need for him. In the shadows of the night and by the glow of firelight, it had seemed to Cait that their mating had gone beyond mere lust even though Michael never professed to loving her. For

Cait it had been a wonderful experience of love. As she touched Michael's ring on her hand, she could only wonder what their coupling meant to Michael. In the light of day she was forced to admit that to him it was probably just carnal gratification.

Michael returned her searching gaze, but she knew nothing of his thoughts.

The wind blew with renewed fervor, parting Michael's mantle. The amulet glinted from its nest of crisp black chest hair.

"Your amulet," Wynne said.

Cait glanced over to see the seafarer staring intently at the gold medallion. She tensed. She worried when anyone showed unusual interest in the amulet. She feared its secret would be revealed for all to know. She also felt a deep sense of guilt. Her father had entrusted the Breastpin to her keeping, and she had failed to safeguard it.

" 'Tis unique craftsmanship," Wynne said.

"Aye," Michael replied, his tone casual. He picked up the amulet between his thumb and index finger and held it out.

"I gave it to him," Cait said, staking her claim to Michael, not liking the interest that Wynne the Seafarer was taking in her husband. "It was designed and crafted by a religious woman who lives in a grove cloister."

Wynne peered intently at it. "Aye, the Dryads. They are renowned goldsmiths. I also wear a talisman crafted by . . . one of them."

Trevor, strolling along the river, glanced over at them, heightening Cait's concerns. She did not appreciate the way Michael seemed to flaunt the amulet. Michael dropped it and drew his mantle more closely about himself.

Trevor waved and kept walking. Wishing Michael

would return the pin to her, wondering what he planned to do with it, Cait left them and entered the cave.

She loved Michael, and she trusted him. But he had once told her that he did not believe in her gods. Thus, he did not revere the cloister or its possessions. To Cait the treasures were sacred objects. To Michael they were booty to be taken.

Cait was rolling up their pallet and tying it when she heard Trevor call.

"Come in, Guardian Priest."

"I'm concerned about sailing with this woman, Cait. We know nothing about her. She could be Gilbert's accomplice."

"Aye, my lord, I have been giving that possibility some thought myself." She picked up hers and Michael's clothing that had dried in front of the fire. "Did you hear the good news about Rob, Dettra, and Bhaltair?"

He shook his head.

"Lady Gwynneth said all three are free. They're sailing with Lang."

"Of course," Trevor said softly, "this is what Lady Gwynneth claims?"

"Aye."

"Where does she claim Lang is going to land?"

Cait thought for a moment. "She didn't say. But we're going to sail up the Treacherous—"

Trevor's eyes rounded. "By the gods, my lady, the seafarer will get us all killed!"

Cait laughed. "I'll talk with Michael about it."

Trevor clasped her hands. "Please do, Cait, and remember *you* are the queen."

By the time Michael joined her, their satchels were at the mouth of the cave waiting to be strapped onto the ponies.

"Good," he said. "You're ready to go." His helmet was tucked under his arm, his mantle blowing in the morning breeze.

"Aye." She pulled her hood over her head. "Do you think it wise to trust this woman? She is an admitted seafarer, Michael, and Gilbert's accomplices were seafarers. And we have only her word about Lang and Rob and the other Silver Daggers."

"Aye, I believe she's trustworthy," he answered, "but even if she weren't, I'd chance using her."

"At the risk of having her sail us into a trap of Gilbert's making?"

"For a chance to save your kingdom." Michael gazed into her eyes. "At the moment, lady, we need to get to Glenmuir as quickly as possible. I'm your champion, and will protect you. Let me worry about the rest."

"If you emptied your personal coffers to save my kingdom," Cait said, "I shall repay you doubly when—"

Softly Michael said, "Have your forgotten that Glenmuir is also my kingdom, lady, now that I am king?"

Cait answered just as softly. "For a moment, I had."

"Then what we do, lady, is for *our* kingdom."

She nodded.

"If I am to reclaim your throne for you, lady, and stop Gilbert from killing innocent people, I must reach the village posthaste. Whether Wynne is trustworthy or not, she and her ship offer the quickest method of transport."

"Aye." Cait wrung her hands.

"Cait—" Michael reached out to her, and she went into his arms "—you must trust me."

" 'Tis difficult to do, lord, when I'm not sure of your motives." She laid her head against his chest.

"No matter what you think, no matter what happens, always know that I'm your champion, Cait, here to fight your dragons. I shall save your kingdom, but I must have your trust."

He was a hard man, born in the rugged grandeur of the Highlands but raised in the harsh coldness of the Northland. Yet Cait had seen the gentle side of him. And she knew he was a man who never went back on his word. She did trust him.

"Gwynneth is a beautiful woman," she said.

"Aye, she is," Michael admitted. He tucked his hand beneath Cait's chin and raised her face. "But she is not nearly as beautiful as you are, Cait. You are the fire a man needs to keep warm."

"A man, my lord?"

"You are the fire *I* need to keep warm, Caity."

She lifted her face to accept his kisses. Long. Deep. Thoroughly arousing, with the promise of more to come.

"Ah, my lady," he breathed, his voice husky, "I cannot touch you without wanting you."

"I'm glad I have set you afire with the same desire that burns within me, my lord husband."

"Michael," Kolby shouted from the distance, "the ship is loaded. We're ready to set sail."

"Aye, my lady and I shall be along directly."

The voyage was rough, and the river treacherous, true to its name, but Wynne was an excellent captain. Her men respected her and followed her orders without question. Michael and Ulf were seasoned sailors, but Malcolm and Trevor turned green, and Cait hung over the side of the ship and retched.

She was grateful when, after two days' and a night's journey, they sailed into a small cove to the south of Glenmuir. She felt a moment of intense anger when the wolf, friskier than ever, bounded off the ship, while she was so weak that Michael had to help her. As soon as they were ashore, Michael, Malcolm, and Cait went to spy out the king's village and harbor.

Keeping under cover of the trees, they climbed the rise. The morning sun glistened gold against the horizon and ripped across the water.

"We're approaching from the back of the village," Cait explained. "Our harbor is located at the Shelter Stone, and the Great Hall faces it. No one will expect us to have sailed in on the Treacherous River."

They topped the next incline and halted. The trees had begun to thin out, and below them lay the beautiful glen of Muir. Dotting the landscape for as far as the eye could see were individual farms.

"The largest rectangular building is the Great Hall?" Michael said, drawing Cait's attention back to the village.

"The smaller one is for the king's men who are unmarried. Those are workshops," she added, pointing to a cluster of buildings along the main street. "The round ones with the thatched roofs are individual homes."

The villagers had just begun stirring, moving in and out of the cottages and along the pathways.

"Gilbert will know we're coming long before we arrive," Michael said.

Malcolm nodded. "We'll have to go in with a show of force."

"Under no condition must he get Cait," Michael said, a steely ring to his words.

As soon as the two warriors had memorized the

terrain and landmarks, they returned to the ship, where the warriors were breaking their fast. Michael and Malcolm called them all together. They described the village and explained their plan of attack.

Munching on dried fish and fruit, Cait listened. His brow furrowed, Trevor paced.

"You know what you're to do, Wynne?" Michael asked.

"Aye," she answered. "And I shall give your instructions to Lang so that he and his warriors know what they are to do."

"You're sure you can spare some of your own men?"

She nodded. "You need them far more than I do."

"That we do," Michael agreed.

Malcolm said, "Counting yours, Wynne, we will have eighty warriors riding with us. But that leaves you and Lang to protect the ship with less than twenty."

" 'Twill be enough," Wynne assured him.

"How much time do you need to reach Lang?" Michael asked.

"I can reach him before noon," she said.

Michael nodded. "At noon we march."

"My lord," Trevor said, "you are making a mistake. By marching against Gilbert, you are putting the prisoners' lives at risk. Gilbert will not hesitate to kill them."

"Aye, priest," Michael said. "That is why we cannot delay our attack."

"Cait!" a young masculine voice called from the forest behind them.

"Rob!" Cait whirled to see a young man step out of the trees and come toward her. She had thought it was Rob. The voice sounded like his. But this man looked nothing like her cousin.

A large turban was wrapped around his dark-skinned face. He wore a shirt with full sleeves, and equally baggy trousers. On his feet were sandals. He carried a flute in one hand, a basket in the other.

Cait moved closer. "Rob?"

He laughed and opened his arms for her. Laughing and crying at the same time, she ran to him.

"Oh, Rob, I have been so worried about you." She pulled back. "Why are you dressed like this?"

"I've been spying in town and at the cloister," he answered. "Remember what Sholto told us. The most obvious is the most unnoticed."

Cait patted his turbaned head.

"Caity!" Rob protested, dodging her touch.

"Lady," Michael said, joining them, "you're embarrassing the warrior."

"But I'm loving the cousin," she said, unrepentant but stepping away. Catching Michael's hand, she tugged him closer.

"Well, Northlander," Rob said, "we meet again."

"But under different circumstances," Michael said. "I am now your cousin's husband."

"So your father explained," Rob said. "He also told us that you and High King Malcolm of Northern Scotland are identical twin brothers."

"Aye."

"Rob!" Trevor walked up to where they stood.

"Guardian Priest," Rob said, returning the greeting.

"Your father and I have been worried about you."

"You had a right to be worried," Rob retorted. "You and Sholto no sooner left that evening than Gilbert's men were after me. It's as if they knew where I was going."

"They did," Trevor answered. "Blar told them."

Rob rocked back on his heels. "Blar?"

"Aye, he's the traitor priest."

"Nay," Rob answered, "he can't be. The night you escaped I found him—"

"No matter what you think," Trevor interrupted, "Blar has betrayed us. He attached himself to you so that he would know when Cait arrived back in Glenmuir."

"Does my father accuse Blar?" Rob asked.

"Father has always known that one of the cloister members was a traitor," Cait answered.

"Did Father say it was Blar?" Rob persisted.

Cait shook her head. "Nay, but he was weak, Rob, and he did not disagree with Trevor when he announced Blar's betrayal."

Rob frowned in uncertainty and changed the subject. "I owe a great debt of gratitude to Gwynneth. She made sure I was not recaptured."

"I have a keen sense of fairness," Wynne explained. "I came here to trade and was sailing out of the harbor when I saw six warriors pursuing one. Six to one is not a fair fight. My men and I evened the odds for Rob. We invited him to sail with us, but he chose to remain behind to help his friends."

"Who are Gilbert's others prisoners and where are they being held?" Michael asked.

Rob answered. "The ten members of the High Council are being held at the cloister. We would have freed them, but Gilbert still has a formidable army, well trained and well equipped."

Pulling Rob down with him, Michael squatted near the ground. Other warriors, including Malcolm, Kolby, Brian, and Gwynneth, gathered around. Cait and Trevor listened.

Michael picked up a stick and began drawing.

"Here's the village and the two rivers. Here we are, and here's how we plan to attack."

When Michael was finished speaking, Trevor said, "My lord Michael, send me and several warriors to the Great Hall. Let us tell Gilbert that Cait is the heir to the High Seat and that she and her husband have come to claim it. Mayhap we can still prevent bloodshed." He wrung his hands together. "Never in my day has Glenmuir been at war."

"I don't trust Gilbert," Michael said. "My brother believes that he has dishonorable warriors in his service, outlaws from Northern Scotland. We cannot bargain with such people, Guardian Priest. Furthermore, I don't intend to expose Cait to danger."

"You cannot stop me from riding with you, my lord," Cait said quietly.

"Nay!"

"In the Highlands women often go into battle with their menfolk."

"You have not been trained as a warrior," Michael argued.

"I have been trained to use the sword and lance and daggers. More important, lord, I am the queen, and I shall lead my forces."

She gave him a measured gaze, letting him know that she would not change her mind.

"She is right, Michael," Malcolm said quietly. "As queen of Glenmuir, she has a right to lead her warriors."

"So be it," Michael said dully.

"Cait," Trevor said, "I wish to talk with you."

"What about?" Michael asked.

Trevor glanced from Michael to Cait. "I think, sire, that under the circumstances, someone else should be entrusted with the sacred cloister pin . . . in case."

"Aye, Michael," Cait said. "Mayhap—"

"Your father entrusted it to you," Michael said. "You have put it in a safe place. Also, my lady, your father lives as does the secret."

"My lord Michael—" Trevor began.

"I have spoken on the matter."

Cait wished she had been more careful with the amulet, that Michael had never taken it from her. Like Trevor, she worried about its safety, but she had no choice except to trust Michael.

" 'Twill be a sad day for the kingdom, lord, should that amulet fall into the wrong hands," the guardian priest warned.

"Aye, Trevor, it would!" shouted a deep masculine voice from the depths of the forest.

As if struck with a cudgel, Trevor jumped. "Blar?" He looked about wildly. "Is that you, Blar?"

"Aye, Trevor, 'tis me. Are you surprised?"

The massive warrior-priest stepped out of the trees. Clothed in a shirt and trousers, he had strapped a sword and dagger about his waist. His cloak was tossed negligently over one shoulder. His face was darkened with bruises, his lips and forehead swollen with cuts. Blar's smile was hard and cynical.

"Perhaps you thought I was dead. A priest, a man I thought was a friend, tried to kill me."

"He is a traitor. Kill him!" Trevor shouted.

Shocked, Cait stood there gaping. Michael and Malcolm didn't move. Dettra and Bhaltair stepped out of the forest and behind Blar. Rob stepped over to join them. And then a woman wearing a hooded cloak also materialized out of the woods.

Trevor pointed at Blar. "He's the man who betrayed us. Now he intends to take the sacred amulet so he and Gilbert can steal the cloister riches."

Blar crossed his arms over his chest in an immovable stance. "Your lies will get you nowhere this time, Trevor. The High Council of Priests has already met."

"How could they? Gilbert's warriors are guarding them."

"Nay, Gilbert's men became frightened, and many abandoned him. We took care of the few who were left. We know you betrayed us."

"You're lying."

"I wish I were, my friend. You betrayed your gods, your friends, and most of all yourself for a chance to become the high priest of the shrine and the Ancient of Nights and Days."

"You have no proof of that," Trevor said. "It is your word against mine."

"I have a witness." Blar motioned, and the old woman stepped forward. She pushed the hood from her head. "Nay," Trevor whispered, the color draining from his face.

"Aye, 'tis the servant woman who heard you conspiring with Gilbert in the Great Hall."

"She lies!" Trevor shouted wildly.

"She could not have known about the brooch case in which the sacred amulet was hidden if she had not seen it and heard someone talking about it. You, Trevor. She heard you and Gilbert."

"Nay!"

"Aye, my lord guardian priest," the woman said, "you are the one who came to see Lord Gilbert. I heard him telling you about the Northman named Michael Langssonn who had come to the Highlands to kill Malcolm mac Duncan."

Stunned, Cait listened as the old woman repeated the conversation between Trevor and Gilbert, relating details of Malcolm and Jarvia's marriage, the payment of the rupture-endowment, and its subsequent theft by pirates.

"Enough, good mother," Blar said.

He motioned, and the three Silver Daggers circled Trevor. "What are you going to do with me?" he cried.

"Rob, Dettra, and Bhaltair are going to take you to the shrine," Blar said. "There you will await judgment."

"Nay." Trevor trembled. "You know what they'll do to me, Blar. Kill me now. Don't let them throw me into the Hag's Lake."

As Trevor continued to plead and wail, the Silver Daggers dragged him away. Blar turned to Cait. "Ah, Caity, I am glad you are home and that Sholto is well."

"My lord Blar," Cait said, "I am glad that you are well and safe." She shook her head. "I believed Trevor. I had no idea it was he who had betrayed us."

"None of us knew until the night Trevor and Sholto escaped," Blar said. "I also escaped, but Trevor found me in the forest behind the cloister. He pierced my shoulder with a dagger and left me for dead. Had a good woman not found me, I would have died. By the time I was able to travel, Sholto and Trevor were too far away to catch them. I prayed that Trevor would not learn the location of the sacred Breastpins."

"He didn't," Cait said. "Nor did my father tell him I am heir to the High Seat until after they had arrived safely in Malcolm's village."

"And Sholto is well," Blar said.

"Aye," Cait said. "All is well." She caught Michael's hand and drew him close. "Guardian Priest,

I would like to introduce you to my husband, Michael Langssonn."

"Rob told me about your marriage," Blar said. His gazed moved from Michael to Malcolm.

"Lord Michael, you and your brother do look alike." Then Blar turned back to Cait. "My lady queen, I plight my services to you and your husband. Shall we march into the king's village so that you may claim the High Seat?"

"Aye, my lord guardian priest."

To Michael Blar said, "I have twelve men who offer their services."

"Thank you, Guardian Priest," Michael replied. "We have no idea what opposition we will encounter when we march into the king's village."

"Nor do I," Blar answered. "We have been unable to ascertain how many warriors have remained loyal to Gilbert."

"My lord Michael," Wynne said, "I shall depart now."

"May the gods go with you, Lady Gwynneth," Cait said.

"Aye, my lady queen, and may they also be with you." Wynne smiled and waved as she slipped into the woods.

Michael put his arms around Cait's shoulder and hugged her to him. " 'Tis time, my lady queen."

"Aye, my lord husband, 'tis time."

Chapter 23

⁓◦⁓

Just before noon, their army was assembled and ready to march.

"My lady wife," Michael said, "I wish you wouldn't ride with us. I fear for your safety."

"I know," she murmured. "Because I am the queen of Glenmuir."

"Nay, because you're Cait," he said. "The woman I love."

"The woman you love?" she repeated slowly.

"Aye, Cait nea Sholto, I love you," Michael said quietly, "and I believe I have ever since I saw you with Ardac and his men."

She raised her head, he lowered his at the same time, and their lips met in a hot, demanding kiss. Cait dug her fingers into Michael's shoulders; he hugged her so tightly, she couldn't breathe.

"Oh, Michael," she whispered, "I love you so much."

He kissed her cheeks, her forehead, the tip of her nose. Then he reclaimed her mouth. At last he gently set her aside, keeping hold of her waist. "Please stay here, my love. I must know you're safe."

"I can't." She begged him to understand.

"Then know, my ladylove, I shall protect the Lydian Stone Breastpin with my life."

These were the words Cait had longed to hear.

"Aye, my lord, I know. I trust you with it implicitly."

"You no longer think I want the treasure?"

"You may want it," she said, "but you won't take it."

Michael grinned. "In the beginning, my little bard, I had designs on both you and your cloister treasure. Now I have designs only on you. And I shall do whatever is necessary to keep you by my side."

"Even surrender the sacred Breastpin to someone else for safekeeping?" Cait looked at him in question.

"I gave it to Blar," Michael said.

"Thank you, my lord husband." Her expression was replete with love and trust.

"Now, wife, 'tis time to go." Michael gave her a brief kiss and swung her upon her mare.

Bracing her hands on his shoulders, Cait smiled impudently. "Lord, don't you think a warrior should mount her own steed?"

Michael grinned, and his eyes twinkled with mischief. "Aye, my ladylove, I most assuredly do."

When Cait realized what he meant, her cheeks flushed.

"You are most infuriating, my lord," she said, "but I love you."

"I have to admit you're also infuriating, my lady, but I love you."

Leather creaked. Mail clinked. Hooves thundered as one hundred warriors followed Michael and Malcolm across the sweeping glen to the king's village. Leading the procession were the piper, the horn blower, and the standard bearer. Behind them rode Blar.

The sun shone brightly, and a gentle breeze furled the green and yellow banner. Cait looked at Michael and smiled.

"When I left here, lord, Glenmuir had no king."

"Now, she has a queen."

"And a king ... The village is quiet," she murmured. "Too quiet."

"Aye," Michael agreed.

The village was smaller than Malcolm's, but not less grand. Above the shoulder-high fence that surrounded the town, Michael saw the towering roof of the Great Hall. Here and there he glimpsed the thatched roofs of other buildings: residences, storehouses, workshops. But he saw no people. As they neared the open gates, they were greeted by silence.

"Michael," Cait whispered.

"Don't be frightened," he said softly.

Blar slowed his pony until he was riding beside Michael. Before they marched through the gates, Michael held up his hand, halting the army.

"My lord priest," Cait said, "what if Gilbert is holding all the villagers as prisoners?"

"Nay," Blar replied. "I can feel their eyes on me. I suspect they are so frightened, they are hiding in their homes."

"Aye," Michael agreed. "They fear we are another invading force, my lady wife. They do not know they have a queen."

"Then we must tell them," Cait said. Aloud she called out, "Piper, play the song of the Galloways. Let the people of Glenmuir know that they have a queen."

Shrill music filled the air. "Kolby," Michael called out, "take some of the men and move through the village looking for warriors Gilbert might have hidden. Brian, take a group and encircle the village. The rest of us will ride down main street toward the Great Hall."

Riding beside Michael, Blar shouted, "People of Glenmuir, I am Blar, guardian priest of the Shelter Stone. I have come to tell you that you have a queen, an heir to the High Seat. Cait nea Sholto." Still shouting, Blar recited Cait's genealogy so all would know she was of royal descent.

As they rode farther, the piper continued to play and Blar proclaimed Cait the queen of Glenmuir. Glancing around, Michael saw a few doors crack open. Tartans were pushed aside from windows.

"Do not fear, people of Glenmuir," Blar shouted. "High Queen Cait and her husband, High King Michael, have come to claim their High Seat. Cait nea Sholto is the rightful ruler of Glenmuir. Gilbert is a usurper, the man who murdered your king and his entire family. He is the man who has imprisoned your councilmen and the priests of the Shelter Stone Cloister. But he is not your king and he can no longer harm you. Riding with your queen is High King Malcolm mac Duncan of Northern Scotland."

Doors were flung open and people stepped into the street. Gradually their wariness turned to shouts of joy and adulation.

"Where is Gilbert?" Blar shouted.

"He was in the Great Hall earlier," one of the women answered.

As Michael and Cait rode by, the people touched and blessed them, thanking them for their rescue. Michael saw no warriors and no ponies before the Great Hall. The silent building looked stark and empty. He didn't like it. It was the building where

King Ido and his entire family had been slaughtered. He would not allow Cait to live there.

Cait's face was white, her hands clenched into tight fists. "Are you frightened?" he asked.

"Aye."

He captured her hand in his.

"All shall be well, my wife," he promised her, never letting up his guard. "We shall build a new Great Hall, one that belongs to us, my lady wife."

"Will it be finished before a year and a day, my lord?"

"It doesn't matter. I'll still be here."

Cait's eyes changed from golden to russet. "You're staying, lord?"

"I have no choice, my lady."

Did he see a flicker of disappointment in her eyes?

Softly he added, "You have my heart. If I left you, I would leave it behind, and I can't live without my heart."

"I love you, Michael."

"I love you, Cait.

The warmth of her smile chased away his apprehension. Silently they rode, holding hands, basking in the wonder of their love.

"Look yonder, lord." She pointed to a distant peak. "That is the Shelter Stone Shrine."

They were too far away for Michael to make out any details, but it was strange how much of what he was seeing here in the Highlands seemed familiar to him. He had not seen it in his dreams or with the naked eye, but he felt as if he had arrived home. He was marching into battle, yet he felt utterly at peace. Northland was his father's kingdom. Northern Scotland belonged to Malcolm. Glenmuir was his and Cait's.

"Do you feel it, lord?" Cait asked. "The wonder and beauty of Glenmuir?"

"Aye."

Blar halted in front of the Great Hall. "Gilbert, come forth," he called out. "Cait nea Sholto is the rightful heir to the High Seat of Glenmuir. She has come to make her claim."

They waited.

Blar shouted the words again.

Still there was no response.

Michael motioned to several of his men. They dismounted and entered the building. Tensely he awaited their return. Cait remained pale but erect on her mare. Finally the warriors returned, shaking their heads.

"It's empty, sire," one of them reported.

Blar dismounted and approached the double doors. He flung them open and walked inside as Michael slid off his stallion and assisted Cait down, then escorted her into the Great Hall. Ulf followed, sniffing out the corners.

They strode to the center of the room. "It hasn't been empty long, Michael," Cait said. The blazing fire and aroma of cooking food told of the recent occupants' hasty departure.

Blar emerged from the kitchen with a lad dangling from his fist.

"When the others saw you, they rode off and left Gilbert," the boy confessed as he kicked and flailed "Then he ran off too."

Blar deposited the boy in front of Michael.

"Where did they go?"

He shrugged. "His men headed toward Athdara He went to the shrine."

* * *

Cait leaned over her mare and urged her on toward the Shelter Stone Cloister. Riding beside her were Michael and Malcolm, followed by a third of their warriors. Another third remained behind to defend the village while Blar led the last third in pursuit of Gilbert's scattered and fleeing men.

By the time they reached the shrine, night had fallen, though the moon was full and bright. At the cloister village, they saw no signs of the warriors. Cait slid off her mare and ran into the Great Hall. It was empty. Malcolm and Michael, the wolf at their side, checked the other buildings, but found them empty also. With Cait in the lead, they raced to the shrine itself, then spread out in search of Gilbert. Minutes later, holding the torch aloft, Rob came running out of the Shelter Chamber, the first of the cavern's rooms.

"Gilbert!" he shouted, and pointed toward the mountain that rose above them. "He's escaping."

"Where are all the prisoners?" Michael called out.

"They're in here," Rob answered. "Gilbert's men have abandoned him. Follow me."

"Nay, Rob," Michael said. "Gilbert belongs to me."

He heard a shuffling noise and looked up to see a dark shadow scaling the mountainside. He studied the natural rock bridge that spanned the waterfall. He had seen it before in his dreams. If Gilbert crossed over it, there was a good chance he would escape into the mountain wilderness.

"I'll cut him off on this side," Michael called out to Malcolm. "You approach him from the other side."

Both brothers bolted off in opposite directions.

Several minutes of hard climbing left Michael winded at the top of the hill. He paused, sucking air into his lungs, and listened. Ulf bounded over to stand beside him. It was hard to hear above the roar of waterfall, but Michael closed his eyes and concentrated. Gilbert was nearby. Michael sensed his presence ...

On silent feet he and Ulf moved through the shadows.

In the distance Cait screamed.

Ulf tore away, and Michael spun around, running back the way he had come. He had to run faster. He couldn't see her, but he heard the sounds of a terrible struggle. He rounded the bend and saw her fighting with Gilbert. She grunted. She screamed. They rolled on the narrow path. He had to get to her, had to save her.

"Cait," he called out.

"I'll kill her before I let you have her," Gilbert shouted.

Michael saw the glint of silver as moonlight caught the dagger Gilbert brandished.

"Ulf!" Michael commanded.

The wolf was a silver arc in the air as he lunged at Gilbert. The man screamed. The blade entered the wolf, and it howled with pain. Gilbert fell off Cait, and she pushed to her feet. He lunged, grabbing her ankles. Cait twisted free, but lost her balance.

"Michael!"

Blood streaming down his back, the wolf clamped his mouth around the loose material of her trousers. And before Michael's horrified eyes, both figures thrashed and twisted and disappeared over the side of the cliff.

"Cait!" Michael shouted.

Gilbert's laughter mocked Michael. "She's dead Langssonn. There is no way she could have survived a fall like that."

"I'll kill you," Michael swore.

Gilbert leaped lithely to his feet. "Nay, Northman, I shall kill you first."

In the bright spill of moonlight, Michael saw the man's grin. He saw the dagger blade, now stained with Ulf's blood.

"If it hadn't been for you, I would have the Cloister Breastpins and all the cloister treasure. I am meant to be king of Glenmuir, and I shall be." Gilbert snorted bitterly. "Aye, Northman, I shall kill you myself."

"Michael," Cait called from afar, "I'm all right. Gilbert can't touch me now. I'm safe."

"After I kill you," Gilbert taunted. "I shall kill Malcolm mac Duncan. I outsmarted him once, and I'll do it again." Gilbert laughed. "Tell Malcolm that Ghaltair sends his greetings."

With a mighty lunge Gilbert pounced on Michael, causing him to stumble. But Michael shifted to the side and quickly regained his balance. His dagger in hand, he studied the huge warrior before him. Cornered, Gilbert was a desperate man . . . and therefore highly dangerous.

Gilbert lashed out, his blade catching Michael's right shoulder. Pain sparked through Michael's body, and he almost lost his grip on his own dagger. He clenched his teeth and forced the pain away, forced the muscles in his arm and fingers to hold on tightly.

With renewed strength, he danced back, sending pebbles skittering over the cliff edge. Gilbert raced forward. Michael jumped aside. His hand flew out, and he pierced Gilbert deep in the arm.

Gilbert grunted, then cursed. Michael saw the stain of blood on his shirt sleeve, but the rest of Gilbert remained in shadow. Michael forced himself to breathe deeply and listen carefully. Gilbert jumped forward, his blade whizzing past Michael's face. Michael jerked to the side, his hand hitting the jagged edge of a boulder. It cut into his flesh and jarred his wounded shoulder. This time he dropped his dagger.

Gilbert laughed. "Now I've got you where I want you, Northman."

He raced in for the kill.

Using his other arm and hand, Michael grabbed Gilbert's wrist, and grunted as he tried to twist the knife out of his grasp. A strong man, Gilbert refused to let go. He pressed downward until the tip of the blade rested against Michael's heart. Michael felt the prick of the point against his clothes.

Drawing in a deep breath, he pushed his hand between them, twirled mightily, and hurled Gilbert over the side of the mountain. Gilbert screamed, and Michael heard several thuds as his body bounced off boulders before it landed on the ground below.

An awful silence followed. "Michael," Rob finally called. "Where are you?"

"Over here. Bring a torch. I need to get Cait." He straightened. "Cait," he called, "where are you?"

"Down here," she called. "Are you all right, Michael?"

"Aye, a little worn, but fine, my love. How about you?"

She laughed with relief. "Ulf and I landed on a narrow ledge."

"Is it sturdy?" Michael asked.

"Aye," she answered, her voice shaking, "but if we move at all, we'll fall off."

"I'll be right down to get you."

Michael shouted for rope and torches. He searched frantically for something on which to tie the rope. The rocks were too loose, the trees too small. By this time Malcolm and many of their warriors had joined him.

"There's nothing to anchor the rope to," Malcolm said. "We'll hold it while you climb down."

Six warriors clasped the rope at intervals along its length. Michael held on to the other end and began to climb slowly down the mountainside, pushing away with his feet to avoid sharp, projecting boulders and rough scrub. Finally his feet touched the ledge where Cait lay. Keeping the rope in one hand, he reached for her with the other.

"Michael," she cried, "I knew you would come for me."

"Cait!" He crooked his arm around her and spread kisses over her face. "Oh, Caity, are you hurt?"

"A few cuts and bruises," she answered, "but nothing major. Ulf is badly hurt though. He's fallen into a stupor."

In the darkness Michael knelt and examined Ulf. He had sustained a deep cut in his right side, and seemed to be losing a great deal of blood.

"First I'm going to get you off the ledge," he said, tying the rope around her waist. "When I tell Malcolm to pull you up, use your feet to climb and push."

He gave her a quick kiss, then called, "Malcolm, pull her up."

Slowly she rose into the air as Malcolm's men brought her to safety. As soon as Malcolm lowered the rope again, Michael secured it around the limp wolf's belly and sent him up.

"We're ready for you now, Michael," Malcolm called down.

Michael grasped the rope and began to climb, but

as he looked up, the torchlight revealed where sharp rocks were cutting into the rope. A fiber gave way. He heard another snap and felt the rope give again.

"The rocks are cutting the rope," Michael yelled up.

Malcolm looked over the ledge. He let loose the section of rope on which he was tugging and reached below the weak spot, relieving some of the pressure on the fraying line.

"Climb a little higher, Michael." He grunted. "Then catch my hand."

Gathering his strength, Michael struggled upward and wedged his foot onto a rock ledge strong enough to bear some of his weight.

"My hand, Michael," Malcolm shouted. "Take my hand."

But just as brother locked hand with brother, the rope broke. The warriors holding the other end went crashing backward. Malcolm, leaning over the edge, was pulled forward by the weight of Michael's body.

"Brian, grab my feet," he shouted. "I'm slipping."

The rock beneath Michael's foot broke loose. He fell a few inches as Malcolm took his full weight and slipped farther over the edge. If he didn't let go, they would both fall to their deaths into the sacred rock-lined pool far below.

"Turn me loose, Malcolm!" he shouted.

But it was too late. Pebbles spewed over Michael's face. With an anguished shout Malcolm lost his precarious position on the ledge and hurtled over the edge. The tension on the rope gave way and Michael plunged with him.

Michael hit the water first. The cold sliced through him with cutting savagery. His eyes burning, his lungs screaming for air, he battled the current. He thrust up above the surface and sucked in air.

"Malcolm!" he shouted.

"Over here."

Michael heard the faint call and swam after it. He was a strong swimmer, but the water was numbing, the current swift. He fought, but the water fought back, seemingly determined to take his life.

"Malcolm," he called out again . . . and again.

This time he received no answer.

The whirlpool was sucking him under. Michael went down, then surged upward again. His arms hurt. He could hardly breathe. He swam on. He called his brother's name over and over.

He saw a dark shadow. With a burst of energy, he surged forward and reached out, but found nothing.

His lungs aching, his arms so tired he couldn't lift them one more time, he sank under the water and gave himself over to the swirling current. He couldn't fight any longer. He was too tired. His eyes closed. The river goddess beckoned.

"Michael!" he heard Cait call. "Michael!"

He wanted to swim to her, but he couldn't. His arms wouldn't obey his command. His legs were heavy. They were pulling him down . . .

Priests of the cloister who knew the pathways around the shrine volunteered to hunt for Michael and Malcolm. Among them were Cait, Rob, and Blar. Muted orbs of light dotted the mountainside. But after several hours, they all returned. They had seen and heard no signs of the men.

"Nay!" Cait cried when one of them suggested

the men had drowned. "Michael is not dead. He's not."

"Of course not," Blar comforted her. "Come, Cait, let's rest in the Great Hall and get out of these wet clothes. You need a cup of warm heather tea . . . or perhaps some ale."

Cait shook her head. "Thank you, but I shall stay here."

"You can't," Blar argued. "It's cold and wet."

"Michael is here," she answered, her voice firm. "I shall stay with him."

"Aye," Blar murmured. "I'll bring you some blankets and hot tea."

Blar returned shortly, and Cait bundled herself and the wolf in the blankets, then savored the hot tea. But she steadfastly refused to leave the mountainside.

"I've done the best I can, Ulf," she whispered, examining the deep cut she had bandaged on the wolf's side. "I only wish Michael were here to care for you."

Tears ran down her cheeks, and she buried her face in the animal's fur. "Michael can't die. He can't."

Ulf whimpered softly, and Cait cried harder. She didn't think she could face life without Michael. Glenmuir was their kingdom. She needed him. She loved him.

She cried and cried.

Finally she had shed all her tears. She was spent. She sat stroking the wolf and praying for her beloved. Straining to see through the darkness, she willed morning to come so she could resume the search. She would find him. She would.

Slowly dawn began to silver the night-shadowed sky. She heard a faint noise. Michael? She leaped to

her feet and raced down the narrow pathway that
led from the mountaintop to the pool below. She
heard voices. Someone was ahead of her. Others followed. She slipped and fell. She pushed up and ran
again.

"Down here, Cait," Blar called. "We've found
them."

Cait pushed around jutting boulders, her feet
barely touching the ground as she ran. She saw a
lifeless body lying on the shore of the Shelter Stone
Pool. Her heart stopped beating, but she didn't stop
running until she was bending over Michael's wet,
supine body.

"Is he dead?" she cried. Before Blar could answer,
she was holding Michael, rocking him back and
forth. "Oh, Michael. Oh, my love."

He groaned.

Cait held him tighter. He laughed weakly.

"Lady, you're suffocating me."

Cait pulled back and looked into her husband's
wan face. "I love you, Michael."

He touched his hand to her cheek. "I love you,
Cait."

They smiled at each other.

"Malcolm?" Michael asked.

"I'm here." Limping, Malcolm joined them, tossing down a shield and collapsing on the ground.
How strange that he had held on to his shield all
this time, Cait thought fleetingly.

As the brothers clasped hands, tears ran down
Cait's cheeks and she began to laugh with relief and
joy.

"Gilbert?" Michael asked.

"Gilbert's dead," Brian answered.

"Good." Michael sighed.

"So is Ghaltair, Malcolm," Brian added, a touch of excitement in his voice.

"So he *was* here," Malcolm said.

"He was here," Brian replied. "Ghaltair and Gilbert were the same man. Some of our warriors captured Ardac last night, and he confessed that it was Ghaltair who stole the rupture-endowment from your father and massacred his crew."

Michael looked at his brother with the relief of a great weight lifted from his shoulders. Then he turned to Blar. "Guardian Priest, I think it's time that my brother and I had a look at the cloister treasure."

Blar frowned. "My lord king, I mean you no disrespect, but this—"

"Please, my lord Blar," Cait said. "Michael and Malcolm have reason to believe that stolen goods are among the gifts of the gods. If the rupture-endowment is there, then a duel to the death will be unnecessary."

Blar thought for a moment, then nodded.

As they stood, Brian picked up Malcolm's shield. Puzzled, he asked, "Where did you get this, Malcolm?"

Malcolm looked blankly at the golden disk. "I found it." He took it from his best-man and studied it. "Or mayhap it found me. I was in the pool and I thought I was dying when my hand struck something. My fingers curled around the smooth edge, and my hand slipped through the arm piece. The next thing I knew, I was lying ashore."

"Some warrior must have dropped it into the pool," Blar said.

"Aye," Malcolm said slowly. "But when I found it, it seemed to be more than just a shield. It was as if something stronger than I was in control, as if the gods ..." He broke off and shrugged.

"As if the gods were in control," Cait murmured.

"Aye, my lady," he confessed, looking a little embarrassed.

"They are, my lord Malcolm, whether we admit it or not."

Malcolm tucked the shield beneath his arm, and Michael clasped Cait's hand as Blar opened the amulet he'd kept safe for Michael and began to read the instructions aloud. Shortly all four of them, carrying torches, were deep in the maze of underground caverns, winding their way ever farther into the bowels of the earth. They twisted and climbed. They descended and rose again. Finally the directions on the amulet guided them to a hidden niche in the wall of a small chamber, where they found the second Breastpin. Blar's hands shook as he unfastened the latch and opened the Bloodstone amulet.

Once again they meandered, circling, going deeper, the air getting damper and chillier. The torch glow barely cut through the darkness. Finally they stood in front of a solid wall. Once, twice, three times Blar read the directions, but they couldn't find the opening that was described.

"Here," Michael said, "let me look at the amulet."

He studied the inscriptions and reread them, using different inflections of his voice. Once. Twice. Three times. Four.

"That's it." Blar snapped his fingers. Long steps carried him across the cavern to the back wall. He brushed his hands over the flat surface. "I've found it." He grunted, and a huge stone began to slide out, revealing a low doorway.

All four of them stood for a moment in stunned

silence, staring into the dark chamber before them. They had found the Secret Chamber.

The men remained in the doorway as Cait walked fully into the room. Torchlight splashed over the cloister riches. Michael had traveled over much of the world, he had seen countless wonders, but he gasped as he beheld the gifts of the gods. He had heard tales of the vast treasures of the Shelter Stone Shrine, but he had never imagined that so much wealth could exist in one place. The room was filled with gold and silver and precious gems and a costly array of fine fabrics that glittered in the torchlight.

Excitement tingled through Michael as he stepped into the room. He kicked something and looked down to see a gem-encrusted tankard roll across the floor. He stopped, picked it up, and held it. He ran his thumb over one of the jewels. Malcolm and Blar joined him.

"I've never seen anything like this," Malcolm murmured, gazing around him. The shield slid from his hand and landed on a purple robe. "Never."

Cait lit the other torches in the room until golden light flickered all about them. Michael's heart beat faster. His blood rushed through his veins. He laid down the tankard and moved about, running the tips of his fingers over the riches.

He stepped over gold and silver dishes and brushed against richly embroidered mantles and cloaks. Precious stones winked at him.

"My lords," Cait said in a hushed voice, "I think this is what you are searching for."

Michael looked over to see her holding out a helmet. It was made of gold and silver and bronze, and was inlaid with precious jewels.

Malcolm pushed past Michael. "By the gods!" he swore softly.

"And here is the sword that matches it," Cait said.

Blar and Michael stood beside them, staring at the magnificent weaponry.

Reverently Malcolm touched it. "But it's not Lachlann's," he said, his voice rising. "It can't be. He's wearing his, Michael. Evidently Ghaltair had a helmet and sword crafted that were so similar to Lachlann's that none could tell the difference."

Malcolm gently waded through the treasures, moving from trunk to trunk, opening lids and peering at the contents. Michael did the same, admiring the beauty of design and craftsmanship.

"The rupture-endowment," Malcolm said. "It should be here if Ghaltair hid his stolen hoard among the cloister treasures."

"It is, my lord," Cait said. Her trousers brushed against the trunks as she gingerly wound around them. She eased in front of Malcolm and went to stand beneath one of the wrought-iron torch holders. She waved her hand. "Is this what you are looking for?"

All three men stared transfixed at the five huge trunks filled with riches. Cait lifted one lid after the other.

"The rupture-endowment." Malcolm laughed in relief. He spun around. "Michael, these five trunks hold the rupture-endowment. They—they—"

"I know," Michael said, and he and his brother embraced. Michael bit back tears at the full significance of the discovery.

Malcolm pulled away and gazed into Michael's face. "All along it was Ghaltair."

"And he is dead," Michael said. "I have honored my vow to Thor. I have killed the man who brought dishonor to my father's name. And in so doing, I have found my brother."

"My honor has also been restored," Malcolm said.

"Aye, my lords," Blar said. "The gods have spoken."

Malcolm turned to Cait and Blar. "Guardian Father, I shall have to take these trunks. They were not gifts meant for the gods. Rather they are gifts intended for Lang."

"Of course, my son," Blar said. "You shall have them."

Michael held out his arms, and Cait ran into them. She laughed, her eyes misty, and led them to a linen-draped table on the far side of the room. On it lay a beautiful golden sickle sword, its crescent inlaid with silver.

"Our symbol," Cait said, recalling her father's words. "The sickle sword belonged to the god Night, and the golden shield to Day."

Michael picked up the sword and studied it as Cait retrieved the shield Malcolm found in the pool and brought it to the table. The three warriors crowded around her.

"Cait," Michael said, holding up the sword, "the inscriptions on the shield are the same as those on the sword."

Her hands trembling, Cait nodded. "Aye, they are the same."

She laid the shield beside the sword.

Whether or not they were magical, they belonged together. The gods had spoken.

The fire in the hearth of the sleeping chamber of the Great Hall of Glenmuir burned brightly. Ulf, enjoying his mistress's pampering, lay in a basket filled with heather and covered with a blanket. He lazily cocked open an eye and looked at Cait and Michael, who stood in each other's arms.

"Will you marry me, Cait?" Michael asked. "A year and a day with you won't be long enough. I need a lifetime."

She was drowning in his beautiful blue eyes. How could she ever have thought they were cold?

"Forever won't be long enough," he added.

"Aye, my love," she whispered, lifting her mouth to his.

Michael felt his hardness against her softness as he held her in a crushing embrace. But Cait didn't resist. He stroked down her back to caress the slim line of her hip. He kissed her again and again; he inhaled the scent of her. He wanted to make her his for all time, to brand her with his body and with his name. But more than anything, he wanted to make her happy and to protect her. She whispered his name, her soft voice a song that touched both his heart and his soul.

Again he caught her mouth in a kiss. Slowly, so slowly, he poured his love and his need into her.

Her mouth tasted of sunshine, of flowers, of a honey that fired his passion to new heights. He tempted, enticed, built her trembling response.

But when she pressed her hands against his chest and laid him back on the mattress, when she began to make love to him in the same way, Michael surrendered to his wife.

Her hair brushed his chest and his stomach. Her hands touched him intimately, driving him to distraction. When he thought he could stand no more, he cried out, "Cait. Now."

Cait levered herself over Michael and received him into her body. He cupped her buttocks, and they began an urgent rhythm that promised fulfillment.

Michael never took the initiative from her. He allowed his love to lead, and he followed. He gave himself to her joy and her passion. He no longer insisted on being in control.

"Cait," he cried as she rose and fell over him, as he held her buttocks tightly against him, "I first loved you because I needed you."

"Aye, Michael." Cait leaned down, her damp hair falling about his face. She thrust one of her breasts into his mouth. As he sucked, she felt the pull in the deepest recesses of her body. She was on the brink, but she wouldn't go until she had brought Michael.

He tensed, his fingers biting into her hips. He arched against her. He shuddered and filled her with his seed. She cried out as she reached her own fulfillment.

They rolled over until Michael was leaning over her. "Now, my ladylove, I need you because I love you."

A long time later, Cait and Michael emerged from their sleeping chamber and joined Malcolm, Lang, and Gwynneth, lounging on the guest settle in the Great Hall.

Lang grinned. "Well, my son, I thought Malcolm and I were going to have to leave without saying good-bye."

"Nay."

"My lady Gwynneth," Cait said. "I want to thank you for helping me reclaim the High Seat of Glenmuir. Without you, we might not have succeeded."

"I'm glad to have given my services, my lady queen," Wynne replied.

Brian glared at the seafarer. "And you shall receive quite a prize, my lady, after you help Lang transport the rupture-endowment back to Northern Scotland."

She laughed, refusing to be chastised by the burly warrior. "Aye, my lord Brian, I shall."

"Now that all is well in your kingdom, Michael, I shall be returning to Northern Scotland," his brother announced. "There are matters that need my attention."

Michael nodded. "But Cait and I shall expect you back shortly."

"For the coronation?" Lang said. "Of course, we'll all be here."

"Nay," Michael said, "for our marriage. Cait and I love each other, and we are going to be married." He smiled at Lang. "At long last, my father, you will have the grandchildren you've desired."

"Aye," Lang muttered, his voice gruff, "grandchildren to carry on the House of the Wolf."

Michael nodded.

"We also invite you, Lady Gwynneth," Cait said.

"I shall be here, my lady queen," the seafarer said. "Now I shall see to my ship." As she strode from the Great Hall, sunlight glistened on her golden hair, and her cloak swished about her booted feet.

"She is a beautiful woman," Kolby said.

Brian shrugged. "Mayhap, but she doesn't appeal to me."

"Best-man," Malcolm shouted, "let us see to the loading of the ship. We must be on our way."

The crowd cleared out of the Great Hall, leaving Michael and Cait alone once more. The fire in the central hearth blazed brightly behind them, and sunlight glimmered through the open window to one side. But no light shone brighter than their feelings for each other as Michael swept her up in his arms and carried her to their sleeping chamber, where they affirmed their love far into the night.

Epilogue

"Aye, the gods always know," Feich mumbled as she followed the pathway outside Malcolm's village. The autumn wind blew briskly, fluttering her cloak. But she enjoyed the cold; it assured her that she was alive ... and soon would be going on a journey.

She walked more slowly these days, but that was to be expected. She had seen many winters come and go. But there was work yet to do.

She stopped beneath a rowan tree. Ah, the berries that had fallen from the tree had stained the earth red.

Babies would be born.

Chanting softly, Feich returned slowly to her cottage. She slipped off her mantle and hung it on a peg inside the door. Then she shuffled to the wood-box and searched until she found two fir branches. She had cut them when the Great Mother God had revealed to her that there would be two new lives in the Houses of the Wolf and the Horse.

Now it was time to make the cradles, to decorate both with the wolf and the horse. She would deliver each babe, then bless mother and child by carrying the burning fir torch around the bed three times. She would clean the babe and hand it to its father.

Aye, she had plenty of work ahead of her.

* * *

Lang and Muireall stood in their sleeping chamber in Malcolm's village.

"Are you sure, my ladylove?" Lang asked.

"Aye, my lord. I'm looking forward to living with you in the Northland. Home is wherever you are, my lord." Muireall cupped her husband's face in both hands.

He caught her in his arms and swung her through the air. "This day, my lady, I am the happiest man in the kingdom."

Muireall guided his lips to hers. She kissed him sweetly.

"And I am the happiest woman." She laughed, then grew serious. "My lord, are you sure you don't wish to marry a younger woman, one who could give you a child?"

"You have already given me a son. In loving me, you have blessed me with far more than I ever dreamed possible."

Malcolm and Jarvia stood in the sleeping chamber of the Great Hall of Malcolm's village.

"Are you sure, my ladylove?" Malcolm stared into his wife's green eyes.

"Aye, my lord," Jarvia answered. "I have not seen my moon for two months."

"My love, you have given me more happiness than I ever dreamed possible."

"When I lost the last babe, Feich promised I would conceive again and would carry the child to full term."

"Did she tell you if we're going to have a boy or girl?"

"Nay, she said the gods didn't reveal that to her, but . . ." Jarvia paused. "I think they do. She just doesn't want to tell us because that gives her a certain air of superiority over us."

"Will this keep you from returning to Glenmuir for Michael and Cait's marriage?" Malcolm asked.

"Nay, my lord, I won't be too far advanced. And we have promised the Ancient of Nights and Days that we will accompany him on his return journey to the Shelter Stone."

"Lang and Mother will travel with him," Malcolm reminded her.

"Well, your mother and Lang have insisted that we go too."

"That doesn't mean you have to go."

Jarvia laughed. "You, my husband, are the one who doesn't wish to make this trip. You shouldn't have promised Michael that you would play the flute while he danced."

Malcolm chuckled. "I'm learning, but my fingers seem to be too big. Nevertheless, by the time of the wedding, I shall be quite good at it . . . well, at that one song."

"Your mother said she heard you playing the other day, and she had to put her hands over her ears. Lang isn't so sure Michael will want you to play at the wedding."

"My mother and that Northman," Malcolm said with a shake of his head. "She was a levelheaded woman until she met Lang. Now she's as giddy as can be. I never thought I'd see the day when she would act like clay in his hands."

"But she's happy."

"Aye."

"And, lord, 'tis all right to be like clay in the hands of someone you love, if at times they are like clay in your hands."

"Aren't you the wise woman today?"

Jarvia laughed. "Oh, Malcolm, your mother is far happier than I have ever seen her. I remember when I first came to the village, I saw shadows in her eyes. Now I don't. Lang has taken her sorrow from her."

"I know my mother can be overbearing," Malcolm said, "but I truly love her. I'm not sure I approve of her going to live in Northland."

"If I remember," Jarvia said, a twinkle in her eyes, "she didn't ask your permission."

"Aye." Malcolm grinned also. "As high king, should I deny her permission?"

"I would love to see you try, love," Jarvia said. "I think your mother, mayhap Lang also, would reduce you to a lad again."

"Aye," Malcolm said with a frown. "Despite the many winters I have seen, Lang's iron gray eyes and stern expression do set me back on my heels."

"Someday, my lord, you'll have a son who is as concerned about you and you are about your mother."

"A son?" Malcolm asked, arching a brow.

"Aye, lord, didn't you promise long ago to give me a son?"

He laughed softly. "That I did, lady."

"Are you sure, my ladylove?" Michael asked as they lay abed one morning in one of the sleeping chambers in the Shelter Stone Cloister. He ran his hands through the silken strands of hair that hung below her shoulders.

"Aye, my husband," Cait replied. "My moon has not come upon me for two months."

Michael buried his face in the crook of her shoulder and neck. He loved this fiery woman. And now she carried their baby.

"My lord, if you approve, I should like to ask Old Mother Feich to deliver the babe for me."

"Aye, 'tis fine with me," Michael said, "but I believe, my love, that you are going to have more midwives than you want. Feich, Muireall, Jarvia, all of them will be here telling you how to birth this baby."

"Will that bother you, lord?"

"Nay, I like Muireall. She can be overbearing, but that shall stand her in good stead as my father's wife."

"Aye, your father is overbearing himself, lord." She laid her palm against Michael's cheek. "Besides, they are in love."

"Aye."

It was still hard at times for Michael to accept that his father and Muireall were as much in love as he and Cait. Lang had been kind to his first wife, but he fairly doted on Muireall.

"Soon all of them shall be here for the wedding," Cait said.

"Aye." Michael pulled a face. "And I have to learn to do that sword dance."

Cait laughed. "Mayhap, my lord, you should play your flute and let Malcolm do the dancing."

"Nay, lady. If that brother of mine can dance like that, then so can I."

"Mayhap it's not something you want to do at our wedding, lord."

"Why?"

Cait arched her brows, and Michael grinned.

"You think I shall injure myself, lady?"

They laughed together and snuggled closer.

"Do you miss traveling, my lord?"

"Nay. In the winter and spring Northlanders always stay in the village," Michael said. "In the winter we rest and remain indoors, preparing our equipment for the coming warm months. In the spring we plant our crops and tend our animals. Only then do we go a-viking."

"Will you be going a-viking this summer?"

"Nay, we shall spend the winter and spring preparing for the arrival of the babe. In a few years, my love, you and I—and our babies—shall travel the seas together during the summer. I shall take you to many faraway lands and teach you how to draw maps."

"I brought your map satchel here for you," she said. "I thought you would like to work on them today."

"You did?"

"I thought I might look at them with you." He grinned and she sighed. "Our life is going to be wonderful, Michael. I have always wanted to travel."

"But we shall always return here. Glenmuir is our home."

"Aye, it is."

"My lord and lady," Blar called as he knocked on the door. " 'Tis time for the coronation ceremony."

"So it is," Michael murmured. "But, madam, first things first."

He clasped her shoulders and drew her against his chest. And he touched his mouth to hers in a deep, leisurely kiss.

Avon Romantic Treasures

Unforgettable, enthralling love stories,
sparkling with passion and adventure
from Romance's bestselling authors

FORTUNE'S FLAME *by Judith E. French*
                                76865-8/ $4.50 US/ $5.50 Can

FASCINATION *by Stella Cameron*
                                77074-1/ $4.50 US/ $5.50 Can

ANGEL EYES *by Suzannah Davis*
                                76822-4/ $4.50 US/ $5.50 Can

LORD OF FIRE *by Emma Merritt*
                                77288-4/$4.50 US/$5.50 Can

CAPTIVES OF THE NIGHT *by Loretta Chase*
                                76648-5/$4.99 US/$5.99 Can

CHEYENNE'S SHADOW *by Deborah Camp*
                                76739-2/$4.99 US/$5.99 Can

FORTUNE'S BRIDE *by Judith E. French*
                                76866-6/$4.99 US/$5.99 Can

GABRIEL'S BRIDE *by Samantha James*
                                77547-6/$4.99 US/$5.99 Can

The Incomparable
ELIZABETH LOWELL

"Lowell is great!"
Johanna Lindsey

ONLY YOU
76340-0/$5.99 US/$6.99 Can

ONLY MINE
76339-7/$5.99 US/$6.99 Can

ONLY HIS
76338-9/$5.99 US/$6.99 Can

UNTAMED
76953-0/$5.99 US/$6.99 Can

FORBIDDEN
76954-9/$5.99 US/$6.99 Can

LOVER IN THE ROUGH
76760-0/$4.99 US/$5.99 Can

And Coming Soon

ENCHANTED
77257-4/$5.99 US/$6.99 Can